I0823862

Tidespeaker

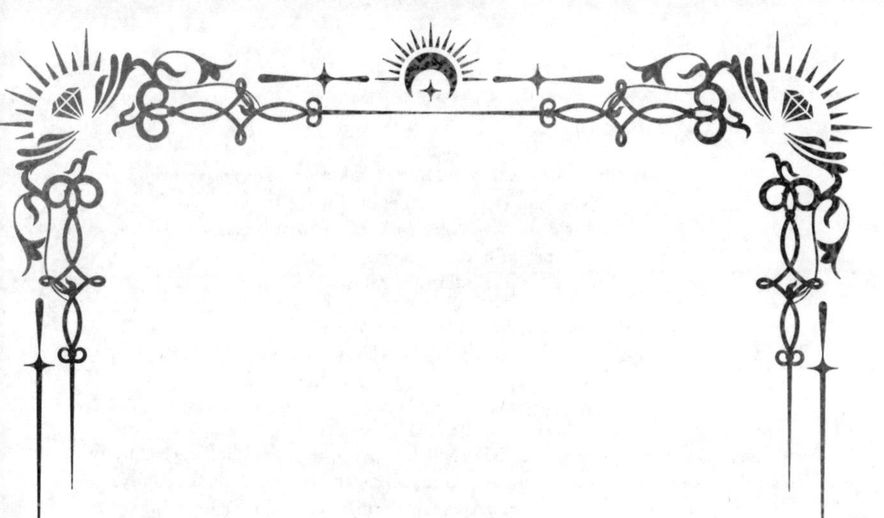

Tidespeaker

Sadie Turner

Delacorte Press

Delacorte Press
An imprint of Random House Children's Books
A division of Penguin Random House LLC
1745 Broadway, New York, NY 10019
penguinrandomhouse.com
GetUnderlined.com

Editor: Lydia Gregovic
Cover Designer: Trisha Previte
Interior Designer: Megan Shortt
Production Editor: Colleen Fellingham
Managing Editor: Tamar Schwartz
Production Manager: Liz Sutton

Library of Congress Cataloging-in-Publication Data is available upon request.
ISBN 979-8-217-02422-3 (trade) — ISBN 979-8-217-02423-0 (lib. bdg.) —
ISBN 979-8-217-02424-7 (ebook)

The text of this book is set in 10-point Requiem Text.

Manufactured in the United States of America
1st Printing

The authorized representative in the EU for product safety and compliance is Penguin Random House Ireland, Morrison Chambers, 32 Nassau Street, Dublin D02 YH68, Ireland, https://eu-contact.penguin.ie.

To the library dwellers,
the daydreamers, the "different"

To Pen Aryn
Breawr
Strakemoor
Great Cradle
The Glens
House Osprey
River Irna
Mirror~in~the~Vale
Shawmarsh
Black
Calder Crags
W
Arbenhaw
Tresteny
Glangell
River Rhala
Great Sinking Grounds
Quaglands
River Bray
House Crake
House Dunlin
Sword Estuary
N E M

Gods' Hollows
Eastwilds
Esterdale
River Fian
House Turnstone
The Channels
Hollow Falls
River Tiva
THAL'S CROSS
Port Rhorstin
House Shearwater
Drowning Woods
Bower Island
Bower Bay
Kestrick
Bannerman's Bluffs
Bone Forest
Point Lorn
Chorus Coast
House Cormorant
Calder Dales
River Luad
Pontarth
Lanniton
Stormshields
House Mallard
Saltwoods
T R A

The last day of summer, and my eighteenth birthday, found me suspended upside down in a tank of water.

It was hardly the coming-of-age I'd hoped for, but no one celebrated birthdays at Arbenhaw. Here, all days were filled with the same three things: training for our service to the Queendom of Nenamor, history lessons on why that was the only life fit for us, and—far more frequently than seemed fair—practical examinations, testing our control.

Today, I was facing one of the last. The flutters of panic I'd been feeling all morning intensified as I blinked through the water at my classmates. Their blurry figures, weirdly inverted, were lined up along the walls of the hexagonal chamber, and I knew every one of them would be smirking at the tank, hoping to witness my spectacular failure.

I was the only Floodmouth being examined today, and I'd never been tested like this before. This ordeal was reserved for our final year, for the day we turned eighteen and were deemed ready for service—and the pressure of all the eyes fixed on me was almost worse than the pressure of the water. As my heart hammered out the familiar beat that always accompanied anything new or unexpected, I felt the telltale burning in my lungs and knew that in about sixty seconds I'd be drowning.

Perched in the gallery, like a row of roosting vultures, were the Instructors who'd come to oversee my exam. They hadn't bothered to heat the water, of course, and it chilled my skin as I wriggled in my restraints. I knew they would all be watching closely; better performance at Institutions like Arbenhaw meant better positions out in the Queendom after graduating. I was acutely aware that poor or even mediocre results would mean serving out the rest of my years doing something dangerous, or downright horrible: protecting the harbor builders down south, irrigating flooded farmland, clearing the sewers in the cities out east . . .

It didn't help that one figure was conspicuously absent from the room, a person whose attendance would have made this much easier.

For a decade, Zennia, my only friend at Arbenhaw, had been a stalwart presence in these echoing chambers, her steady brown gaze—as familiar to me as a sister's—the anchor I needed to remind me *I could do this.* But a month ago, my friend, my anchor, had been whisked away after her own final exam to serve some noble family on the coast.

I knew the chamber outside the tank would be silent, perhaps only the scuff of a slippered foot breaking the quiet. Squeezing my eyes shut, I tried to feel out the water. After ten years in this place, the water we practiced with, drawn from the mountain springs outside the complex, was nearly as familiar to me as Zennia was. But today it seemed implacable, almost haughty.

Without Zennia, I felt like a shipwrecked sailor. Since she'd left, I'd struggled through our practicals, slogged through our lessons, but this—this was new. My fear was snowballing. And the water, coldly cocooning me, seemed to know it.

There were only two things that could render us Orha useless:

laconite stone, and emotions. Strong emotions. I needed to wrest control of mine, or my eager classmates would get what they hoped for.

I knew what my friend would have willed me to do, had she been out there in the line with them, watching. I forced myself to clear my thoughts, to ignore the cold pressure, the unfurling fear, and tried to picture my emotions in my mind.

It was a trick Zennia taught me nearly two years ago, when I'd floundered in one of our eighth-year tests. Since then, it had helped me impress the Instructors—but I wasn't sure it would save me today.

"What do your feelings look like? As an image?"

Mine always looked chaotic, even frightening. And sure enough, they burst into my mind's eye like a firework: a shivering, scarlet ball of panic, bolts streaking out into the black like lightning.

"Squeeze it. Shrink it. Smother it to nothing."

Her words came back to me as I grappled with the ball. The idea was to slowly force it inward, mentally crush it to the size of a pinprick. But all I could see, overlaid upon it, was my friend's sad smile as she was led away.

Seconds passed. My body shook. The need to breathe was like a hunger, starvation, a burning torch held too close to my skin. I didn't have long. I needed to *control* this, but in my head, I could only relive Zennia's exam. The sight of her hanging, serene, in the tank, black hair scrunched and tied into bunches. The glint of light on the brooch I'd given her for her own eighteenth birthday fastened tight to her blouse.

She'd excelled, of course; flown through it with ease. Since we'd all been thrown together at Arbenhaw, having passed the test that granted us entry—and a route to the best possible service placements after graduation—Zennia had surpassed the rest of us in practical after practical, and many of our classmates disliked her for it. Well, that and the fact that she refused to dislike *me,* the watchful one on the periphery who could never seem to say the right thing.

But though Zennia had landed her prestigious placement, mine was even now slipping from my grip.

With a heave, a spasm, my mouth jerked open, my lungs now searing, desperate for air. But instead of gulping, dooming me to drown, I spoke instead. Commanded the water.

"Part," I choked out, bubbles streaming from my mouth. "Give me air. Let me breathe."

My chest, my body—all was pain. This must be what it felt like to be crushed under a boulder. Ordinarily, when my emotions were in check, the water obeyed me readily. But today . . .

I waited three seconds. Five. My torso shuddered, my limbs twitching wildly. Ten full seconds now since I'd spoken to the water. It wasn't listening. I'd known it wouldn't.

I opened my eyes, felt them sting with the cold. When we were little, the trainees in the years above us tried to scare us with lurid stories about this exam. They claimed that if you failed, you were left to drown. An Orha who couldn't perform at all wasn't even useful in the mills, mines, or military: the lowest tier of employment for our kind. Why bother sending us back to our families, draped in humming, scarlet laconite, when there was no place in society for us without work? Staring out at the blurry figures of the Instructors, I wondered if I'd been foolish to scoff at these tales.

It was over. The craving for air was too strong. My lips stretched wide, my chest sucking inward, and cold water gushed down my throat.

But at the same time, around me . . . something was happening. A shift in the water; a sudden great heaving.

I was buffeted as bubbles of air broke against me, my breeches rippling and my long sleeves billowing. My red braids whipped around my face like loose rigging as the water rumbled, groaned . . . and *displaced.*

The gap of air above me, at the top of the tank—through which I could just see a shimmering silhouette—moved downward, and my now-dripping face was left clear. The water sloshed against the crown of my head, and I coughed and coughed, gasping in rasps of air.

One thought broke through: *That shouldn't have worked.* Emotions that strong should have smothered my power, since nature, unimpressed by feelings, balked at them. Either the water had taken pity on me—which was impossible, unheard of; it didn't work like that—or somebody in the chamber had.

Firm hands hauled me up, sending hot relief spiking through me. Below, the hovering water crashed back down, slopping noisily against the tank as though enraged.

A wooden platform had been erected against the tank, with a rickety ladder leading down to the flagstones. It was Rhama who'd pulled me out—the bald, bespectacled Instructor had also been the one to lower me in and must have been up here the whole time, watching. I collapsed at his feet, spluttering water. He picked me back up, sat me upright, and slowly, my breaths began to come a little steadier.

I waited as his deft hands worked at my bindings. I was glad it was him. He was one of the fair ones, and we shared a serious, thoughtful demeanor. I wasn't his favorite—he had no favorites among us—but he'd always put a firm end to the needling from my classmates. Not like Instructor Caerig, who could be downright vindictive and was currently lurking at the edge of the gallery, her hawk's gaze pinned on us from the shadows.

Rhama, I noticed, was watching me carefully. His eyes betrayed neither approval nor disappointment, but I detected a faint line etched between his brows: frustration. The clock above the gallery marked me at sixty-eight seconds. I should have done better—clearly Rhama thought so, too—and in the end, had I even succeeded at all? The water's delayed reprieve still confounded me.

I was offered no cloak or cape to warm me as I climbed down the ladder and faced my classmates. Along the line of them, there were lifted eyebrows, quirking lips, eyes flashing with delight. I made my stare as poisonous as I could, though behind it simmered a horrible shame.

Rhama, who'd come down the ladder behind me, still watched me, and I quickly schooled my expression. We were expected to maintain strict control at all times, not just when we were communing with our element. Outbursts of feeling, aside from hampering our abilities, were a sign of weakness and punished harshly.

"Thank you, Corith," he said dispassionately. "That concludes your final examination. You'll be informed when a suitable placement becomes available. Until then, you'll attend lessons with the others, as normal."

"A suitable placement."

My skin tightened painfully, and not from the chill of my soaking garments. Sibilant whispers started up in the line. I heard a few shuffles, a stifled laugh.

"Silence," came Caerig's voice from the gallery: curt, emotionless. A hush descended. "Anyone," she continued, "who so much as *clears their throat* will find themselves in the Confinement Locker from dawn until dusk tomorrow."

Traditionally, the exhausted examinee was permitted to leave while their classmates emptied the tank and mopped water from the floor.

But Caerig's lip lifted as her gaze met mine.

"Now, *all* of you: Clean up this room."

With a thumping heart and trembling hands, I lagged behind my classmates as we wound through the halls, dodging a couple of whispering Sparkmouths clad in their flame-resistant wools and leathers. As keen as I was to get out of my sodden clothes, I knew if I kept up with the others, there'd be biting words and barbed jokes.

Through the corridor's only window, I spotted Mudmouths in the grounds, practicing carving furrows in the earth, and beyond them a knot of wind-lashed Gustmouths, listening attentively to a barking Instructor. But I barely paid the sight any attention. My mind was in turmoil, turning over what had happened. Why had the water eventually listened, and how, with my emotions so out of control? *Had* it even listened, or had someone intervened?

Our quarters—a full ten levels of rooms along galleries with sentries stationed at every corner—faced out into a great, cavernous chamber, the better to keep an eye on us at all times. As tenth-years, we had small, single rooms on the top floor, and I shivered as I hurried along the walkway to my own. Zennia's room had been right next to mine, but now it was bare, the door standing open.

I stalled and lingered, staring into it.

A month ago, after Zennia's final exam, I hurried straight here, desperate to see her. We hadn't spoken since the previous day, since before Rhama kept her back after our last class to discuss an essay we'd handed in recently. She'd missed dinner, which was unusual for her—in spite of her short stature, she ate like a wolf—and I didn't have a chance to speak to her before curfew. Then, at breakfast, before her exam, we were too near the Instructors' table to exchange our usual whispers, too rushed to scrawl messages in our made-up code. But I saw how tired, how drawn, she looked, despite the fierce determination in her eyes. And I caught the fleeting looks she was giving me—looks that, for once, I found hard to interpret.

She'd impressed in her exam, as I knew she would, but I couldn't shake the thought that something wasn't right. And sure enough, when I reached her room afterward, Rhama stood guardlike at the open door. Inside, I spotted my friend's compact figure. Her back was to me; she was packing clothes into a trunk.

Rhama shot me a warning look, but I decided I would take the punishment. "Zen," I said urgently. "What's going on?"

She whirled around, dropping a nightshift onto the floor, and an odd expression flashed across her face—a look that seemed meant to convey something important, though what, I still had no idea.

"Rhama says I'm not to talk to anyone," she said. We both glanced at the watching Instructor.

"Sixty seconds," he said flatly, his gaze sliding to Zennia, but he didn't move; he wasn't going to give us any privacy. I turned back to her. I didn't care what he, or anyone, heard me say.

"What's happening? Why are you packing that trunk?"

"A placement," she replied, flitting another glance at Rhama. "Corith, listen. If we don't see each other again—"

Rhama must have looked like he was going to interrupt. She stepped forward, gripped my arm, looked hard into my eyes: "You have to know, you're like a sister to me. And I know you'll be fine. You'll get a good placement—"

"No," I protested, clutching her tightly. I'd known, of course, that we'd be parted eventually, but I'd convinced myself we had at least a few weeks left. "Where's the placement? Where are you going?"

Her eyes darted to the doorway, to Rhama. "Somewhere out east. One of the noble Houses. A place called Bower Island, I think."

I was dimly aware of heavy footsteps, a hand on my shoulder, Rhama's deep voice: "That's enough."

"You can't go," I murmured numbly. Then, louder, to Rhama: "She can't go. Not yet. I don't . . . You can't send her away."

I'd been about to say, *I don't know how to* be *without Zennia.* But the words got stuck on something in my throat. Something vast and terrible—emotion like I'd never felt.

"Here," Rhama said to her, picking up the fallen nightshift. "It's time. Bring your trunk. And you"—he turned to me—"I won't report this to the other Instructors, provided you turn around and leave. Right now."

I wanted to defy him, to pull Zennia into a hug and refuse to let go until they peeled me off her, but I knew, deep down, it wouldn't change what was coming—only ensure I saw the inside of the Confinement Locker for a week.

Instead, I watched with steadily blurring vision as Zennia stuffed the nightshift into her trunk. "Wait," she murmured, then dashed over to her nightstand, where she snatched something up and pinned it to her shirt: the brooch I'd given her, plain hammered metal, imprinted with the image of a sailing ship. I'd saved up a year's worth of chore money for it, picked it out on one of our rare trips to town. Ever since I'd known her, Zennia had wanted to see the sea.

"Come," Rhama ordered. And to me: "Your room—this instant."

I was shocked at how lenient he'd been already. Caerig would have imploded by now. He must have seen, over the years, how close we'd become. But it didn't stop the flare of anger I felt toward him.

I walked backward down the gallery, feeling my way along the wall, unable to wrench my gaze from Zennia. Rhama was inscrutable as he hefted her trunk and ushered her toward the stairwell.

I was left to stare after my only friend, the closest thing I had to family, knowing that once she rounded that corner out of sight, I'd be utterly and completely alone in the world.

The night after my exam found me cross-legged on my bed, having abandoned the first few scribbled lines of an essay. It was due in two days, but I couldn't concentrate. My head felt foggy, bogged down by uncertainty.

The near disaster of my test that morning—and the question of what, or who, had eventually saved me—had left me reeling all through our remaining lessons. There was a tedious history lecture on some battle or other between the constantly quarrelling Hundred Houses, then a tutorial on emotional control. Finally, we were put through another grueling practical. Caerig, perhaps as punishment for the whispering in the exam, had us run extra laps of the yard while splitting the flow of water from its fountain.

I did poorly, of course, and sensed Caerig watching me; I flattened my features, but my thoughts were fizzing. Awful possibilities flitted through my head, each one more disturbing than the last. Would I end up in one of the Hundred's private navies, be blown apart by ships' cannons in another pointless skirmish? Or succumb to the monstrous tides that ravaged the coastlines as I helped build harbors or drain marshes in the Quaglands?

Getting into Arbenhaw should have meant a good placement, but failures ended up no better off than the Orha who hadn't passed the test for entry. As tough as our schooling here was, it wasn't as though there were many alternatives. Drudgery, danger . . . or no work at all. The last was the worst: a life lived in laconite.

At some point in my fretting, I must have lain down on the bed, as I woke an hour later to an insistent knocking at my door.

I heaved myself up, bleary-eyed and confused. We were never disturbed or summoned after curfew. It had to be something important—or something bad.

A nervous-looking boy poked his head around the doorframe. One of the younger Floodmouths—they often ran errands. "Instructor Caerig's sent for you," he whispered, brandishing a note of permission to walk the halls. He dropped the note into my damp, outstretched palm and hurried off, leaving me to grab a night rushlight. Fingers of fear clawed at my stomach as I left my room and headed down the walkway. I could think of only one explanation for this summons: The Instructors had decided I deserved some punishment for my lackluster performance in the tank that morning. Sixty-eight seconds . . . slower than nearly all the others.

I had to show my permission slip, which trembled as I clutched it, five times as I made my way across the complex. Arbenhaw was shadowed and silent at this hour, and the Instructors' Wing was no exception. There, I stopped at a tall, forbidding door, its brass plaque—engraved with INSTRUCTOR MARIN CAERIG—glowing a dull orange in the light from my candle.

I paused for a moment to use Zennia's trick. My nerves were a shivering ball in my mind's eye, and I mentally cradled it, compressed it. My hold felt precarious, but it would have to do. I knocked.

"Enter."

As I stepped through the door and nudged it closed behind me, I glanced around fleetingly at Instructor Caerig's suite. There were neat bookshelves, piles of paper on a desk, a painting on the wall, and a practice aid in the corner, made up of glass tubes and vials of water.

"Corith," came Caerig's clipped tone. "Do sit."

A large round table stood in front of the fire, and I was shocked to see not just Caerig sitting there but Rhama, too. I caught his gaze as I sidled over to a chair, but the Instructor remained as expressionless as ever.

It felt wrong, oddly intimate, to be sitting in this suite. The Instructors were usually so remote, so draconian. To see Caerig's personal items, her bric-a-brac, was discordant, and I twisted my fingers in my lap.

Neither of them said anything for a few long moments. Rhama's eyes were fixed on some parchment on the table, but Caerig, leaning back in her chair, studied me thoughtfully. It was unnerving, being the sole object of her attention. I wondered what punishment they'd see fit to hand down.

"You disappointed us in your examination this morning," she said, watching me closely for a reaction. I fought to keep my features neutral. "But," she continued, face creasing into a chilly smile, "Instructor Rhama has just been reminding me of the fact that your performance has been, in general, very impressive, for the better part of your time here at Arbenhaw."

I looked at Rhama, unable to hide my surprise. He'd been watching me, his gaze weighing, almost assessing, but now he glanced back at the parchment beneath his fingertips.

"Your control and concentration has waned, these past weeks," Caerig continued, "but, as Rhama has pointed out, it *has* been a period of . . . some upheaval. I understand you were very close to . . ." She seemed to search for Zennia's name and, unable to recall it, shot me a tight smile. "Well, in any case, I am willing to concede that this morning may have been an . . . unfortunate lapse."

Before I could say anything, Rhama leaned forward and spun the parchment, showing me the wax seal at its base. A letter, inked in a deep, regal violet.

"House Shearwater," he said. "You'll remember them from your lessons."

I didn't, but I gave no indication of the oversight.

We'd had countless hours of classes on the Hundred Houses, the dynasties who'd ruled Nenamor for the past few centuries after leading their Great Revolt against our kind. Endless history lessons on how, with the help of laconite, they'd grappled back control from Orha who'd let power go to their heads. And long lectures, too, on how we Orha now had a duty to use our gifts productively—furthering prosperity, bettering the Queendom—or else refrain from using them at all.

I was sure House Shearwater would have been mentioned at some point, but by now the Houses, and their skirmishes and rivalries, had all muddled together in my mind.

"Of course," I said, hoping there were no follow-up questions.

"Given the capabilities you've demonstrated thus far, we've decided to assign you a placement with the Shearwaters. A placement that has, as of very recently, become . . . available."

I blinked. The red spark in my mind's eye sputtered, flaring into brilliance. I grappled with it, my breath coming faster.

"A placement?" I couldn't help repeating. "Already?"

"Congratulations," Caerig intoned. That frosty smile again.

Zennia was sent out straight after her exam, but that was unusual, almost unheard of. It was normally a few weeks, sometimes months, before a role was assigned and a transfer arranged.

I'd been of age for not even a day.

And I'd never expected to be placed with the *Hundred*. A chill crept over me as Rhama's words sank in.

Such placements came up only rarely. Normally, only a couple of us per year would get the "honor," reserved for the very best of us, the Zennias. With her talent, I always suspected she'd end up back in that world, much as she muttered mulishly that she'd rather take her chances with "lesser" work than serve the Hundred Houses—at least the contemptible ones her mother had done business with. But me? I never quite reached her heights.

Caerig must have seen my features sagging, because her smile rapidly disappeared. "It's a prestigious position any Orha would be grateful for. Rhama assures me you're the right trainee for the job. You will not disappoint us, as you did this morning."

She was right. Serving the Hundred as a member of their prized "sets" was touted as the highest position one could reach as Orha. It meant a life spent in luxurious surroundings, even if we didn't get to sleep in the four-poster beds ourselves. But it was tedious, too. I'd seen Floodmouths in town made to keep the rain off noblewomen's heads, shrink puddles so their hems stayed dry, part streams so they didn't have to ride to the next bridge. Some nobles paraded their sets like voguish accessories.

And there were worse stories. Zennia was a merchantwoman's daughter. She'd told me what she'd seen in the Hundred's parlors: one of Regent Shrike's Sparkmouths beaten black and blue for not lighting a visitor's pipe fast enough; a set forced to perform ridiculous, demeaning tricks to entertain guests at one of House Blackcap's soirées. It was why Zennia had always said she'd refuse a placement with the Hundred. But when that day had come, she hadn't. I wondered why.

Swallowing, I tried to keep the disquiet from my face.

"Shearwater, as you know, is one of the Coastal Dozen," said Rhama, pushing another document toward me. It was larger than the letter and faintly creased, covered in snaking lines and carefully inked labels. A map of Nemestra, the easternmost province of Nenamor. "They hold Port Rhorstin and all the lands around Bower Bay."

Bower Bay.

Why did that name set bells jangling in my head?

"One of the wealthiest Houses on the coast," said Caerig, "along with House Crake, of course." She and Rhama exchanged glances. "There's a . . . rivalry there. Things are a little tense at present. Suffice it to say, this is a very important posting. Rexim Shearwater is particularly influential, and he finds himself in need of a new Floodmouth. Right away."

"What happened to the old one?" The words tumbled out before I could stop them. The unexpected news had made me careless, blundering.

Caerig stared at me for a long, drawn-out moment, while Rhama's dark eyes flicked down and away.

And then, with a sharp slap of shock, I remembered.

"Somewhere out east. One of the noble Houses. A place called Bower Island, I think."

I gripped the table to steady myself.

Zennia had been assigned the Shearwater placement. So why was *I* being sent out there, too? I knew enough about the Hundred to know that their sets included one each of the four types of Orha. House Shearwater wouldn't keep *two* Floodmouths.

The realization settled over me like a shroud: Something had happened. I was Zennia's replacement.

Caerig's lips thinned at my impertinence. "We wouldn't normally share such information, but given your predecessor was a particular friend . . ." She glanced at Rhama. "It seems she had an unfortunate accident. Out in the bay. Got caught in the tides. Brigant Shearwater"—Caerig's fingertips tapped the letter—"writes that this was caused by her foolhardiness. Her ineptitude." She held my gaze in the wavering lamplight. "Not something you'll allow to happen, I am confident."

I opened my lips, but nothing came out.

"An unfortunate accident."

Zennia. *My* Zennia.

At last, I managed to find my voice, but it came out as a whisper: "I won't, Instructor."

Silence descended, heavy and grave, and after a few seconds, Rhama added, "I'm sorry."

His words only deepened the chill in my core. It was what people said after someone had died.

"Shearwater wants our very best," Caerig said curtly. "He'd prefer a more experienced Floodmouth, but with the nature of the placement system . . . well, all our past graduates are already employed. And time is of the essence." She looked at Rhama.

"They have an island," he said. "Nearly nine miles off the coast. Accessible via causeway when the tides are right."

I glanced at the map, dazed, and saw it there: a little coat of arms nestled in the half-moon of the bay. A clever defense from hostile Houses, but no doubt a hindrance without a competent Floodmouth. I'd heard that the shape of the coast out there meant the tides moved faster than a person could run.

As though from far off, I heard Rhama say, "You'll want to go and get some rest. We're organizing an escort to the island for you, but everything should be arranged by dawn. Leave a pile of the belongings you wish to take with you in your room. I'll ensure they're loaded onto the coach at sunrise."

Sunrise.

I couldn't believe it had come about this suddenly—this stark setting-out of the rest of my life. And it seemed like a particularly cruel twist of fate that I was heading to the same place my friend had disappeared to, only for her not to be there when I arrived.

I thought of Zennia, of the last time I'd seen her—the glint in her eyes, that meaningful look, her words: *"You have to know, you're like a sister to me"*—but I only felt numb, like the truth of it hadn't hit me, like my grief was waiting in the wings for later.

And there was something else, too. A niggle of doubt. *"Her ineptitude."* That just didn't sound like Zennia.

With a dark, weighty dread, I rose to my feet, the prospect of tomorrow hanging over me like a death sentence. Caerig flashed me a tight, pursed-lipped smile. She held out her hand. "Your permission slip, please. And you'll understand if we post a guard outside your room. Now that we've told Brigant Shearwater to expect you, we wouldn't want anything to befall his new Floodmouth."

I stared at her. Running off would be virtually impossible, but clearly Caerig was taking no chances. Eventually, my shoulders dropped, and I handed over the crumpled permission slip. "Yes, Instructor."

"Good. I'll see you back to your quarters."

I threw one last, wretched glance at Rhama: a final plea for some sort of reprieve. But he avoided my eyes, leaning back in his chair, his gaze still on the parchment in front of him.

With Caerig as my shadow, I shuffled from the suite.

The coach waiting at the gate at dawn had clearly seen better days: Its paintwork was scuffed, its wheels were well-worn, and its body was speckled with the dry mud of countless travels. It had perhaps been robust and elegant once, but looking at it now, I had little hope of a comfortable journey.

It was the first day of Tịma, the Turning to Autumn, and the air was crisp this early in the morning. I had donned the black uniform all trainees had to wear on the rare occasions we left the Institution—but black also seemed an appropriate choice after what I'd learned in Caerig's office.

I blinked. My eyes were swollen from crying, and unused to the brightness: There were few windows in Arbenhaw. The complex rose up like a mountain behind me—its walls the smooth black of nabyrium, a tough stone impervious to damage by Orha—while ahead, beyond the deep ditches and watchtowers, the tops of the larches shivered in the breeze.

Rooks and jackdaws eyed me beadily from the ramparts. Their

presence was an uneasy reminder of the Hundred, for all the Houses were named after birds: They claimed they were descended from the leaders of ancient clans who'd taken birds as emblems and inked them on their banners. There seemed no escape from reminders of House Shearwater, of Zennia, of the island that was to be my new home.

When I finally saw Caerig and Rhama walking toward me, a heavy sense of foreboding settled in my chest.

A pair of armed guards strode along behind them. One was pale, squat, and heavyset, with grayish hair pulled back into a greasy ponytail and a face that bore an uncanny likeness to a toad's. Judging by the squint-eyed look he gave me, he, like most people, harbored a deep distrust of Orha.

The second guard was taller, gangly, and sharp-eyed, with a matchlock gun strapped to his belt. Unlike his companion, he barely spared me a passing glance.

"Corith," said Caerig as they came to the gate. "These fine gentlemen will be keeping you company on the journey."

Keeping me from running off, more like.

Rhama stepped forward. Something glinted in his hands. As he lifted it toward me, guided its cord over my head, the telltale hum of laconite filled the air. Dark, blood-red, with pale, threadlike veins, the pendant nestled against my chest, and I felt its faint vibration through my clothes. Should I attempt to speak to any water, my pleas would go unheeded, my gift thoroughly deadened.

I wasn't used to it; we rarely set foot outside these gates. All Orha had to wear laconite when travelling, but we couldn't exactly don it when we were training or working. I wouldn't be permitted to remove the pendant until I reached Bower Island—and my service placement.

Caerig spoke: "I hope you realize how fortunate you are, Corith.

Your classmates would give anything to be posted with such a family." Perhaps she'd noticed the grim downturn of my mouth.

I gave no reply, merely tried not to wince. *Fortunate.* After last night's news, that word cut deep.

Rhama, I saw, was studying me closely. He looked tired; days-old stubble dotted his jaw. "You should know," he said evenly, "that the ocean is a . . . different beast. These mountain springs, the pools in your practice chambers . . ." He paused, seeming to grope for the right words. "Just remember your training. It takes time, and respect."

If I hadn't known better, I'd have thought he was concerned. But though Rhama had taught us for years, he'd never been one to display much warmth. No doubt he was thinking of Zennia's accident, of how displeased Shearwater would be with another . . .

I searched his expression, burning to ask more questions about my friend—I was leaving anyway, they couldn't punish me for impertinence now—but he seemed to sense it and flattened his features. The minute shake of his head that followed made it clear I'd be getting no answers from him.

The squat guard, whom Caerig introduced as Egard, hiked up his sword belt. "Let's go," he said brusquely. "The sooner this one gets to where she's going, the better."

And the sooner you'll get paid, I wanted to shoot back, *and can spend your wages in the dice and ale houses.* As the pair walked past me, I thought I caught a stale whiff of drink.

Once the three of us were installed in the coach, Rhama leaned in and held out a sheet of parchment, stamped with the Institution's official crest. "A letter of passage, in case you're stopped on the road. Informs anyone who cares to know of the purpose of your journey and why there is an Orha with you."

Egard pocketed it, shooting me another suspicious glare.

Before Rhama moved away, he caught my gaze, holding it just a fraction too long. There was meaning there. A reminder of his warning.

And perhaps, I imagined, something a little like *Good luck*.

Despite Egard's thinly veiled hostility, he eventually let me glimpse the map he carried. The journey was fifty miles as the crow flew, but with our route requiring a loop around the southern foothills of the Cradle, we'd be on the road for more like sixty-five. Five nights in coaching inns until we reached Port Rhorstin.

Before he could snatch the map away, I traced down the coastline with my eyes to the Saltwoods, to the city of Pontarth and the tiny village marked YSTREN.

My birthplace.

A knot had formed in my insides. My mother might still be there, I thought, working the little apothecary's garden my father left us after he died. He'd been killed when I was six in a pointless skirmish for a local lord who held tenured land from House Mallard. Skewered by a polearm, then dragged behind a cart. Even before I heard Zennia's grim stories, I had reason to resent the Hundred's deadly politicking, their bickering.

But though the thought of my mother made my eyes burn uncomfortably, I doubted she would ever welcome me back, even if I wanted to return to my hometown. The law forbade Orha lacking sanctioned employment from ever using our gifts again, and tales of the Revolt still lurked like a shadow in people's minds. I'd be shunned, the object of deep suspicion, forced to wear laconite everywhere I went.

It wouldn't be much of a life at all.

My sparse belongings barely filled the leather case they'd been packed in—by one of the Instructors' servants, maybe—and I had nothing, no books, to pass the time on the journey. Egard and his companion, who it turned out was called Belamy, amused themselves with card games and crude chitchat, neither of which I had any interest in joining. Instead, I stared out at the passing scree slopes and stands of birches, by turns mesmerized and terrified to see the world outside Arbenhaw.

This was a world hostile to my kind. Though Arbenhaw had felt akin to a prison, it had also, for a decade, been my home. The bell tolls directing our movements every day. The Instructors: harsh, but always there, like strict parents . . . That was all gone. And it made my chest hurt a little.

As we trailed through Glangell, the great forest hugging the mountains, I tried to stave off my anxiety about the island, and my misery over Zennia, by daydreaming about running: imagining myself leaping out of the coach and disappearing, living amid nature, using my gift to draw up water.

But I knew the likely reality would be starvation. Winter was on its way, and nobles hunted in these woods. I'd eventually have to buy food, seek out shelter. And with laconite everywhere, humming whenever I came near, I'd quickly attract attention and be questioned.

I shivered as I watched fir trees flit past the window. Arbenhaw had been a veritable hotbed of rumors, and one was that there *were* Orha living in the wilds. Rebels. Insubordinates who called themselves the Cage.

I knew it was one of the few rumors that were true, because I'd seen the headlines screaming across the pages of the news pamphlets that Zennia—and I, more reluctantly—had pickpocketed during our rare trips to town: BRUTAL ASSASSINATION BLAMED ON CAGE TERRORISTS. CAGE STRIKES AGAIN IN QUEENDOM'S CAPITAL. REGENT SHRIKE VOWS TO ROOT OUT REBELS.

And then, of course, there had been Owyn.

Zennia and I had sometimes whispered about running. Made up silly stories about where we'd hide out. Then, for the first and only time during our training, one student had absconded. An older boy called Owyn.

He had been sixteen, Zennia and I only twelve. Someone found out later, from a pamphlet plucked out of a gutter, that Owyn had been caught in just two days. They'd made an example of him, said he'd wanted to join the Cage. He hadn't turned up at Arbenhaw again. None of us knew what had happened to him. Those suspected of being linked to the Cage tended to disappear without trace.

Egard grunted. "You look like you're being carted to the gallows, girl."

I met his sour gaze and gave no reply.

Daydreaming about fleeing was a welcome distraction. But in the end, I knew I much preferred a straw-and-linen mattress, a hot breakfast at the bar of a coaching inn, to roughing it in the woods, knowing that at any moment the same suspicion that had fallen on Owyn would fall on me—and the same fate, too.

That night, I staggered up to the eaves of the only guesthouse that had had a spare room, my tailbone burning from the jolting of the coach and my ears assailed by unfamiliar noises. We were on the outskirts of the city of Tresteny, and despite the late hour, there were people guffawing, dogs barking, carts clattering by below. I had no idea how I was going to sleep. At least I could take off my laconite pendant, which had purred against my breastbone all day, stopping me from dozing.

Egard narrowed his eyes as I set it on a table.

"We'll be right down there, between the stairs and the door, so don't even *think* about scuttling, little Orha rat."

"I wasn't," I said shortly, squashing a spike of anger. I wished I *could* run, if only to deny Egard his payment.

After he and Belamy stomped down to the dice tables, I crouched and opened the leather case of my belongings. As I lifted the nightshift that lay on top, something fluttered out: a folded scrap of parchment. Unfolding it, I saw words inked in a precise hand across it:

IF YOU WISH TO KNOW WHAT HAPPENED TO YOUR FRIEND, GO TO THE VEIL, PORT RHORSTIN, ON 14TH TIMA. SUNSET EXACTLY. BRING A MASK.

I stared. Heard my breath over the rumble from downstairs.

With shaking fingers, I put the note aside and dug through the rest of my luggage. But there was nothing else, only my clothes, a pair of slippers, candles and rushlights, a tinderbox . . .

I sat back and reached for the note again.

Zennia.

The fourteenth of Tima was less than two weeks from now. And Port Rhorstin . . . that was the closest town to Bower Island. The embarking point for the nine-mile crossing to House Shearwater.

I had no idea what the Veil was, or why I had to bring a mask, or even if there'd be any possibility of getting there, but I already knew I'd do everything I could to make this meeting.

A meeting that someone at Arbenhaw must have arranged.

Loud thumps on the staircase made me jump to my feet. I crumpled the parchment into my palm, stood there frozen.

A rap on the door, Belamy's voice issuing through it: "Forgot my coin purse. You decent in there?"

I angled my face away as he rummaged in his pack and hoped he couldn't see the feverishness in my eyes.

That niggle of doubt I'd felt in Caerig's office; that wrongness that had struck me at her words, *"unfortunate accident"* . . . My instinct had been right. There was more to all this—to Zennia's accident—than I'd been told.

And in two weeks, I was determined, I would find out what it was.

On the fifth day, with a nervous lurch in my abdomen, I spotted gulls circling over the treetops of the Drowning Woods. The roads looked sandier, the people windburned, and the air had taken on a strange new freshness.

My whole body ached. I was exhausted from lack of sleep, not merely from the scritching of mice in our guest rooms but from lying awake each night for hours, my mind raking over the note in my case.

It had to have been left by someone at Arbenhaw. Egard and Belamy had been in the coach with me all day, and I'd had to lug my own bag up the steep steps to our room.

There was whoever had been ordered to pack my things, but at Arbenhaw, most chores and odd jobs for the Instructors were performed by the younger trainees, in preparation for service. They wouldn't have known either me or Zennia, nor had the means to arrange a meeting on the other side of Nemestra.

It seemed more likely that someone else had packed my case. Caerig had known I was bound for Bower Bay, but I simply couldn't imagine why *she* would have a hand in this.

That left Rhama.

I recalled his too-long look at my departure, him standing guard outside Zennia's room. He alone had seemed to understand how close we were. Perhaps he had taken pity on me after all, arranged for someone to share the details of her fate.

But why not simply seek me out and tell me? Much as I tried, in those long hours tossing and turning, I couldn't square what I knew of Instructor Rhama—who'd been a stalwart presence at Arbenhaw for far longer than I'd been there—with the mystery, the clandestine unorthodoxy, of this note.

It was dark when we finally rattled into Port Rhorstin. The moons were close, almost touching—at the beginning of each month, one eclipsed the other—but tonight, their faces were swaddled in thin cloud. As I limped from our coach through the doorway of our last inn, the note crumpled small and hidden in my pocket, I saw only the dark outlines of gables and weather vanes and the uncanny glow of hanging lamps.

For the first time on our journey, I slept like the dead, the accumulated fatigue of four nights of poor sleep at last overcoming my racing thoughts. My grief, too, seemed finally to have blunted: no longer the raw, open wound of a few days ago but a yawning black hole I now teetered on the edge of.

The next morning, I woke late, groggy and disoriented. Daylight, dulled by a heavy blanket of cloud, filtered in through the window and beckoned me from bed. I opened the catch, pushed the casement wide, and with a sudden thrill felt the bracing briskness of the breeze, smelled salt on the air, heard the snapping of ships' sails.

We were on a main thoroughfare that dropped east to some docks, just visible between the walls of weather-beaten whitewashed buildings. Over the rooftops, marsh reeds marched into the distance. I craned my neck but couldn't yet see the sea.

Egard and Belamy had the room adjoining mine and in their drunken state hadn't even closed the door. They sprawled, snoring, on canvas-covered cots. An empty wine bottle lay on its side near the window, and a few stained playing cards were scattered over the floor. I eyed their slumped figures, disdainful.

Perhaps it was time to give my "guardians" a little scare.

Downstairs, the taproom was noisy and bustling, but my uniform—and the laconite pendant against his chest—alerted the barman, drawing his eye to me immediately. Those who could afford it often wore protections against us.

"Orha," he said. "Another one o'you. You're alone."

I sidled to an empty space at the bar. "My guardians sent me down to get breakfast." I held out the letter of passage from Arbenhaw, which I'd eased from one of Egard's pockets. "Could I have buttered eggs in bread? And cold meats?"

His eyes roved the parchment; then he nodded, handing it back.

"What did you mean, 'another one of us'?" I asked, my pulse picking up.

He threw me a quick glance as he poured out two ales. "Last month," he commented. "One from *there,* just like you." He nudged his chin at the letter I held. "Same uniform an' all. Just that we don't see many of you."

He sloshed the ales onto a tray with some bread and hefted it, making to head down the bar.

"How did she seem?" I said desperately, heart drumming. It was the only thing I could think of to ask. But with a shake of his head, he was gone, tray held high.

Half an hour later, I heard the inevitable ruckus: shouts from upstairs, then the thumping of boots. Egard appeared first, eyes raking the taproom. Belamy, behind him, looked to be nursing a painful hangover.

"You." Egard stalked up to me, face bright red. "Thought you'd try

your luck giving us the slip? Thought you'd treat yourself to a little something on our tab?" He scowled at the remnants of egg on my plate.

"You looked like you needed your beauty sleep."

I felt a little thrill at my words, knowing he couldn't harm me if he wanted his coin. I'd never talked back to the Instructors at Arbenhaw. Now I was outside its walls, I couldn't resist.

Egard looked as though he was about to explode.

"Come on," Belamy said, steering me roughly away. "Tides mean we need to get going across that causeway."

A tingle went through me: half anticipation, half apprehension. I hadn't seen the sea since I was eight years old. And I knew the tides here were different from those down south.

Outside, the clouds had lowered and a brisk wind blew, bringing the scent of oncoming rain. As my case was loaded onto a cart pulled by a gray mare, I watched sailors loitering in fraying linens and wool caps, rusted whistles slung around their necks. Servants lugged sacks and ewers of water, picking their way with practiced ease around the wagons and over the ruts in the road. A knight on horseback nearly clipped me as he passed, two men-at-arms behind him, broadswords strapped to their backs.

And above the din, I heard a distant roaring.

We walked east, toward the docks I'd seen from my window, passing through a cobbled square surrounded by narrow shop fronts and houses. One of the shops was selling news pamphlets, and I slowed my pace, eyes roving the headlines.

But there was nothing, of course, about one drowned Orha, even though it had happened right here in this bay. Deaths in service were a common enough occurrence. Instead, it seemed, the pamphlets were going wild about the declining health of one of the ruling Regents: WHO WILL FILL CHAMBER SEAT LEFT BY DYING DUNLIN?

"Hoi, get moving," came Egard's low growl.

But something else in the square caught my eye: a line of great metal plaques affixed high on the walls of the buildings. Each was engraved with symbols and figures, and I hesitated, staring up at the dense rows and columns. It was like another language; I could make no sense of it.

This time, Egard butted me from behind, and I grabbed at the cart to keep from falling. I'd seen no sign of a place called the Veil, the establishment my mysterious meeting would take place in, but I couldn't exactly look for it now . . .

Besides, once we emerged from between the buildings, all thoughts of the Veil flew out of my head. A wide vista opened out before us, and all around were the endless marsh reeds. I looked down the hill, beyond the docks, and saw it there—

The high tide, battering the coast.

It filled the bay from end to end, dull daylight glinting off boisterous waves as clouds of seabirds wheeled above us. Even up here, I felt a thin mist on my face.

If I remembered right from my lessons at Arbenhaw, every month was split into archwater and pallwater. This had to be archwater, when the tides were fastest, flooding the bay with frightening speed. The stone docks we'd emerged onto were deserted; no one took boats out when the sea was this wild.

"I don't understand," I said to my guardians, trailing them down to the water's edge. Rhama had said there was a causeway to the island, but there was nothing in the bay save churning waves. "Don't we have to wait for low tide?"

"There," said Belamy, nudging his chin up. Following his gaze, I finally saw it: the beginnings of a stone track raised above the marsh, snaking out from the reeds into the water. "Tides move fast here. It's goin' out already."

He was right—the sea was receding in front of us, each swell breaking well short of the last. By now there were stretches of mudflat exposed, strewn with glistening seaweed and shells.

"Better get a move on," he added to Egard. "Innkeeper said to follow close behind the tide."

"Oh, *we* won't be leaving," Egard replied, tightening the ropes that held down my case. He shot me a disconcerting smile. "Nowhere for her to go this time but onward. So she can cross by herself while we sit here and watch. And she can tell them nobles up at the castle to have the cart returned to its owner tomorrow." He clapped a hand onto the mare's flank, making her jump. "Up we get, then," he said, lip curling, "Orha filth."

My heart thudded painfully as I looked out at the tide. Although it was receding, it was still unruly, slapping at the dull stone, sending spray up over the track.

"You were contracted to see me *all* the way to my destination." I had no desire to spend another second in Egard's company, but the thought of heading into the bay alone made me uneasy—the very place where my friend had met her end.

"That may be," Egard retorted, "but you can't exactly tattle on us now, can you?" He shaded his eyes, looking out to where the island must lie, and shook his head. "Hells if I can guess why anyone'd choose to live out there."

I half expected Belamy to protest, or at least look discomforted by the plan, but he seemed relieved; I suspected his head was still pounding. Idling by the bay's edge with some breakfast no doubt sounded far more inviting than bumping along that causeway and back.

I climbed, with as much dignity as I could muster, into the cart.

"Farewell, then, Floodmouth," Egard called, already seating himself heavily on a low wall.

"Enjoy your well-earned wages," I shot back, but goading him was far less satisfying this time. My nerves fluttered and my neck was damp despite the breeze.

Egard chuckled as Belamy folded his long body down next to him. I was left to urge the gray mare onward, and my cart slowly trundled off into the bay.

The salt marsh was a vast tapestry sprawling along the coastline. Marsh reeds speared skyward like pikes around me, while waders and wildfowl were buffeted by the surf. Eventually the stone track spilled me out onto the causeway, which looked to have been reinforced with durable nabyrium to offset the tides' relentless erosion. Gradually the reeds thinned, the bay opened out in front of me, and I was faced with an expanse of steel ocean beneath a dull sky.

Bower Island was a dark smear, a suggestion, on the horizon. It looked immensely far away. Nine miles, I recalled Rhama saying back at Arbenhaw—a three-hour journey at the plodding pace of this mare.

I swivelled, but Egard and Belamy were hidden by the reeds. I supposed I might have fled over the mudflats, but the tide wasn't going out all at once—it was ragged, rivulets snaking around me. I saw ditches in the sand, great frothing pools, areas of mud that looked like they might swallow me . . .

Egard had been right: I had nowhere to go but onward. Besides, there was no way I was going to miss that meeting, miss the opportunity to find out more about Zennia—and that meant surviving this placement, at least for the next week. So I sat and watched the endless uncovering of the causeway ahead, seaweed laid across it like clumps of dark hair.

An hour passed by, then an hour and a half. The clouds thickened and thunder rumbled in the distance. Behind me was a constant cacophony of screeching: gulls feasting on the delicacies left behind by the tide. It was clear, I thought as I watched redshanks wheel above me, why this whole stretch of shoreline was called the Chorus Coast.

About halfway along the causeway, I came to a stone harbor, which looked to be built entirely of nabyrium. The sea sloughed off it in sheets as it emerged. There were no boats, of course, not at archwater—only iron rings set into the stone.

The harbor must have cost a fortune to build. Nabyrium—volcanic and almost as strong as diamond—was rare and not widely available. The coastal Houses used it to counter the tides, while the rest of the Hundred liked it because *we* couldn't damage it—though a very determined Mudmouth might shake a nabyrium tower down.

The waves broke ahead of me, drew back out, came back in again. It was monotonous by now, even a little mesmerizing. I found myself gazing at the emerging sands, wondering if here, or there, was where Zennia had struggled . . . I was sinking back into that black hole of grief, wallowing, pulled under by the movement of the cart. I closed my eyes, almost nodding right off, when abruptly—

Crack!

The cart jolted violently.

I clung on as the mare reared, nearly upending the cart—and me. The wheels groaned; something scraped against the stone. Before the mare could send us toppling onto the mud, I sprang down, tottered briefly, and caught hold of her reins.

“Steady. *Steady.*” I had no idea how to manage horses, but I spoke as calmly and firmly as I could, and she seemed to respond, whickering gently. Once she was still, I went to inspect the damage.

“Hells,” I muttered as I dropped into a crouch. A fitting had splintered near one of the wheels, and something else important-looking had cracked right through. I mentally cursed Egard and Belamy for securing the cheapest cart-for-hire they could find in Port Rhorstin.

As I straightened stiffly and gazed out at the island, closer now but still some distance off, I saw the tide drawing inexorably away from me, the gap between us lengthening even as I stood there. The mare had no saddlebags, not even a saddle—no means of carrying either me or my case.

I chewed my lower lip. I'd just have to walk. The broken-down cart—surely no loss to its owner—would fall victim to the next tide, smashed to splinters and scattered.

I unfastened the mare and used some of the rope to fashion a makeshift handle for my case, then took her by the bridle, yanked the case down off the cart, and began to drag it behind me up the causeway—just as a thin rain began to fall.

“Hells, hells, hells.”

A far-off growl of thunder answered me.

We plodded along, our pace hampered by my case. But the mare seemed happier to travel this way; with no bulky cart to pull and the tide disappearing, she seemed calmer and even nudged my hand companionably.

It wasn't long, however, before a new sound reached my ears.

I turned, squinting back through the drizzle to the mainland. Two dark shapes, speeding toward me down the causeway. The noise I heard was the beating of hooves.

Riders. I would have to make way.

I moved to the edge of the causeway and stepped off it, yelping as icy water curled around my boot. I teetered for a second, then sat down hard on the stone.

The gray mare whickered as I scrambled to my feet. By now, the riders were almost upon us, and I turned to face them, my cheeks growing warm. They'd already had to pick their way carefully around the cart. Now the mare and I would slow them down further.

The first of the riders pulled up abruptly, reins snapping, his stallion's mane tossed wildly by the breeze. For it was a man—a young man—standing in his stirrups to peer at me. I caught an impression of fine clothes, fashionably cut. A lean, rangy frame. A practiced ease in the saddle. I quickly brushed the grime from my travel-worn garments.

Cantering up behind him came a much shorter and older man, suntanned, his long dark hair streaked with gray. He was dressed in servants' livery, a deep, rich violet.

"Who are you? Why do you trespass on our land?" The young man's voice was frosty, his accent well-heeled. He pulled his steed around, and I could see him more clearly. Brown-gold hair, slicked back but tousling in the rain. Smooth featured, striking, but in a fine-boned, birdlike sort of way. He was dressed in deep navy, a froth of lace at his collar; laconite glinted down his chest and on his cuffs.

"Corith Fraine," I said, raising my voice above the din. "House Shearwater's Floodmouth." I swallowed painfully. "Their *new* Floodmouth."

His lips tightened. "Brigant Shearwater is my father."

I'd suspected as much. I wondered if I ought to bow.

"That broken-down cart back there," he continued. "That was yours?"

I nodded, knowing my cheeks were still pink.

He tipped his chin, indicating the gray mare. "You and your horse will drown if you continue as you are. You do realize it is the middle of archwater? That the returning high tide will catch you in"—he consulted a pocket watch grimly—"a little over a quarter of an hour?"

I blinked, then turned to look out at the dark island. Certainly more than a quarter of an hour away at the glacial pace the mare and I had been maintaining.

"Why are you alone?" called the long-haired man behind him. He had a low voice, neat features, weathered and furrowed skin. "You should have at least one guardian with you if you came all the way from Arbenhaw."

Hearing the name of my former home felt strange.

"They . . . preferred to remain on the mainland," I said diplomatically.

He shifted in his saddle, a shade of suspicion entering his gaze.

The Shearwater studied me, looking over my grubby garments, and I flicked my eyes away, uncomfortable under that close stare. But he only shook his head, as though something far more pressing occupied his thoughts. As though my presence—my predicament—was an irritating interruption. "You didn't think to at least look at the tide tables in Port Rhorstin? Everyone in this region knows the tide times by heart. Those who don't dice with death, sooner or later."

My face heating, I thought of the engraved plaques in the square, the dense rows and columns of symbols and figures. And I thought, too, of Zennia. She'd surely have learned them, at least by the time the accident happened.

I caught the young man try to throw off a small shudder.

"We left on time, but . . . well," I answered stiffly, gesturing to the broken-down cart. It wasn't *my* fault it had fallen to bits.

"If you'd known the tides, you'd have known to ride your mare, or turn around and return to the mainland if you couldn't."

The man behind him cleared his throat. "Speaking of the tide, my lord . . ."

"Hells," the Shearwater whispered. He darted another glance at his pocket watch, then beckoned me. "Come on, quickly. Hand that case up to Tigo. We don't have time to idle here any longer." He eyed me, suddenly wary. "You'll have to sit up with one of us."

"I'll take her," said the man called Tigo. "Pepper here is bigger." And indeed, his black stallion was the largest I'd seen. Circling Pepper, who harrumphed at me dubiously, I passed my case up, then clambered into the saddle.

In the distance, I realized, I could no longer see the sea.

The Shearwater brought his horse around expertly and grabbed the reins of my puzzled mare. "It'll be a tight one," he said to Tigo, sounding strained. The rain had turned his hair dark; the breeze buffeted it into his eyes.

"We'll be fine," came the rumble of Tigo's voice behind me, and we set off, my thrumming heart like wings beating in my chest.

I could see my mare was slowing them down considerably. At full gallop, and with such powerful horses, I imagined this trip was usually quite quick for them. The Shearwater and Tigo had probably calculated their crossing perfectly.

Now I, and my poor mare, had made it far more perilous.

Thin rain soaked my face as we clattered down the causeway, my braids and Tigo's hair streaming out behind us. All around were the glimmering, weed-strewn mudflats, great dark headlands erupting to the north and south. Craning my head to peer back the way we'd come, I saw only a shadowed line where the coastline was, the far-off greenish tint of the marshes, and the causeway curving behind us like an eel.

My breath came faster as we neared the causeway's end. There was still no sign of any waves up ahead. The island reared now as though bearing down on us, its rocks, black and sea slick, thrusting up from sodden sands. The mass of land spiralled upward to a pinnacle, where an ancient-looking castle perched. Its walls were dark and weather-beaten, its ramparts crowded with flocks of white birds. Banners in the

House colors—deep violet, navy, and gold—flapped so violently they seemed about to take off.

Other squat buildings were clustered on the shoreline. There was another stone harbor, a small shingle beach. In just a few moments, we'd reach their safety.

And then—a spray of white against the rocks. With a jolt, I saw that the tide was coming back for us, already slopping shallowly at the shore.

The Shearwater pulled up, his steed's hooves skittering on the rain-slicked causeway. It was shocking how quickly the waters were rising. Pepper rattled up behind him, and we made the mistake of hesitating a moment. Channels filled, waves reared, surf fountained against the rocks. The swells broke over the causeway ahead, growing deeper by the second, threatening to cut us off entirely.

The Shearwater, I noticed, was looking at me. With horror, I realized it was a look of expectation. My eyes flicked to his laconite, and he nudged his horse back, only now appearing to realize the stone might hinder me.

I stared at the water and tried to call on my training, but Arbenhaw seemed a thousand miles away, Zennia's emboldening gaze even further—lost forever. My emotions were boiling, my heart a thudding drum. There was no use pleading with the water in this state, even if it had been inclined to listen.

I closed my eyes, knowing I had mere seconds to control this, and saw my ball of light flaring bright as a bonfire. But with the churning tide creeping ever higher and the Shearwater's gaze boring into my back, it was useless. I couldn't do it. I snapped my eyes open.

"Let us pass!" I gasped to the water anyway, but it was wild as a bear, implacable as stone. Tigo tensed behind me as a wave sloshed in front of us, making Pepper snort and toss his huge head.

Rhama's words came back to me: *"The ocean is a . . . different beast."*

He'd been right: This was nothing like the pools at Arbenhaw, where I'd had few problems succeeding in practicals. Where Zennia had always been standing to one side, reminding me that I could do this. Here I felt none of that strange, faint connection I usually felt when I spoke to water. None of that sense that we were somehow kindred. This water felt vast and alien. Wrathful.

"Come on," Tigo called, "before it gets any deeper." And with one solid arm steadying me in the saddle, he nudged Pepper forward, into the surf.

The Shearwater was no longer looking at me. He urged his horse and the gray mare onward, face pale under the iron sky. The sea buffeted us, swirled angrily over the causeway. Soon it was knee-high on our mounts and still rising. I was anxious about the mare—I could see the whites of her eyes—but she followed us dutifully, almost nose to tail with Pepper.

"Steady," Tigo said to the horses. "Steady now."

I nearly choked with relief as we made it to the beach. Our mounts staggered up the shingle, drenched to their bellies in seawater. Tigo tugged Pepper around, looking back out at the tide. Gulls rose in great flocks ahead of it, and a tidal bore burgeoned in one of the riverbeds. In the far distance, I saw tiny figures on the mudflats. Foragers, maybe, heading back to safe ground.

Twisting in the saddle, I caught the Shearwater's eye. He pushed back his rain-slick hair, staring at me.

"Welcome to Bower Island," he said, his tone clipped. "Tigo will show you your living quarters." Then he kneed his steed in the direction of the path upward and was off, riding hard up to the castle.

I bent my head to hide the burning in my face as Tigo and I hiked east from the beach. We'd dismounted to give the horses a rest, and were climbing a dirt path that switchbacked through a dense wood, curving around the castle to the far end of the island.

"Arbenhaw," Tigo said quietly behind me. When I looked back, he was shaking his head. "Thirty-five years, and I still dream about that place."

"You're Orha," I said, surprised, taking him in.

"Mudmouth," he replied shortly. "Your arrival completes the four of us."

The Shearwaters' set. The set I was now a part of. Cold nerves curled up from somewhere below my chest.

The silence between us dragged on for a few minutes. I almost felt that the specter of Zennia was here, striding up the path alongside us. I burned to ask about her—had they liked her? And she them? But the set of Tigo's shoulders told me the subject was closed.

Instead, in a clumsy attempt to be companionable and to redirect the conversation elsewhere, I asked, "What business took you to the mainland this morning?"

No answer was forthcoming, and when I looked back again, Tigo's stony gaze was fixed determinedly on the path.

I turned away, face heating once more. Yet again I'd made a misstep, said the wrong thing. Another in the long list of traits my classmates, save Zennia, had seemed to find so infuriating.

Through the ash trees, the tide marched on toward the mainland, and I paused, watching how quickly it moved. Tidal bores boiled up the sunken riverbeds, sending clouds of seabirds soaring in great arcs to collect in the branches and along the castle's ramparts, their screeching unceasing over the roar of the waves. I would find little peace and quiet here, it seemed. Suddenly I longed for Arbenhaw's weighty silence.

"I have a spare copy of the bay's tide tables," came Tigo's voice. He must have noticed me staring. "I suggest you commit them to memory tonight."

I swallowed, remembering the Shearwater's disdain. "Does it always come in that fast?" I asked.

"At archwater, yes," Tigo said, stopping near me. He shaded his eyes, gazing out through the trees. "We have four high tides a day, like everywhere else, but the bay speeds them up. Funnels the water. At peak archwater, the tides sweep the farthest—miles and miles in just a few hours—and for a week or two around it, they're still pretty dangerous. At low tide, they pull back so far they uncover the whole causeway, but only for a short time. You don't want to get caught."

"And pallwater?" I ventured, remembering my lessons.

"Much calmer," he replied, glancing at me. "But because the tidal range shrinks down so small, the sea comes in and settles in the bay, so part of the causeway's always covered."

"So no high tides and no low tides."

"Barely," he said, "for a week or so, at least. It's actually more trouble for the family than archwater, because the causeway's blocked and they have to take boats."

I wrenched my gaze from the far-off deluge and trailed him up the remainder of the path, toward a thin tower that rose in the east. It loomed steadily nearer and nearer until, after the track dipped downhill, we crossed a scrubby, gorse-strewn slope to its entrance. It looked down over a deep, rocky cove, the booming ocean only a few hundred yards off.

"*This* is where you live?" I couldn't help commenting. The tower was ivy choked, nearly crumbling in places. Some of the cracked stone had been reinforced with wooden beams. At its pinnacle, three stone protrusions curved inward, and there was empty space within them, letting in the rain.

"Take the steps up," came Tigo's voice as he relieved Pepper of the weight of his saddlebags. He hefted my case. "The ones straight in front of you."

But a little way over the tower's threshold, I paused. There were etchings here on the worn stone floor: the two moons, Arior and Amnhain, the first small, the second larger. This had been a temple once, I was sure.

At Arbenhaw, we learned that our ancestors had believed Arior and Amnhain to be the seats of the gods. The givers of moonslight. The origin of our calendar. And the divine directors of the world's great tides, which seemed to match the twin moons' movements uncannily. But apparently, now that noblemen-astronomers were pointing their new telescopes up at the heavens, we knew that the moons were merely rocky bodies. No godly dwellings of any kind. It was one of the reasons these temples had been abandoned.

Ahead of me, spiral steps wound upward. I hurried up them, conscious of Tigo waiting behind me, and passed a stained glass window in shades of blue and purple.

At the first landing, I glimpsed a small but tidy bedchamber, with soil-stained clothing hanging from a hook and rows of seedlings crowded into rough-hewn pots, along with jars of what looked like tea leaves. "That's me," came Tigo's gruff voice from the stairs. "You're up one farther." I hastened onward.

The next narrow window revealed more of the horizon. Below, near the deep cove, I caught movement through the glass: the suggestion of a tall, willowy figure on the clifftop.

The room on the next landing was stark, its walls bare. The fireplace was swept, the bed made up severely, and a chilly-looking stone seat nestled beneath the window. A forlorn pile of items sat beside a pockmarked dresser: a single framed painting, a few dog-eared books, items of simple clothing, folded.

Tigo lugged my case in and set it down on the bed.

"This was your predecessor's room," he said. "We didn't really know what to do with her things, after . . ." He gestured to the sad pile, then gave a helpless shrug. "We weren't sure if she had family, where they might be . . . or even if they'd want to know what happened."

My insides wrenched. I gazed around the room. It was hard to connect this spartan space with the warm, dynamic presence of my friend.

"Miss Catua, the youngest Shearwater, sorted through her belongings. Felt terrible about it all. She's a good girl, that one. Some of the things we sold at market. The rest are yours, if you can make any use of them."

I stepped to the pile, stared down at it wretchedly.

"I knew her," I said, my voice splintering. Somehow I couldn't bring myself to reveal just how close we'd been. "And trust me, her mother wouldn't much care."

Tigo glanced across at me, stoic, and for a moment there was silence, save the rumble of the waves outside. Then he cleared his throat and stepped to the window. "Mawre's our Gustmouth. She has the top room, upstairs."

Looking out, I caught sight of the figure again. A woman: tall, bony, brown skinned, with a long black braid that streamed out behind her. She was standing near the cliffs that encircled the cove. In front of her, secured to a large wooden frame, were linen shirts and breeches, flapping wildly in the wind. Laundry, I guessed, and by the look of it, the family's.

"There's Rhianne, too, our Sparkmouth—she's down in the cellar—but I don't know—"

As though his words had been a summons, the light patter of feet on the stairs reached our ears. Tigo slipped out the door. I heard whispers.

After a moment, a diminutive figure appeared. Dressed in the same purple livery as Tigo, she had a shock of red hair, an elfin face, an easy smile.

"Hurrah," she said on seeing me. "Another redhead. Soon we'll take over the world." She held a saucer of what looked like roasted sweetnuts, but when Tigo moved in and shot her a warning look—*Don't get too friendly*—her shoulders dipped.

Handing him the snacks and stepping over to my grate, she produced a pocket tinderbox, struck up a small flame, and murmured something to it. I jumped as it erupted with a roar.

"Easy there," Tigo muttered.

"Sorry," said Rhianne, warming her hands next to the fire. "I'm used to the big hearths up at the castle. Speaking of which . . ." She glanced out the window. "I'm due to help Cook with supper, and hells welcome me if I'm late."

"We'll leave you to get settled," Tigo said. He glanced down at the sweetnuts, then placed them on my dresser. "And I'll tell the housekeeper, Miss Haney, you're here."

As they turned toward the door, I couldn't help feeling suddenly very alone.

"What's it like?" I asked quickly before they could leave. "Working for them. House Shearwater, I mean."

I was thinking of Zennia's stories about the Hundred. Of the young man's cool regard on the causeway.

They exchanged a glance. Tigo seemed to deliberate. "It's good, solid work," he said simply, slowly. As though he were trying to convince himself as well as me.

"They leave us alone to get on with things, for the most part," added Rhianne. "It's Miss Haney we deal with day to day."

I thought they would go then, but Tigo hesitated, eyes flicking to the pile of items on the floor. "Zennia's . . . passing caused a lot of turbulence," he said. "Brigant Shearwater—he wasn't best pleased."

At Tigo's word—*passing*—my stomach flopped. Hearing it spoken aloud, at last, felt like a blade piercing my skin.

"It's usually a good idea to avoid Rexim's attention. But he may take a little more interest in your performance, these first few weeks, in the wake of . . . well"—Tigo scrubbed a hand over the back of his neck—"as he sees it, in the wake of Arbenhaw's failure, thus far, to provide him with a capable Floodmouth."

Anger stung me, while shame warmed my cheeks. Tigo had been there on the causeway; he'd seen me fail. If I couldn't persuade the ocean to listen to me soon, if this feeling of floating adrift got worse, Brigant Shearwater would surely notice. I'd be sent off somewhere else, perhaps somewhere far worse. I'd never make it to my meeting at the Veil, never find out anything more about Zennia.

"Zennia was the best of us," I said into the silence. "Top of our year. She was more than capable."

At that, Rhianne darted a quick look at Tigo. But the Mudmouth carefully avoided her eyes.

"We're needed at the castle," he said, grim faced. "I'm sure Miss Haney will contact you soon."

He took Rhianne's arm—a gentle steer—and the two of them padded out into the hall. Tigo pulled my door closed behind him.

As I stood there, every intake of breath hitching, their murmurs echoed up the stone steps. Quickly, I slipped off my boots and darted to the door. I eased myself through it, footsteps silent, and moved to the top of the spiralling stairs.

"How did the drop-off go?" Rhianne's voice, drifting upward.

Tigo's deeper one: "Fine, apart from the crossing back. Turnstone agreed to half the gold now and half in two weeks, on market day."

A pause. "Do you think he'll go out again tonight?"

"Undoubtedly."

The sound of a faint, shallow sigh.

Rhianne: "Did you hear what she said in there? About Zennia?"

I sidled forward, creeping down another stair.

But Tigo's answer, when it came, was short: "Not now."

And with that, their footsteps faded to nothing.

I stood there a moment, listening to my breathing, and thought of the Shearwater Tigo had been accompanying. Was that who they'd been talking about? And why had Rhianne been so struck by what I'd said?

Gripped, now, by a sudden fervor, I hurried to my room and stared around at it. There had to be something here of Zennia's—something other than that sad pile of items. But I went to them first, rifling through them.

The painting I'd noticed was a picturesque scene of the bay, its docks crowded with ships' masts. Maybe Zennia had bought it with her wages, but it seemed unlikely—we were hardly paid anything. I pried it from its frame, searched for any notes or names, but there was nothing. Perhaps it had come with the room.

The books were slim and looked well thumbed. One of poetry, the other of local legend. After flipping through them, chest tight with grief, I placed them carefully on my dresser, for later.

I couldn't make myself handle her clothes, some of which I recognized, painfully, from Arbenhaw, so I left them and set about searching the rest of the room.

I wasn't even sure what I was looking for, really. Anything else—anything that *meant* something. A hidden journal my friend might have kept; initials scratched somewhere on wood or stone . . . Something personal that would thread me to Zennia, help me picture her last weeks in this world.

But though I crawled under the bed and peered under the dresser, searched all the drawers for hidden compartments, tapped on the floorboards looking for loose nails . . . there was nothing. Only bare chill and emptiness.

I was left to sink onto the bed, where she'd slept, and stare at the ceiling through a thick haze of tears.

A summons arrived for me just before sundown, borne by a footman from up at the castle. He was dressed impeccably in navy livery embroidered with the House crest: a soaring, white-bellied shearwater.

His arrival interrupted my fevered practice in front of a basin of cold water in my room. Anxious to confirm I hadn't lost all my ability, I'd commanded the water to form a whirlpool, made waves in it, parted it, told it to spring into a fountain. It had heeded me, which was both reassuring and unsettling—though it collapsed as soon as the footman's knock sounded.

The summons turned out to be from Miss Haney. She wrote, in tiny, careful script, that the family had requested my presence at dinner. I was to present myself at the gatehouse at eight of the clock and was not under any circumstances to be late.

My hands trembled as I placed the note on my dresser. I hadn't touched the sweetnuts next to it; I was too nervous. I rifled through my garments—and, in desperation, Zennia's—trying to decide which were the least objectionable.

Eventually I settled on a plain ivory kirtle over a linen blouse with ballooning sleeves. It was nothing special, intended as workwear, but with my bodice laced over it and my hair brushed and braided, I hoped I wouldn't be turned away in disgrace.

It was too early to leave, but I knew that if I stayed, I would only end up anxiously pacing my room, so I grabbed the note and headed downstairs.

Tigo's room still stood empty, and Rhianne must be off stoking some stove somewhere. I ventured warily out of the tower, finding that the rain had finally eased off, and headed toward where I'd spotted Mawre from the window.

She was still there on the clifftop, speaking to the wind.

As I approached, I saw she was perhaps in her early thirties. In service, I knew from my lessons at Arbenhaw, younger Orha worked alongside older. As placements out in the Queendom became available—whether drying the Hundred's laundry or guiding merchant ships into harbor—graduates from the Institutions were sent to fill them. Most Orha grew old doing the same menial job.

We were born equal, none naturally any better than another, and though more years under our belts did mean more experience, nature didn't care whether we were eighteen or eighty—if we didn't temper our emotions, it would resoundingly ignore us. And the reason for that, we'd been taught at Arbenhaw, was that nature itself was merciless, unconcerned with our feelings; it preferred to commune only with like minds, with those who respected it.

How good we were, therefore, was down to nothing but control and our rapport with our element. Both of which, out here, were newly eluding me . . .

For her part, Mawre looked serene as a statue, a small pair of spectacles perched on her nose. Her vibrant purple livery matched Tigo's and Rhianne's. She noticed me out of the corner of her eye but didn't turn, merely offered a shallow nod.

"So you come to fill Zennia's boots," she said eventually. I felt the wind die a little in the absence of her coaxing.

I wondered how well they'd all gotten to know Zennia. Tigo and Rhianne had been wary, reserved, but for me that reaction was nothing new. Zennia had been easier to talk to, to laugh with; the only reason our classmates hadn't liked her was envy.

"I can only try," I said tentatively. "We were friends, Zennia and I. Back at Arbenhaw."

Mawre didn't seem surprised by this. Perhaps the others had conferred with her earlier.

"My sympathies," she said simply. "It must have been a shock. We were sad to lose her." She adjusted the linens.

I was desperate to ask what had happened—*how* it had happened. If the note in my case was to be believed, Rexim Shearwater had held something back in his letter to Arbenhaw, or at least didn't know the full story. *Foolhardiness. Ineptitude.* It just didn't square. Zennia had been confident but far from a fool. I'd never known anyone to learn so quickly.

Mawre turned and looked at me, but not in the eyes. "You're welcome here," she said with the ghost of a smile. "I'm sorry. I don't get on well with gossip or chitchat."

"Nor do I," I answered automatically.

I got the feeling that she was telling the truth; that it wasn't just an excuse because Tigo had warned her off.

I also got the feeling, suddenly and powerfully, that we were similar in some strange, indefinable way; that we shared some thread in our temperaments. I usually felt like a different species around people. But with Mawre, already, I felt a vague sense of understanding.

I held up the note. "The family wants me to dine with them." I couldn't quite keep the waver from my voice.

Mawre squinted at it, then briefly caught my gaze. "Probably Vercha, the eldest girl. If you're not careful, she'll make you her latest . . . project." She paused to rehang one of the shirts on the rack. "Or the Brigant. Perhaps he wants to get your measure. I've rarely seen him so angry as after Zennia died."

So Tigo had implied, back in the tower. Nervously, I wondered what "get your measure" meant.

But I recognized the closing of Mawre's features, the averted gaze, the slight lift of her shoulders, and I left her alone, as I'd have wanted to be.

Turning away, I took a deep, steadying breath and began the climb up the hill to the castle.

The sun was just setting, limning the damp island in gold. Already it was low tide again, the sea lurking beyond the cove, and the great expanse of seabed between here and the mainland was bare mud, cut through with meandering silver streams.

I guessed my way toward the gatehouse, past kitchen gardens bursting with cabbages and onions, and glasshouses filled with succulent-looking fruits. The castle itself squatted ominously on the rock, seabirds bickering and shuffling on its rooftops. It was ancient and built of a murky gray stone, darkened and roughened by the weather and salty air. Clearly the Shearwaters' reported wealth didn't extend to reinforcing their home with nabyrium, but it had a curtain wall surrounded by a deep ditch and round corner towers peppered with arrow slits. As I approached the gatehouse and the tall keep beyond, I saw lamps burning in the lofty windows, the flash of a figure moving behind leaded glass.

A thin woman I guessed was Miss Haney was there to meet me. She was nearly as tall as Mawre, though, unlike the Gustmouth, she stared full into my face, scrutinizing me carefully. With brown hair scraped back tight under a cap, a long nose, and a stack of well-worn frown lines, she had the look of a person perennially stressed.

"You must be Corith," she said as I came near, her accent as clipped and neat as her handwriting. "I'm so relieved. It's been a challenge, these last couple of weeks without a Floodmouth."

Couple of weeks. So that was when it had happened. We spent nearly a week on the road to get here, meaning Zennia died just a week before I left.

The Brigant had been quick to demand a replacement.

Miss Haney came toward me, put her hands on my shoulders. I tried not to flinch as she looked me up and down. Being touched, touching others, had never come easily. The only person it hadn't felt wrong with was Zennia.

The housekeeper didn't seem too happy about my attire, but, lacking the means to do anything about it, she sighed and said, "Never mind. We'll get you fitted for some livery. And you can accompany Miss Vercha to the next market day, on the fourteenth. I'll advance you your first wages to get some new clothes."

I fought to betray no reaction to her words. *The fourteenth.* Of course. Whoever had arranged my mysterious meeting must have known market day would be a good excuse to visit Port Rhorstin.

I nodded, which seemed to satisfy her, and she beckoned me onward. "Right. This way."

The gatehouse gave access to a wide, grassy outer ward. Through the barbican gate was a smaller inner ward, its ground tramped down to bare, packed earth. After the rain, it was sticky with mud, and I held my ivory skirts—in hindsight, a poor choice—as high as I could without baring too much wrinkled stocking.

When we reached the keep's entrance, Miss Haney seemed to dither.

"Ordinarily, we'd use the servants' door," she said, frowning, "but since you're the family's guest this evening . . ."

At that, my stomach knotted unpleasantly, my heart striking up a patter against my ribs.

She led me into a gloomy, high-ceilinged hall, all wood panelling, gilt edges, and candelabras. The walls were hung with dozens of dour portraits, intricate tapestries, cruel-looking weapons of war. An imperial staircase dominated the space, and perched on each of its wooden newel posts was a carved shearwater: beak open, wings raised.

As Miss Haney ushered me through the hall, I spotted a girl coming down the stairs. She was about my age, wide framed and round faced. Her blond hair, done up intricately with pins, glinted in the lamplight, her earrings winking, and her snub nose was buried in a dog-eared publication.

"Miss Catua," the housekeeper said in an undertone. "The youngest. Never without some periodical or another. She picks them up in Breawr, when the family visits the city. Giving her some funny ideas about things, if you ask me, but it's not my place to say anything, of course . . ."

Soon we came to some carved double doors, and before I could take even a second to steady myself, Miss Haney was rapping smartly on the wood.

"Do not speak unless asked a question," she whispered. "And do *not* refer to your predecessor. At all."

My insides jumped as the doors were pulled open, revealing two stiff-backed, navy-clad footmen and, beyond them, the Shearwaters' banqueting hall.

"Corith Fraine," Miss Haney called, "presenting for dinner."

I stared, beginning to sweat beneath my blouse.

The vaulted ceiling was two stories high, and a gallery ran across the far end of the room. The walls, whitewashed between deep-black beams, hosted the heads of stags; wolves with hungry gazes; even a bear, teeth bared, silently bellowing. Along one wall was the biggest hearth

I'd ever seen, big enough to warm a giant, surrounded by carved stone. Two lanky wolfhounds lounged in front of it. When they spotted me, their tails thumped lazily on the floor.

There'd been murmuring in the room as the doors were pulled open. Now an expectant silence fell. All eyes turned to me. I felt Miss Haney prod me forward.

"Ah," came a deep, rich voice. "At last. Miss Fraine."

Opposite me, sitting at the head of the huge table, was the man I presumed to be Rexim Shearwater.

Tall, and thick around the chest and middle, he wore a lace ruff, a decorated doublet with slashed sleeves, rings on his fingers, a heavy chain around his neck. He gazed piercingly at me with grayish eyes, his thin mouth downturned, face craggy with his years.

I saw little of his son in him—the one I'd met on the causeway. The young Shearwater sat with his back to the great hearth, a single empty chair separating him from his father. Perhaps he took after his mother instead, of whom I could see no sign at the table. Hair now dry and swept back off his forehead, he'd changed for dinner into well-tailored ebony. He watched me, too: aloof, assessing. The candlelight sent shadows pooling beneath his cheekbones.

"Introductions, I think," Rexim said with a slow smile. "I hardly think I need to tell you who *I* am. But here is Vercha, my second eldest"—he gestured to a young woman sitting to his right—"Catua, my youngest. And Llir, my second son."

The blond girl I'd seen, Catua, had slipped into a seat. She still had her book and was hiding it in her lap, racing to finish the page she was reading.

To her left, nearer Rexim, was the older daughter. Beautiful, with shining mahogany hair, Vercha studied me with a twist to her pert lips. She and her brother could almost have been twins: They had the same arch countenance, the same narrow, sculpted features.

“My eldest, Emment, is . . . otherwise engaged this evening.”

Rexim’s eyes flicked to the empty chair beside him and a slight awkwardness seemed to descend on the table. The seconds stretched out; then he added, “Do sit, my dear. Or would you prefer to stand there and eat?”

I blinked, coming back to myself. Vercha gave a tinkling laugh. With heavy legs, I sidled to a chair, and as I slid into it, Catua flashed me a reassuring smile.

Seeming to want to fill the silence that followed, Llir cleared his throat. “We met already, actually.”

“Oh?”

At Rexim’s curious gaze, Llir lifted a hand nonchalantly to the windows. “On the causeway this afternoon, when I was returning from town.” Nearby, servants hovered with carafes of wine, and at a glance from Rexim, they moved forward to decant them.

“Surely you didn’t *walk* here?” Vercha said to me, leaning forward. Her bright gaze was unnerving; I was reminded faintly of Caerig. “Poor thing. Are your guards from that school really so negligent?”

“Of course not,” Llir said with a fleeting frown. “Though their choice of transport did turn out to be very poor.”

“Whatever do you mean?” Vercha said, her lips quirking. “There’s a story here. Don’t keep us waiting.”

I couldn’t flash Llir a desperate gaze without it being spotted. But Vercha—and Rexim, who lifted an expectant eyebrow—would not be put off. I glimpsed Llir’s lips working.

“Her cart broke down,” he said eventually. “Halfway along. That’s all.”

“Gods, how dire,” said Vercha eagerly.

“That’s *all*?” put in Catua, looking far more concerned than her sister. “You must have had a close call with the Shadow Tide, then?”

“Yes,” Llir said, “it did get a bit dicey, but you know how good Tigo is with the horses.”

Rexim gazed at me, his gray eyes roving my face, as the servants carted in great silver platters. There was something new, something almost dangerous, in his expression. "It sounds like we almost lost you before we had you. And what a blow that would have been, so soon after the last . . ."

My stomach clenched, but I kept my face neutral.

"But of course, a truly *talented* Floodmouth should have few issues on the causeway, even at archwater. And you *are* a talented Floodmouth, I am sure, for I specifically requested the best Arbenhaw had to offer."

"I am, sir," I replied, fighting to keep my voice steady.

He hadn't technically asked a question—I'd probably broken Miss Haney's first rule—but the way they were discussing me back and forth over the table had grown almost unbearable. And I was angry now, too. Had Llir brought up the incident on the causeway on purpose, or simply not realized how it would look?

"So you *do* speak," Rexim said, still assessing me closely. "I was beginning to worry they'd sent us a mute." He took a deep sip of wine, patted his lips with a napkin. "Which would hardly be better than the specimen they sent last time."

The puff of a laugh escaped Vercha's nose.

I flinched as a deeper rage shot through me. *She had a name,* I wanted to hiss.

Catua, however, clinked her glass down firmly. She caught Llir's gaze with a look I couldn't decipher, but from the corner of my eye, he gave a narrow shake of his head.

"Well," Rexim said, surveying the feast before him. "We shall see. I look forward to witnessing your work." That small smile again, vaguely threatening.

My ears were ringing with what I'd assumed was anxiety, but now I realized it was the family's laconite. Rexim had small beads of it mounted down his doublet. Of the rings he was wearing, several bore the blood-red stone. Llir had a pendant on a chain around his neck, Vercha a jewelled carcanet above her gown. At first I didn't spot any on Catua; then I noticed her fiddling with her scarlet earrings, as though unused to their relentless buzzing.

It was Vercha who eventually changed the subject. "You will find this an excellent situation for service. I told Father we simply *had* to have you for the evening, to get to know you better. I take an interest, you see. We treat our set well, and they, in turn, do well by us." She smiled. "You know we pay better wages than nearly all the other Coastal Dozen?"

But still a pittance, I thought, staring around at the heavy silver, the golden candelabras, the meats piled on china plates. There were fish in sweet spices, a whole roasted crab. Tureens of sauces and gravies and cream.

The crystal goblets were finely engraved, and I wondered if they were Tresteny glass. Zennia had told me about her mother's glass-making business, the best in Nemestra, beloved by the Hundred. It was how Zennia had found herself in their company so often: Her mother visited the Houses, and the Houses came to her.

And Zennia had whispered to me, too, about the Sparkmouths working her mother's glass furnaces, paid a nominal few coins for their hazardous work. Fires had ripped through the furnaces often. No one cared enough to make it safer.

"I only wish," Vercha continued in a wistful tone, "we had more engagements in our social calendar we could take you to. Alas, we are a little too isolated out here. We visit the nearest city, Breawr, whenever we can, and we host friends and parties and even balls on occasion. But if you were imagining a life like the Hundreds' Orha in, say, Pen Aryn, I worry you may be a little disappointed." She darted a glance at her father under her lashes. I got the impression there was resentment simmering there.

"Just wait, Verch," said Catua, her eyes still on her book. "When Father wins the Chamber Seat, it'll be balls and soirées and theater trips all day. So many you'll get bored of them."

"I highly doubt she will," said Llir.

"Now, now," Rexim admonished as he tucked into a glazed pie. "Let's not get ahead of ourselves. And remember, Vercha, we have the luncheon next week." He flicked a glance at me over his raised cutlery. "But in any case, no politics at the table, remember?"

"Quite right," said Vercha. "We don't want to start Cattie off on one of her lectures."

As Catua rolled her eyes, my gaze snagged on Rexim's face.

A Chamber Seat?

The Chamber of Regents effectively ruled Nenamor. Queen Annig was only nine years old and, the rumors said, chronically sickly. There were five Seats in the Chamber, so that votes on policy were never tied, and the nobles who held them wielded immense power, especially the Queen's uncle, Regent Shrike: the man they called the Puppeteer. Zennia said Annig's reign had seen a lot of upheaval—more skirmishing, more jostling for influence, for patronage—and that lately things were coming to a head. I remembered the headline of the pamphlet I saw: DYING DUNLIN. The Hundred would be voting for his replacement, and Rexim must be in the running for that Seat . . .

Thoughts whirling, I tried to cover my surprise by reaching to serve myself from the nearest platter. Some rich meat dish, braised in heavy cream. We'd never had anything like this at Arbenhaw. Though I was still taut with nerves, my gown sticking to my back, I took mouthful after mouthful, savoring the exquisite taste.

The rest of the dinner passed with little attention paid to me; it seemed Rexim and Vercha had decided to stop prying. But that didn't make the evening any less agonizing, didn't stop me from feeling acutely out of place, as the family spoke of inconsequential matters, like what shade of drapes they would install in the ballroom to replace those too gnawed by moths to repair.

After a dessert of pears in ginger syrup—sweeter than anything I'd tasted before in my life—Vercha ushered me through a side door to a parlor, where a footman waited with a tray of more wine.

"We call this our snug," Vercha said, draping herself on a couch. "A bit pokey, and it doesn't get much light, but it was Grandmother Velda's favorite room."

The "snug" was little smaller than our practice chambers at Arbenhaw, with a high, plastered ceiling crisscrossed by beams and another great hearth, above which hung a portrait of a frightening-looking matriarch with the same grayish, calculating gaze as her descendants.

Vercha patted the couch next to her, smiling, and I forced myself to perch beside her, hands clasped.

"My," she said, moving a copper braid behind my shoulder. "You could be very pretty if you tried."

Llir had come in behind us, the wolfhounds at his heels, and his gaze caught mine fleetingly as he rounded the couch.

I remembered Mawre's warning: *"If you're not careful, she'll make you her latest . . . project."* But what choice did I have? I needed to stay here, impress in this placement, keep all of them on side, if I was going to get to my meeting in Port Rhorstin.

And so, as Vercha wondered aloud whether my hair would clash with the Shearwater livery, I said nothing, merely sat straight-backed and listened, occasionally nodding when she paused to draw breath.

Later, when even Vercha had run out of things to say, I was dismissed, Rexim waving a hand at me from his chair. "Do ensure you get enough rest, Miss Fraine, for you're likely to rouse early tomorrow. The Waking Tide can be merciless in the mornings."

"Not to mention the bloody birds," muttered Catua.

The Brigant had spent most of the evening settled by the fire, surveying me silently and a little unnervingly. Catua's head had been bent over her periodical, and Llir had seemed restless, stalking the bookshelves.

Now, as I stepped out into the empty banqueting hall, I heard murmurs behind me. An admonishment from Vercha.

I paused. The remnants of the feast had been cleared away. There were no servants about; it must have been past midnight.

Turning, I sidled back toward the door, keeping far enough away to be out of range of their laconite but close enough that I could just about hear their voices. My ears still rang with an after-echo from the stone.

"—like a hare being chased down by the hounds." Rexim's voice.

Vercha: "Oh, stop. I like her. I'll make something of her."

"Gods help her." A barely there mutter from Llir.

A moment of quiet, the only sound the spitting of the great fire.

Then Llir spoke again: "What of Regent Dunlin's condition, Father?"

I heard the clink of a glass, the faint panting of the wolfhounds. "It won't be long now. A matter of weeks—or days. My correspondents inform me he is declining rather rapidly."

A huff from Vercha. I pictured her lounging on the couch. "I *do* wish he would hurry up so the rest of us can just get on with the vote."

"Now, Vercha. Dunlin has served the Chamber well." There was the creak of a chair as Rexim shifted position. "Levelheaded man. Kept the others in line on many an occasion."

"But the longer he hangs on," said Llir, "the longer Crake has to catch your lead."

At that name, I remembered Caerig's words: *"There's a . . . rivalry there. Things are a little tense at present."*

"Crake can't catch up now, can he?" Catua this time. "Most Houses don't want someone so reactionary, surely? He's stuck in the past, especially about Orha. Just look at Breova—the same thing will happen here soon enough."

Breova. The kingdom that neighbored ours. Our lessons had covered their bitter infighting, which had raged, on and off, for a century now, but glossed over the social upheaval that came after.

"Will it really?" Vercha, an edge to her voice. "I rather think that's your own progressive sensibilities talking. *Misguided* sensibilities, I might add."

The rumors, spread by trainees whose families had read the pamphlets, were that Breovan Orha now had almost as many rights as common folk. None of us knew for sure, since our border was closed, had been since Breova's latest war, decades ago. The Regents kept voting to keep it shut, claiming the decision was for Nenamor's safety.

"Crake's losing because of the land grab he's planning with Shrike," said Llir. "Not because his policies would be harsher on Orha. The Houses don't care what happens to Orha, but they don't want to end up at war with Breova."

"That's right," murmured Rexim. "Crake's always been a warmonger, and I believe the appetite for that is drying up somewhat. Annig's reign has depleted the Houses' resources . . . They're tired of all the skirmishing. They're looking to me to move us forward."

"Yet you'll still let society be dictated by the Great Revolt?" said Catua. A few seconds of tense quiet followed.

"Well, anyway, Crake's not the real threat, is he?" Vercha again. "You heard the latest from Tresteny, I assume? Brigantess Blackcap, *poisoned* at her own breakfast table?"

"Indeed." Rexim's voice had turned grave. "We must be more

watchful than ever. Especially on the mainland. I keep telling Emment—"

"Wasn't one of their hidey-holes blown up in Pen Aryn last week?" Llir, who sounded like he was pacing the room. "Doesn't seem to have slowed them down much, by the sound of it."

My skin prickled all over. They must be speaking of the Cage.

"Forget Crake," Vercha said. "Those *murderers* are trying to destroy our society. Don't they know what things were like before the Great Revolt? Don't they realize what would happen if Orha were given free rein?"

"They know the histories," Llir murmured. "They just don't believe them."

Vercha scoffed. "It was our ancestors who saved this realm from ruin. If anything, I'd say we need *stricter* controls."

A mutter from Catua: "You're starting to sound like Crake himself."

After a short pause, Vercha's tone grew a little more conciliatory. "It's very unfortunate, but the Orha at those Institutions are just too powerful, too valuable, to be left to their own devices. To direct their own destinies. Don't you agree?"

A huff from Catua. Silence from Llir. If Zennia had been here, she'd have marched right in, too angry to worry about the repercussions.

Our lot in life made me angry, too, of course. But unlike Zennia, I'd felt mostly fear. Fear that I'd displease whoever I worked for and wind up in a wagon bound for Crake's Quaglands. Fear that if I pleased the Instructors *too* well, I'd end up as one of Regent Shrike's black-eyed servants . . . And fear that Zennia, if she'd been foolish enough to run, would have met her end on the gallows—as Owyn likely had.

"Perfectly stated," Rexim was saying. "I'd be willing to consider minor concessions to Orha rights . . . but not these bizarre reforms Regent Finch is pushing. Breova has made a grave misstep, in my opinion. The Hundred need someone they can trust in the Chamber, someone as steady handed and, yes, *predictable* as Dunlin. Particularly since whoever wins this Seat will have the power to sway policy one way or the other."

Without warning, a patter of footsteps approached the door. My insides clenched, and my breath hitched in my throat. There was no time to run. I reeled backward—

As one of the waist-high wolfhounds slipped through the door.

Amber eyes gazed out at me from a shaggy mass of gray fur. I held my breath, steeling myself for a bark, or at least a growl, but after a few seconds, he padded quietly past me, clearly deciding I was no threat and of no interest.

"You know it's late when the dogs go to bed before you," Catua commented.

"Indeed," came Rexim's voice. "Where in hells is your eldest brother?"

I'd been stupid to linger at all, let alone for this long.

Without waiting to hear what any of them said next, I hurried after the hound, keeping to the shadows.

Outside, the air held the tang of the ocean. Lights still burned in the castle windows behind me, but ahead and around, all was cast in deep shadow. Aside from the far-off glow of Port Rhorstin, the flats and the mainland beyond were solid black.

I picked my way back through the kitchen gardens, through the silent gatehouse with its scant night watchmen, and was about to turn north, circle around to the Orha's tower, when I heard it:

A strange noise in the darkness ahead of me.

It came from the dirt path that wound up from the pinewood, from the shingle beach, where the low tide murmured against the rocks. Something, or some*one,* was heading up the track.

I soon made out the clopping of a horse's hooves, and the strange sound I'd heard resolved into a song, albeit a slurred and slightly out-of-tune one. A moment later, its singer materialized: a broad-shouldered man sitting unsteadily in his saddle. He was dressed in an embroidered emerald-green doublet with gold stitching, a frilled silk shirt collar poking out. He had a thatch of dark hair; handsome, regal features. As I watched, he listed heavily to his left, then jerked suddenly upright as he spotted me standing there.

"Great gods," he exclaimed, squinting at me through the shadows. He'd paled, his fingers gripping the reins. "Just a girl. I thought you were . . ." He paused, collecting himself. "I thought you were a wraith. A fetch, or something."

With a nervous chuckle, he stilled his horse, then dismounted heavily, staggering a little. "Oops." He steadied himself against the beast. "Perhaps a bit too much of the Myrnian red . . ."

I said nothing. So this was Emment Shearwater. I now knew who Tigo and Rhianne had been talking about. *"Turnstone agreed to half the gold now and half in two weeks, on market day."*

He peered at me with silver eyes bleary with drink and hung on tightly to his steed's reins to stay upright. "You're *not* a wraith, are you?"

"No," I said. "I'm your family's new Floodmouth."

At that word—"Floodmouth"—the planes of his face hardened, and he swallowed queasily as he looked me up and down. For a second, his eyes seemed to dart out to the mudflats, which were wreathed in black. Distantly the sea blustered.

"About time," he muttered, starting forward, his horse dutifully matching his weaving path. "Maybe my shirts won't take three days to come back to me now."

As he passed me, he waved a hand dismissively in the air. "Welcome and all that, I suppose. You know."

He hiccupped—and then disappeared into the darkness.

I snapped awake before dawn to a thumping on my floorboards.

"Here. Bind her hands. Get that blindfold on."

"And gag 'er. 'Case she tries somethin' stupid."

For a moment or two, in my groggy, disoriented state, I assumed I was back in my room at Arbenhaw and that someone was banging insistently on my door. All was dim, the glass in the window deep navy. It took me a second to realize the thumps were boot steps.

Then hands were hauling me roughly from my bed, looping a gag around my face, muffling my cries. I remembered where I was—the island, the tower—and smelled the musty, outdoorsy scent of the intruders. Not Caerig and Rhama. Not anyone I recognized from their voices.

I bucked and struggled, grunting with the effort, but there were three of them, and they were strong. Soldiers, maybe.

"That's it," said one, a woman's deep voice.

As I lashed out with an elbow, tried to stop them binding my ankles, a man laughed right next to my ear. "She's a whippet, this one, i'n't she?"

I cringed away as I was tugged to standing and propelled from the room, toes bumping over the floorboards. They began to drag me down the steep tower steps.

In the blackness of my vision, my crimson ball of emotions sparked. There had been no point in gagging me: With my adrenaline spiking, my heart rate speeding, no water would heed me, even if there had been any close by.

Footsteps sounded on the stairs behind us. Another set, lighter, coming up from the cellar.

"Hoi, what's going on?" Tigo's gruff voice.

And Rhianne's, groggy: "Where're you taking her?"

Metal rang faintly, like a weapon being hefted. I tried to call out around my gag.

"Back, Mudmouth. There's a good man, now." It was the woman. There came another scrape of steel. "Brigant's orders. He wants the Floodmouth. Don't you worry, it's all in hand."

My ribs thumped violently. It was *Rexim* who'd ordered this?

They dragged me backward out of the tower.

Cool air hit me. The scent of the sea. The cold solidity of the tower's stone floor turned softer, bumpier: packed earth and grassy hillocks. Then the ground dropped away—we were descending rapidly.

The realization came over me like a sickness. After learning from Llir what had happened on the causeway, the Brigant must have decided I was useless and was already packing me off back to Arbenhaw.

But with nothing on save a nightshift? Bare feet?

Nearby, I heard the shushing of the ocean, building its strength before it rushed into the bay. "Not far, little whippet," came that horrible voice, and I shuddered, going limp, forcing them to half carry me down the steep cliff paths.

At last the ground levelled, went spongy beneath my feet. Freezing water pooled around my toes. I staggered on, hearing the sea's susurration, but it was muted, as though on the other side of a wall.

I was shoved forward roughly and fell to my knees.

"Ticktock," said the third man as he loosened my wrist bindings. He pressed something cold and hard into my palm. "You'll want to make use of that sharpish, I warrant."

Chuckles from the others. I heard them squelch away.

Bewildered, I fingered the object they'd given me and pricked myself on its pointed tip. A knife, small, not particularly sharp. Trembling, I raised it and hacked away my blindfold.

When my eyes had adjusted to the predawn murk, I turned in a circle, or as best I could with my ankles still bound—and stared up at the nearly sheer cliff faces around me.

They were twenty, maybe closer to thirty, feet high. I'd been dumped in the deep cove, its only entrance to the east: narrow, like a winding alley, the rocks overlapping and concealing the bay beyond. Three sets of footsteps led out that way, but they were already starting to disappear in the wet sand. Above, the sky was just beginning to pale, thin clouds cloaking the waning moons.

My thoughts darted, whirled, like a shoal of fish. Why had they dropped me here if Rexim had sent for me? Why give me a knife to free myself with?

I bent down to saw at the rope around my ankles, intending to follow them as soon as I could. My gag still bit into the sides of my mouth, and my hair and nightshift were damp with a cold sweat.

"Good morning, Miss Fraine."

I jumped, dropped the knife. Craning my neck, I saw figures on the clifftop.

Rexim Shearwater stood closest to the edge. A little way back, just their heads and shoulders visible, were Vercha, Llir, a stricken-looking

Catua. The eldest, Emment, whom I'd met in the night, wore a velvety night-robe and a nauseated expression.

Llir stared down at me, face unreadable. Vercha looked thoroughly entertained, eyes glittering, her high collar sprouting with lace.

"I hope you slept well last night, as I advised." Rexim's voice carried well despite the distance—a quirk of the way the wind was blowing. "My apologies for the rather uncouth method of bringing you here. But you see, if I'd asked you, I think you would have refused."

I tried to call out, to demand to know why I was here, but the gag turned it into a series of muffled grunts. I snatched up the knife, intending to cut the gag away. But the Brigant appeared to grasp my meaning.

"Just a simple test," Rexim said with a smile. I froze. Behind me came an ominous, growing roar. "I have to be sure, you understand. After what happened with your predecessor, I can't take any chances. And when I was made aware of what happened on the causeway . . ."

My eyes flashed to Llir, my body tense with panic. He blinked, just once, his features pulled taut.

"After all," Rexim continued, "I have my family's safety to think of. And I need to know now if you will also disappoint us."

Behind him, Catua snapped out a few words, but the others ignored her. The roaring grew louder.

I stumbled, turned, stared out at the cove's entrance. I could hear it clearly now.

The rising tide.

Gripping the knife harder, I sawed frantically at my gag. It soon came away, and I pitched it onto the sand. But there was still a rope looped tight around my ankles. I squatted, my pulse pounding heavily in my skull, and as I got to work on it, another noise reached my ears: the first great *boom* against the rocks outside the cove.

My palm was burning with the motion of the knife. The rope resisted, frayed, then began to come apart.

Another *boom.* I glanced up, saw the first fountains of surf.

Then steel-gray water came barrelling down the gorge.

Funnelled by the bay, and now the cove's twisting entrance, the Waking Tide raced in like a horse at full gallop.

I barely had time to cut through the rest of the rope before the trough of the next wave fanned out around me, white veined and frothing. I was misted with spray. I staggered back, saw the next wave already rearing, but knew I should steer clear of those jagged cliff walls . . . I could be dashed against them, knocked senseless. And drowned.

The wave loomed, made monstrous by the gorge ahead of me. I braced myself, and a second later, it crashed down, knocking me from my feet, sweeping me with it. I caught a fleeting glimpse of Rexim's broad silhouette, the wide eyes of the siblings, the still-murky sky, before I was under, bitter salt filling my mouth, my eyes stinging and my body seizing with the cold.

I was a strong swimmer—all trained Floodmouths were—but this was a far cry from the practice pools at Arbenhaw. I broke the surface, flailing in a desperate dog paddle, but the dark water was rising, bearing me toward the cliffs. Rather than take the next wave head-on, I ducked under, my body lurching with the current.

At last, a single thought broke through: *You have to get hold of yourself. You have to* do *something.*

"Please," I choked, bubbles streaming from my mouth. "Still your waves. Grant me passage."

But it was laughable to think the tide would heed me, with my panic spilling over, consuming me completely. It was stubborn, belligerent, a bull charging its fences. And I couldn't shake that overwhelming sense of its immensity. By comparison, I was a fly buzzing at the bull's ears.

Frantically I surfaced, took a huge, gulping breath, then sank again, preferring the muted buffeting underwater. I squeezed my eyes shut, tried to conjure my red ball of panic, but all I kept picturing were the Shearwaters' faces. Vercha's wide smile. My own messy demise.

With a wrench, I forced myself to picture Zennia's face. But already, even though I'd seen her only a month ago, it was fuzzier at the edges; I couldn't bring her into focus. I was adrift here, in this wild, lonely place. Cast out like a fishing line, but never to be reeled back in.

Another wave broke then, tossing me backward. Stone scraped my spine, and I cried out in pain. With the next wave, I knew I'd be flung against the cliff face.

Again I braced myself. This time for my death.

But then I felt a sort of . . . *ceasing.* Not in the raging sea around me but in my own mind. My body. A shutting-down of sorts.

I would die here—I was as certain of that as of the sunrise—and that was all right. There was nothing I could do. And because I was powerless to change my fate, surely there was no point agonizing about it?

A memory came to me. Zennia's face, clearer now. The first time she taught me the calming trick, explained to me how she pictured her emotions. We'd been paired off in one of Caerig's classes, and as usual, the Instructor had showed no mercy. I'd panicked, convinced this was the day my mask slipped and Caerig saw the turmoil that churned within me.

I remembered Zennia's whispers as we treaded water in the pool, our blouses ballooning, our hair slick against our faces.

"Mine looks like a hole ripped into a piece of paper. I repair it, bit by bit, until there's just the tiniest tear . . ."

I swayed in the tide's current, waiting for the next wave, content that my friend's face would be the last one I saw—and as I sensed the growing swell, my red ball popped into being.

In this new, serene acceptance of my end, the ball was smaller, wavering. Pinkish, like a sunset. Curious, I prodded at it. Shrunk it to an acorn. Then I cracked my eyes and lips open and said, "Please."

The wave looming above me paused, teetering right on the edge of breaking. With my panic now tempered, the tide seemed to be *listening*, though I got the sense this was a begrudging reprieve. It shrunk a little, then shattered, shoving me back toward the cliff. I still impacted hard against the wall behind me, my clothes snagging, my bare limbs bruising, but I was able to cling onto an outcrop of rock.

I tried to dampen any jubilation—joy, relief: they were still emotions, they could still hamper my plea, turn the tide back against me—but the sea's rage ramped up again almost immediately, the next building wave looking to be the biggest yet. Hastily, I concentrated on climbing. One hand, one foot, one *haul* at a time.

A wave smashed into the rock face, barely missing me, its spray stinging my grazed knees and calves. Turning, I risked a glance out at the cove. The water was furious, its waves head-high and merciless, climbing the cliff face almost as fast as I was. I forced myself upward, my muscles on fire.

It took what seemed an inexorably long time, but I finally neared the lip of the steep wall. I was well above the tide now—it had risen to its peak—but the pain from the scrapes on my hands and feet, the burning in my arms, tipped beyond unbearable, and I slipped, my body swinging out over the drop.

A brisk gust of wind, strong as a hand on my back, blasted into me, nudging me back against the wall. A fortuitous sea breeze, I guessed as I clung there. More powerful up here, without the shelter of the cove.

Finally, arduously, I flung a hand up over the cliff. An arm appeared, enrobed in velvet, and heaved me upward, seeing me safely over the edge.

I crawled forward on my hands and knees, hair sodden and nightshift dripping, and peered up to see Emment Shearwater above me. He looked like he might expel the contents of his stomach, but whether that was down to the events just passed or his activities last night, I had no idea.

"A somewhat fraught pass," came Rexim's voice, "but a pass nonetheless, I suppose. I congratulate you."

Pass. He couldn't know that I'd utterly failed. That the only reason I'd survived was because I'd . . . given up.

I sat back on my haunches. A croak escaped my lips: "You're twisted."

I instantly regretted it, but Rexim only chuckled. "As I said previously, I had to be sure."

Eager to gather up some shreds of my dignity, I forced myself to stand and hugged myself, shivering. Water pooled beneath my shift's hem.

Llir was standing some distance away, staring. Vercha seemed delighted by the whole sadistic display: Her gloved hands were clasped as though she'd been applauding, and her expression was disconcertingly proud. Catua, on the other hand, was nowhere to be seen—she must have left, perhaps in protest.

"See? What did I tell you?" Vercha said, stepping forward. "I knew she'd get there eventually." She tipped her head. "Come now, don't let hard feelings fester. There was no way to test you without its being a surprise. And you passed, didn't you? No need to dwell on what *might* have happened . . ."

"You'd have let me die," I whispered, trembling. "All of you."

Emment had moved a few feet away, his hands on his thighs, his face oddly grayish. He swallowed, and Llir put a hand on his shoulder, but his brother shrugged him off. He avoided all our eyes.

"We'd have pulled you out before it came to *that,*" Vercha said.

She gestured to three hulking figures nearby. I'd overlooked them, perhaps mistaking them for rocks. But they were my kidnappers, I was certain of it: a woman and two men. Beside them rested a comfortable-looking litter.

"We don't expect you to walk back, of course."

I moved a few steps away. "I'm not getting in that."

Rexim's dark eyebrows dipped in displeasure. I'd somehow gotten away with my first outburst, but now he looked irritated, dangerously impatient. The rational part of me berated myself.

When Zennia told me her stories back at Arbenhaw, I admittedly wondered if those early memories might have blurred together with the wild imaginings of a young child. I wondered if the Hundred really considered us that lowly. Now it didn't seem far-fetched at all.

But I knew that if I made an enemy of the Brigant, I'd be straight back to Arbenhaw today—or worse. I'd never know what awaited me at the meeting in Port Rhorstin, never know what had happened to Zennia in the bay.

"I meant to say," I tried again mildly, "that I'd prefer to walk. Thank you."

"As you like," Rexim replied after a pause, and snapped his fingers at the waiting guards. They jerked to attention and lifted the litter, bearing it up the stone-strewn path. "Today," he added, "your real work begins. I expect you to report to Miss Haney without delay."

Though my body pulsed with pain, and Rexim must have known it, I forced myself to stand straight-backed as the family moved away, trailing after the soldiers. Rexim and Vercha walked together, speaking quietly. Emment looked relieved to be heading back to his bed.

Llir left last, troubled gaze out on the ocean. I glared at his back. This had all been his fault. If he hadn't mentioned the causeway last night, Rexim might never have gotten this idea into his head.

I waited until they were far enough ahead of me, then took a deep breath and limped back toward the tower.

But it wasn't until I was halfway there, and heard the waves battering the cliffs behind me, that I realized I had forgotten to thank the Waking Tide.

It took me an age to pick my way painfully up the slope.

My palms and soles were raw from the climb, my muscles screaming, my nightshift sodden and heavy. In the distance, the Shearwaters disappeared into the castle, no doubt to enjoy a sumptuous breakfast. My stomach growled, but I ignored it, pressing onward.

The base of the Orha's thin tower came into view, three figures outside it, two short and one tall, dressed for the day in their violet livery. Tigo had a hatchet resting against one shoulder. Rhianne shaded her eyes against the rising sun, her face screwed up, wincing, as she watched me approach. Mawre, standing slightly apart from the others, had her arms folded tightly over a fringed navy shawl.

I balled my fingers into fists, more to hide the tremors in them than anything, and slipped on my mask: that stony schooling of my features that was second nature after my training at Arbenhaw.

"I'm sorry he put you through that," Rhianne said, taking me in. "We saw everything from up there." She nudged her chin toward the top of our tower—the steps must have spiralled all the way to its pinnacle.

"I knew he was angry about what happened with Zennia, but I didn't think he'd . . ." She shook her head, gave a shrug.

Tigo surveyed me, his brows pinched together. Reticence and concern fought for dominance in his expression.

"I'll dry those," said Mawre, gesturing to my wet nightclothes. "You should go up and change. I'll wait downstairs."

I appreciated that none of them fussed. Grateful to escape their gazes, I hurried up the steps and donned some dry workwear, wringing my nightshift out over the basin. The smell of brine made my insides turn over as it hit me just how close I'd come to drowning—like Zennia.

Downstairs, Mawre took the sodden pile and left. Behind her, Tigo and Rhianne still lingered. Rhianne had been hissing something to Tigo as I descended.

"I brought some breakfast from the kitchens," she said suddenly. "It's not much, but I thought . . . well, that you'd need it after all that."

My jog to and from my room had left me lightheaded, and my stomach burbled, giving me away. I nodded warily and followed her down into the cellar. Tigo leaned his hatchet against the wall and came down behind us, like a watchful chaperone.

Rhianne's cellar room was surprisingly cozy, with a crackling fire, brightly colored wall hangings, a circle of mismatched, tired-looking chairs, and a narrow, blackened stove on which a kettle was already boiling.

"If it's any consolation," she said, handing me a plate, "he'll probably ignore you now, like he does with us. Just keep your head down, get all your work done . . ."

I perched in one of the armchairs with my food: slightly stale bread with butter caked on it, dried fish, a hunk of cheese going hard at the edges.

"D'you think it was all his idea?" I said. "You don't think the siblings helped him plan it?"

Tigo folded his wiry arms.

"Vercha, maybe," Rhianne said quickly, "but definitely not Catua." Rosy spots bloomed on her cheeks. "She hates anything like that. Orha mistreatment. Actually, she's quite progressive."

"Emment only returned in the early hours," said Tigo. He'd moved to the stove and was clinking cups around, tense shouldered. "He wouldn't have had time to confer with his father. And Llir certainly wouldn't have been involved."

I frowned. "I think he was. Llir, I mean. He mentioned at the dinner that we'd already met, then ended up practically *telling* Rexim about yesterday . . ."

Rhianne dipped her head over the tea Tigo handed her. From the way she carefully avoided my eyes, I guessed he'd told her what happened on the causeway.

Tigo paused a moment, then placed my tea on an end table. "As I said, Llir wouldn't have had a hand in something like that."

I quirked an eyebrow skeptically. "What's his problem, anyway?" I ventured. I had so many questions, I couldn't keep them from spilling out. "He seems to have taken against me from the start. And he stalks around the place like the weight of the world's on him . . ."

I caught Rhianne flicking her eyes at the Mudmouth.

"If you mean Llir's lecture on the causeway," said Tigo shortly, "he was right that it's foolish to be ignorant of the tides."

My face warmed as I dropped my gaze to my tea. I hadn't had a chance to look at his tide tables.

"And if you really must know, he and I were on the mainland yesterday to sort out the latest of Emment's gambling debts."

I glanced up, surprised, but Tigo had his back to me, busying himself with the breakfast things. "The Brigant, of course, would never go himself, though he seems happy to keep covering his eldest son's 'expenses.' And he won't send his daughters or any other servants. He doesn't want them to know."

"Though we all do," put in Rhianne.

"So if Llir seemed preoccupied . . ." After a pause, Tigo shrugged. "The boy has his challenges, like any of us."

I swallowed the scoff that threatened to spill out of me. What true challenges could someone like Llir have? Born into luxury. The freedom to go anywhere. All his whims catered to by servants like us.

"Fine," I said. "But something's going on with Emment. There was something wrong with him up on the cliffs, and it wasn't just the hangover. And I ran into him on my way back here last night. He was drunk, but as soon as I said who I was, it was like a shutter came down . . ."

Another fleeting look between them.

"He hasn't been the same since the accident," Rhianne said tentatively, keeping one eye on Tigo. "He was out there, after all. Saw . . . saw her drown."

"Wait," I said, dropping a crust onto my plate. "What?"

A few seconds of silence, then Tigo sighed heavily. "Zennia accompanied Emment to Port Rhorstin so he wouldn't have to row; so the crossing went quicker. The accident happened on the way back, at night. Big waves, he said. They got into trouble."

Rhianne had paled and was fiddling with her mug. "He was shaking harder than I've ever seen anyone . . . Got us all up, made us go out there looking . . ."

"You searched for her?" I whispered, thinking of the bay: its miles-wide vastness, its deep, choppy waters.

"Didn't find anything," Tigo murmured. "But that's no surprise. She'll be out east by now, I expect. At rest."

His words left me cold and oddly comforted at the same time. "I didn't realize someone had seen," I croaked. "She's really gone."

Tigo nodded, his gaze far off. Rhianne, however, still looked jittery.

"We should go," she said to Tigo, eyes darting to the doorway. "It must be getting on for seven by now."

"I'll be there soon," I said, getting up to rinse my cup.

The two of them seemed stiff shouldered, closed up. I often sensed a remove when people were with me, when they detected that strange frosted glass between us. But I didn't think the Orha's reserve was born from that. It seemed to stem from suspicion, from things still left unsaid. The gambling, the accident—all that was no doubt true—but I got the impression Tigo had used them as a cover, to try to put down my prying about the brothers.

For something about the Shearwater family nagged at me.

There were secrets on this island. And I found myself hungry for them.

I didn't have long before Miss Haney would miss me, but I couldn't bring myself to face the day just yet. My limbs throbbed as though I'd been churned in a barrel. I trudged up the steps to my third-floor room, the sea breeze whistling through the cracks in the windows, and lay on my bed, staring up at the ceiling.

The revelation about Emment and Zennia hung over me, a shadowy cloak stifling the tiny part of me that had secretly hoped my friend might just have survived. But Emment had seen her drown. They'd searched and hadn't found her . . .

She wasn't hiding. She hadn't run. She was truly gone.

I lay there gazing at the wall above my bed, watching the way the light pooled in its crevices, the nooks and crannies between the rough stones. As I did so, a memory came to me suddenly: standing tiptoe on my bed at Arbenhaw, a week or so after we'd been moved to single rooms. Tapping on the stone and hearing Zennia tap back. Hissing through a crack, *"Are you there? Can you hear me?"*

I blinked, my pulse sounding louder in my ears. A tingle ran over the skin on my arms. Clambering up, I peered into the clefts in the wall.

Some were mere cracks—too thin for what I sought—but others were slightly crumbled and gaping. Feeling at once fevered and foolish, I stretched up, ran my fingers across them.

And then, with a twang in my chest like a bowstring, I saw it: something pale in the blackness. Something that looked a lot like paper, rolled up tight and pressed into a fissure.

I scrabbled, picking at it, easing it out. I told myself it would likely be nothing—a blank page stuffed there to keep out a draft, or a lover's letter from a previous inhabitant.

But when I finally drew out my prize and carefully unrolled it, smoothing the creases, my heart began to bang against my ribs. For writing covered the sheet of paper. And some of it was in a code I recognized.

I jumped down, ignoring the jar in my muscles, and ran to the window, where light speared in. Now I could see the writing more clearly. Or, rather, the lines and numbers and shapes.

It had been one of the first things we'd done in lessons, after I'd finally realized we were friends. A code, concocted in total silence, achieved by sneaking glances at each other's papers. We weren't permitted to speak in lectures, but we were allowed to sit side by side. Eventually we could have secret conversations just by inking symbols in our margins.

There was only one person who could have written what I'd found. My fingers shook as my eyes roved the paper, easily translating the code—into a letter.

13th Illir, Bower Island

Corith,

I'm not sure why I'm writing this to you, since I can't imagine a circumstance in which you'll ever read it, but you know I've never been one for introspection. It feels easier, somehow, to "talk" to you instead.

I miss you. I even miss Arbenhaw, if you can believe it. I thought it would feel good to escape to somewhere new, even if a tough job awaited me there, but this place . . . it's hard not to feel trapped out here. And the people—well, you know how I feel about the Hundred.

I probably shouldn't have written that last part. I so wish I could talk about everything I want to, but I worry about this "journal" being discovered and then being forced to translate its contents. Rexim Shearwater seems like the type to do that. I can already tell he, and his eldest daughter, don't like me.

But it's not just the fact that I don't feel welcome, and how cut off we are out here. It's that I can't seem to shake the feeling that everyone on this island knows something I don't.

I can see up to the castle in the early hours from here, and sometimes I make out lights in odd places. Like the culverhouse, where they keep crows to send their letters, and one of the towers in the curtain wall, which Miss Haney says aren't used for anything anymore.

Anyway, like I said, I shouldn't be writing this, and it's probably nothing—maybe the isolation is getting to me.

I really just wanted to say that I miss you. And actually, I think I already feel better for it.

Your friend, always,

Z

I read the journal entry again, then a third time, eyes burning with the beginnings of tears. I flipped it over, hoping to find more, but there was nothing, only a couple of scrawled dates. Maybe Zennia had intended to write more, but she'd never gotten around to it or she'd been interrupted . . . and then the accident had happened. A shiver passed through me. *"Everyone on this island knows something I don't."*

Abruptly, footfalls sounded outside, and I shoved the paper deep into my pocket. Mawre, coming past my room. Time for chores.

On my way down the steps, I paused to stare out a window that faced west, to the castle. The curtain wall had countless towers; there was no way to tell which one Zennia had meant. And maybe she *had* been seeing things: the gleam of gold-tinged moonslight on glass . . .

But whoever had invited me to the meeting at the Veil seemed certain there was something I ought to know. And now, after reading Zennia's letter, I was more sure than ever that I needed to be there.

Miss Haney had a small office on the western side of the inner ward. From there, it seemed, she helmed the running of the entire household and oversaw all the servants, including us Orha.

As I'd sped through the gardens, I'd seen Tigo, bent backed, furrowing ditches for autumn seedlings. He'd been walking slowly alongside the beds, speaking quietly, the earth churning gently. A little way off, great stones stood piled by the circular foundations of a folly he was building.

Mawre had vanished before I could greet her, no doubt to blast more laundry on a clifftop somewhere. Rhianne was likely down in the kitchens, getting an earful from Cook for being late. So I turned up at Miss Haney's door alone, adrenaline still pumping from discovering Zennia's letter.

"There'll be little for you to do out in the bay until pallwater," said the housekeeper, leading me on a brisk tour through the labyrinthine corridors. "Has anyone explained the tides to you yet?"

"Briefly," I said, trying to remember Tigo's "lesson."

"Pallwater is the period of the month when the sea comes in and settles in the bay. The family take boats sometimes, and they'll need you to propel them. Or clear part of the causeway if the sea's shallow enough."

I swallowed and nodded. *If it ever decides to listen to me . . .*

"No one takes boats out at archwater, of course. But our Floodmouth always accompanies the family on crossings, in case anything happens to their horses on the way." She pursed her lips. "Well, the siblings are *supposed* to take you, anyway . . ."

Sweat broke out across my shoulders. "And if that does happen," I said breathlessly, hurrying to keep up with her, "what exactly am I expected to do?"

She turned to me, looked down her long nose through her spectacles. "Why," she said, "keep them alive, of course."

I blinked rapidly as she turned down another passage. Was that why Zennia had died out there? She'd put her all into saving Emment and had nothing left to save herself?

"This is one of the libraries," said Miss Haney, beckoning me past a series of doors. "And the Master's study . . ."

I paused, glancing in. Rexim wasn't there, but I glimpsed ceiling-high bookshelves, a vast, shining desk, a leather-covered chair. Pamphlets and parchments were strewn across the desktop. Letters. Accounts. Perhaps a diary.

I knew one son was a profligate gambler. What else might I learn from that desk, from those papers? Something more about Zennia, perhaps? I was certain Tigo and Rhianne had been hiding something . . .

"Do keep up," Miss Haney prompted, and I started, then trailed her to another door. "Until pallwater," she continued, "nearly all your duties will be here in the castle or out on the grounds." We exited into a wide, muddy courtyard, overlooked by four stories of mullioned windows. There was a well at its center, a huge wooden vat, barrels and buckets stacked in wonky piles.

"Tigo will need your help with irrigation. We need water from the well at all hours of the day. The latrines, of course . . ." She broke off, looking apologetic. "Then there's the laundry, and a lot of it, I'm afraid." She seemed harried, a few strands of hair coming loose. "You Orha . . . well, you're gods-sent, in my eyes. We're all *very* pleased to have a Floodmouth again."

I looked at her. Of all the people on Bower Island, here was the one it was perhaps most vital to please. Miss Haney would no doubt report back to Rexim. If I was going to impress enough to see out this week—to be able to get to my meeting in Port Rhorstin—I would need the housekeeper's trust above anyone's.

I drew myself up, surveying the courtyard. "I'll get started right away. A barrel of water to last the morning. And I'll fetch the breakfast dishes for washing, and speak to the maids and valets about the family's clothes."

She looked at me, relief softening her stiff shoulders. "Very good," she said. "And . . . thank you, Corith. The work is long and tiring here, but I'm sure you'll find it as rewarding as the others do."

I forced as genuine a smile as I could. "I'm so grateful for this opportunity. It's a placement my classmates could only dream of." Parroting Instructor Caerig was galling, but it was worth it to see the approval in Miss Haney's eyes.

She hesitated, flicking her gaze to the windows. "The Master of the House has asked me to pay special attention to your performance these first few weeks."

"I won't disappoint you," I said firmly. "Nor him."

She nodded, gratified, and turned to leave.

"Is there a Mistress of the House?" I ventured before she could disappear.

She turned to me in astonishment. "Has no one told you?"

When I shook my head, she stepped closer, lowered her voice. "Belisama Shearwater died after having Miss Catua. Childbed fever. Never mention her name. It hit the three eldest very hard indeed. Master Llir was but four years old, Miss Vercha six. And Master Emment . . . well, he hasn't been the same since." Her gaze wandered; she pressed her lips together. "A very great shame. The heir to the Brigancy . . ."

With a shudder, I tried to imagine being raised solely by Rexim Shearwater. He had probably palmed off most of his offspring's care onto his servants.

Miss Haney swept away through a narrow door, and I approached the well, gazing down into its depths.

This water was glass clear, sitting lazily at the bottom, and though it took a few tries, it responded to my entreaties. Miss Haney's confidence in me had calmed my rattled nerves, and this was a task we'd practiced hundreds of times at Arbenhaw. This water, drawn from the rock below, was far closer to the cold springs I'd worked with for a decade than the violence, the frenzy, of those archwater waves.

When the groundwater rose, spilling into my waiting bucket, hot relief sparked briefly in my chest before I tamped it down and concentrated on my chores. My muscles still burned from my climb, and my palms stung where they gripped the handles of the buckets, but before long I found a kind of rhythm in the work.

As I coaxed water into the vat, preparing to churn laundry, I caught movement behind a window on the second floor. A figure was passing, and they paused, glancing down at me. It was Llir, his smooth features distorted by the leaded glass.

I forced myself not to be the first to break the stare. To give every impression that this morning's test hadn't bothered me. And after a few long seconds, he turned and disappeared.

10

I toiled all the rest of that day, late into the evening, then sat up trying to memorize Tigo's tide tables. But my thoughts kept zipping from Zennia's letter to the story Tigo and Rhianne had told me, and then to my meeting, now a mere week away. I'd already heard Vercha mention market day more than once. I'd need to make sure I was still in town at sunset, slip away somehow . . . *and* acquire myself a mask.

My work was exhausting in spite of my ability. Though I could persuade the groundwater to go where I willed it, I couldn't tell the wire brushes to scrub off stubborn stains. I couldn't tell the tubs and ewers to haul themselves around. Despite whipping through my duties faster than a normal servant could, I still went to bed that night half dazed and aching, doubly tired after my ordeal with the Waking Tide.

All the same, I forced myself to rise before sunup the next morning and hurried down the rocky path that led to the shingle beach.

Worry was gnawing at me, a growing unease that before long, nearer pallwater, my services would be called on. The family would expect me to steer their boats, clear the causeway. After what had happened in front of Llir and Tigo, and in the cove, I had to *do* something. I had to keep trying.

I'd chosen this particular time of day for a reason: The Waking Tide was still a quarter of an hour off, and the waves were low, receding around the island. The causeway shone under ivory moonslight, and either side of it stretched the endless mudflats, empty and ominous in the predawn dark.

I shuffled to the water's edge—it would soon retreat beyond the island—and crouched, staring at it, trying to get a sense of it. It lapped at the shingle, rippling almost with a purr.

"I'm Corith," I said tentatively. "It's good to meet you."

I sensed only a vast weightiness, an indifferent disregard.

"I'm sorry we got off on the wrong foot the other day. But I really hope we can learn to work together."

I thought I detected a weak answering swirl, but it was gone before I could be sure I'd really seen it. The water seemed bent on its withdrawal from the bay, on building its strength for the assault to come.

"Form a whirlpool," I whispered. "Please. Or a wave."

But there was something so removed about these archwater swells. As though the ocean's purpose was so great, so consuming, that my entreaties didn't register at all.

What would Zennia do if she were here instead of you?

The thought surprised me, made my breath catch in my throat. I gazed out at the waves and realized I didn't really know. Zennia was lost; I could barely think of her without crumpling.

But what I did know was that my friend would *never* have given up.

"I'll be back tomorrow," I said to the surf, "and the next day."

And even though the tide hadn't deigned to respond, I murmured a quick "Thank you" as I rose and backed away.

* * *

Late morning found me in one of the fine halls I'd padded down the day before with Miss Haney. My duties included washing the floors, and I was hauling a bucket of lavender water. This part of the castle seemed oddly quiet, and when I passed Rexim's study, I was surprised to see the door standing ajar, no sign of him within.

I'd been told the Brigant answered correspondence here in the mornings, which was why it was the best time to collect laundry from his bedroom, but today he was absent, the study still and silent. I lowered the bucket and inched forward, gripping my washcloth tightly in my hand.

The thought came again, insistent, tugging at me: What clues about Zennia might this room hold?

I turned my head, listening, but no one was about. A clock on a side table clucked a steady rhythm. Moving to the great expanse of mahogany that made up Rexim's desk, I glanced quickly through the papers scattered across it.

A letter, half written, to someone called Orlagh, its topic some dense, philosophical rebuttal that I could make no sense of. I shifted it aside. Another, this one addressed to Rexim, bearing a House crest I didn't recognize. Again the subject was uninteresting—no mention of the family, just people I didn't know—but beneath the letter lay a large, leatherbound book, splayed open, its pages covered in figures.

An accounts book.

I leaned in, scanning it closely. My eye snagged on a couple of lines: *"Emment—Illir allowance. Emment—Tíma allowance."* Substantial sums at the start of each month. Plenty of figures inked in red. I was certainly no mathematician, but I got the impression the Shearwater finances weren't exactly robust. The "savings" figures were steadily declining.

There was a scribbled note in the margin: *"Can't crack open hoard."* What did that mean?

Creak.

I whirled, my stomach pitching, to see a figure standing in the doorway.

Tigo was dressed in his purple livery rather than his usual earth-stained overalls. His gray-streaked hair was neat, tied back with ribbon, and his dark eyes narrowed as he took me in.

"I've been sent to find you," he said. "You're late. The guests have arrived for the Brigant's luncheon."

Of course. That's why he was so put together, why Rexim wasn't here, why the halls were so quiet . . . Vercha had mentioned some visitors were coming, and Miss Haney had said something about it yesterday—I'd been so distracted by Zennia's strange letter, the secrets swirling beneath this island's surface, that it had flown right out of my head. I swallowed.

"I'm sorry," I said. "I completely forgot."

His gaze moved slowly to the desk behind me; I hoped my body blocked his view of the ledger. Quickly, I held up my grimy washcloth. "Damp dusting," I added, forcing an awkward smile.

"Did Miss Haney not tell you this room is off-limits?" Tigo folded his violet-clad arms. "She cleans it herself. The rest of us cannot enter."

I lowered the washcloth, my cheeks growing warm. Miss Haney's tour had been swift, overwhelming. It was certainly possible she'd mentioned that rule and that, as with her instructions for the luncheon, my darting mind had failed to register it.

"I don't think so," I squeaked, looking apologetic, and Tigo held my gaze for a few seconds more.

"Well, now you know," he said, stepping back. "You'd better come quickly. She's right on the verge."

* * *

We arrived to find the housekeeper barking orders. When she spotted my grubby breeches and creased blouse, she immediately sent a maid to fetch my new livery, which they'd measured me for the previous day.

"You can use my office," she said, thrusting the clothes at me. "Well? Don't stand there gaping like a fish! Hurry!"

I changed rapidly, catching a fleeting glimpse in the mirror of a high violet collar, the embroidered House crest.

When I returned, Rhianne and Mawre were there, too, and Miss Haney directed us to the Painted Chamber. With its high, ornamented ceiling, opulent chimneypiece, and floor-to-ceiling windows, it seemed built to receive guests. And indeed, Rexim Shearwater was there, sitting easily in a carved gilt chair near the fire. A few plush couches were arranged artfully around him, and on one sat the siblings, pristine in their finery.

"As part of our set," Miss Haney whispered in my ear, "you're expected to be present at audiences like these. This one . . ." She swallowed. "Well, just follow the others' lead."

She positioned us off to one side of Rexim, whom I eyed with a mixture of wariness and loathing. His "test" still lurked in the back of my mind—and my limbs were still laced with cuts and bruises.

I glanced at the siblings. Emment looked bored, Catua expectant, and Llir oddly tense. Llir's gaze passed over us Orha, lingering on me, taking in my new livery. Vercha, smiling, fingered her laconite, and I noticed just how much of it they were all wearing. In the presence of us Orha, the stones whined faintly, their high, discordant notes putting me on edge.

"What is all this?" I whispered to Rhianne, hoping we were far enough away to go unheard. "Just a social call?"

She shook her head narrowly. "Politics," she murmured. "He's been having them every few weeks for a while now."

Miss Haney, who had vanished a few moments earlier, now reappeared and pushed the doors wide. "Brigantess Osprey," she announced, stepping aside, "and the eldest son of Brigant Turnstone."

The first to enter was a small, slim woman, though, despite her size, she exuded a strong presence. Striking, with pale hair piled onto her head, she flashed with jewels and more laconite than the Shearwaters. Her ice-blue eyes swept the room, then all of us—a sharp intelligence, almost a cunning, in her gaze.

Behind her sauntered a man around Emment's age: olive skinned, well-dressed, with black curly hair. With a smirk, he caught the eldest sibling's eye, and in response, Emment offered a tight, awkward smile.

Turnstone. I'd heard that name before, when I'd eavesdropped on Tigo and Rhianne in the tower. He was the one Emment owed money to. But this hardly seemed an appropriate occasion to talk debt.

I didn't expect anyone else to come in, but abruptly a group of figures appeared. I blinked. Four of them were done up in livery like ours, but in fire orange, with a different House crest. They fairly shone, their postures impeccable as they trailed close behind Brigantess Osprey. The next four, far more sedate in livery of dark green, were no less stiff and grave of expression, though one—a solid man with a scar on one cheek—was sporting a nasty-looking black eye.

"Damona," said Rexim, briefly standing. He gestured to the couches. "Madox. You're very welcome."

"I'm sorry my father couldn't make it," said Madox Turnstone, throwing himself onto the plump blue velvet. "You know how he is. Hates to travel these days."

Damona Osprey settled in a chair, accepting the welcome with only a nod. Their sets of Orha collected behind them, framing their mistress and master like a painting.

“Of course,” came Rexim’s smooth reply. “I only hope you’ll convey my warmest wishes and the salient points of our discussion today. But first—” He tilted his head at Miss Haney, who hurried to the doors and disappeared through them. A moment later, footmen trooped in, bearing silver trays crowded with china and teapots.

“Come on, then,” said Turnstone, leaning back on the couch. For a man so young, he was confident with his elders. “You know my father’s always been a hard-liner, whereas *I’m* more inclined to vote for you. So we’ll cancel each other out, unless you can help me persuade him.”

Rexim’s lip quirked. “Well, let me begin by—”

A scrape from the doorway made us all look around.

Miss Haney was back, her face pale as linen. Her thin lips opened and closed a few times. Rexim blinked once and narrowed his eyes. “Yes?” he said softly, with simmering anger.

“My lord,” she breathed, “you—you have another visitor. *Visitors,* I should say, as there are in fact two of them.”

Rexim froze. The siblings frowned. Catua stretched, trying to peer out of the tall windows. I looked, too—they offered a view of the inner ward—and saw guards bristling under the barbican’s arch.

“Your father?” Rexim said, flashing a glance at Turnstone.

The boy looked horrified. “Surely not—he was abed—”

Miss Haney hurried across the polished marble floor and bent to whisper in Rexim’s ear.

It was the first time I’d seen the Shearwater patriarch look anything less than supremely assured. He flicked a glance at his offspring, then us Orha, and then at Osprey and Turnstone, hesitating. His tension, the wound-tight stiffness of his shoulders, spoke of rage he was fighting to hide from his guests, while his darting gaze betrayed uncertainty. Eventually he waved Miss Haney away. “Well,” he said, his voice now smooth, “send them in. No reason why they can’t join our party.”

Miss Haney retreated, soles clacking on the floor, leaving silence as thick as a winter muffler.

"A pleasant surprise," Rexim said through his teeth. "One I shan't spoil." He sat back and waited.

A moment later, the doors again opened, admitting, this time, only two individuals.

Though the younger towered over the older, I saw clear similarity in their features. A father and a son, the older squat and heavy. Sixty, perhaps—a little older than Rexim—but fit and strong looking despite his years. He was pale, with reddish hair graying all over. Plain looking—none of the regalness of the Shearwaters—but as his watery blue eyes raked over the room, I almost shrank away. There was something daunting about him.

And that was magnified tenfold in his son.

A bear of a man, surely six and a half feet, he had deep-black hair cascading to broad shoulders. I suspected his mother might be very beautiful indeed, as although he'd inherited some of his father's unevenness, his features were arresting. He stared only at Rexim.

"Uirbrig," Rexim said to the older man. I noted that, this time, he didn't stand. "To what do we owe this unexpected pleasure?"

Damona Osprey's lips pursed in a tiny smile, while Turnstone's mouth had dropped right open. Despite still reclining, Emment clenched his jaw, and Catua's curiosity had turned to bare shock. Llir and Vercha exchanged a glance, their expressions unreadable, though Vercha had paled.

"My goodness," the man called Uirbrig said, narrow lips quirking. "We didn't realize you had guests." He nodded an easy greeting at the siblings, at Osprey and Turnstone; he ignored us Orha.

"Did you not?" Rexim grated, shifting in his chair. "And how do you all do, down at Castle Crake?"

Beside me, Rhianne stiffened, a hitch in her breath.

Crake.

I forced my face to remain neutral.

"We are not quite where we would want to be," said Crake with a slow smile. "But I think you know that. And yourselves?" He looked at the siblings again. "A handsome family, I've always thought so. We do miss your company out there on the mainland."

A muscle twitched in Rexim's cheek. Vercha's eyes flicked to Crake's hulking son, who studied her impassively, still as a statue.

"If things aren't going the way you hoped with the vote," said Catua, "that's really *your* problem to try to solve, isn't it?"

I felt a flash of admiration. Crake also seemed to appreciate the challenge. His eyes twinkled. "Getting right to it, are we? Very well." He stepped forward, began a slow walk around the couches. The Orha on either side of me tensed.

"I'm here to ask you to stand down, Rexim. Be a good sport. For the benefit of the Queendom."

I saw this register in Rexim's eyes. Then he chuckled, glancing genially at his other guests. "Forgive me, but the Queendom will hardly be best served with a . . . well, if you don't mind my uncouth turn of phrase, a warmonger in the Chamber." He leaned back in his chair. "A man who once told me we should challenge Breova. Who wants to send nearly all Nenamor's Orha to the front."

My eyes, along with everyone else's, flashed to Crake.

"Quite right," put in Turnstone, though he looked somewhat rattled. To Crake, he said, "I read your letter to Father. Are you really proposing to steal land from Breova? And fight them for it when they—understandably—retaliate?"

"They don't need that land," Uirbrig Crake said simply. "The Redback Mountains are desolate—just laconite mines. Breova don't use much laconite anymore. Not since they started coddling their Orha."

"That's still no reason to—" Turnstone blustered, then shook his head. "But look. Like Shearwater said, isn't it also true you want to funnel more Orha into Annig's armies, *and* your own, and Regent Shrike's? What about our sets? All the Orha in the mills? Who's going to till the fields, clear the mines? Steer the ships and power the smithies? Who's going to protect coastal towns from the gales?"

"It would be temporary," Crake countered, "until we had the land we need. Mudmouths and Sparkmouths to the front lines out west. Floodmouths and Gustmouths to the navies down south."

I glanced to my right and caught Mawre's gaze. Her eyes had widened behind her spectacles. Tigo and Rhianne exchanged a fleeting, somber look. Even the Orha behind Osprey and Turnstone at last seemed to show some emotion on their faces.

"Would you prefer Regent Finch's reforms?" said Brigantess Osprey to Turnstone. She sat there, cool and still as a lake. "Raising the age Orha go to the Institutions to twelve, with only six years of training? Then giving them more choice over their placements? And a day off a week?" She gave a light laugh.

"Of course not," said Turnstone, his cheeks turning rose. "But—"

"Look," said Rexim, leaning forward in his chair. "Whichever of us is elected will have the deciding hand—in Shrike's ambitions as well as Finch's wild schemes. Understand me: I'm no warmonger, nor a radical. You can trust me to keep all these preposterous ideas out of the Chamber."

He turned to Crake, who was still pacing slowly. "I'm sorry, my friend. But your journey here was wasted if you really hoped to persuade me to step down."

"I told you this was useless," came a flat murmur from the son.

Ignoring him, Crake said to Rexim, "Well, I thought I'd ask." Oddly, he seemed, if anything, cheerier, nearly bouncing on the balls of his feet. "I thank you. You couldn't have made your position clearer. Now, I hope you will not turn us away without luncheon, otherwise our trip really will have been wasted."

With reluctance, the guests were led through to a parlor, where pastries and sundries soon appeared. I pictured Cook toiling away over the stove, given barely any notice, cursing the Crake name.

Guards had now appeared and flanked Rexim tightly, while Tigo, Rhianne, Mawre, and I were covertly directed to stand behind the family.

Under my breath, audible only to Rhianne, I murmured, "Crake didn't bring any Orha with him."

As the visitors engaged in stilted conversation, Rhianne side-eyed me and replied in a whisper, "The son's a Mudmouth. His father's general. Iovawn Crake. The only Orha among the Hundred."

I looked at the younger Crake in shock. Of course, laconite always hummed in our presence, so I hadn't been able to tell he was Orha. Rhianne must have heard the family discuss it.

My eyes traveled over him. *An Orha among the Hundred.* I'd never even heard of such a thing. The Hundred despised us, considered us below them, no matter how many pretty words they couched it in, like Vercha's after the dinner two nights ago.

"Too powerful, too valuable, to be left to their own devices."

Now I realized it must be possible for our kind to be born into the highest echelons of society. Zennia, after all, had been a wealthy merchant's daughter. Why not the Hundred? We could pop up anywhere.

"They accept him because his father does," Rhianne added, turning her head to hide her murmur. "Because he's the only one. It's like his niche."

And, I thought, a man with such power—both political and elemental—must be feared, too.

His towering figure was silhouetted against the window, removed from the others, watching them dispassionately. Vercha approached him, a cinnamon tart in her hand. She said something, and his eyes slid slowly toward her. He replied—something short that made Vercha smirk—and they entered into an inaudible conversation.

Soon Cook stopped sending tidbits from the kitchens, and Rexim cleared his throat, letting the conversation die away. Uirbrig Crake brushed the crumbs from his hands and inclined his head to Brigant Shearwater and his children.

"I'm very grateful for the courtesy of your hall," he said, sweeping a disquieting look over us. "I'm sorry we couldn't come to an agreement."

Turnstone's eyes flicked from Rexim to Crake. Both he and Brigantess Osprey seemed as eager to leave as Rexim was to be rid of his guests.

"As am I," Rexim said, flashing eyes at his guards. They moved toward the Crakes, preparing to escort them. "I shall see you out to the gatehouse myself."

"Let me," said Vercha, who was already near the door.

Rexim's face betrayed a flicker of relief as his eldest daughter strode out behind the visitors.

Llir, scrubbing a hand through his tan hair, joined Catua at the window to watch them leave. Emment sat down heavily, a goblet in his hand. "Gods," he said to his father, "what was that all about?"

Rexim's sideburns were damp with sweat. He opened his mouth, then seemed to remember we Orha were there. "You," he snapped at us. "Out. Now."

As I returned to my chores, I passed Vercha in a hallway. Her eyes were narrowed and her face was pinched in thought.

A man who wants to send all our Orha to the front.

I shivered, remembering Crake's dangerous smile, the flat stare of his battle-hardened son.

As much as I disliked—almost despised—Rexim Shearwater, after today I was beginning to suspect that the Brigant of Bower Island might be the lesser of two evils.

11

Autumn bedded in over the week that followed. The air crisped, and I found myself in need of my cloak. Gold and bronze leaves littered the lawns and pathways, and I helped Tigo harvest giant squashes from the kitchen gardens.

I made sure to excel at anything and everything Miss Haney tasked me with. In the face of my nagging uncertainty about Zennia, here, at least, was something over which I could exert glorious control. I polished the floors until they shone like mirrors, scrubbed the linens so hard my palms turned pink. My voice went hoarse from cajoling the water—and I even tackled jobs no one had mentioned to me at all. One morning I sent fountains up over the glasshouses, washing the panes down inside and out. When I showed Miss Haney the gleaming results later, her face glowed, and I knew I was getting there. Gradually.

All the same, as the days ticked by, I woke in the mornings under a growing shadow of unease. I'd long since burned the scrap of parchment with the details of my meeting in my room's narrow grate, fearful it would be discovered, but its mysterious instructions were branded on my brain. The fourteenth was creeping nearer and nearer, and I spent my days dwelling compulsively, anxiously, on whether I'd make it and what awaited me there.

Zennia's letter I couldn't bring myself to burn, so I scrunched it tight and returned it to its crevice. Occasionally I watched the castle at night, but had seen no sign of the lights she'd mentioned.

In the wake of the Crakes' surprise appearance, the family was jittery, particularly Rexim. He walked the halls distractedly, head bent over his correspondence, or shut himself up in his study for hours. I glimpsed the siblings speaking quietly in corners and caught a new frown line etched between Miss Haney's brows.

Ever since I discovered that Emment Shearwater had been the last person to see Zennia alive, I found myself noticing him, distracted by his presence. He, in turn, avoided me for the most part, so much so that it began to seem pointed. There was a certain tensing of his features when he spotted me, a tendency to change direction rather than pass me, and the suspicion seeded itself in my mind that the sight of me reminded him of my predecessor; of the accident he'd witnessed in the bay.

Vercha, by contrast, I had to *try* to avoid. She'd begun to seek me out, seemed to have taken a shine to me. In the mornings, she often requested me especially to bring her bathwater instead of her lady's maid, Debry. She brushed dust from my uniform. Corrected my poor posture.

"None of this 'my lady,'" she said. "You must call me Miss Vercha. And if you ever need anything, you must come *straight* to me. Miss Haney is so stretched, poor thing, she's sure to neglect you." I soon saw how she delighted in new things, in appearances and perceptions, in society and tradition.

The day before my meeting, drear clouds rolled in and the island was curtained in a thin, misty drizzle. With Tima marching on, the tidal range was shrinking, the waterline beginning to encroach into the bay. At pallwater proper, the sea would settle at the bay's midpoint: the little stone harbor I'd seen on my crossing. Then, I gathered, there'd be barely any difference between high tide and low tide—much safer for sea travel. Gentler waves already greeted me each morning when I visited the ocean before starting my chores. And I didn't know if I was imagining it, but I was starting to sense some of its fierceness, its frightening remoteness, ebbing away.

Vercha cornered me as I was collecting laundry, beckoning me out into the haze of gray rain. "Come," she said. "I'm hunting for Father. I've had a letter I must speak to him about right away. This velvet, you understand, it simply *can't* get wet . . ."

I trailed after her nervously, tugging up my high collar.

Rain was notoriously tricky for all Floodmouths. There were so many tiny, disparate drops, and they all seemed to have minds of their own. Generally, the smaller the body of water, the easier it was to coerce it to our will. But beyond a certain point, the tinier it got, the less it seemed able to hear our words. It was as though its capacity for connection dwindled and it became more chaotic—slow-witted, almost. Like a mayfly compared to a dog or a horse.

As Vercha strode across the puddle-strewn ward, I breathed out, long and slow, then whispered to the rain. It half heeded me, just sparing her hair and velvet bodice, but damp patches slowly appeared on her skirts. Thankfully, she didn't seem to notice as she hoisted her hem high above the mud.

Rexim soon appeared, coming in the opposite direction, a sheaf of papers clutched in his hand.

"Ah, there you are," he said. They stopped out in the open. I pleaded with the rain in a desperate undertone and managed to persuade it not to soak Rexim's hat. "News just this morning." He held up the papers. "Dunlin's succumbed—died night before last."

He flicked a glance over me, only now registering my presence, but I avoided his eyes, concentrating on the rain.

"How terrible," Vercha said, not sounding as if she meant it. "And sooner than we'd thought—has the vote been arranged?"

"Ballots to be cast in just a few weeks," the Brigant said. "I've been speaking to Ferda about organizing a coach. I must go to Pen Aryn. I've been away too long."

My eyes flicked across the ward to the stables. Ferda was the island's stablemaster, though he also performed countless other odd jobs.

"All the way to the capital? Because of what Crake said?" Vercha's nose wrinkled. "But you have a solid lead, and he clearly knows it."

"All the same," Rexim replied. "That lead could dwindle. If I am out of sight this close to the vote, I am out of the Hundred's minds. I must go. Besides, the funeral will be held in Pen Aryn, and I need to be seen there, speak to those present."

"What a blow," said Vercha, pulling an envelope from her bodice. "For *I* have just heard from our old friends, the Cormorants. We've been saying for some time that we should meet on the mainland, but today they write to say they miss us, and the island. They ask if they can stay. And what a good excuse for a party . . ." She ran a thumb over the letter, forlorn.

Rexim took in his daughter fondly. "Invite them anyway," he said. "I shall be back in a few weeks. I should be glad to know they are keeping you occupied in my absence, and on my return . . . Yes, I think I have decided. We shall host a ball in the Cormorants' honor and try to make up for that disastrous luncheon. I want to see Osprey again, *without* Crake, and the other eastern families—as many as can come. A final push before the vote. What do you say?"

Vercha's whole countenance glowed.

"A *ball,*" she gushed. "Oh, I must meet with Cook immediately, and Miss Haney, and, oh dear, none of my dresses will do—"

Rexim waved a hand. "Tell Madam Mora she may bill me directly. And don't forget to order one for your sister."

Vercha was almost vibrating with delight. "You are too good to us, Father."

He shook his head distractedly. "Now, where is your elder brother? I must tell him in no uncertain terms that neither he nor any of you are to leave this island while I'm gone." His eyes roved the windows, brows drawn down. "Things are far too unsettled for any of his usual nonsense. I have no choice but to leave him to hold down the fort, but I'm counting on the rest of you to help keep him in line. No Veil, not until—" His eyes suddenly shot to me. I'd blended into the background: quiet, unassuming. "Well, if you run into him, you send him straight to me."

He strode off, boots squelching in the mud, and I looked at Vercha, pulse thudding in my throat. "What's the Veil?" I asked as innocuously as I could.

She cocked an eyebrow before squinting up at the drizzle. "Oh, just a place we all meet in Port Rhorstin. Our . . . circles, I mean." She flicked me a glance. She must mean the Hundred. The local nobility.

Why in hells was my meeting there?

But she was already beckoning me back toward shelter, and I could only hurry after her, fighting to hide my dismay.

The next day, with a mixture of nervous energy and cold dread, I went to meet Vercha and Debry on the beach.

I'd had to don my livery for this, but I knew I couldn't wear it into the Veil: a haunt of the Hundred, according to Vercha. From what Rexim had said, it seemed Emment, at least, was a regular, and I didn't want to risk someone recognizing the crest and mentioning the fact that I'd been there to the Shearwaters . . . I'd need another outfit. But I had a plan for that.

Vercha's revelation had kept me up in the night. Was it one of the Hundred who'd slipped the note in my luggage? But how was that possible? It had been packed at Arbenhaw and remained unopened until we got to Tresteny.

I'd also been fretting about the crossing itself. With pallwater a week away, the causeway was covered, nearly a third of its length now sitting beneath the waves. And though a gale had whipped up that would help nudge us westward, I still suspected my services would be called on. I pictured all the practice I'd done coming to nothing. The sea roundly ignoring me. Vercha, right there, witnessing it . . .

But at dawn that morning, for the first time, I'd made a breakthrough. Crouching on the shingle, I'd made a whirlpool in the surf, the calmer ocean seeming more receptive to my cajoling.

As I jogged down the path to the harbor's small jetty, a quiet voice in my head said, *It's easier because it's pallwater.* I squashed it down. I knew archwater would come around again soon, but I didn't want to think about that. It made my stomach twist with fear.

Vercha and Debry were waiting at the harbor, but to my shock and unease, Llir and Tigo were there, too. It was only as I picked my way over the shingle that I recalled Tigo's words from the day of my arrival: *"Half the gold now and half in two weeks, on market day."*

As I approached the little party, Llir's eyes caught mine. His hair, dark brass, was breeze blown and fluffy; his cloak fluttered around the tops of his boots. Tigo gave me an evaluating stare, and I suspected he was remembering our encounter in Rexim's study. Over the past week, I'd been far more careful. I just had to hope our paths didn't cross in town . . .

Vercha was immaculate in a deep-emerald coat, elbow-length gloves, and hair pinned so tightly that the gusts off the ocean barely shifted it. Neither she nor Llir wore laconite, of course—my efforts would have been hamstrung if they did. Perhaps because of the lack of protection, Debry eyed Tigo and me suspiciously as she helped her mistress step into the vessel. Most of the non-Orha servants avoided us. They seemed simultaneously afraid of and scathing toward our "gifts."

"*Such* a relief," Vercha said, "to have a Floodmouth again. We hardly managed after pallwater last month."

Llir said nothing, watching the ocean, but his sister's eyes were glittering excitedly. "Corith, you must be *dying* to hear about the ball. It's all in motion; the Cormorants have confirmed. Old allies of ours. You'll love them—everyone does."

The boat moved off, buffeted by waves and wind. I stared at the green-gray water, trying in vain to focus.

"If they set off directly, they'll be here at full pallwater, so they'll be coming by boat, but they'll bring their own Floodmouth, of course. And they're to stay for three weeks, with the ball on the thirty-eighth . . ."

She was clearly exhilarated; she'd barely paused to draw breath. The boat lagged. I fought to block out her chatter.

At a flashed glance from Tigo, Llir reluctantly interrupted. "Orha need quiet to concentrate, Sister." I met his eyes, feeling a flicker of gratitude, but he settled back, watching me expectantly—disconcertingly.

"Gosh, sorry," Vercha said. "Me and my mouth!"

All of them sat and stared at me in silence, which was hardly any better, but at least it was quiet.

I angled away, trailed my fingers in the water. I brought to mind my small success with the pallwater current, sought that brief moment of connection I'd felt. "Bear us westward," I murmured.

For a long, stretched-out moment, our trajectory didn't change. The boat still bumped at the same pace through the swells. I wrestled with the nerves that threatened to bubble over. *"Please,"* I mumbled, staring hard at the water, wishing keenly it was Zennia at my back instead of Vercha and Llir.

Eventually, we tilted more toward the mainland, and though it was hard to tell with the rolling of the waves, the water—with the same vaguely docile air as this morning—rippled against the boat's stern, nudging us forward.

Vercha seemed satisfied, or perhaps she just wanted to keep talking, as she soon took up her prattle again.

"There's just so much to *do.* The ballroom isn't ready. I tried to persuade Father that we need new flooring, but he says what we have will do well enough. And the drapes, let me tell you . . ."

This continued for some minutes, punctured only by the odd noise of feigned interest from Llir.

"Sounds wonderful, Miss," Debry said wistfully. "I only wish *I* could go." She shot me a strangely disgruntled look.

We soon neared the waterline, where a black carriage waited, much smarter than the coach that had brought me from Arbenhaw. Horses with violet plumes stood ready to bear us onward. A coachman helped the others into the vehicle, but our livery marked Tigo and me out as Orha, and as a result, we were avoided, which suited me fine.

We clattered into Port Rhorstin in a spray of dust and gravel, where Llir and Tigo immediately disembarked. Market day meant the small town was bustling, and pallwater meant its residents could trek to the sea's edge, take boats out, catch fish, or forage on the dry flats.

Vercha, Debry, and I stopped first at the posting house, where Vercha produced a letter from her pocket. "I'll only be a moment," she said, stepping from the carriage. She glanced both ways down the street before entering. Why she hadn't sent the note from the culverhouse on the island like everyone else, I had no idea. Probably a letter for her friends, the Cormorants.

The dressmaker's—Madam Mora's—was just across town, a small, neat shop with velvet bodices in the windows. As we entered, a bell tinkled, but it was hardly needed. As soon as *I* stepped over the threshold, a great humming assailed us from all sides. There was more laconite here than I'd ever seen in my life: a glass case of laconite jewelry and brooches, adornments on headpieces, embellished doublets, even a studded ceremonial saber.

The din brought a figure hurrying out of the back, a short, compact woman I presumed was Madam Mora. Her raven-black eyes widened on seeing Vercha.

"Miss Shearwater," she gushed over the drone of the laconite. "Such a pleasure. I'm *honored* you would think of us again." She shot me a swift look. "Come, back here where it's quieter . . ."

We trailed after her to a cluttered workroom. There were bolts of fabric piled on a table, sheaves of paper covered in shorthand. "What brings you to my door?" she asked, shutting out the racket.

"My sister and I trust only you to outfit us for a ball we are hosting in three weeks." Vercha tugged off her gloves and accepted some papers Debry held out to her. "I've taken the liberty of listing some shades, noting some styles . . . There are a few sketches here . . ."

The papers were covered in Vercha's elegant hand. I somehow doubted whether Catua had been allowed much input at all.

"And our new Floodmouth here will need an outfit, of course."

Vercha pointed out some cramped notes in the margin, turning a winning smile on me.

I blinked. "Miss?"

Madam Mora was hovering, beginning to scrawl down some shorthand of her own.

"One's set always attends social occasions like these."

Debry's grumpiness suddenly made sense.

We'd had a few dance lessons at Arbenhaw. At first I hadn't

understood why we might need them. Then, once I'd learned about service with the Hundred, I'd never believed I'd get the kind of placement that required them.

A memory came to me: a worn timber floor, a harpist plucking out a melody in the corner. An Instructor called Albach—tall, white-haired, spindly—barking at us as we twirled and stepped in formation. Zennia's bright gaze; her barely suppressed grin. The unbearable feeling of a laugh threatening to burst out of me.

I wanted to flee, to shrink from their gazes. Madam Mora was assessing my figure, already mentally measuring me for a gown.

Vercha stepped up to me, fingering my braids. "And we shall have to do something with this lovely long hair." I cringed, my senses clanging like a servant's bell, but I knew—as sure as I knew I would hate this ball—that I had to keep her happy. At least until my meeting.

My eyes flicked to the sketches in Madam Mora's hands, but Vercha moved her slim body to block them. "Let it be a surprise," she said with a knowing smile. "A gift to you. Out of my own allowance."

Rexim must have refused to cover it. I met her gaze. "Thank you, Miss," I forced out.

I was beholden to her now. And she wanted me to know it.

She patted my arm as though we were old friends. "We shall make a proper Hundred's Floodmouth of you yet!"

The sun was dipping low in the sky as we exited onto the steep cobbled street. Though sunset—the time given in my mysterious summons—still looked to be an hour or so off, I glanced at Vercha and Debry nervously. I still needed time to locate the Veil.

"Now, to market," Vercha said, consulting a list. "There's the glovers to visit. But oh, first the drapers . . ."

I dug around in my pocket, fervently hoping my plan would work.

"Miss Haney asked me to get some new clothes," I ventured, bringing out a few coins. I'd left some in my pocket, but Vercha didn't need to know that. "Simple things, she said. Workwear and shifts. But I don't know which stalls are best to try . . ."

"Goodness," said Vercha, staring down at the paltry sum. "That won't do. That won't do at all." She frowned. "Didn't I say you should always come to me? Here." She fished around and brought out a heavy coin purse, round as an apple and straining around its contents. "This should do it. Make sure you get some nice outfits—a gown or two, some smart bodices and hose. Try Crengar's, on East Street, *not* the market. *Stalls,* indeed." She looked me up and down. "Really, I should come with you. I have a fine eye for fabrics and tailoring, you know."

"Oh, no," I said, panicking. "You have so much else to organize."

"She's right, Miss," said Debry, eyeing my funds jealously.

Vercha gave a sigh. "Yes, I suppose so. But later, you must come and show me everything, and if it's not quite right, we'll send it back with Ferda."

Heart pumping now, I forced a grateful nod.

"Meet us back at the carriage at sunset," Vercha called as she beckoned Debry down the street.

Sunset. My stomach swooped.

I'd have to hope this meeting—whatever it had in store for me—was quick.

An hour later, I lurked in an alley and gazed out at the Veil, which glowed rose gold with the setting sun.

I'd had to ask directions, but I was careful to approach someone who looked about as far removed from the Hundred as possible: an old, grizzled sailor hefting a crate of hardtack. He'd squinted at me, taking in my fine livery, and pointed me toward a street called Queen's Wharf.

The Veil had immediately caught my eye: a large, proud, four-story mansion, all red brick, white plaster, and black timber detailing. Vines wreathed its walls and curled around its windows, behind which I could just see heavy scarlet drapes. A sign hung above its carved double doors, depicting a masked jester peering from behind a curtain. I heard chattering, high laughter, the tinkling of glasses.

Patrons, impeccably dressed and, of course, masked, were queuing outside, filing past two burly doormen. There were Orha there, too—liveried and straight shouldered—but they were all accompanying someone or other.

Hells damn it. How would I get in alone?

First things first: I had to look the part.

Crengar's had been a lucky suggestion from Vercha: An entire wall of the establishment was covered in masks. The tailor seemed to cater particularly to the fickle fashions of the Hundred, and my Shearwater livery meant I attracted no comment.

Retreating deeper into the alley, I changed behind a barrel, stuffing my bag of clothes well out of sight. I'd chosen carefully: an embroidered blouse, a new brushed bodice, and a pair of velvet breeches.

The mask had taken me even longer. There were eye masks, full-face masks, masks with long noses. Masks of feathers or lace or ceramic . . . even the terrifying visage of a dragon. I skipped over the grinning, blue-green likenesses of niskai, ribbons trailing from their edges like water, and masks made of bark to symbolize tree men.

In the end, I picked the sharp-beaked mask of a bluebird, drawn to its bluish-violet and gold feathers. I hoped the colors—which nearly matched the Shearwaters' banners—might clue in my contact as to who I really was.

Now I fastened it over my face and checked my hair in the glass of a cracked window. I'd ditched my usual braids for this, twisting my red locks up into a knot. I'd never in a hundred years pass as a noble, but I hoped, even in the absence of my livery, I'd pass as just another of those haughty Orha.

It wasn't quite full sunset, but I was horribly conscious that Vercha and Llir would soon be waiting at our carriage. I sidled around to the rear of the building, finding that it backed onto a pretty little yard. It was quieter here, and shadowed beyond the streetlamps, but there was a single bored-looking guard standing sentry, overseeing an entrance I assumed was for staff. The door hung open, raised voices drifting out.

There was a well in the yard and, around a corner, some large barrels. I kept to the shadows. An idea budded in my mind.

The barrels were standing just out of the guard's eyeline. From my hiding place, I took a few deep breaths—imagined it was just another practical at Arbenhaw—and whispered a few choice words under my breath.

Nothing happened at first. I murmured again. The quiet was broken by a long, ominous *creeeak.*

"Who's 'at?" The guard squinted into the dimness.

And then: Two splintering explosions rent the air.

The barrels burst open like overripe fruits, shedding shards of timber, spraying arcs of amber fluid. I could smell it on the air—it was ale, not water—and the guard, who looked as though his heart had seized, raised his torch high and stamped off toward the ruckus.

Silently, nimbly, I stayed close to the wall and darted through the doorway. Into the Veil.

I found myself in a narrow, panelled corridor, an open door to my left, a heavy curtain ahead. From the doorway came the sounds of clinking pans and shouted orders. Smoke and the mustiness of spice filled the air. As I hastened past, a palm covering my mask, I glimpsed black stoves, stacked caskets of wine, milling figures, also masked, decked out in dark uniforms.

"Hoi!" came a shout. A servant moved toward me, but I was gone before they could make it two steps. Up the hallway, through the curtain . . . and into a maelstrom of color and light.

If the mansion's exterior had been impressive, its interior took my breath away.

I had stumbled into an enormous hall, three tiers of galleries and black-railed balconies projecting out over its mirror-polished floor. Everything here was gilt-edged and gleaming, from the ivy-twined pillars rising to a painted ceiling, where a stained glass skylight shone scarlet in the sunset, to the velvet couches and spindly-legged tables set out in front of the mahogany bar. There was music playing: a string trio in the corner and someone on a higher floor plucking a harp.

All around the walls were luxurious red curtains, similar to the one I'd just slipped through. Some, held back with lengths of gold rope, gave access to passageways, nooks, and hidey-holes. I moved away from the servants' entrance—and found myself well and truly part of the masquerade.

There were dandies in ridiculous-looking fashions—expansive ruffs, ballooning pantaloons—and nobles in sleek gowns and padded doublets that looked like they'd cost me fifty years' worth of wages. It was so far removed from the nabyrium halls of Arbenhaw that I felt I'd stepped into a different world. Even the Shearwaters' finery on Bower Island seemed drear, conservative, compared to all this.

The thought of Arbenhaw, of the island, brought me back to myself. *My meeting.* I'd been so distracted by the spectacle that for a moment I'd almost forgotten why I was here. I slouched a little, swiped a glass from an end table, and tried to look as though I came here every week.

There were other Orha trailing after their employers, and the drone of laconite was clearly audible. They'd attempted to cover it up with music, but the quantity of the stone on display was astounding. Earrings, carcanets, rings, embellishments . . . even a full-on laconite headpiece. All for show, a ritual of the rich.

Then—a feather touch at my elbow. A low voice, male, murmuring in my ear: "You're early. This way."

My stomach flip-flopped. A young man in a lion mask—maybe

only a few years my senior—was leaving my side, heading for the nearest spiral staircase. He had a bright golden-blond ponytail, a black uniform like the other servants.

This had to be the person I'd been invited to meet. It was a little worrying, how easily he'd identified me . . . My chest thudded dully as I thought of Zennia. *Please,* I thought. *Please say this wasn't all for nothing.*

Casually I trailed him up the metalwork steps.

On the second floor was a trio of veiled contortionists, slim bodies bent into impossible positions. A jester, her white mask frighteningly blank, juggled five glass balls as she watched me pass.

Then, up ahead, coming right toward me—

"You tell him they're having a rematch next week. He should come. So should you. It'll be a good night."

I recognized that confident drawl, the black curls sprouting from above a boar mask. It was Turnstone, the young man who'd come to Rexim's luncheon. And beside him . . .

My heart began to knock on my breastbone; my skin turned clammy, my next breath snagged. A figure that looked a lot like . . . no, *was* Llir—rangy, lean, in the same clothes as earlier—weaved his way down the gallery, face half covered by a carved silver mask. Behind him came Tigo in a mask of his own, in the unmistakable purple livery of the Shearwaters, and next to him one of Turnstone's Orha—the one with the scar, black eye hidden beneath his mask.

"I'm not sure that's wise," came Llir's measured answer.

Turnstone glanced at him, lips quirking upward: "I knew there was a reason we used to call you Stick-in-the-Mud Shearwater."

What were they *doing* here? I half turned away, trying to force my legs to obey me. Then the realization finally registered: The remaining half of Emment's debt . . . of course they'd have chosen *this* as a meeting place.

I ducked my head, feigning a sip from my glass, hoping my mask and new clothes would conceal me. And sure enough, when the quartet swept by, none of them picked me out from the crowd.

Pulse racing, I hurried after my contact, toward one of the heavy velvet curtains. There, the lion-masked man held it open, brow raised at the delay. I shook my head, panting.

Within, I found myself in a dim, pokey cubbyhole: no more than a round booth with a low, curving ceiling, a bench, and a table with a burning candle. There were etchings of birds in the wood on the wall—a sandpiper, a falcon, an osprey. And a shearwater.

"Interesting choice of mask," said the man as he slid in after me, closing the curtain. His tone was light, his voice youthful. "A cuckoo might have been more apt." He cocked his head and studied me with interest, a small smile on his lips, just visible beneath his mask.

"Why?" I said. "And who are you?" After that close call, and with sunset imminent, I was keen to get on with it. "I found a note inviting me to come here—"

"Yes," he said, businesslike. "Placed by our cuckoo in Arbenhaw. And you'll be our newest one—we hope—on Bower Island."

I stared at him. The candlelight flickered on his jaw.

"I'm sorry," I said slowly. "How can a person be a cuckoo?"

But with a creeping horror, I was beginning to understand.

"That's what Leadership have taken to calling us," he said, leaning back, stretching one arm along the bench. "A bit of a dig at the Hundred, I suppose. You know that cuckoos lay their eggs in other birds' nests?"

I shook my head, but not because I hadn't known it—more to ward off the revelation I knew was coming.

"'Stay close to your enemy and you have more chance of tripping him.' That's why they place us, or recruit us, right under their noses.

Parts of the system we're determined to bring down." He paused. "Don't tell me those Instructors run such a tight ship that none of you have ever even heard of the Cage?"

"Of course I've heard of you," I whispered skittishly. "You want better rights for Orha, like they're getting in Breova, but you blow things up to try to get your way."

"Sometimes violence may be necessary to shock an oppressive system out of stasis."

Under my blouse, the hairs on my arms prickled.

It was said the Cage were named in defiance of the Hundred, a riposte to their tradition of taking birds as namesakes. It was said they wanted to corral the Houses, to hamstring them, to curb their influence. And some said the Cage Orha wanted that influence for themselves. That it would go to their heads, just like before the Great Revolt.

"Actually," he said, "we're people who want fairness. We're not just Orha but common folk, too. The histories are clear on what caused the Great Revolt—Orha amassing too much power, abusing it—but who wrote those histories? The Hundred did. When their ancestors got their hands on laconite, realized just what they could do . . ."

He left the disturbing line of thought hanging.

"Anyway," he added, "the Revolt was centuries ago. We want a fresh beginning. To start from first principles."

I was suddenly acutely aware of the curtain, of the feet occasionally passing beneath it. The words he was saying could get us both killed, but the music and the laconite together drowned our voices.

"Why here?" I said, glancing around, feeling trapped, knowing that Llir and Tigo were out there somewhere. "Why couldn't we meet in an alley somewhere?"

"Why here?" he repeated, grinning. "I work here."

I took in his servant's uniform, its crest: a masked jester. "You're pretending to work here? Won't somebody notice?"

His eyes flashed a brilliant blue through his mask. "No, I really do work here," he said, grinning again. "Cuckoo, remember? I hear a lot, treading these floors. The Cage always has someone stationed here. It's a place the Hundred can 'disappear' for the evening . . . talk business, or pleasure, without showing their faces."

Somewhere beyond the curtain, a woman laughed shrilly. It reminded me of Vercha. My abdomen clenched.

"I don't know what this is," I said, shifting away from him, "but they're waiting for me. The Shearwaters. I can't stay here." I began to clamber awkwardly from the booth. "The note said you had information about my friend, but I didn't realize . . ." That it had been from the *Cage.* That these rebels—*murderers,* the pamphlets said—wanted me to do something for them on the island. A weight had settled on me, dark and miserable. Did they even know anything about Zennia at all? Or had the note just been a way to lure me here?

"Ah, yes," the man said. "It was . . . Zennia, wasn't it?"

My chest constricted. "What do you know about her?" I whispered. I wanted to rip off that lion mask, try to read in his features whether he was stringing me along.

"An information exchange," he stated. "That's all we're proposing."

I gazed at him, unable to respond.

"*You* tally the types and quantities of laconite on Bower Island and report on the family's usual movements, and in return, *we* tell you what we know about your friend." He watched me in the wavering light from the candle. "It's information only a resident of the island can provide accurately. There may be laconite in their fortifications that we can't see; they'll have garments with it, armor, maybe weapons . . . And to properly study the family's routines?" His eyes twinkled. "Well, as I'm sure you've noticed, the island's location makes spying . . . somewhat difficult. Unless you're a member of the family's inner circle, or otherwise, one of their trusted servants."

His eyes flickered over me, perhaps wondering if I was yet trusted enough.

"Laconite," I repeated, my thoughts moving sluggishly. "The Cage is going to do something. Something to the Shearwaters. I don't understand—what could destroying them achieve? There are ninety-nine other Houses out there, some much worse." I thought of Crake. Of Shrike, whose innocent-looking namesake was infamous for impaling its prey on spines and twigs . . .

The man merely smiled, infuriatingly good-humored.

"You're not going to destroy them," I said, scrutinizing him. "It's something else."

"We cuckoos don't get told a whole lot. Probably because, like I said, we're right under the Hundred's noses. I don't know any more than I've just passed on to you."

I didn't believe him, but I let him go on.

"And if you were thinking of reporting me—which it looks like you might be—you should know there are only a couple of contacts I could give up, and the authorities would be hard-pressed to find them, assuming they believed you. Then, of course, I'd meet my death, whether by my own hand or that of the Cage, or the Hundred." *Along with any chance of finding out more about Zennia.* "It's a risk I—*we* are willing to take."

I wondered what it must feel like—to be ready to die for an idea. Something that seemed so impossible, so utterly unachievable. The Hundred's grip on Nenamor was strong as nabyrium. Wasn't it?

A cold thought clawed at me, memories now surfacing: Zennia's musings about running from Arbenhaw. Her mutinous mutters about her mother's noble clients. "How do you know what happened to my friend?" I said, my voice dipping to little above a whisper. "Did she seek you out? Did you know each other?"

His gaze, behind his mask, didn't alter. "I said it was an information *exchange,*" he replied. "But I suppose there's no harm in telling you this much: We played no part in the death of your friend."

At that word—*death*—my stomach dropped. And then, for the first time, his gaze flicked to the curtain. The candle was burning low, inviting in the shadows. "Your answer," he said. "I need it now."

I felt hemmed in, like a sheep being herded. I thought of Owyn, of his swift disappearance, and wondered whether that would be *my* fate if I accepted.

But the knowing glint in the man's eyes made me pause. To walk away now might be to walk away from Zennia, from ever finding out what had happened in the bay. I tried to imagine getting on with my chores, living out my placement, getting to Mawre's, then Tigo's, age. Never knowing what had befallen my near sister, but knowing I'd had the *chance* to find out—and squandered it.

And Rexim . . . as a master, he didn't exactly inspire loyalty. Though the thought of him discovering I was a spy was terrifying, I couldn't deny that some sort of comeuppance was tempting. I remembered his steely face staring down from the clifftop. His readiness to half drown me and make a spectacle of it.

Trying to ignore the roiling of my insides, I nodded shallowly. "Fine. I'll do it." I eyed him warily. "How do I get you the information? And when?"

He surveyed me critically, seeming to ponder. It was the same look he'd given me when he'd spoken of "trusted servants."

"We need to be sure you're really in on this," he said, "and that you possess the skills to do it. At pallwater, send a tally of what you've found so far, by crow, to the Veil, marked with a 'K.' Keep it simple. Vague. Just a list of numbers. There'll be no way to tell it's come from the island."

K. His first name's initial, I guessed. I rapidly counted off days in my head. "Pallwater's only a week away," I said.

"Events are happening in the Chamber, among the Hundred, that mean we need to act quickly on this."

The Chamber.

Whatever the Cage was planning must have something to do with the vote. I remembered the letters Rexim had brandished. The strain in his face. *"Ballots to be cast in just a few weeks . . ."*

My pause must have seemed like hesitation, because he added, eyes glinting, "And by the way, if I don't receive that note, this deal is off the table."

My stomach jumped. I couldn't let that happen.

"All right," I said thinly. "Pallwater, then. And what happens after? I tally the rest?"

"Exactly," he said, glancing again at the curtain. "I'll write back to you with details of a second meeting, where you can hand over everything else we need."

"And you'll tell me about Zennia," I stated, staring at him.

He held my gaze and gave a bare nod.

My clothes were damp with sweat where they clung to my skin as my contact stood up and reached for the drapes. "Come on. I'll show you a servants' exit you can slip out of."

It was over so quickly I felt dizzy, stunned, and I almost stumbled as I shuffled from the booth. The warmth, the music, the hum of laconite: It all assailed my senses, making my head buzz. But the prospect of that second meeting stood out like a beacon in my mind.

If I just did as he asked, and did it quickly, I'd find out what had happened to my friend.

Wouldn't I?

In the end, I was only twenty minutes late to meet the siblings. I claimed I'd gotten lost taking a shortcut through the alleys, which cut like rat warrens behind the smart shop fronts. Llir and Tigo seemed oblivious to the fact that I'd walked right past them back at the Veil. And Vercha didn't appear to mind my tardiness. She looked approvingly at my bag from Crengar's—I'd changed back into my livery in an alley—then returned to fawning over fabric samples with Debry.

On the crossing back, I had to fight hard to clear my mind. My strange task, my tight deadline, kept swimming through my thoughts, interrupting my tenuous connection with the water. And I had a new, uncomfortable awareness of the siblings—two of the people I was now *spying* on. In the bobbing glow of our boat's hanging lantern, I couldn't stop my eyes from drifting to Llir's chest, to Vercha's neckline, where their laconite pendants usually sat; to their fingers and wrists, where the stones usually hummed. I was already trying to tally their number in my head.

Back on the shadowed island, every piece of laconite stood out to me. I'd already spotted some around the grounds: inlaid into the barbican, on spikes in the dry moat. Inside the castle, I'd noticed more: the eyes of the statues lining the main corridor—which meant, annoyingly, I had to scrub those floors manually—and embellishments on the arches of important rooms, like the armory and the cellars that held the locked coffers.

But overall, the stones were few and far between, and by now, I was beginning to understand why.

Laconite was a soft stone, hopelessly vulnerable to the elements. To be used outdoors, it had to be regularly replaced or encased in some other durable material—both of which, I knew, incurred great expense.

With the Shearwaters out here, protected by the tides, I guessed they hadn't thought it worth bothering with much laconite. They relied on their indoor protections—and their garments.

To truly know how much laconite they had—of what kind, and where it was generally kept—I'd need to search the family's bedchambers. One by one.

And it made sense to start with the most dangerous of them: Rexim's.

Stone-gray clouds hung low over the island as I hurried to West Tower a few days later. At this time, late morning, the upper reaches would be quiet—the family occupied, its patriarch sequestered in his study.

There were chores calling, of course, a hasty lunch to be grabbed, but I hoped I could disappear for just fifteen minutes. On my way, I swiped a few linen shirts from the laundry house. They were Emment's, not Rexim's, but an observer wouldn't know that. They should suffice as an excuse if I was seen.

My pulse began to flutter as I ascended West Tower. All the family's bedchambers were up here. As I passed a long gallery I rarely had cause to enter, I heard scuffs, grunts, and the clanging of blades. I paused, glimpsing floorboards worn pale with footsteps, and two figures—Llir, and the fencing master, who visited from Port Rhorstin every week—facing each other with rapiers held aloft.

"And the Devil's Riposte," barked the master, twirling his blade.

Llir's hair was sweat dark, his linen shirt baggy. His doublet lay on a bench by the wall. I lingered a second, caught off guard by his unkemptness; before now, I'd only seen him buttoned up in high collars. He parried a thrust by the fencing master, then twisted, striking out swiftly with his saber. The movement was so fluid, I felt a strange little thrill. But before either of them could spot me, I hurried on my way, sweat prickling across my shoulders. Better not to be seen here at all.

As I'd hoped, the upper floors of the tower were silent, but that didn't stop the blood churning in my ears. I was acutely aware of the last time I'd snooped in one of the Brigant's domains . . . What if, this time, he himself came and caught me?

I paused outside his double doors. Nothing stirred. Stepping inside, I found myself in a lush suite: three rooms connected by two stone archways.

I'd rarely set foot here before; I didn't need to. Rexim had a veritable army of valets who trooped in and out every morning and evening, helping him dress, ferrying his meals, bringing hot tea, bearing letters on silver trays.

The room I'd entered was a circular lounge. Plush couches lined the walls, velvet drapes framed the windows, and solemn portraits of ancient Shearwaters gazed down on me with hooded silver eyes. Over a desk was a painting of a girl—tiny, pale, perched on horseback—and it took me a moment to realize it was our Queen.

I didn't have long. I drew in a breath and crossed to the right-hand door, which led into the bedroom.

A four-poster bed dominated the opulent space. Arrow slits

looked out to the distant mainland and the dark northern headlands that sprouted from its shore. The Brigant had not one but three towering wardrobes, an elaborately carved dresser, a gold-tiled washstand. Approaching the wardrobes, I was rewarded with a familiar hum, and indeed, on opening them, I saw laconite winking. It was inlaid into doublets, into buttons on his cuffs, stiff collars with jewelled edges, a decorative ruff. Even some sort of ceremonial cuirass, spiralling designs looping around the crimson stones.

I took a scrap of parchment from his writing desk and scrawled down an inventory, my fingers trembling. Remembering Zennia's coded letter—*"I worry about this 'journal' being discovered and then being forced to translate its contents"*—I used the same code, planning to translate it later. But though the symbols would be nonsense to anyone else, still the act of putting quill to paper made my nerves flitter like moths trapped in a glass.

I moved to the other wardrobes, then the dresser. I began to worry that the singing of the laconite would alert anyone passing by to my presence, but I fought the urge to check at the door. The sooner I got through this, the sooner I'd be out of here . . .

The dresser's lower drawers contained yet more laconite. I tallied it, rifling through it with my fingers, ensuring I placed everything back where I'd found it.

Then I paused.

Something was wrong. I stared down at the laconite.

It took me a moment to force my thoughts into order, to realize what it was that had struck me as odd. The stones here: They looked just like laconite, had exactly the right blood-red shade, the thin white veins, the glimmering sheen. But they were utterly motionless under my fingers. I touched one, feeling only its smooth, cold surface instead of the buzzing vibration I was used to. I bent to it, placed my ear to it. No telltale hum.

I straightened, my heart drumming a ragged rhythm in my chest.

A porcelain ewer stood by the washstand, an inch of water sitting at the bottom. I carried it, along with the false laconite I'd found, out into Rexim's living quarters. There, far enough away from the bedroom, I sat with the strange stone lying in my lap and spoke to the water, commanding it to swirl.

To my shock, it whirled a few times, then settled idly. The stone wasn't preventing my words from being heeded. I stared at it. Why on earth would Rexim have adornments that *looked* like laconite but had none of its properties?

As I sat there, bewildered, I heard a noise nearby.

I jumped, almost knocking the ewer to the floor, but managed to steady it just in time. I leaped to my feet, throat closing in fear.

The noise came again: the padding of footsteps.

Snatching up the stone and hefting the ewer, I hurried back into Rexim's bedroom, where I dithered, weighing up whether to hide under the bed, but being found there . . . it didn't bear thinking about. I dropped the stone back into the drawer—there was no time to make sure it was precisely where it had been—and returned the ewer to its station by the washstand. Darting back to the living room, I grabbed the shirts I'd brought with me as a decoy and hovered by the door, straining my ears.

The footsteps were coming down this corridor.

A faint whine still issued from the wardrobes behind me. Whoever was coming would hear it, too, would come in to check . . . there'd be no hiding. And they'd hear if I closed the door; they were almost upon me . . .

Heart hammering, making a split-second decision, I strode into the corridor and away from the footsteps.

A second or two later, a voice came: "Hello?"

Turning, I called on all my years of training. Schooled my face into an expressionless mask.

Llir Shearwater had rounded the corner into the corridor and stood staring at me, saber held loosely in his hand.

"My lord," I said, dipping my head shallowly.

His green eyes darted from me to Rexim's door. "You," he said quietly. "What were you doing in there?"

I gestured with the shirts, hoping they hid my shaking fingers. "Mawre gave me these to return to your father's rooms, but I've realized they are Emment's. Can you point me to your brother's chambers?"

He watched me in the dim light spearing through the arrow slits, shadows moving over his sharp-edged features. He hadn't yet changed after his fencing session: His hair was rumpled and his cheekbones were shiny. With the usual tight collar of his doublet absent, his damp linen shirt gaped open at the neck, exposing an upturned triangle of smooth, pale skin.

I'd always found it painful to hold eye contact with anyone—it felt like slowly lowering my palm over a lit candle. But the longer I forced myself to hold Llir's gaze, the more an odd, exhilarated feeling bubbled inside me. And it wasn't an entirely unpleasant sensation.

His eyes picked over my pristine livery. Then, sliding his saber into his belt, he padded toward me. "You're settling into your new role?"

I tensed, remembering his swift swipe with that sword. If any of the Shearwaters found out what I was doing, would they even wait to turn me over to the authorities? Or would they lock me under the castle, exact their own justice?

He stopped in front of me, and, as with Vercha at Madam Mora's, his nearness distracted me, amplified my nerves. But there was something different about *his* nearness.

Before the awkward silence could stretch out any longer, I shifted the pile of shirts, keeping my features neutral. "Yes, I'm settling in well. Thank you for asking."

“Miss Haney sings your praises,” he said, folding his arms.

I finally had to look away, my face warming slightly, my heart still pattering. That restless silence descended again, a theme in most conversations I had.

He hesitated a second, as though mentally debating something. Then he said, “I’m . . . sorry for what my father did last week. When I said I’d run into you on the causeway, I didn’t think—” His eyes flicked from me to Rexim’s door. “Well, I suppose I said it *without* thinking. Then, later, he asked me—”

“It’s only natural,” I interrupted, my tone chilly, “that you would all be concerned about your new Floodmouth’s capabilities.”

After what happened. The unsaid words hung in the air.

His brow twitched. “I wasn’t—”

“If you don’t mind, my lord, I am expected in the washroom.”

He blinked, clearly unused to interruptions. But I felt spiky now, remembering Rexim’s test. Irritated, exposed . . . and a little ashamed.

His gaze had hardened. He tilted his head. “You know, I’ve been told we ought to be wary of trusting you. That you ask too many questions and stray where you shouldn’t.”

I stared at him. *Tígo.* He must have said something. I remembered the Veil, how narrowly I’d escaped.

“Asking questions is surely expected of new staff? And as for straying where I shouldn’t . . .” I felt my cheeks heat, knowing I was once again in Rexim’s domain. “I’m allowed to be up here. How could I do laundry otherwise?”

The corner of his mouth curled upward very slightly, but it didn’t reach his eyes, which were fixed, assessing.

“Emment’s rooms,” he said eventually, scrubbing a hand through damp hair. “Up there, turn left, then take the steps to the next floor.”

“Thank you,” I said, turning away. I was finding it harder to suppress my nerves. My heart thumped; I could feel his gaze on my back. The notepaper I'd scribbled my findings on, now crumpled and concealed deep within my bodice, felt like a brand being seared into my skin.

As soon as I was around the corner, I paused, closed my eyes, and leaned weakly against a cabinet. Then I sidled back to peer narrowly around the wall.

Llir was at his father's cracked-open doorway, fingertips resting on one of the handles. I watched him stop there for a moment, seeming to listen.

Then, to my relief, he closed the door and walked away.

14

My run-in with Llir left me shaken, and I knew I had to be more careful next time.

Rexim left for Pen Aryn the next morning—one less member of the family to pose a threat—but as one day passed and then another, I suddenly found myself saddled with extra chores. House Cormorant would be arriving at pallwater, and the entire island seemed to be bustling. Miss Haney was even more exacting than usual, her eagle eyes spotting every smear, every watermark. She patrolled incessantly, like a bear guarding a kill, scuppering any chances I might have had to slip away. As I worked, I mentally ticked off the hours, my chest growing tight with a new, weighty pressure. It grew increasingly difficult to focus on my chores. The water in the well seemed slightly more sluggish, the slop for sluicing the pigpens a little slower to react.

Everyone, it seemed, was feeling more fraught, and it appeared to have come to a head one evening when I walked in on the siblings quarrelling in the entrance hall.

"—*expressly* forbade any of us from going out for the night—"

“And how exactly will he find out? Are you planning to write to him?”

“Perhaps I will!” Vercha’s face was pink. She faced off with Emment at the bottom of the great staircase, Llir at her side, his arms tightly folded.

Catua sat at the base of the stairs, chin resting in her hands. “Just leave it, Verch.”

“I won’t!” Vercha said shrilly. “Father left you in charge, Emment. You’re the *heir*—you’re supposed to be the sensible one. It’s the younger son who should be off cavorting.”

“I can go with him,” said Llir, taking a step toward his brother.

Emment rounded on him. “You’re not coming,” he said with an odd half smile. “Not without—”

But Vercha had spotted me by then. I’d frozen on the top step, tray in hand. “No,” she said determinedly. “You’ll take the Floodmouth.”

Emment went distinctly pale. He wheeled, looking up at me. “I certainly won’t.”

“Yes, you will,” said his sister. “Or I’ll send a crow to Father now.”

“I won’t let you near the culverhouse,” Emment bit out. But Vercha was striding away from him already, snatching up a quill from an end table by the doors.

“It’s *pallwater,* Sister,” he tried, blocking her way. “I could *swim* there and back if I really had to.”

“Don’t be an idiot,” Llir said warningly.

“Just take the bloody Floodmouth!” Catua nearly shouted. Then she turned where she sat, looking sheepish. “Sorry. It’s Corith.”

“It’s fine,” I said stiffly, picking my way down the stairs. But unease and irritation were prickling at me. Full pallwater was only two days away, and I knew I needed more information for my contact. So far, I’d managed to search only Rexim’s rooms. With Emment gone, tonight would have been the perfect opportunity to slip into his chambers . . .

"Gods above," Emment said, dragging a hand through his dark hair. There was a strained sort of desperation in his expression, almost a queasiness as he watched me approach. I noticed now that he was outfitted in finery: his doublet elegantly cut, a thin sword at his hip. A bulge at his side spoke of a full-to-bursting coin purse. "I'll take the Floodmouth. Will you put that down now?"

He pried the quill from a slightly calmer Vercha, though she still glared at him, lips twisted in disapproval. Before he could move away, she grabbed his arm, hissed in an undertone, "You need to get a grip on this, Emment."

Her brother huffed out a dismissive laugh and avoided her eyes as he brushed down his doublet.

"Just take it easy tonight," Catua said lightly. She flashed me a glance.

Emment turned, looking me up and down quickly. "I'd fetch a cloak if I were you. Meet me at the harbor in fifteen minutes."

It was indeed a frigid evening, and despite my cloak, I shivered as I climbed into the boat. The vessel was lit by a single hanging lantern, which enveloped us in an eerie, pallid glow.

I'd changed into my violet Shearwater livery and also picked up my bluebird mask, shoving it deep into a pocket of my cloak. I remembered Rexim's warning to his son: *"No Veil."* If Emment went there, I meant to keep an eye on him.

I watched the eldest Shearwater with a mixture of wariness and intrigue as he clambered in after me, making the boat rock. We hadn't spoken since I'd run into him the night of my arrival, and I was sure now that he'd been avoiding me, that seeing me was a reminder of Zennia. This past week, the heir's moods had seemed even blacker, so much so that I was sure Rexim had cornered his son before departing.

"He was shaking harder than I've ever seen anyone . . ." I burned to ask Emment about that night—if he'd seen anything odd; if Zennia had said something . . . But I was already known for asking too many questions. Would it get back to Llir? Would his suspicion of me snowball?

My contact seemed confident there was more to the story, and I was desperate to discover how the Cage had come to know it. Had Emment said something to someone at the Veil? Had somebody else been out there that night, watching?

"So you've been rowing yourself there and back at pallwater?" I inquired.

Since you lost your last Floodmouth. The unsaid words hovered between us.

"Of course not," he replied, settling back against the boat's bow. "Ferda ferries me. And I top up his wages." Through the gloom, he flashed me a disarming grin, pulling out a silver flask and swigging from it. But as he watched the ocean, there was something dark and distant in his expression.

When he belched and offered the flask to me, I stared at him flatly until he shrugged and tucked it away.

"I suppose it interferes with all your—you know." He pinched his fingers back and forth in an imitation of speaking, to which I could only give another deadpan stare. I had no idea if it would or not; liquor hadn't exactly flowed at Arbenhaw . . .

In truth, with full pallwater only days away, the ocean was like a lazy cat by a fire. I could still sense its alien quality, its vastness, but it was no longer hell-bent on ravaging the bay. By now, the tidal range had shrunk down to mere feet, and the sea stretched along the midpoint of the mudflats. Around the island, it was deep but peaceful, and though it still took some cajoling—a little discomfiting with Emment watching—it listened. We meandered off, rippling along next to the flooded causeway, and I wondered if my own paltry allowance would see a few extra regals this month.

Before long, we disembarked at the little stone harbor, halfway between the mainland and the island. There stood a large horse and a puzzled-looking errand boy. Emment must have messaged ahead for a mount.

"My master said there'd only be one of you," the boy complained. "Now I'll have to walk back."

"Bad luck," said Emment bracingly.

I wanted to offer the poor boy my seat in front of Emment. But then I wouldn't be able to keep a close eye on the Shearwater.

"Sorry," I muttered as we mounted and set off. The boy's outline quickly disappeared into the darkness. Emment was a confident horseman, and he rode fast. The beast clattered down the causeway, mane tossing, as the lights of Port Rhorstin grew brighter and brighter. When I glanced about us, I saw nothing but blackness: The mudflats were shrouded, the crescent moons veiled by cloud.

The town front was busier this close to pallwater. Golden light streamed from windows, and lamps lined the streets. We emerged from the pale marsh reeds, night toads croaking, and into the bustling dock area, where fishermen sang sea shanties. Groups of people thronged on street corners, music spilling from open doorways up the hill.

Dismounting, Emment brushed himself down, straightened his collar. "Our stables are over there," he said, pointing to a low building. "Meet me back here at"—he checked his pocket watch—"about midnight."

"What?" I said, jumping down after him and staggering. What was I, a lone Orha, supposed to do until then? "No. I'm coming with you." I stepped toward him.

Emment wheeled, and I started at the look on his face: lip curled, eyes flashing. "Stay away from me," he barked. Then, seeming to remember himself, he blinked and tugged his coin purse from his belt. "Here," he said gruffly, emptying out gold. More than Vercha had handed over for my clothes. More than I'd ever seen in one place.

When I didn't reach out, he grabbed my hand, pouring the coins into it. "For a drink and a meal somewhere. Argyle's is a safe bet—just tell them you're one of ours."

Frowning, I shoved the coins into my pocket. I couldn't deny it was a tempting prospect: whiling away the evening on my own, enjoying a good meal, leaving Emment to the cards . . . But the fact that he was so keen to be rid of me made me even more determined to see what he was up to.

"Fine," I said lightly, smoothing my features. "I'll meet you at midnight."

Seeming satisfied, he turned and strode into town, and I grabbed the horse's reins, jogging north to the stables. As I went, I kept my eyes trained on Emment's back, noting which street he was turning down.

I dropped the horse off with a single tossed coin and darted back out as quickly as I'd come in.

Then, keeping the milling townsfolk between us, I tailed Emment Shearwater into Port Rhorstin.

It soon became obvious where Emment was headed. West from the docks, up the hill—to Queen's Wharf.

Twice he turned and scanned the street for me. The first time, I ducked behind a burly dockhand, tugging my hood up over my face. After that, I made sure I kept to the road's edge, slipping into an alley when he looked around again.

It seemed I'd managed to escape his notice, as he strode to the Veil without another backward glance. In the evening dimness, the building glowed: red brick contrasting with bright-white plaster, firelight gleaming from diamond-leaded windows. As I watched from an alley across the street, he skipped past the queue, the doormen nodding at him. Clearly, being heir to the land it was built on stood him in special favor with the establishment.

I cursed under my breath. He was lost to me now. Unless . . .

I tugged my mask from my cloak.

The queue was long and moved slowly. It seemed to take an age to reach the door. In that time, I was acutely aware that no other Orha here was unaccompanied.

"You with them?" one doorman grunted with a frown, nudging his chin at the nobles behind me. Their expressions must have told him I wasn't, for he shifted his bulk in front of the door. "No Orha without their employer," he stated, eyeing the crest stitched onto my breastbone. The squawking shearwater finally registered, for he raised an eyebrow, glancing at my face. "You, of all o' them, should know that rule."

"I stopped off a moment to run an errand," I said, hiding my fingers, which were clammy and trembling. "Lord Shearwater said he'd meet me inside."

Both doormen assessed me, faces like stone. "You can either wait here while I go in and check," said one, "or piss off till he comes out and gets you himself."

I pressed my lips together, eyes flicking over their shoulders. It was no use sending them in to ask Emment. It would only raise the Shearwater's suspicions of me.

At the impatient clearing of throats behind me, I nodded and stepped away from the doors, but the doorman who'd spoken kept his stare trained on me, and eventually I sidled back to my alley.

Hells. This had *not* gone well. Whatever Emment was doing in there, whatever he was saying, perhaps revealing . . . I'd never know. I flopped down onto a barrel.

I had no pocket watch to track the time, but hours must have passed as I sat there brooding, not wanting to leave in case Emment emerged. The distant music grew louder and messier. The shouts turned angrier, the laughter wilder. Behind me in the alley, rats tugged at old refuse.

By now, fatigue clawed at my eyes, and patrons were trickling out of the Veil. It had to be getting on to midnight, or past it. But there was no sign of Emment. Had he gone out the back?

Cursing softly, I slipped out of the side street. If he'd left from the rear, I'd have missed him entirely. Perhaps there was somewhere I could see both exits. Or maybe I could sneak in again, like last time.

As I walked, I peered into the Veil's burning windows, but the scarlet drapes hid its interior from view. I wondered if my infuriating golden-haired contact was working tonight. I wanted nothing more than to march back in there and demand to hear what the Cage knew about Zennia. But I knew it would be useless. First I had to give him what he'd asked for.

As I skirted the Veil and approached its rear, I could tell immediately that something was different.

Voices—boisterous, with noble, clipped tones—floated out of the high-walled backyard. The archway I'd entered through last time was blocked by a woman in leathers, thick arms folded. She looked tired and bored, but her eyes still roved, watching for anyone trying to get near.

I shrank into shadow, heart kicking up a flutter.

"Shearwater!" I heard a familiar voice caw. "Don't tell me you're going to sit *this* one out."

I'd last heard that voice in the Veil itself, and before that, at Rexim's luncheon on the island.

Why were Turnstone and Emment out back? Whose were those other murmuring voices? And why was this woman guarding the yard? From memory, it held only a well and some barrels.

If Emment gave an answer, I didn't hear it. There were only raucous cheers; the scraping of boot soles. Pulse picking up, I moved through the darkness. I had to find somewhere I could see what was happening . . .

The Veil itself was choked with ivy, but so were the outbuildings arranged around the yard. One, a low, single-story structure, must have been a stable or storehouse of some kind. Thick vines grew up it, trailing to its roof, and—astonished at myself—I found myself climbing them.

The ascent was nothing compared to the cove's cliffs, the creepers easy to hook my feet onto. They must have been colonizing these walls for years, as their stems were almost as wide as my wrists. Only a few hauls took me up to the shallow roof, where I crawled to its edge, keeping my head low.

From there, peering through a cluster of vine leaves, I had a good view of the Veil's backyard and its occupants: a circle of chattering nobles, mostly young men in various states of disarray. Turnstone was there, clutching a goblet of wine, and I soon spotted Emment beside him, hair askew, collar unbuttoned, brandishing a palmful of winking regals.

"That's more like it." Turnstone grinned as a man in a black mask patrolled, collecting coins. "Don't worry, Bryce never lets me down. You'll see."

A liveried figure stepped into the circle: dark-green tabard, tall, bulky frame. It was the Orha I'd seen with Turnstone before. His bruised eye was healed now, but he still squinted slightly, flexing his fist as he paced a few times.

Opposite him hovered a rose-clad woman with pointed features and darting eyes. She had an elaborate crest on her livery: a bird of prey with a rat in its talons. Some of the men were smirking at her, a few exchanging snide-sounding murmurs, but she ignored them, slowly circling Turnstone's Orha.

"To first blood," barked the black-masked overseer.

"First blood!" the other revellers echoed, sloshing their drinks, a few cheering loudly.

Ice lanced through me as I picked out Emment. He was hood-eyed, propping himself against a barrel.

“Put her down, Brycey,” a blond man heckled, and Turnstone’s Orha began to mutter.

As I lay there, the damp seeping through to my knees, a wind whipped up, blowing leaves from the gutter. It swirled around the yard, making some of the men yelp, and blasted right into the liveried woman.

She staggered backward, tottering on one leg, but her lips moved, too, now, and a torch on the wall flared. My eyes followed the pair, a sickness in my stomach. Making us fight, purely for their entertainment . . .

At least the two didn’t have weapons on them. Turnstone’s Gustmouth had his sleeves pushed up, and he raised his fists as he ducked toward the woman. By now, however, a series of sparks had flown from the torch and burgeoned into flames. They shot toward the larger man, causing him to wheel and bat at them frantically.

Taking advantage of his momentary distraction, the Sparkmouth zipped in under his arm, spun, and snapped her elbow into his nose.

It all happened so fast, I barely caught it. A second later, another cheer went up.

“First blood!” shrieked a man in a padded silver doublet. More a boy, really, hardly older than I was. “My Sparkmouth wins! Bad luck, Turnstone.” He was hopping on the balls of his feet with excitement. At the sight, my scalp tightened, needling all over, flickers of anger curling up from my belly.

Turnstone’s Orha had stumbled backward, smears of blood under his nose, on his fingers. The Sparkmouth turned away, massaging her elbow. She was frowning, and I got the distinct impression she’d intended to make it quick—and relatively painless.

Across the yard, Turnstone stood white-faced, his goblet hanging, forgotten, at his side. Wine stained the cobbles alongside flecks of blood.

"And bad luck, Shearwater," said another of the men as the masked overseer distributed winnings. "Second loss in as many weeks, now, isn't it?"

"Let's hope it's not a Shearwater curse, eh?" said the Sparkmouth's young, silver-clad employer, tucking a weighty purse into his breeches. "Not with the vote in just a few weeks. Don't worry. If Daddy wins, he'll be swimming in regals. No more raiding the coffers for ill-advised wagers."

"Our coffers are none of your damned business," Emment slurred, and stalked across the yard to the exit. There he leaned briefly against the stone wall, waiting for the burly guard to step aside, then pushed off from it—and disappeared into darkness.

Hells. I wriggled backward, sliding off the roof, feet casting around for purchase on the vines. When I'd reached ground level, I took off after Emment.

There he was, about fifty yards ahead of me, tracing a weaving path down the street. I jogged to catch up with him, staring daggers at his back. The rage—the *outrage*—that had kindled within me was simmering now, heading for a rolling boil.

"Hey," I said sharply, catching his elbow.

He jumped, perhaps assuming I was someone nefarious, but when he saw it was me, his shoulders sank heavily. "Oh. I thought we were meeting by the stables." He peered at me through the lamplit gloom. "What are you doing here?"

"Searching the streets. Do you realize what time it is?" I glanced around us. "You said midnight. It's well past by now."

"Really?" he muttered, listing to one side as he tried to focus on the pocket watch he'd pulled out. "Must've . . . lossht track. Cards weren't in my favor."

"Cards," I repeated flatly, eyeing him.

He nearly dropped the watch—I swiped it from him—and tugged out his coin purse, which was now totally empty. "Huh," he said; an interested little noise. "Washh going to offer to buy you a drink, but—"

"Come on," I said bitterly, "we have to go." Supporting his arm, I urged him away.

Our horse was ready, had even been fed and watered. I shoved Emment upward as he attempted to mount—it took three tries, but he eventually kept his seat.

"Here," said the stablehand, handing me a lantern. "No moonslight tonight." He looked resigned. This must be just one of many times he'd seen off the Shearwater heir in this state.

"Thank you," I said, affixing the lamp in front of Emment. I was jittery, anger still coursing through me, as I climbed up behind him. I'd have to hold him steady. "If you're going to be sick," I muttered, "please warn me first."

His only response was an echoing belch.

I nudged the horse onward, and we clopped down to the marsh, where our lantern bathed us in a pool of dim gold. The stone track stretched away ahead of us, walled in with marsh reeds, uncanny in the darkness. I set our pace at a solemn trot. It would take twice as long as the crossing here had, but I was an inexperienced rider—and I had unsteady cargo.

As we trailed through the marsh and out over the flats, I heard strange noises off in the night. A grating birdcall. An animal coughing. And then, somewhere not too distant, something that sounded a lot like a howl.

I fingered the reins nervously. Would wolves really venture here? Prowl down out of the Drowning Woods in search of roosting birds to pick off?

As if to ward off the creepiness, Emment took up a lilting song, his tenor off-key, his words bleeding together. It seemed he'd thrown off any moodiness about the fight, as every now and then, after a particularly bawdy line, he chuckled to himself and swayed one way or the other. I pressed my arms in tight to his sides.

Then, closer now, another howl. A sliver of ice speared through me to my belly.

I urged the horse onward, picking up our loping pace. We were maybe halfway to the harbor by now. I was eager to reach the waterline, where wolves couldn't follow, and in my agitation I pressed the stallion into a canter. Emment's song cut off. He gave a low moan.

"Hold on," I said, irritated. "It can't be long now."

Abruptly, our lamp jolted, came loose, and flew downward. A tinkling crash sounded over the beating of hooves. Our light was gone, the blackness around us total, and the stallion reared up suddenly, blind now to the path ahead.

I yelped. Emment was dislodged from the saddle. He toppled with a grunt of surprise to the ground, where I heard him slam onto the stone and cry out.

Trying to keep from falling, I pulled the reins taut. The stallion sidestepped and snorted in alarm. Then, to my dizzying relief, he settled. I jumped down, disoriented, jarring my knees. Somewhere behind me, I heard Emment cough, then retch, then finally empty the contents of his stomach.

I swore. Still gripping the reins tightly, I picked my way carefully back down the causeway, searching for him in near-total darkness.

"Emment! Where are you?"

A groan from ahead. A hoarse voice: ". . . Zennia?"

My blood went cold.

I heard shuffling, then a worrying *flumph.*

“Emment!” I shouted. “It’s Corith! Don’t—”

But it was too late. I guessed that in his drunken confusion, he’d toppled right over the edge of the causeway, as I heard the *shush shush* of his boots on the slick sands.

He was moving, but in completely the wrong direction.

16

"Emment!"

I dithered for a moment. Swore again.

Dropping the reins, I left the track's comforting solidity, stepping down onto the flats with a twist in my gut. My eyes were finally adjusting to the dark, and I could just make out the faint gray line of the causeway, the shadowy smears of clouds above. Port Rhorstin was a cluster of fireflies in the distance. Of Bower Island, to the east, I could see nothing—only black.

I hurried after Emment, following the squelches of his footsteps. My own soles sank shallowly into the sands. I heard his harsh panting, caught him whimper again: "Zennia." With his longer legs and stronger build, he was faster than me despite his ale-addled state.

"For gods' sakes. Emment!"

I'd heard no more howls, but that didn't mean much. The pack could be circling, drawn by the noise. I staggered on, expecting at any given second to see the eerie pinpricks of eyes in the night.

Then: a shout of panic ahead.

I stalled, gasping for breath, then picked my way forward. The sand was growing softer, wetter, under my feet. The clouds shifted, letting through a few spears of moonslight. And by them, I at last spotted Emment ahead.

But he looked odd. Shorter. Bent over double. He was struggling, arms flailing, twisting at the waist. With a sick jolt, I realized what he was doing. His legs were stuck; sinking. He was trying to get free.

"Emment!"

I inched my way forward.

I'd known there were sinking sands out on the mudflats—swathes of the bay turned sodden by lazy streams—but unlike the fishermen, the mud pickers, the foragers, I'd not yet had cause to worry about them, to learn where they were and how to avoid them.

"Here!" I cried, stepping toward him, reaching out. But straightaway I had to dart back again. My own boots were vanishing into the gritty mulch. I wrenched them out, hopping, heart pounding a wild rhythm.

As I watched him struggle, a part of me thought, *Good.*

It was as much as he deserved, after what I'd seen at the Veil. Maybe I should just leave him to the sands, claim to the family that he'd vanished in the blackness.

But then I thought of my Cage contact. My agreement. If something happened to Emment out here, Rexim Shearwater would have his revenge. I'd be packed off to a mill, or maybe a cell, any hope of learning about Zennia lost to me.

Emment yelled something incoherent. He was exhausted now, sunk up above his knees. There wasn't much time. I could save him by speaking, by telling the water to leach from the sands . . . but I didn't.

I sensed a dark flicker of opportunity.

"I can help you," I said hoarsely, "but on one condition."

He reached out, raking fingers over the sand, but his hands only disappeared into the soggy mire.

"What?" he gasped. I could no longer see him; the clouds had shrouded the moons like thick smoke.

"Tell me what happened," I said, inching forward as far as I could without sinking myself. "That night, when Zennia . . . I *know* there's more to it."

Though I couldn't make him out, I could sense his confusion, his panic. "I don't know what you mean. I told—I told everyone what happened. We searched—"

"I saw you back there," I interrupted coldly. "I saw those fights you bet on with your friends. Did you take her there to try to make her fight? Did something bad happen to her—and you covered it up?"

The awful possibility had only just struck me. Even more awful after seeing those nobles laughing and joking and teasing the Shearwater.

"What?" His voice had cracked like glass. "No. Gods, no. I don't do that any—" He cut off and let out a breath, harsh and shaky. "Okay," he continued, his words running together, "I admit, there's more to what happened that night, but believe me, I haven't brought ours along for years. It was . . . wrong. It's all wrong, I know . . ." He sounded broken.

"Tell me," I demanded, shocked at myself. I didn't recognize the voice coming out of me. But I needed to know. I burned for the truth.

Emment let out a strangled sob. "She saw it, too," he said through rasping breaths; he was still trying, unsuccessfully, to get free. "I brought her in with me, but not to fight. The other Orha, they all stand there watching, but she—she suddenly got really angry. Marched right in, tried to break up the fight. She was"—Emment paused, took a great gulping breath—"saying things to my . . . my friends. Things I couldn't countenance."

I could picture her anger, clear as water. The way her nose—her whole face—would've screwed up. The flare in her eyes. The hunch to her shoulders.

"I dragged her away, back to the causeway. Said Father would hear of it first thing in the morning, that her placement with us was already at an end . . ."

The clouds shifted again, letting through pallid moonslight. I picked out Emment's grimace in the gloom.

"And then, look, I promise you, it's what I told the others. The water, it turned choppy, then . . . wild. Must've been a sudden squall off the ocean. Our rowboat couldn't cope, and we both went over. When I climbed back in, she was nowhere to be seen."

My eyes raked his face for any duplicity, but all I could see was drunken misery, and—to my horror—a cracked-open honesty.

"No," I forced out. "There's something else."

"There's nothing else," Emment said, sagging. His panicked wriggling had only made him sink further; there was no way he was getting out of here without help.

"How did you get back?" I pressed. "If Zennia was . . . gone?"

"There were oars in the bottom of the boat," he said weakly. "The water had calmed by then. I rowed back."

My legs felt weak. I crouched on the sand, my own black misery draping over me.

"Please," he choked, "don't leave me here."

I raised my eyes, taking him in.

If I punished Emment Shearwater, I'd be punished, too. My contact might never know what had happened to me. Whatever the Cage was hiding about Zennia—and I found myself even more desperate to know now, to see if their story simply matched Emment's or if he was keeping something from me—I would never find out.

I wouldn't let that happen.

Squeezing my eyes shut, I conjured my emotions. They were starbright right now, red as blood—red as laconite. Emment wasn't wearing the stone tonight. Together in our boat, it would have hindered my efforts.

There was nothing preventing me from saving him but myself.

I tried to squash my anger, my grief. Instead, I imagined myself back at Arbenhaw. This would make a good exam, a detached part of me observed. And the thought of Arbenhaw brought Zennia's face to my mind.

Two days, I told myself. In just two days, I'd get the time and location of that second meeting, and there I'd finally find out the truth. No more drifting along unmoored; no more of this terrible, all-consuming uncertainty. The thought calmed me. I breathed out, long and slow.

"Displace," I said to the saturated sands. And to the meandering stream: "Divert your course."

This slow-moving water, soaking the sands, was a world away from the raging torrents of archwater. It was sluggish and heavy but permissive, too. Pliant. I felt the sand shift and constrict around my soles. Emment yelped in surprise. He must have felt it, too, that tightening around him.

From somewhere came the eerie echo of a howl, and I wasted no time in staggering forward.

"Help me," I gasped, scooping handfuls of sand. The ordeal must have sobered him, as he joined me in digging, grunting with exertion, heaving himself upward.

At last he stumbled out onto the flats, his fashionable breeches mud-blackened, ruined. He sank down, buried his face in his hands. He was crying, I realized. Murmuring something between the sobs.

"Zennia. I'm sorry. I'm sorry, Zennia."

"Come on," I hissed, dragging him up. We had to get out of here. I urged him toward the causeway.

But as we neared it, my stomach sank like a stone. Our stallion was gone, no sign of him anywhere.

And then, when I turned and peered behind us—

Eyes.

"This way," I whispered, tugging Emment along with me. The lights of Port Rhorstin flickered to the west. Ahead of us must lie the lapping water, but how far I no longer had any idea. The clouds shifted again, dappling the bay with moonslight, and another glance back revealed black shapes on the sands. Three, maybe four. Even taller than the wolfhounds.

I broke into a run, shoving Emment ahead of me.

"Wha—What is't?" He stumbled, craning his neck.

"Just go!" I shouted, then turned, jogging backward.

The eyes were getting nearer. I sucked in a breath.

Another exam. That was all. I could do this. I called to the nearby streams, to the wet sands, "Cut them off! Block their path to the causeway."

I didn't wait around to see if it had worked.

Whirling, I took off after Emment. And together we sprinted onward into the night.

More howls sounded as we raced along the causeway, but no eyes winked in the surrounding darkness. I hoped that meant the wolves couldn't cross the soaking sands.

When we finally made it to the little stone harbor, I collapsed into the boat, relief searing through me. Emment lay back in the vessel with a groan. I peered at him as we slid through the water, thankful that at least he wasn't crying anymore. I'd never been a natural at comforting people. I'd always felt utterly unhelpful and awkward, guiltily wishing I could just slip away. Not that Emment deserved any comfort, not after his antics back at the Veil.

I soon picked out the island rearing above us, a deep black against the navy curtain of night. As I looked keenly for the beach, for the planes and angles of its harbor, I saw a single light there, hovering in the darkness. A lantern, being held aloft by a cloaked figure.

I nudged Emment with my foot but elicited no movement. To my annoyance, a loud snore emanated from his slumped form.

"Who's out there?" came a hoarse call from the beach. Over the sloshing water, I didn't recognize the voice.

"It's us," I called back stiffly, trying to shake Emment awake. I heard a bitten-off curse, the *swoosh* of someone wading into the surf.

Emment finally stirred, blinking into the thick darkness. "Wha—?" His bleary eyes took me in.

A cold hand touched my back, and I wheeled, caught off guard. For a second, the light of the lantern blinded me. Then the figure who was holding it resolved: Llir.

His cloak's hood was up, shadowing his face. As I took in the smooth lines of his features, he yanked it back. "Emment," he said, staring wildly past me. He'd waded up to his waist into the water, his doublet darkening, his hair wet with spray. "Is he all right?"

"Functional," I said, glancing back at the sorry sight, "if incoherent."

"Help me get this boat in," Llir said tersely, handing me the lantern. He gripped the boat's side and began to haul it along with him. Though he wasn't as broad at the shoulder as his brother, his tall frame still exuded a lean, wiry strength.

When I spoke to the water, it heeded me quickly, seeming almost to sense my weary impatience. I was too fatigued to be hampered by anxiety, too fed up with Emment to let the nerves creep in—though

Llir's presence *had* sparked an odd flittering in my navel. Probably I was conscious of failing in front of him, like last time.

Together our efforts easily grounded the boat, and I helped as best I could to drag it clear of the water. By now, Emment was up, trying to clamber out of the vessel, and Llir darted around to him, slipping a shoulder under his arm.

"You let him get like this?" Llir said, hoisting his brother to standing.

"Me?" I said. Surprise gave way to brittle anger. "He gave me the slip. But even if he hadn't, it's not like he'd have listened to *me* if I'd said anything."

The revelation about the fights was on the tip of my tongue. I wanted to spill out my bitterness to Llir, but I was willing to bet he already knew all about them.

Llir kept his eyes down, navigating the shingle. He looked strained, the corners of his mouth pulled taut. "What happened? Why is he . . . ?" He gestured to Emment's breeches.

I eyed our filthy, soaking garments. The two of us must have presented quite a sight. I let out a shaky breath. "The sinking sands," I admitted. "There were howls, and I pushed the horse too hard. Emment fell. He took off over the flats—I had no time to stop him. He wandered right into one of those wide streams."

Llir's head whipped round; he gazed at me through the murk. "You got him out," he said. It wasn't a question.

Saved his life. Eventually.

I nodded guiltily, meeting his eyes.

Llir blinked, as though seeing me properly for the first time. I wavered under that piercing stare. After a pause, he said, in a hoarse rush, "Thank you."

I said nothing, merely moved to Emment's other side, and in silence we helped the heir up the path to the castle. He shuffled along like a walking corpse, only just making it up the West Tower steps without collapsing.

On reaching his rooms, we steered him over to the bed. He made no attempt to undress. Didn't even take his boots off. He collapsed face down and lay there unmoving, leaving streaks of sand and mud on the coverlet. I was certain his valets had seen much worse.

I folded my arms, darting a glance at Llir. "He does this often," I said. Again, not a question.

Llir didn't tear his shadowed eyes from Emment's form. After a heavy silence, he murmured, "He was eight when our mother died. Remembers it all. It was slow. Drawn out. We think all this started as a way to . . . block it out."

He was stock-still, trancelike, lost in memories. He almost seemed to have forgotten it was me he was talking to.

"And now?" I ventured, recalling Rhianne's and Tigo's dark looks. What had Emment been trying to escape from this time?

"Zennia. I'm sorry. I'm sorry, Zennia."

The heavy quiet was broken by a sudden, grating snore.

Llir blinked, and a veil drew across his face. Whatever reverie he'd been caught in had dissipated.

"We should get to bed, too," he said. "I'll check on him in the morning."

"Of course." I hung back to let him go first.

But as I made to leave, hearing Llir's quick steps fade ahead of me, I suddenly realized where I was.

What I could do.

Heart scudding, I looked back at the regal four-poster. Another snore emanated from that thatch of dark hair.

Silently, carefully, I went to Emment's wardrobe and rifled through the garments within. My crumpled ball of paper was tucked into my bodice—I'd decided it was safer not to hide it in my room. Unfolding it, I used a quill from Emment's writing desk to scratch out a list of all the laconite I found.

I moved to a slim closet. An end table. A dresser. And there, in a box in a top drawer, I found it:

More of that same false laconite.

It was set into a few earrings, a brooch, some rings. A long, heavy pendant wrapped in thin tissue. I touched them all hesitantly. Silence. Stillness.

A grunt from the bed; Emment shifted in his sleep. I jumped, slipped the drawer closed, and scrambled to my feet. What if Llir decided to come back after all?

Quickly I made sure everything was as I'd found it. Then, feeling even more puzzled than before, I stole out of the room and down the dark, silent stairway.

I saw little of Emment in the days that followed.

He didn't return to the mainland again. I got the sense something in him had broken that night and he wouldn't be back at the Veil in a hurry. Instead, he brooded in solitude around the castle. As I worked, still striving to impress Miss Haney, I glimpsed him in drawing rooms nursing glasses of wine; folded into armchairs, unread papers in his lap; or stalking the gardens, feathered hat gripped in his hand.

Whenever he spotted me, he quickly looked away, and I couldn't stop dwelling on his story about Zennia. The way he'd said she behaved rang true. But the accident . . . I still couldn't picture it in my mind. Steadying a boat should have been well within her talents. Perhaps Emment's threats, the prospect of banishment, had thrown her off, made the water refuse to listen.

I got no spoken thank-you from Emment for rescuing him. But my next wage pouch, handed over by a puzzled-looking Miss Haney, had nearly double the amount of regals I'd expected. I harbored suspicions that this wasn't just a reward, that it signified a demand for my silence about the Veil. Though I was still bitterly angry, I knew I had to comply. I certainly didn't need attention right now, not with my task to complete for the Cage. I carefully folded the secret away, sequestered the pouch under a floorboard in my bedroom, and left the eldest Shearwater to his melancholy moods.

Instead, I puzzled over the false laconite I'd been finding. But try as I might, I just couldn't fathom why Rexim and Emment might need it, or want it.

Expense? Laconite wasn't cheap, it was true. But the false stone hadn't looked inexpensive either. It might even cost more than laconite itself to create its mirror image from other materials, like ruby, garnet, or even red diamond.

No. There had to be a different reason. Maybe my contact at the Veil would know.

My contact.

Full pallwater was here already, and that meant I needed to send my first tally.

I had figures for Rexim's and Emment's rooms and a few other locations around the castle, and I fervently hoped that would be enough for now. I just had to get to the culverhouse in North Tower—a place I rarely had cause to venture—sometime in the next day, without anyone noticing.

The morning had dawned clear and chilly, the bay quiet, its waves whispering against the rocks. I was up in South Tower with a few of the maids, and as I plumped a pillow, wondering when I could get away, I spotted a guard hightailing it across the inner ward. Moving to a narrow window that looked west, I saw two boats on the water, one flying a blue flag.

"It's them," said Debry eagerly, coming up behind me. "At last. Go on, you'd better get downstairs."

"Them?" I repeated, turning to look at her.

"The Cormorants, o' course!" she replied, flapping her hands at me. "Quickly. You'll be needed. You hadn't forgotten?"

I flushed. Between my task and Emment's breakdown, I had.

Recalling how we Orha had been summoned to Rexim's luncheon, I hurried to the entrance hall, hearing voices below. Whatever this involved, I hoped it would be quick.

Miss Haney soon appeared, Rhianne and Mawre trailing after her. Tigo, I guessed, had gone to change into his livery. I shrugged off the smudged apron I'd been wearing over mine.

"Here, I'll take that," Miss Haney said, frazzled. "Go on, then, out to the gatehouse with you all. The family want to be the first to greet their guests."

Outside, the air was fresh, faintly salty. The gulls that perched along the battlements squalled. Beyond the gatehouse, on the path rising from the beach, the Shearwater siblings stood together, resplendent—all velvet and lace, ornamented in laconite.

I brushed down my livery, skin tingling with nerves. Llir spotted us coming and murmured to Vercha, who turned, bright-eyed, and beckoned us forward. "There you are at last," she said. "They'll be alighting any minute."

I glanced at Llir as we joined their little group. We hadn't run into each other since the night I'd saved Emment. He seemed tense, gaze fixed on the path ahead. As I watched, Catua leaned briefly against him, and he turned his head a fraction, shooting her a tight smile.

Emment, on the other hand, was a man transformed.

These last few days, he'd looked dishevelled, almost wretched. The servants had whispered about him in hushed tones. Now he stood immaculate, every inch the strapping heir, a smirk on his face, his posture relaxed. Perhaps, I thought, the act of confessing had, in the end, tugged him out of the darkness.

"Now," said Vercha, "you all know the protocol. Rhianne, over here. And Mawre. Remember—"

"Where's Tigo?" Llir demanded, eyes flicking between us.

"Bringing up the rear," came the Mudmouth's deep voice, and he jogged into view, slowing to a stop close by Llir.

Like accessories, I thought with a stab of indignation. Llir was no better than Vercha for it.

"Very good," Vercha said, running narrowed eyes over us. In the thin, cool air, their laconite sang faintly.

A moment later, a party appeared on the path. Two figures out front, sitting casually in their saddles, on mounts I recognized, borrowed from our own stables. I shaded my eyes, for their laconite, their finery, winked in the sunlight, obscuring their faces.

Behind them came others in bright cobalt-blue livery, along with a wagon piled high with leather trunks.

Curious, I shifted to get a better look. A baritone voice reached us, carried by the sea breeze. "Hail, Shearwaters! Here we are, at long last!" It was joined by a woman's laugh: deep and delighted.

Vercha stepped forward, held a palm up in greeting.

The pair that rode up to us were startlingly alike. Twins, I guessed, taking in their fine countenances: one a slim-shouldered man in a peacock-green doublet, the other a woman in a silver-gray gown. They had the same rich tan skin, the same handsome features, the same dark, sparkling eyes, the same wide, easy smiles.

"Avrix. Morgen," Vercha said warmly.

"Darlings," Morgen Cormorant replied. She dismounted elegantly, kissed the siblings on their cheeks.

"My, look at you all," said her brother, Avrix. He hopped down with a flourish, tugged off his riding gloves. "Little Cattie. You were nigh out of muslin nappies when we saw you last, I'm certain of it."

Catua flushed; the others all laughed.

"You are *most* welcome," Emment said, clapping his friend on the back. He had an air of almost desperate relief. Gratitude, perhaps, for the coming distractions.

"You *have* all grown up, haven't you?" Morgen said slowly. She had just pressed a kiss to Llir's right cheek. Standing back now, she took in his frame.

Llir was smiling like his siblings, but there was a tightness to his jaw that the others didn't share. "And you're as magnificent as ever, Morgen." He dipped his head, and she grinned at him, eyes glittering.

As my stomach tugged oddly, Avrix's eyes roved his hosts. "But where is your dear father?" he said with a frown. "Not indisposed, I hope? What a stroke of bad luck that would be."

"Not at all," said Vercha hastily. "He is over in Pen Aryn. Business, you understand. He sends his deepest apologies."

Avrix's eyebrows twitched. "Of course. The Chamber."

Exchanging a barely there glance with her brother, Morgen looked sorrowful. "Shall we not see him at all?"

"I'm confident you will," Emment replied, smiling. "He fully expects to return for the ball."

The visitors looked mollified, and they all moved off. With a strange, jagged feeling I couldn't explain, I watched Morgen fall in close beside Llir, Tigo hiking behind them like a shadow.

Avrix's voice drifted back toward me: "You have a culverhouse up at the castle, yes? Later I should like to let our long-suffering mother know we didn't perish on the crossing, as she predicted we would."

My insides jumped at the mention of the culverhouse, at the reminder of the message I still had to send.

Vercha's eyes twinkled. "Dear Lady Cormorant. Of course. How is the dowager doing these days?"

My nerves were multiplying by the minute. But then I was distracted by the figures that came next: the blue-liveried servants we'd seen behind the twins. Here, I realized with a spark of curiosity, were the Cormorants' own Orha: a set of four, like us.

They were cool faced, unsmiling, done up in high collars. The crests on their livery showed an ebony bird: long necked, wings raised, on top of two crossed sabers.

The group was fronted by a burly woman. Taller than Mawre, she was pale, rose-cheeked, her flaxen hair braided tightly to her head.

"Well met," she said to Rhianne and me—we'd strayed behind the others to stare. She had a blunt, biting accent I couldn't place. "I am Nemaine. This is Ebba, Orran, and Daiman." Behind her clustered a woman and two men, all of whom looked older than us.

It was Rhianne who replied, after a momentary pause. "I'm Rhianne. This is Corith. And that's Tigo and Mawre." But when we glanced around, our Mudmouth and Gustmouth had drawn away.

Nemaine's ice-blue eyes swept us up and down once. Then she beckoned to her companions, and they disappeared through the gatehouse.

Before the luggage cart could overtake us, too, we followed, exchanging a fleeting glance.

"This ball," I said quietly, watching the visitors ahead, seeing Morgen Cormorant throw her head back, laughing. "Are we really expected to go to it?"

"Of course," said Rhianne. "Along with everything else. When the Hundred are together, it's . . . like a performance. It started after the Great Revolt. For their protection, at first, from rival Houses, but then, eventually, it became tradition. Exhibition." She'd lowered her voice to little more than a whisper. "It's stupid, really. Lots of standing around."

"Wait," I said with creeping trepidation. "What do you mean, 'Along with everything else'?"

"Tours of the island. Musical evenings. Cards, dice. Formal dinners, dancing, readings . . ."

"What about our chores?" I knew I looked panicked. But it wasn't only my chores I was worried about having time for.

"Oh, we'll be expected to keep up with those, too. When they're sleeping or bathing." She quirked a bronze eyebrow. "Why d'you think Miss Haney's been so frantic? And Tigo working extra time in the gardens? Because he knows he'll have so little now."

Unseen, I dug my nails into my palms. I'd hoped now that the Cormorants were here, everyone would be distracted seeing to the guests and I'd have more opportunities for sneaking around. Instead, it seemed, I might not have any at all.

"That does seem stupid," I said in a forced monotone, and followed her up the steps into the keep.

Vercha led us through to the room she'd called the snug, where a fire crackled cheerily in the grate, and the wolfhounds, who'd been basking in front of it, shot up and bounded around the visitors' ankles. I was acutely conscious of the clock's loud ticking. I needed to get to the culverhouse. Today.

"I can't tell you how gratifying it is to see your faces," said Avrix Cormorant, throwing himself into a chair. His sister stayed standing, peering from the windows. "And that crossing—the sea breeze, the view over the bay . . . I feel rejuvenated already." He grinned at the siblings.

The Cormorants' Orha lined up along the wall, beneath a portrait of a Shearwater ancestor. Their movements were practiced, almost automatic. Clearly, the twins were social people. I followed Tigo and Mawre's lead, joining them on the opposite wall. Rhianne padded over to murmur into the hearth—I was sorry I didn't have her excuse to sidle off.

As Vercha poured tea, the other siblings took up positions on the couches.

"It was snowing when you were last here, wasn't it? Do you remember?" Emment leaned forward, a glint in his eyes. "You accidentally caught Father with a snowball meant for me."

"My gods," Avrix said. "I *do* remember." He laughed, a rich peal that seemed to warm the room.

Morgen was patrolling, inspecting the portraits. As she stopped in front of me, my skin went taut.

"*This* one's new," she murmured, gazing at me. Her skin was flawless, glowing in the firelight, her eyes dark pools ringed by thick lashes.

Vercha had come up behind her with her tea. "Corith's just wonderful," the Shearwater said sweetly. "Our housekeeper says she'd be lost without her."

"What happened to that grizzled old lady you had?"

"Muiry? Oh, she got sick, poor lamb. Went to a brewery in Lanniton, I think. Somewhere she could sit down and work."

Morgen made a sympathetic noise as nausea clawed its way up from my belly.

"We had a terrible time last month, before Corith," Vercha said, not even lowering her voice. "The first girl they sent . . ." She glanced behind her. "Well, let's just say that was a *short-lived* placement."

The atmosphere in the room cooled, turned brittle. Llir threw a knifelike glance at his sister as Emment's jaw clenched and his teacup rattled.

"You sometimes get duds," Morgen said airily.

My eyes flashed to her. I was coiled like a spring.

"Well, in any case," the Cormorant continued, clearly sensing she'd trodden in murky waters, "this one looks hale enough, if a little skinny." She smiled at me. "I wish you every happiness here."

"Great gods," came Avrix's voice. He was lounging in his chair, patting one of the wolfhounds. "Leave the poor girl alone, will you, Morgen? She's not a new painting." He shot me a small wink.

Despite myself, I felt a flicker of gratitude. It had taken everything I had to remain impassive; I wasn't sure I had a shred of restraint left.

"Now, look," Avrix continued, jumping up and staring out into the bay. "We simply *must* get back out on that water—and take advantage of this excellent weather. What do you say we meet down there tomorrow and give your father's sailing boats a spin?"

Morgen clapped and circled the couches. "Not just a spin—a race. I demand it. Let's see how your Orha measure up!"

"We can take the dogs out," Catua said with a grin. "They love a splash around." The hounds' tails thumped.

Renewed anxiety crept back in, chasing the wisps of relief from my midriff. *Sailing.* That was the Floodmouths' purview, though Mawre and the Cormorants' Gustmouth would help.

"It's settled, then," said Avrix, sitting back down. "Now. Where are those pastries you promised us?"

As the day crawled by, Rhianne's prediction bore out.

The Shearwaters and the Cormorants sat up late that evening, reminiscing about capers past. It seemed it had been a few years, at least, since the families had spent a long stretch together, and they were clearly keen to make up for lost time.

When the guests began to yawn and we were finally released, my spine was throbbing from standing to attention and my ears were stinging from the ring of laconite. I wanted nothing more than to fall into bed, but I hadn't forgotten my contact's warning: *"If I don't receive that note, this deal is off the table."*

An eternity seemed to pass once I returned to the tower and waited for my fellow Orha to fall asleep, but at last the final lamp went out, and I stole silently back up to the castle.

All was quiet as I wound my way up North Tower, darkness mantling the steep spiral stair. The autumn chill had seeped through the walls, and my shivers made my rushlight's glow flitter eerily.

The circular culverhouse was musty and shadowed, scant moonslight spearing in from a hole in the ceiling. As I entered, I heard the susurration of feathers and could just make out black humps in the darkness, pairs of sharp, beady eyes trained on me.

My heart thudded dully as I took out my note, onto which I'd carefully translated my code, and hurried over to the recess marked THE VEIL. The "K" I'd etched on the note stood out sharply, and I wondered what it stood for, what my contact's name was.

The crow watched me attentively, shifting its dark bulk. It knew to expect morsels of bread on arrival and was clearly impatient to receive its reward, but as I fastened my message to one scrawny leg—

The scrape of a sole from behind me reached my ears.

Whirling, I saw the outline of a figure in the doorway, faintly lit by their own candle. I nudged the crow frantically, whispering, *"Go!"*

With a beating of huge black wings, it took off, streaking up out of the hole into moonslight. I reared back. Behind me, the figure dropped their light, the flame extinguishing, the candle rolling.

My own rushlight still glowed faintly, and by it, I saw a striking face, warm brown skin, dark eyes stretched wide.

"Hello," came one of the well-heeled voices I'd been forced to listen to for several hours earlier.

Avrix Cormorant, dressed in a night-robe.

"He-hello," I stuttered, heart galloping, gazing at him through the thick gloom.

A smile lit his features as he took me in. "I'm sorry for surprising you. What a place to get a scare!" His eyes flicked upward. "Creepy, isn't it?"

I offered no reply, stepping back to make space. The culverhouse wasn't exactly roomy. As he moved inside, he had to stand close.

"Couldn't sleep myself," he said, still sounding apologetic. "Never can the first night away from home. I thought I might as well post our letter to Mother, given I was wide awake anyway." He smiled. "What's your name? I remember you from the snug."

Despite my horror at being discovered, and my racing thoughts—how would I explain this?—I couldn't help feeling a flicker of warmth. He was looking at me with genuine interest, not the cool, predatory regard of his sister.

"Corith," I said. "The Shearwaters' Floodmouth. I—" My mind grasped desperately for *something.* "Everything's been so hectic today, I didn't have a chance to get here until now. I—I had a letter to drop off, too." Well, that much was true, I thought. "For my friend. She has a placement down south. We write to each other, and I owe her a message."

Avrix looked pained, his brows dipping down. "That'll be our fault, I expect," he said gently. "I'm sorry we've lumbered you all with more chores." He glanced at my clothes; I was still in my livery. "Must already be quite the load, with five in the family." He paused. "Lots of laconite to polish, too, yes?"

My thoughts snagged, panicked. But he couldn't have known. "Yes," I half whispered, managing a smile.

"Got to be annoying. All that buzzing." He grinned as he spoke, tugging an envelope from his pocket. "Well, I'd really better get this off to Mother, or she'll think we capsized and send out a search party."

Though my pulse still thumped like a drum in my ears, I felt a warm curl of amusement. "Here," I said, bending to pick up his candle. I lit it using my rushlight's flame and handed it to him, hoping my fingers weren't trembling.

"Thank you," he said, dark eyes on my face. "Will you be sailing with us tomorrow?"

"Of course," I said reluctantly. I'd forgotten about that.

"Then I shall look forward to it even more," he replied, quirking an eyebrow. "Good night, Corith."

"Good night," I forced out, stepping past him, revelling in the heady relief at my escape that almost—but not quite—banished my jangling nerves.

18

I woke with the hope that rain clouds had rolled in, but the sky shone sapphire blue above the bay.

With preparations for the guests complete, Miss Haney was no longer stalking the castle, so after breakfast and my morning chores, which I slogged through heavy eyed and foggy headed, I dashed up the stairs to the culverhouse to check for any response from my contact. But though the crow was back, nestled deep in its recess, there was no reply attached to its leg, nor in the basket where the birds dropped their deliveries. "K" probably hadn't even started his shift yet.

Reluctantly I dragged my feet down to the little stone harbor on the island's west shore. The day was bright and blustery, perfect for sailing, and my high-collared livery was enough to keep off the chill. Avrix had said the water looked inviting, and I had to grudgingly admit he was right. Pallwater meant it was swaddling the island—not quite calm, with the wind from out east, but gently choppy, slapping at the rocks.

The Cormorant twins were already there: Morgen in billowing

breeches and a jacket, her black hair caught in a beaded caul, and Avrix a beacon in a scarlet doublet. Their Orha stood to attention nearby, while Tigo and the others lingered on the shingle. Behind me came excited voices, and I looked back to see the siblings skittering down the path, Catua out front, racing the wolfhounds.

"Marvelous," Avrix said on seeing me. "Our second rudder. We have a complete set."

Despite his own late-night wanderings in the castle, his features bore no evidence of fatigue. Anxiety plucked at me—would he bring up last night?—but he only flashed a white-toothed grin at me. I couldn't help flushing in the face of that smile. The twins were so handsome they were almost hard to look at—like catching the glare of the sun in the sky.

"Ebba, with me," Morgen said easily. "Orran, you can join Avrix's boat."

"Mixed teams?" said Emment, striding toward us. "Excellent idea. We'd outnumber you otherwise. Cat, fancy joining me and Avrix?"

"Good, we get Morgen and Mawre," said Vercha, linking arms with Llir, who was buttoned in dark velvet. The breeze stirred his hair as he glanced from me to Avrix. I was infinitely glad it was the latter I'd run into in the early hours and not the Shearwater.

"With deepest apologies to our spectators, of course," Avrix added, looking over at the others—Tigo, Rhianne, and the Cormorants' equivalents. I caught the eye of their Sparkmouth, Nemaine, but the towering woman only stared back dispassionately. "We'll have to come up with another activity that plays more to your talents." He shot them a winning smile.

Tigo's folded arms gave the impression that he'd much rather be watching from a clifftop anyway, while Rhianne gazed out at the bay with envy. I'd have gladly swapped places with her, but there was no escaping. I trailed after Emment and Catua to the boats.

Rexim's sailing vessels were impressive. A pair of compact fore-and-aft rigs, with bright-white lateen sails made for speed. I wondered what the Brigant would say if he knew his offspring were taking his boats for a spin. At least we were right in the middle of pallwater—no tides to speak of, the sea solid blue.

I eyed Emment's profile as I clambered in next to him. Since arriving, he'd determinedly avoided my eyes. But if the tragic ending to his boat trip last month was still affecting him, he gave no sign of it. His dark hair was wind tossed, his silver gaze keen.

"Corith, Orran, we'll need you at the stern," said Catua, her round face pink from the breeze. Golden locks whipped out from her braids as she tugged at one rope, then fastened another.

She knew what she was doing, and so did Emment, who pushed us off, letting the sails fill and billow. "Vercha's never been a sailor," he said, throwing a glance at our competition. "But Mawre's cool as an icehouse under pressure."

"And Llir always used to beat me in the dinghies," Catua added with the shade of a glower.

I shuffled down the boat, trying to adjust to the waves' pitch and roll. In the other vessel, Llir was murmuring to Mawre, shading his eyes, pointing up at their sails. Vercha had folded herself down nearby, and Ebba, the Cormorants' Floodmouth, peered over the side.

Avrix had stepped to our bow, staring westward. "I really do envy you this bay," he called back. "Our cliffs jut out too far and too high; we rarely get out on the water like this. But I warn you: Though she may not have had much practice, my sister is competitive. A natural rallier."

And indeed, Morgen was striding the deck, barking out orders at Ebba—and Mawre. The latter showed no evidence of displeasure, though I caught her eyes lingering on Morgen's turned back.

"Are we ready?" Avrix shouted across the shallow swells.

"Waiting for you," came Vercha's arch reply.

The Cormorant chuckled. "Very well, then. Once around the island—leeward—on three!"

My abdomen heaved, my heart jumping wildly. I wasn't ready. I hung over the gunwale.

Beside me, the Cormorants' Gustmouth, Orran—thin, white-haired, face faintly lined—set his shoulders and moistened his lips.

"One."

I shut my eyes against the breeze, bringing to mind my leaping anxiety. It shone deep red like a far-off fire, growing by the second, sending out sparks.

"Two."

You can do this.

I plunged my fingers into the surf and felt the shock of cold on my skin. There was an openness to the churning waters, almost a ready eagerness to buoy us along.

"Three!"

I opened my eyes just for a second, darting a look at the second boat. Mawre was standing tall at the stern, black hair whipping against her shoulders, the sails snapping outward, ballooning. Not waiting to see what their Floodmouth was doing, I squeezed my eyes shut and leaned out farther.

Focusing on the memory of Zennia—remembering the encouraging twitch of her lips, the lift of her eyebrows she'd always given me at Arbenhaw whenever I'd thrown her a panicked glance—I gripped my emotions as though I held them in my fist. The red ball sputtered and buckled inward, my panic tempering, my breath coming easier.

"Help us," I said to the waves at our rear, opening my eyes. "Speed us onward." As though in answer, one smacked the boat's side. Whether it was a rebuff or a show of solidarity, I couldn't tell—not until I felt the current. It pushed against my hand, and then the boat's hull, making the timbers creak beneath us.

At the same time our sails filled with a southerly squall, strong as a person pushing on my shoulders. Orran's eyes were closed, his lips moving rapidly.

"There she blows!" came Avrix's voice, joined by whoops from Emment and Catua.

We zipped along, water seething at the bow, but Morgen's team was ahead of us—for now. They'd had a good start. Mawre's winds were powerful, enough to make me marvel at how one Gustmouth could do it.

I eyed Ebba as I clambered back and steadied myself. Hard-faced, the Floodmouth muttered down into the foam, but the tautness of her features and the hunch in her spine told me she felt under as much pressure as I did. The bubbling ridges behind their boat weren't quite as high, as insistent, as ours were, and I felt a brief surge of gratification—before squashing it and concentrating on the surf.

Bower Island was far from large; we'd already rounded its northern shoreline. The rocks were craggier, the clifftops higher, and I suddenly spotted a cluster of figures on a hillock to the east, pointing and waving. Tigo and Rhianne had been joined by other servants—I recognized the willowy outline of Miss Haney; Debry's flapping skirts and white bonnet; even Ferda's short, spry figure, hopping in excitement, graying hair wild.

"Is there any pastime superior to sailing?" called Avrix, who was still standing proudly at the bow. He'd raised one knee, had it braced on the prow like a navy captain, hands on his hips.

"I'd say so, if dice and drink are involved," put in Emment, then, at a glare from Catua, "What?"

I had to admit, it was near to glorious. Clear, cloudless skies, a lukewarm sun, the bracing bluster of wind past my ears. To our left, as we curled around the island's east side, the open ocean stretched out like a blanket, shimmering, its wave tips winking bright white.

We'd left our spectators behind by now, the vast, dour castle hiding them from view. I expected they were hurrying back to the beach to watch our arrival and judge the winner.

I glanced to our right, at our shining twin vessel, and was thrilled to see we'd drawn almost level. Morgen, one arm hugging the mast, leaned toward Ebba and shouted something, her words disappearing amid the rushing spray. My eyes found Llir, who reclined at the stern, resting on bent elbows, hair whipping wildly. As we sliced through the water, he looked at our boat and caught my eye—

Just as a wave bumped us.

"Hoi!" yelled Emment, clinging to the gunwale.

"Cheaters!" Catua shrieked, teetering where she stood.

Vercha and Llir jumped to their feet for the finale. Ebba's stern gaze was fixed on our hull, her lips forming words I couldn't decipher. As we shot past the southern shoreline, with its low cliffs and beaches, I felt another heave, a precarious rocking.

"What did I tell you?" Avrix shouted. "Competitive, that one!" He saluted his sister.

We'd fallen behind again, only a few feet, but suddenly Avrix was looming above me. "Corith, isn't it?" That sun-bright smile. "I think this calls for some . . . underhand tactics. Are you game?"

My wind-scoured face flushed uncomfortably, but within I felt an odd pull to comply. There was no doubt the Cormorant was charming to a fault, but I remembered, too, his warm manner in the culverhouse. And before that, how he'd saved me in the snug: admonishing his sister, redirecting her attention.

"I can do my best," I said breathlessly, and Avrix clapped me gratefully on the shoulder.

Shifting, staring at the other team's boat, I began to weave my own new pleas . . .

We'd rounded the rocks of the southeast headland, the distant mainland a shadow to our left, and now the shingle beach reappeared and the harbor beyond it, pestered by waves.

Tigo, Rhianne, and the others were there, hands cupped around their mouths, egging us onward.

The current propelling Morgen's boat had turned scrappy. Distracted by sabotaging us, Ebba had neglected it, and its interest was clearly waning, its strength weakening. All it took me was a few choice entreaties, and their boat lagged behind, thudding in the water. At the same time, I gazed ahead of us and called to the waves that rolled past us to the beach. One rose high, responding with zeal—and knocked right into our rivals, jolting their boat.

Morgen clung on. Mawre ducked. But Ebba, who'd been perched on the gunwale, tumbled overboard with a splash. Vercha nearly lost her footing, arms pinwheeling, grasping for Llir. And to my horror, in the course of steadying his sister, Llir staggered backward—and went in himself.

The harbor, only fifty yards off, rang with the clamor of cheers and protests. Avrix was laughing, deep from his belly, the others exchanging bellows of blame. "You started it!" Catua was screeching, as Vercha cursed us, murder in her eyes.

It took us all a moment to realize that while Ebba had surfaced, Llir was nowhere to be seen. I froze where I stood, my eyes darting. Catua ran to the side of our vessel and leaned over—which turned out to be a grave mistake.

Her brother, who'd swum underwater to our boat, exploded upward, one arm on the shallow gunwale, hooked her around the waist, and hauled her toward him.

"It wasn't me!" she screamed, but she was laughing. Just before they bombed into the bubbling water, Llir's eyes flashed up and caught mine knowingly.

Our vessel had crossed the finish line and now bobbed close enough to the harbor for Tigo to throw lines and draw us in.

Even so short a dash over the waves made my soles feel strange on solid ground. Llir, Catua, and Ebba had struck out powerfully for the stone slipway and now strode up it with loping steps. My ribs thudded painfully at what I'd done, at the sight of Llir, sodden hair dripping, shirtsleeves soaked and clinging to his arms. But when his moss-green gaze snagged on mine, I could only discern a strange, sharp appraisal. As though he was almost as surprised as I was—as though he hadn't thought me capable of it. It reminded me of the look he gave me a few nights ago when I'd rescued Emment. Like he was seeing me anew.

A touch on my shoulder, a voice at my ear. I swivelled to face a grinning Avrix. "Excellent work," he said admiringly. And then, perhaps because he sensed my reticence, "Nothing wrong with a cutthroat tactic or two. Trust me."

With a wink, he fell in with his sister and the siblings, who were already trudging up the loose shingle, sparring genially about the result.

Rhianne caught my eye, and I moved to join her. I thought my fellow Orha might disapprove, and sure enough, Tigo, nearby, was tense-lipped. But as soon as he'd taken his usual place directly behind Llir, a gleam entered Rhianne's gaze.

"That was brilliant," she murmured with a twitch of her lips. I half shrugged, but inside, my chest warmed pleasingly. "Oh," she continued, digging into her livery and tugging out a slip of parchment as we hiked up the path. "I don't suppose *this* means anything to you? I found it up in the culverhouse this morning. Can't make head nor tail of it. I'll give it to Miss Haney when we get back to the castle, but"—she squinted at it—"it's very odd."

Skin icing over, I stared at the note.

MD SS V BACK K

That was it. The letters were tiny, precise. But it took only a second for their meaning to register.

Market day. Sunset. The back of the Veil. K.

I swallowed, mouth dry, throat squeezing in panic. "Er . . ." I held out a hand for the note, pretending to want to examine it more closely. As Rhianne gave it up, she glanced at my face, and I wrestled to keep my features neutral. "Actually," I said, remembering with a jolt just where I'd seen such shorthand before—symbols and letters often caught my eye—"this looks like it might be from Madam Mora. You know, the ball dresses?" My pulse was clattering. "Maybe she needs an extra measurement."

Rhianne's confusion seemed to clear. "Right," she said. "'*Back.*' That does make sense."

"I can give this to Vercha later," I said, fingertips white where I clutched the note.

The Sparkmouth seemed relieved. "Thanks. I've got so much to do in the kitchens . . ."

As we wound our way upward, my thoughts raced and darted. I'd done it—my contact was clearly satisfied—and next market day was the thirtieth of Tima. Just over a week to finish my tally and present the Cage with what they'd asked for.

But as the castle loomed through the trees above, my eye caught West Tower, where the siblings slept.

I still had three of their bedchambers to search. And the prospect of trespassing in Llir's domain made an odd disquiet flitter behind my breastbone.

Crack!

The noise was deafening, making my heart jolt and my shoulders twitch.

"Ho! Fine shot, my boy." Avrix Cormorant shaded his eyes, gazing down the neatly trimmed lawn to the targets: round sheets of parchment nailed to wooden frames. They were riddled with bullet holes. Smoke tinged the air.

"Kicks to the side a bit," Llir said indifferently, flipping the eight-shot matchlock revolver and examining it closely, running his thumb over the wood.

"She *is* a touch unreliable, it's true." Avrix smiled, his laconite drop earring winking. "But she's a beauty, don't you think? Breovan walnut."

Llir handed the gun to Tigo and Rhianne. They stood close by him, straight-backed, immaculate. The Sparkmouth kept the match burning while the Mudmouth pounded the bullets into the barrels.

I let out a short, frustrated breath. Standing with Mawre off to one side, I was acutely conscious that another day was slipping by.

Opposite us, near the entrance to the rose gardens, the Cormorants' Orha stood in a line, flaxen-haired Nemaine looking on with thin lips.

I watched as the pistol was handed to Catua. She hefted it, intrigued, and Avrix chuckled. Nearby, Vercha, Morgen, and Emment were engaged in a lively debate. I tuned them out.

Two days.

Only two days left until my meeting.

Nearly a week had passed since the sail race, and almost all of it had been spent like this: standing around, just as Rhianne had predicted, any spare moments used to catch up on my work. I was tired and antsy, horribly aware of each hour that passed, as though there were a ticking clock in my mind.

I'd only just managed a fleeting inspection of Vercha's and Catua's laconite the day before, a snatched opportunity while emptying their baths in a rare few moments when Debry wasn't lurking.

But Llir's . . . I'd had no chance to sneak in there. Whenever I found myself with a free half hour, either he was in there, bathing or changing, or his valet was, tidying up after him. Desperately, I'd wondered if I could sneak in while Llir was sleeping, but the prospect of his waking made my stomach clench with horror—no excuse would save me then.

But turning up to the Veil without the rest of my information . . . that made me anxious and nauseated, too. The Cage knew something about Zennia, about what had happened that night. If I failed in this, they'd cut me loose.

Or maybe they'd decide I knew too much about their mission. My contact hadn't seemed particularly threatening, but that didn't mean this "Leadership" weren't. No. I had to fulfill our agreement.

Crack!

I winced.

Avrix applauded. "Best of the lot! You've a fine eye on you, Cattie."

Not long after, the party dispersed. The sky was murky, the air heavy with damp.

"Do let me show you the new harp in the music room," Vercha said to the twins, holding out a gloved arm.

"I think I'll stay out with the dogs for a bit," said Llir, lingering by Tigo and Rhianne.

"Yes, me too," said Catua, handing Avrix his gleaming pistol. The wolfhounds, lying nearby on the grass, thumped their tails as the younger Shearwaters approached them.

Emment followed after Vercha and the Cormorants, and the Cormorants' Orha stepped quickly behind them.

I dithered, unsure which group to trail after, before Vercha said in passing, "Don't worry, you're relieved. We won't need you till dinner."

As Llir lobbed a stick down the lawn for the wolfhounds, a tingle of adrenaline snaked down my spine.

"At long last," Mawre muttered, and strode off, arms folded, no doubt to tackle her ever-towering piles of laundry.

I knew I should dedicate the precious time to chores, too. There was water to draw, linens to churn. But my deadline was weighing me down like an anchor. Heart hammering, I hurried in the direction of the castle, shadowing Vercha and the others to West Tower at a safe distance, so I wouldn't be spotted.

With the sweet notes of the harp drifting behind me, I dashed up the spiral steps two at a time. The dinner bell wouldn't ring for another hour or so, but the siblings would change in their quarters before that . . .

Pausing at an arrow slit, I peered down beyond the gardens. Llir and Catua were disappearing into the pinewood. A peal of laughter rang out from the music room, and I took a steadying breath. I was safe; I was alone.

The tower's upper floors were empty of servants. Only my own soft steps broke the silence. Stopping outside Llir's door, which was shut tight, I listened carefully before easing it open, but all was quiet when I stepped over the threshold. I'd never set foot in his chambers before, and trespassing here felt . . . different to the others. There was a quiver to my stomach I couldn't explain.

Llir had two rooms conjoined by an archway: a study with what seemed to be a walk-in closet, and a bedroom with a window that showed a leaden sky. Everything was rich brown wood, clean and gleaming, the gray drapes pulled closed, no torches burning. The surface of his writing desk was bare, but in one of the drawers I found pencil sketches: of birds, the bay, an older woman's profile.

In the bedroom was a bathtub, a pair of boots on a stool. A silver-embroidered coverlet on the four-poster bed, and a dent in his pillow that drew my eye.

Opening his wardrobe, I thumbed through doublet after doublet, a jittery feeling fizzing in my chest. It felt strange—too intimate—to be touching his clothes, to be breathing the scent that wafted out at me: lavender soap, the bare hint of sweat. Dimly I registered that it was drizzling outside, thin drops pattering on the mullioned windows.

It was only after a minute or two that I realized there was no laconite in his bedroom. Puzzled, I retraced my steps to the study and finally found some, shut up in the closet. It sang at me weakly, a thin whine, like a fly. There was plenty of false laconite here, too, and I clinked through it, frustrated. He had more than his siblings and father did.

It was then that I heard a rustle from the study, the slightest creak of a floorboard outside, just audible over the stones' faint ringing.

I froze.

Llir's valet, maybe, bringing fresh towels.

The closet door was open a fraction, a sliver of the study visible beyond: a tapestry on the wall, part of the rain-spattered window. I waited, stock-still, for a few long minutes, but nothing moved, and there were no other sounds.

I pushed the door open and stepped into the study. It was empty. I huffed a laugh at myself. Perhaps a dislodged doublet had slipped off its hanger. And this castle was old—of course there'd be creaks. Or maybe by now my nerves were so frayed, my sleep so disturbed by my looming deadline, that I was hearing things.

In any case, my duty here was done.

Starting across the carpet to the main door—it was open a crack; had I left it like that?—I paused as a scent wafted suddenly over me. Rain, brine, the tang of pine needles. Something a little musty, like wet fur.

I glanced back, but the window was shut tight. The only sounds were the patter of the drizzle and the familiar crooning of laconite in the closet.

You're losing it, I thought as I tugged the door open.

But as I slipped through it, shutting it behind me, I couldn't seem to shake the sinister sensation of a presence somewhere nearby.

Listening and watching.

The next morning, I presented myself at Miss Haney's office door.

My eyes were heavy. I'd had barely any sleep. I'd needed to tally the laconite in the armory, and the dead of night seemed the best time to do it. But Tigo had sat up long into the evening, the door of his room cracked open, spilling light. I suspected he still harbored suspicions about me, for his early starts and strenuous labor meant he was usually snoring by ten. I hadn't felt safe sneaking past on the stairs until well past midnight, when his lamp finally went out.

It did mean I'd had time to prepare a script in my head. It was market day again tomorrow, and I hoped my excuse for a visit would fly. But before I could even open my mouth, Miss Haney glanced up, spotted me, and said, frowning, "Ah, Corith. Have you seen Ferda about? I've had a crow from Madam Mora. The girls' dresses are ready. I need him to go and fetch them today."

My mouth opened and closed a few times. "I can go," I said abruptly. "I can get them tomorrow. Then I could get a last-minute fitting done for mine."

She blinked at me, still frowning. "I don't think so, my dear. Not if Ferda can get them today."

"But it's market day tomorrow," I persisted, trying to look winsome. Time to deploy the excuse I'd prepared. "Truth be told . . . I was hoping to get a gift for Miss Vercha. Something small, just to say thank you for my dress." I smiled, drawing on the limited charisma I had.

Her expression moved from faintly baffled to charmed. "Well, now, if that isn't a lovely idea." Then she chewed her lip. "But the ball *is* in a week . . ."

"A day won't signify," I said with false confidence. "And if anything happens on the crossing—gods forbid—I'm the best person to protect the dresses. *And* I'll make personally sure that any other alterations are completed in time."

The housekeeper looked gratified. "You certainly are an asset to our little team here, Corith. Thank you." She smiled. "That will be all."

As I walked away, I hid the tremor in my fingers. It had been worth it, all those weeks spent cozying up to Miss Haney. I just had to get through the rest of the day, then ensure I was in town for sunset tomorrow.

I set off to find Ferda, to let him know I'd need the boat, but as I crossed the entrance hall, Llir and Emment were coming down the stairs.

“Come on, Brother, it’s perfect,” Emment was saying. “What better way to end their visit than a play? You know, I’ve always thought I had a talent for acting . . .”

Those words snagged my attention, made me glance sharply at him.

But Llir looked distracted as soon as he saw me. As his brother chattered on, Llir’s eyes tracked my progress, his face carefully blank, impossible to read.

I bobbed my head shallowly and quickened my pace, glancing at the clock as though my chores were calling. But I was thinking of my foray into his rooms, the horrible sense that someone else had been there, the possibility that the rain had brought him in early . . .

At least my sneaking for the Cage was over. Even if Llir was still suspicious of me, if I could keep my head down, give him no more cause to wonder, I hoped that eventually his attention would drift away.

When the date of my second meeting arrived, the sea was choppy, riled by chill autumn winds. I'd spent most of the day either racing through my chores or standing idly by while the Shearwaters and Cormorants played mallet ball in the rose gardens, practiced archery in the outer ward, or talked excitedly of the amateur theatricals they were planning.

By the time the sun was midway to the horizon, they were hotly debating which play to put on: Catua's choice was deemed too satirical, Emment's too racy, and Llir's too tragic. Llir was arguing good-naturedly with Morgen, countering her objections with a lopsided smirk. The sight oddly irked me, and I was glad when, finally, I could make my excuses and hurry away.

My heart pounded as I readied the boat. I had to take a few moments, draw on Zennia's old trick, to calm myself enough for the wind-tossed waters to heed me. I didn't need much propulsion—the strong gusts helped me along—but I could already sense a fickleness to the ocean. Pallwater was waning now, and archwater beginning its slow and ominous encroach.

I stared fixedly at the mainland, at the shadow of Port Rhorstin, as I traversed the final mile or two of the crossing. I'd gathered the information my contact had asked for. I'd translated my code onto a fresh piece of parchment. Now the Cage had to hold up their end of the bargain.

It transpired, when I arrived first at Madam Mora's, that Vercha had left strict instructions not to let me spy my own gown before the ball. The seamstress insisted on blindfolding me before helping me into it and standing me on a stool. She then commenced pinching and pinning it all over, occasional low murmurs escaping her lips. The garment felt cold and tight on me already; its stiffness, its rustling, alien and unsettling.

At last she disappeared into a back room with the dress, and I was permitted to tug off my blindfold. But the alterations dragged on longer than I'd expected, and when she finally returned, my eyes were on the windows, nervously watching the sun meet the horizon.

After stowing the dresses in a cart at the stables—tipping the stable girl every coin I had on me to guard them—I hurried out into the red-gold streets. Across town, the Veil was strung with lanterns, which peeped from the vines climbing its timber-framed walls. A sweet, spicy scent filled the air—wine and sugar—tinged with woodsmoke from the half dozen chimneys. I changed rapidly in the same alley as before, my bluebird mask rasping against my face, my whole body wound taut with expectation.

What was it my summons had said? Around the back.

I circled the building and entered the yard where Emment and Turnstone had bet on the fight. The memory brought a sharp, vinegary anger, sitting at the back of my throat like bile. No young men filled the yard this time—the fights clearly happened late, past midnight—and there wasn't a guard on duty this evening. Perhaps my contact had arranged some distraction.

I looked around and eventually noticed a pair of bulkhead doors set into the ground. One had been cracked open a few inches, and the edge of a golden mask flashed in the glare. "Come on, then." My contact. "We haven't much time."

I lowered myself into dank, dripping darkness.

For a second or two, once the doors were shut tight, we were smothered in shadow and I heard only my harsh breaths. Then: the striking of flint on firesteel. A murmur, and the sizzle of a flame responding. Light flared, illuminating the lion's gold visage. He was a Sparkmouth.

"This way," he said, leading me by his candle's glow.

He was dressed in his black servant's uniform again. "I suggest we keep the masks on, in case someone sees you."

I swallowed. "Is that likely?" I said, my voice thin.

"Shouldn't be," he said cheerily. "We're going to the lowest levels."

He beckoned me down a steep, spiralling stair. The air got colder the deeper we went, and when I touched the wall, my hand came away wet. My contact must have heard my intake of breath, because he said, "Cool and damp. Best way to store wine."

Eventually we came to the bottom of the gloomy stairwell. Ducking through a door, we emerged into a wide, echoing space, filled floor to ceiling with shelves upon shelves.

"Down here's where we keep the good stuff," he said, stepping to a shelf and inspecting a bottle. "Some of these date back to King Judan's reign. Unless we've got someone *very* wealthy upstairs, we shouldn't be disturbed . . . Still, I can't linger long." He turned to me, placing the candle on a shelf. "So let's get right to it. Do you have the final tally?"

I fished in my bodice for the crinkled parchment. Plucking it from me and smoothing it out, he stared at it in focused silence for a moment.

"And there's something else," I ventured. "Two things, actually. First, you should know there are visitors on the island. House Cormorant. I think they're staying until archwater. They have Orha with them. I thought, if your people . . ."

His cheek twitched, his blue eyes still fixed on the parchment. "Not a problem if they'll be gone by next pallwater, which it sounds like they will."

"All right," I said, feeling slightly reassured. "But the Shearwaters, they have . . . well, I don't know what to call it. I've been thinking of it as—as *false laconite*."

That did give him pause, his eyes flicking up to me.

"It looks just like laconite, feels just like it, but it doesn't work. It doesn't *do* anything."

He stared at me, the candlelight wavering on his mask, then shook his head. "I don't know what that's all about. But it doesn't matter. We only need to know about the stuff that *does* work. And you"—he gestured at me with the parchment—"have answered our questions. Thank you for that."

He glanced at the candle, muttered something under his breath. A spark jumped out, arcing toward him, and it lit the paper, burning it to a crisp.

I let out a breath. My information was good, and he clearly had no concerns about the Cormorants. The false laconite still niggled at me like a hangnail, but if the Cage weren't interested, maybe it wasn't so big a deal. Now my part was done, they had to give me what they'd promised.

"Now," he continued, flashing me a genial smile, "for what we need you to do for us next."

I stared. "What do you mean, *next*? That wasn't the deal!"

"You agreed to help us," he said casually.

"I agreed to get you this information. And *you* agreed to give me information about my friend."

"And then—what? You'll go back to trailing after the Shearwaters? You've found you like being a Hundred's Orha?"

I fell silent. I didn't like that I couldn't see his face, but I was glad, right now, that he couldn't see mine.

If there was one thing this placement had helped me understand, it was why so many of us liked shadowing the Hundred. To be immersed in such luxury, to feel part of this gilded world . . . For some, the drudgery was just about worth it for the expensive livery, the elevated rank, the balls, the soirées—even if we were just observers.

His words had caught on something inside me: a splinter of doubt. I pushed it down. "Of course I don't *like* it. They're insufferable, spoiled—"

"All the more reason to aid us," he replied.

"I've done what you asked," I said angrily. Desperately. "I'm not getting mixed up in anything else. An information exchange, remember? That's what you agreed."

I did want change. How could I not? I knew better than most that the way things were was wrong—my father killed in a noble's pointless skirmish, a mother who'd been only too happy to be rid of me. And over half my life shut up in Arbenhaw, told day in and day out that my only worth was in service.

But I hadn't forgotten Owyn. The threat of the gallows. And the siblings' gossip, the night I'd eavesdropped. Poisonings. Murders. A Cage hideout, blown up. That wasn't me. I wasn't *like* these people.

"I should have known you'd go back on your word," I said. "Do you even really know anything about Zennia?"

He surveyed me, lips quirked thoughtfully. "What have you been told?" he asked after a moment.

"That she came here with the eldest, Emment Shearwater, one night. That she saw one of those Orha fights you host here." At the twitch of his eyebrow, my own gaze narrowed. He hadn't expected me to know about those. "And she got into trouble on the crossing back. Drowned in a sudden squall that blew up."

He pondered this, nodding shallowly.

"That was it, wasn't it?" I said hopelessly. "That was the information you were going to give me. But I already found out about it myself."

"No," he said softly, shifting in the darkness. He pulled something out of his black doublet.

The hammered metal shone in the golden light from the candle. A brooch, imprinted with the image of a sailing ship. My chest constricted. The last time I'd seen it, Zennia had been packing it into her trunk at Arbenhaw before coming here, to Bower Island.

I lurched forward, darted a hand out instinctively, but the blond man stepped back, coolly inspecting it. "Pretty enough trinket," he said, turning it over.

"Give that to me," I gasped, wanting to rip off his mask; wanting to read, in his face, how he'd come to have the brooch.

"Certainly," he said. "*After* you've heard me out."

Every breath was a rasp in my throat, and my head was spinning—but eventually I nodded.

"The tale you've been fed is wrong," he said bluntly. "Or, at least, it leaves plenty out. Whether whoever told it to you realizes that . . ." He shrugged. "In any case, I can give you the whole story, *if* you agree to do one more thing for us."

I stared at the shadows moving over his mask. "They already suspect me," I said reluctantly. With an icy prickle, I thought of Tigo. Of Llir.

"Then you'll just have to throw them off the scent, won't you?"

When I didn't respond, he forged ahead anyway. "We have . . . plans for Rexim Shearwater. And as you may know, there's a Chamber Seat now free, so those plans have been, shall we say, accelerated. Just weeks from now, the Hundred will be voting for the person they want to fill that Seat, and our friend Brigant Shearwater is a shoo-in. His voice will have the power to tip the Chamber one way or the other, and the Cage have tasked *me* with putting together a group to pay him and his family . . . a little visit. Have a nice chat about how they might want to use their newfound political sway."

I remembered the luncheon. The proposals discussed there. Shrike's and Crake's ambitions for war. Orha funnelled to the armies, the navies. And Finch's reforms, which Rexim, as a Regent, might end up having the deciding vote on.

"What does that mean?" I said. "You want to try to . . . work with Rexim? Get him to vote the way you want him to?"

He smiled. "Let's call it . . . persuasion, shall we? Maybe his dear children can help him see reason."

The mention of the siblings—of the Cage having *plans* for them—made something bizarrely close to possessiveness rise in me. "You don't understand," I said. "I know them, and I doubt they'll be any more amenable to your cause. Except the youngest, Catua, maybe, but Rexim doesn't listen to her—"

"Well," he interrupted, "we have other . . . avenues we could go down. In fact, that brings me on nicely to your next task. The first part of it anyway."

I blinked at him. *First part?*

"We need you to find out what they're hiding. Every Hundred family has their dirty little secrets. Things they wouldn't want their peers to know. Rexim, his children, even his servants . . . there must be something. Something we can use to convince your Brigant to hear us out. But your word won't cut it—we need proof. Physical items."

Persuasion? No—this was extortion.

"Here's a start," my contact mused. "Why does Shearwater want the Seat so badly? He's never shown much interest in politics before. I doubt it's a strong sense of moral duty. And I doubt it's only to keep Crake out."

I frowned. "But if Rexim refuses to be . . . 'persuaded,' won't spreading his secrets mean Crake wins the vote?"

"We're confident," he said, "of Shearwater's acquiescence. He wants this Seat as much as Crake does."

I thought of Crake's narrow gaze at the luncheon. *"Floodmouths and Gustmouths to the navies down south."* "Does Crake really want war?" I ventured nervously. "Or is he just trying to impress Regent Shrike?"

"Both," said my contact, his voice turning brittle. "We have people stationed down in the Quaglands. Crake already seems to be calling up forces. As for Shrike, I'm sure you've heard the rumors about Queen Annig . . . The Hundred are thinking about who will come *after*. And Shrike's no exception. He's Annig's uncle. Everyone knows he's desperate for that crown. But there are other contenders for it, including the Breovan King—another of Annig's relations, albeit distant. Shrike hates Breova because of its Charter, but war would take out a competitor for the throne, too."

K shook his head. "Shrike's always thinking one step ahead, and Crake's like a moth to a flame—he's cozying up to him. With Crake in the Chamber, war is almost certain. And I expect you've figured out what that means for us Orha."

I'd gone cold all over, but before I could respond, a dull thud sounded from somewhere above. My contact's blue gaze flicked up to the ceiling. "We have to wrap this up," he said, handing me two items. "The next part of your task is to make use of these."

I stared down at the diminutive objects in my palm. Dark in color and exactingly made, they reminded me strongly of a hammer and chisel. Except the chisel narrowed to a wicked point, its tip made of a blacker, shinier material.

"Fashioned of pure nabyrium," he said. "Designed to crack laconite in a very particular way." He took them from me briefly, mimed tapping the chisel. "Just a few taps will cause hairline fractures . . . You can practice first. Get a sense of how long it takes. Eventually the laconite degrades, stops working. The stone's so dark it's hard to tell it's damaged, but the family might notice if you do too much too soon. You'll need to time it so the stones stop working *just* before we get there, on the sixteenth of Undalh. Pallwater. Makes it easier, with the tides. Oh, and don't forget that when we get there, we'll need whatever skeletons you've pried out of their closets."

I looked at him, incredulous. Another date. Another deadline.

"Why didn't you give me these in the first place?" I hissed. "I was there, in their rooms . . . I could have done it *then.*"

"Three reasons," he said brusquely, looking impatient. "First, we didn't know if you were up to the job. We couldn't risk your being caught—and with Cage tools on you. Second, we didn't know how long Regent Dunlin had left. No point your getting started until we knew when we were coming.

"Third, and most important, we didn't have your little tally. Didn't have a clue what we'd be walking into. Turns out"—he tipped his head at my bodice, where I'd stashed my notes—"it's not that much. Certainly not as much as some other Houses. Meaning, this plan is cranking into motion."

He watched me carefully in the glimmer from the candle. I felt like a marionette twirling on a string, the Cage looming, blank faced, above me.

But I had to admit it: My choice was made. Had been as soon as

I saw Zennia's brooch. As soon as he said the tale I'd been fed was wrong.

I thought of Tigo and Rhianne's shared glances. Of Llir's watchfulness; his tenseness. Of Emment: *"I've always thought I had a talent for acting."* I was sure they were still hiding something. I needed to know it.

"Okay," I said, the word feeling weighty. The thought that the next time I saw my contact would be on Bower Island, with a group of Cage rebels, made my stomach churn with nausea.

And what then? After the Cage's "visit," after Rexim agreed to their demands . . . what of *my* future?

"But you need to promise me something in return," I said. "That the Shearwaters won't find out it was me. That you'll keep your source for this information to yourself."

A dark, knowing smirk tugged at his mouth.

"You'll go back to trailing after the Shearwaters? You've found you like being a Hundred's Orha?"

Right now I didn't care what he thought of me. I needed to know I could get out of this alive—and with my sanctioned employment intact.

"Very well," he said. "If that's really what you want."

"And what if I need to contact you?" I added. "If something unexpected happens?"

Another soft thump from somewhere above. His eyes flashed upward. "Same protocol as before. And by the way, the 'K' stands for Kielty."

He was trusting me with his name. My work must have impressed him. I nodded, stowing the tools in my pocket. "The sixteenth of Undalh?" I said, squashing my nerves.

"The sixteenth," he said. "Come on. I'll see you out. Oh, and—" He glanced at the brooch, tossed it to me. I fumbled but managed to catch it, heart leaping. "You can have that, I suppose. A reminder. To be ready."

With a wrench, I shoved the brooch deep into my jacket, where its edges pushed comfortingly against my skin.

"This way," he said, adjusting his mask. And I let him lead me out of the cellar.

I TOSSED fitfully that night, my dreams tense and confusing. Zennia's face melded into Emment's and back, into Kielty's lion mask, then the Veil's blank-faced jester. In the early hours, I lay staring up at the ceiling, turning the brooch over and over in my fingers. I wished more than anything that Zennia was here, in a bunk above me, as she had been for most of a decade at Arbenhaw. I wondered, if our places were reversed, what she'd be doing. How she'd be feeling.

Zennia had always been the brave one.

An image popped into my mind unbidden: a lean-limbed girl, a full head shorter than me, with a world-weary air borne from a childhood among the Hundred. Thick black hair scrunched into buns, wrapped with cord. A round face that moved from scowl to smile in an instant.

My first week at Arbenhaw, I uttered not a word. Not even when the others called me Mouse, then Ghost. I had the bunk beneath Zennia in our first-year dormitory and the seat beside her in our history lessons.

Despite the fact that I rarely replied, she whispered to me of her mother, of her brothers, and how she'd always longed for a sister. How her house in Tresteny was filled with glass: a dozen crown glass windows, spun glass lamps in every room. How her mother's customers—and some of her mother's friends—hated people like us. Called Zennia "unfortunate."

Another memory. Eight years later. A tedious lecture from Instructor Rhama on the alleged causes of the Great Revolt. Zennia's tan arm snaking into the air. "Is it true we used to call ourselves Tidespeakers, sir?"

Rhama staring at her. "Where did you hear that?"

"A book at a house my family visited. If it's true, why did they change our name, sir?"

Rhama's eyes on her back as she left the classroom, bound for a stretch in the Confinement Locker.

I blinked at the ceiling, tears blurring my vision. It was clear I wouldn't be getting any more sleep, so I dragged myself out of bed, pulled on my work clothes, and slipped out into the predawn chill.

The scent of tea herbs hung around the tower door. Tigo must be up already, though I'd heard no shuffles or pots clinking in his room. I was glad it was quiet. After my forays to the Veil and a full week of attending to the Cormorants and the Shearwaters, I was strung out, drained by the constant need to perform. All I wanted was to be alone.

I trailed down the dirt path that led to the cove, past dwarf gorse and heather and hillocks dusted with sand. Gulls skimmed by on the air currents above me. All was shadowed; the sky bloomed lilac like a bruise.

I'd half planned to scramble down to the water to practice. Archwater was a dark, heavy presence in my mind, sitting just out of sight, yet sidling ever nearer. But as I approached the boulders that marked the start of the steep path, I caught a low laugh, the murmur of voices below me.

Dropping down, I peered around the edge of a rock and saw them clearly, despite the dimness: the backs of a fiery-red head and a blond one, standing out starkly against the gray-black cliffs.

One was Rhianne; that hair was unmistakable. And the other . . . For a wild moment, I thought it was Kielty, my half-formed dreams still lurking in my mind. But the figure was too short, too wide-framed. It was Catua. They sat on a rock ledge, close together. Both clutched near-empty cups of tea.

Rhianne muttered something, and Catua laughed, leaning sideways, bumping the older girl with her shoulder. Their heads turned, and I saw their lips meet briefly.

A needle of static shot right through me. Heart drumming, I shrank back, pressed my spine against the boulder. I thought of Rhianne's pink cheeks after my "test," her rapid defense of the youngest Shearwater, denying her part in it.

After the shock came a creeping cold. Here it was already: a skeleton in the closet.

Catua Shearwater, daughter of Rexim, in a secret relationship with an Orha servant. The Hundred only married within the Hundred. Liaisons with a commoner were a very great scandal. Liaisons with an Orha were something else: unthinkable.

This was just what Kielty had asked for. But could I use it? The cold stabbed deeper. Catua and Rhianne had been nothing but kind to me. I'd even begun to think of Rhianne as a friend. Would I really betray them to fulfill my bargain? And if I did, how, exactly, could I give the Cage proof?

I glanced back down at the pair again. They'd finished their tea and set aside their empty cups. They swung their legs out over the bubbling surf. They kissed again, lightly teased each other. Catua stretched and gazed up at the circling shearwaters.

Eventually they clambered stiffly to their feet, and I tensed, ready to flee should they both come this way. But instead, Catua headed left, taking a low track that wound north to the castle. Rhianne began the hike up to the boulders, toward me, but rather than running, I moved ten paces or so back.

The Sparkmouth was smiling faintly to herself as she crested the ridge, her eyes on the path. When she finally glanced up—saw me standing there, arms folded—her face turned bone white, each freckle standing out.

For a few long seconds, we faced off, silent. Then her shoulders drooped, her gaze lowered, and she trudged toward me, cloak trailing in the mud.

"You won't say anything," she said as she reached me, her brown eyes pleading. "You can't tell *him.*"

"I won't," I replied. It was technically true. Even if I did end up leveraging this secret, it wouldn't be *me* who'd reveal all to Rexim . . . "But"—I searched her face—"aren't you scared?"

It was Rhianne, of course, who would be viciously punished. Catua might be confined to her room, have her allowance cut off, but she wouldn't be banished. Wouldn't be sent back to the mainland in disgrace, to a workhouse or maybe a cell, if Rexim could swing it.

Rhianne shrugged unhappily. "What are we supposed to do? Live side by side here and just ignore how we feel?" She began to traipse back to the Orha's tower. "We tried that at first. It . . . didn't work out."

I paused, a new thought nagging at me.

"I know Catua's interested in Orha rights," I ventured, jogging after her. "Is there more to it than that?"

Rhianne frowned. "What do you mean?"

"It's just . . ." My skin tingled; I was skirting too close. "She challenges the others. Says we should follow Breova. Do you think she's in contact with . . . anyone radical?"

Rhianne looked shocked. "If you mean who I think you mean . . . Moons, no. She would have told me. I know she wants some of the same things *they* do. So do I, I suppose." She shot me a nervous glance. "But she always says big change has to happen slowly. Through the Chamber. Through sympathetic Regents like Finch.

"And the Cage . . . well," Rhianne continued, "they want things to happen far more quickly than that. And the only way to do that"—her face twisted—"is to hurt people. Catua would never want anyone to get hurt."

I blinked, staring intently at the path, hoping my features gave nothing away.

"So if you're Catua's secret," I said as we walked, "what are the others'? Emment's? Llir's?"

She threw me a wild look. "What do you mean?"

I glanced around. It was early; we were utterly alone. I'd be taking a risk, confiding in Rhianne, but something told me she harbored suspicions of her own—I still remembered her flashed glances at Tigo, the odd look she'd given me when I'd talked about Zennia. And from the way she'd spoken about Orha traditions, I didn't get the impression she shared Tigo's loyalty . . .

"Listen," I said. "I know what Emment's been up to. But I'm starting to think there might be more."

I told her about the trip. The fights at the Veil. The crossing back and the sinking sands. Emment's story, relayed in choked sobs. The extra regals he'd slipped me later.

By the end, Rhianne's mouth was hanging open. "The valets were gossiping about that night," she said, "but they only said he'd come back sozzled again. I didn't realize he'd nearly *died.* That you—you saved him." She stared at me. She had that same look on her face that Llir had. Like she was suddenly *seeing* me. My face felt hot.

"Did you know about the fights?"

"Yes," she admitted. "Tigo told me. He found out from Llir. It's all just . . . horrible."

She paused, something kindling in her eyes. "His story, though, about what happened with Zennia. The crossing, the waves . . . that's what he told all of us. But these last few weeks, I've been thinking back. I was burning old timber up near the pinewood that day. It was pallwater—did you know that? Calm as could be. Not a storm cloud in sight. Nothing stronger than a breeze."

I gazed at her, hearing the sea shush nearby. "Of course it was pallwater," I murmured, realizing. I'd been picturing the angry swells of archwater, but Emment had said they'd crossed by boat, which didn't make sense if it wasn't pallwater, when the causeway was always part-covered by the sea.

"Sometimes the sands, they can change their shape, and that makes the water swirl in differently . . . but that only really happens at archwater. And then, when *you* arrived and told us about Zennia . . . about how she was top of your class . . ." She broke off.

"It doesn't add up," I finished for her, looking out at the distant bay.

"No, it doesn't," she said intently. "That's what I've been trying to tell Tigo. But he believes Llir, and Llir believes his brother . . . I don't think any of them thought very deeply about it."

"What do *you* think happened?" My voice had turned hoarse. Something dark crouched in the pit of my stomach.

She looked at me, guarded and sad all at once. The quiet, the far-off rushing of the waves, stretched on until I could hardly bear it. Then she folded her arms and said, "I don't know. Maybe nothing. Maybe there *was* a squall." But I could see she didn't really believe it.

What was Emment Shearwater capable of?

We parted ways then, and I headed for the castle. I'd be starting my chores early—very early—but I hoped that meant I could finish a little sooner. Retreat to my room and dwell on what I'd learned. Try to work out how I was going to tackle my new tasks.

For Kielty was telling the truth, I was sure now, and I was even more determined to find out what he knew. If that meant aiding dangerous rebels . . . so be it. And in the meantime, I'd uncover what I could.

The sun was just rising, speckling the gatehouse in bronze as I walked under its archway and into the outer ward. I'd expected to see no one at this ungodly hour, which was why, when I spotted a hunched figure ahead of me, I hesitated, shrinking back into the shadows.

I was soon glad I'd hidden. The figure was Llir, his mantle hanging loose over what looked like nightclothes. His boots scraped on the stone as he crossed to a tower, one of many that made up the curtain wall, round and choked with an autumn-red creeper. My pulse picked up. What was he doing out this early?

And, for that matter, what was he doing *here*? As far as I knew, this tower was abandoned.

As Llir took a key from his pocket and unlocked the door, glancing left and right before entering, I remembered with a jolt: Zennia's letter. The one I'd found in the crevice in my room, with the mysterious dates scrawled on the back. *"Sometimes I make out lights in odd places."* Maybe it had been *this* tower she'd seen the lights in. And maybe the dates were the times she'd seen them.

The *thunk* and *click* of the lock echoed toward me. Then—silence. Llir didn't reemerge.

When I was sure I was alone, I left the gatehouse and picked my way over the scrubby grass. I headed for the keep, where my duties waited, but as I walked my eyes crawled up to the tower's arrow slits.

I knew one of Emment's secrets. I knew Catua's now, too. Rexim and Vercha might have secrets; they might not.

But I still wasn't much closer to learning Llir's.

The day of the ball bore down upon us, and the fevered anticipation in the castle grew.

I couldn't seem to shake off flitters of curiosity, of reluctant excitement, at the thought of the dance. As much as I knew I had a mission to focus on, that this was a distraction, that I wasn't part of this world, I still caught myself looking forward to seeing the decorations and wondering—worrying—how I would look in my new dress.

But as the days passed, I reminded myself that I couldn't leave my next task late like last time. I had to assume that anything could delay me. And that meant getting started on the laconite soon.

Frustratingly, Rexim returned a few days before the ball, preventing me from easily accessing his chambers. I watched his small party trot up from the shingle beach, his craggy face pale against the ocean's stern gray. Archwater was coming, the sea was growing restless, and storm season was already here, the skies cloud choked and dour.

In the days that followed, Rexim was tense, preoccupied. A multitude of letters had begun to arrive for him, piles of them teetering in

Miss Haney's office, great stacks of them delivered to his rooms every morning. Petitions, I guessed, for his patronage and favor in anticipation of his victory in the upcoming vote.

But the Cormorants lifted the mood in the castle, their teasing and laughter ringing through the halls. If they didn't manage to assuage Rexim's absorptions, they appeared to banish Emment's dark depressions, Vercha's frantic fretting about the ball, and some, at least, of Llir's strange and solemn moods.

The evening of the ball, I was summoned to Vercha's room, my heart tapping out a jig. Invitees were arriving from the mainland; I glimpsed them from a window as I ascended the stairs. With full archwater a week off, the tidal range had expanded, and our low tides were just curling around the island, giving carriages clear access—but not for long.

The rain we'd expected all week had arrived and fell in misty sheets over the dark, sodden mudflats. In the distance, angry rumbles threatened a tempest, but the guests had brought their Floodmouths with them: Liveried figures in greens, reds, and golds, stiff postured and confident, trailed closely after the Hundred.

"Come away, Corith," Vercha called. She stood at her door, shivering in a corset and underskirt. "You'll surely catch a chill. Isn't it *beastly*?"

When I entered her room, I saw Morgen Cormorant within, resplendent in a sapphire-blue gown. She was lounging on Vercha's bed, legs crossed, and her dark eyes followed my progress across the room.

Catua was hunched at Vercha's dresser, her nose in a book as her maid, Hana, pinned her hair. As I passed her, the skin on my bare arms prickling, I couldn't help thinking of the cove. Of Rhianne. I avoided looking at her as I perched near Vercha.

"Ready, Miss," came Debry's voice from behind a screen.

Vercha clapped her hands, vanished behind it, and a second later emerged—holding an exquisite violet gown.

It was floor-length and full skirted, the square neckline dipping concerningly low. Its sleeves were tight from armpit to elbow, where black lace dripped, forming wide, sheer bells. The fabric brought to mind the darkest roses in the gardens, the deep, rich purple of blackcurrant wine. It was embroidered with blackwork, gold pearls down the bodice, and on the top of each shoulder rose a little lace-trimmed puff.

I paled on seeing it. Took a small step backward.

"You don't like it?" said Vercha, feigning concern. Beneath it I could hear the tightness in her tone, see the flash in her eyes as she took in my expression. Morgen's presence seemed both a blessing and a curse: Vercha wouldn't get openly angry, but she also wanted to impress her friend.

"No—I mean, yes, of course I do," I stammered. "I just . . . don't think I can do it justice."

"Don't be silly," she said. "Debry and Hana will sort you out. In fact," she added, turning to the maids, "you ought to do that now, before she gets into the dress."

"Yes, Miss," said Debry, casting a doubtful eye over me. From somewhere below came the tinkling of music.

"I've finished over here," said Hana. "You can have this spot."

Vercha propelled me to the chair.

While Catua was clasped and buttoned into her own gown—Shearwater navy with silver embroidery—I stared at my reflection as the maids descended, brandishing gold pins and ebony ribbons.

"These would go beautifully," came Morgen's voice. She held out a pair of dark drop earrings.

I put a hand to my earlobe as Debry commented, "Her ears ain't pierced, ma'am."

"Oh, yes, of course."

Vercha turned, looking faintly uncomfortable, the reminder of my upbringing hanging between us. As keen as she was to primp me like a pet, we were unmistakably different. Her eyes darted over me. "Very well," she said. And to Debry: "Get on, then."

To distract myself as the maids got to work, I half listened to the string musicians tuning up downstairs and turned my thoughts to the long evening to come. Then it came to me in a flash:

The ball.

The family, the Cormorants, the guests, the servants . . . everyone would be downstairs, in the ballroom and the parlors. Dancing, drinking, eating, chattering—occupied and oblivious. This was my chance.

I wouldn't be able to slip away to begin with. But as the hour grew later and the partygoers drunker, I doubted I'd be missed among the crowds. And even if I was, there were myriad excuses—the food hadn't agreed with me, I was unused to the drink, my dress had torn and I had gone to repair it . . .

I stared fixedly ahead in the mirror, avoiding catching Debry's and Hana's eyes.

The maids, too, would be loitering near the revelries, even if they had no specific duties to perform. I'd be alone in West Tower. Free to seek out the family's secrets—and begin the sabotage the Cage had tasked me with.

My fingers fidgeted nervously in my lap as I waited for the maids to finish pinning and prodding.

At last they stepped back and Vercha came to inspect me. My hair had been pulled up to the back of my head and braided in some sort of intricate knotwork, threaded with ribbons and glinting pearled pinheads. In the orange light from the lamps and the fire, it wasn't its usual lackluster copper but a deep, rich bronze picked out with gold.

My cheeks had been rouged, my eyebrows darkened. Vercha watched my reflection expectantly, and I offered her a wavering smile. "It's lovely, thank you."

Her rosebud mouth curled into a satisfied smirk, and she gestured to Debry. "Help us into our gowns."

Vercha's dress was a vision in pale gold, all intricate lacework and jewelled embellishments. Gold ribbon stood out against her long umber hair, and at the edge of my hearing, I caught the hum of her laconite.

From somewhere below us, a clock chimed eight.

"Come," Vercha trilled, holding a slim arm out to Morgen. The Cormorant took it, and they swept from the room. I tried my best to navigate the floorboards with the new weight of my dress, the wide reach of its skirts. My chest felt as though a band was constricting it, and it wasn't merely the tightly buttoned bodice.

"Into the fray," I heard Catua mutter, and we all headed toward the imperial staircase.

On the landing, lamps were burning brightly. A low drone spoke of masses of laconite; below it, the rumble of laughter and conversation.

I brought up the rear, staying close to the sisters, but before I could head down the staircase after them, a hand caught my elbow.

"Floodmouth."

I turned.

It was Emment, steering me into an alcove, clutching a glass of something effervescent. His collar and cuffs were stark-white lace and his padded doublet was a brilliant vermillion.

I tugged my arm away, feeling awkward in my dress, and glared at him, taking in his regal features—the man who'd been the last to see Zennia alive. Facing him brought back flashes of the crossing: his "confession," his silhouette sobbing on the sands.

"You got the regals I told Miss Haney to pass on?"

"Yes," I said shortly. Saying thank you seemed . . . wrong.

He swallowed. "I suppose I owe you my life. I take it you've not spoken of that night to anyone?"

I hesitated, thinking of Rhianne's wide-eyed gaping. But I didn't think she'd tell anyone, except perhaps Tigo, and he, it seemed, was the island's premier secret keeper.

"I haven't." I dropped my eyes to hide the lie. "But I think your family might be grateful if you refrained from almost drowning yourself in the bay a third time." I recalled Llir's wild look, wading out to the boat. The way he'd carefully shouldered his brother's weight.

Emment's gaze was already a little unfocused, but his handsome face flinched as he registered my words. Then the shade of a sneer touched his expression. "Thank you for your concern," he said, eyes running over me, "but wise counsel isn't part of our servants' job description."

My hackles rose. I matched his stony stare. It was back: that dark and ominous feeling, lurking somewhere low in my midsection. The one that had stirred when I'd spoken to Rhianne, when I'd learned that Zennia had died at pallwater, on a day when the sea had seemed serene . . .

"The story you told me," I said, chest thudding. "I wondered if you might have left something out."

He seemed surprised. "What are you talking about?" he replied, careful, despite his tipsiness, to keep his voice down.

"It's just . . . it doesn't sound like my friend. I knew Zennia well, back at Arbenhaw. She should have been able to deal with a few waves."

I knew I was treading dangerous ground. This was my employer, Rexim's heir. I shouldn't be speaking to him like this. But I was angry at his demeanor. Angry about the fights. Angry that his whims had led to the "accident."

It took him a moment to process my words. He frowned, looming over me in the cramped, low-ceilinged space. "What are you saying? You don't believe me? Well, that's up to you. I know what I saw."

"Do you?" I whispered. He'd been drunk after our trip. I was willing to bet he'd been in a similar state when he'd dragged Zennia back to their boat, too. "Maybe your memories of that night were . . . impaired."

Emment's already wine-flushed cheeks grew redder. His gaze drifted to the wall behind me, but I got the impression he wasn't really seeing it, that his mind had flashed back to that night in the bay. His frown now looked more like worry than anger. Then at last, blinking, he seemed to snap back. "That's—that's ridiculous—" he started, but he was interrupted by Vercha calling my name.

"I'm sorry," I muttered. I'd gone too far.

I eased my way past him, nudging his glass, which his fingers were squeezing unnaturally hard. The bubbling drink sloshed over the rim. As I hurried away, I glanced over my shoulder and saw him staring hard at my retreating figure.

23

Normally, in the midst of a storm such as this, the interior of the castle would be drear and dingy. But tonight, despite the rain spattering on the windows, all was warmth and gleaming firelight.

The entrance hall was decked out in hanging banners—Shearwater navy, violet, and gold, alongside the Cormorants' blue, black, and white stripes. Glittering twine and vines from the gardens looped around pillars, along banisters and archways, dotted with clusters of shining baubles, like gold berries.

The parlors had been given over to card tables and cake stands, while the ballroom—its floor polished to perfection by my own hand—was strung with more banners, fresh flowers, and candles.

And all around us . . . the Hundred and their Orha.

It was like the Veil all over again, except the dresses were wider, the doublets extra padded. There were families of nobles, three generations, all trussed up in their House colors and crests. The older women had powdered their faces; the men had oiled and forked their beards.

The air vibrated with the low hum of laconite—everywhere the dark stone winked and flashed at me, reminding me of what I planned to do later.

As I trailed Vercha through the fast-filling halls, pulse still thrumming from my encounter with Emment, my eyes flicked from face to face. There was laughter and shouts of recognition. Men and women with their heads together, exchanging news or secrets or both.

"But you *know,*" an imperious woman was saying, "on our way here, we heard the most troubling rumors. That the knights along the Stormshields, south of Lanniton, have been calling up men. Now, why would that be, I wonder?"

Vercha paused, stepping closer to the group. I saw Avrix Cormorant turn and make room for her.

"That's Uirbrig Crake's land," put in a crimson-clad man. From his features, I guessed he was the imperious woman's son.

"Rumors only," said Avrix easily. His voice was warm and reassuring. "If Crake *is* planning something, it'll be another skirmish with House Mallard. Poor bastards." He shook his head, sipped from his drink. "He's like a dog with a bone. Can't leave 'em alone."

Vercha gave a tinkling laugh, but I was remembering Kielty's dark look. *"Crake already seems to be calling up forces."*

"You're right, of course," said the matriarch. "Besides, no one could catch Shearwater's share of the vote now."

"And Crake seems to know it," the younger man added. "I see he hasn't put in an appearance tonight. Looks like the old dog's given up already. Might as well start celebrating early, eh?" He winked at Vercha and beckoned to a server, who rushed over bearing a tray of more drinks.

"Shush," Vercha cautioned. Rexim was passing.

The Brigant was clad in a black velvet doublet, the sleeves slashed with gold, his cape lined with sable. Llir was beside him, buttoned in deep navy. A high collar tipped with lace just grazed his jawline. Short slashed breeches over black hose and slippers, dun hair swept back, a laconite earring. And Tigo trailing behind him, as always.

Something bitter curled within me. Vercha had been bad enough this evening, pampering me and parading me like an accessory, but Llir and Emment were hardly any better. I recalled Llir's snap—*"Where's Tigo?"*—on the Cormorants' arrival. Since then, we'd barely been let out of their sight. Forced to stick to the family like limpets, to hold to ridiculous Hundred tradition.

But disturbingly, as I watched Llir pass, I realized my irritation was cut through with something else. Intrigue. When his eyes passed across me, I found myself straightening, but he seemed not to recognize me, transformed by my dress. Instead, he glanced around as Morgen fell in beside him, and I couldn't seem to drag my eyes from their figures. The Cormorant murmured something close to Llir's ear, and he smirked, giving an answer that pleased her in return. At the sight, resentment zigzagged through me, and I turned, annoyed at myself. Why did I care?

I began to sidle to the ballroom's perimeter, where I could wait and watch until I had an opportunity to slip away. But abruptly, a quiet unfurled across the crowd. Rexim was standing above us in the gallery, in front of a line of waiting musicians.

"Dear friends," he intoned, his deep voice carrying. "First, I want to thank you all for making the crossing, particularly in such inclement conditions. And particularly since our uncompromising tides give you only two opportunities, tonight, to escape: fashionably early or fashionably late."

A titter rippled through the gathered guests, a few raising their glasses to the balcony.

"Second, I hope you will all forgive me for imparting a few words about the upcoming vote." His gray eyes swept the crowded hall, seeming to pick out a few individuals in particular, perhaps those he knew were still on the fence.

"In a mere few weeks, you will all face a choice. I do not think it hyperbole to label this a choice between order and chaos. Between rationality and self-serving belligerence. Between harmony, cordiality . . . and war."

Another ripple, but of unease this time, mixed with one or two skeptical coughs. Even the Orha stared keenly at Rexim, as though we had any say in the matter; as though we weren't utterly at the mercy of the Hundred's votes.

Kielty's words drifted back to me again: *"Why does Shearwater want the Seat so badly?"* Something half-remembered had been niggling at me, and now it came back. The accounts in the study. The figures in red; the diminishing savings. What was it Catua had promised Vercha once Rexim took up the Chamber Seat? *"Balls and soirées and theater trips all day . . ."* and plenty of regals, I had no doubt.

"I shall say no more here, but I intend to speak further with each House in attendance this evening. Until then, please: Eat, dance, and make merry. You have my hall, and you have my promise to be a steady hand on the tiller through any storms to come."

As though in response, rain lashed at the windows, but its onslaught was lost in the burst of chatter, the tuning of the instruments above. Soon after, the musicians struck up a melody, strings and woodwinds ringing out under the rafters.

"Come, come!" cried Vercha, grabbing Avrix's arm. "First dance of the night. You know what that means."

"The Orha, too," Avrix called out, beckoning. He winked at me as my eye happened to catch his.

My stomach dropped as Vercha spotted me. She gripped my arm, propelling me along. “It’s an old tradition,” she said in my ear, “for the Orha to participate with their Houses in the first dance.”

Of course it was. My skin went cold.

Feverishly I tried to recall our lessons at Arbenhaw. I recognized the piece—it was one we’d practiced—but its players were adding more trills and flourishes.

Nobles and Orha faced each other; many of the Orha even looked excited. Mawre stood nearby in a dark-purple robe, her hair pulled back with gold clips shaped like wings. When our gazes met, she grimaced faintly: *Get me out of here.* I widened my eyes in agreement.

“Gentlemen opposite ladies!” came a call. Morgen Cormorant, sapphire gown glimmering. “Come on, Shearwaters, organize yourselves!”

Laughter rippled along the lines of dancers. The musicians started over, grinning down from the gallery.

With dread, I watched Morgen push and pull at the Shearwaters. A skeptical-looking Catua swapped places with Emment. At last I was prodded into line next to Vercha—and found myself standing opposite Llir.

His eyes flashed over me, then he did a double take. Fighting to stop my cheeks from flushing, I glanced away. I had to copy Vercha’s steps.

As the dance began, my memories of it solidified: forward, back, a half-turn here.

For the most part, it was easy to avoid Llir’s gaze. This first section had us remaining apart. When our eyes did meet, we watched each other warily. His technique was flawless, like that of all his siblings.

I was prickly with sweat as the next section started, heart racing at the prospect of stepping badly wrong. We moved closer this time, held up our palms. Circled each other like fencing partners. But our hands didn’t meet. That would come later.

Sidestep and back. Full turn. And away. The ringing of laconite mingled with the music, odd and discordant. My skin felt too warm.

The dance had us step toward each other, and for a second, we were a mere foot apart. My eyes found his, and I hesitated, nearly missing my next twist, my sweep to the side. A moment later, I moved back toward him, my spine to his chest, palms a hair's breadth apart. His presence behind me filled my whole mind, my senses. From there he'd be able to see every pin in my hair, every freckle on my neck. I swallowed, no doubt visibly.

Down the line, some giggling couples pressed their palms together. They'd gotten ahead of themselves.

I had a verse's reprieve as we twirled away, clapping in sync with the other dancers. Then it was time for the final section.

The strings dipped low, and the rhythm slowed. The dance grew grand and heavy with meaning. Two steps forward, one away. Half turn, sweep right. And come back together.

All at once, we were facing each other, half a foot between our chests. We raised our palms, this time pressed them together. Slowly we circled each other again.

His hand was smooth, and warm from the dancing. I knew that mine would feel calloused from my work.

My gaze crept upward, past his jaw, his cheekbones. As my skirts brushed his leg, I saw his tongue dart out fleetingly, run along his lips as though his mouth was too dry. His eyes, a deep olive green flecked with tan, met mine, and my pulse thudded dully in my ears, out of time with the music, surely loud enough to hear.

Abruptly applause broke through into our bubble. I started and swept down into a low curtsy. The dance was over; the couples were separating. Vercha clapped delightedly at the musicians.

When I rose, chest thumping, Llir had vanished, but I soon saw him standing near Emment and Tigo. He was taking a lengthy swig from a glass flute: a pale-green liquid, a special punch Cook had concocted. He gulped down more, almost draining it in one, and touched his sleeve to his mouth, eyes fixed and staring.

My own nerves frayed, I went in search of a glass myself.

No more dances were sprung upon me. It seemed, bar the traditional first set, we Orha were expected to linger on the periphery, as always. The merriment thereafter was all for the Hundred—and make merry they did, twirling long into the evening. I nursed my green punch, still strung out from trying to remember the dance steps earlier. But I knew there was more to my edginess than that.

It was time to finally admit to myself that Llir Shearwater was affecting me. Rattling me.

He's one of the Hundred, I reminded myself. He'd blabbed to his father and gotten me dumped in that cove. He was stuck up, standoffish, little better than Vercha. Not to mention, I thought nervously, completely off-limits.

But despite all that, when I was in his vicinity, I couldn't help but find myself intoxicated. Snared. I was beginning to find his features bewitching. The way the shadows underscored his cheekbones. The sweep of his lashes; his quick, knowing eyes. His smiles were rare, and never sent my way, but when I happened to glimpse one, my stomach seemed to free-fall.

My fingers trembled as I gripped my glass. I had to squash this, to hide it, while it lasted. It was a silly, fleeting fascination, stoked by the heady luxury of the ball, and it would surely pass as quickly as it had come into being.

I just needed to distract myself.

With that thought, I surveyed the guests. They were tipsier, rowdier from the pale-green liquor. Dance steps were increasingly being missed; hats and headpieces were sliding awry. The roar of laughter and conversation was wilder.

This was my chance.

I placed my glass on a table and slipped away through the crowds, unnoticed.

24

A hard rain battered the stained glass windows of West Tower. Beyond them, I saw nothing, only impenetrable blackness, but I could hear the wind screaming through the battlements like a banshee.

I'd had to brave the storm to fetch my tools from my room: the hammer and chisel I'd stowed under a floorboard. I'd begged the deluge to spare my dress, but it was single-minded in its pummeling of the island. Still, only the silky outer layer was wet, and the pins in my hair had held fast against the gale. I smoothed the flyaways as I hurried up the steps, my dancing shoes mercifully silent on the stone.

Then, out of nowhere, a deep rumble sounded. The spiral staircase jolted and trembled. I put out a hand to steady myself; a tapestry ahead of me now hung askew.

Another faint shudder. Glass tinkled downstairs. A few far-off exclamations—then stillness.

I could hear only my breath and the insistent, driving rain.

A quake, I guessed. I'd never felt one before. We'd learned about the big ones in our classes at Arbenhaw: The Breaking of the Eastwilds, north of Gods' Hollows, which had tumbled House Avocet's citadel into the sea. And, long before that, the unnamed quake that had flattened half of Ulthony, buried House Ibis, and set off a tidal wave that had ravaged southern Breova.

I knew small quakes weren't uncommon along the coast, but I'd never expected to experience one. My breath came fast as I carried on upward.

By the time I neared the family's rooms, the jovial music had resumed downstairs, the chatter was decidedly less excited, and my heart had calmed. There were no more shudders.

I made for Vercha's chamber first.

It seemed the safest place to start: to try out the tools the Cage had handed over and give the room a more thorough going-over in search of something interesting—or incriminating.

The sisters shared adjoining bedrooms with a well-appointed washroom between. Vercha's domain was the most familiar, with its blush-colored furnishings, its heavy gold-trimmed drapes, the glass vases on nearly every surface, bursting with bunches of late-blooming roses. Their scent was heady as I circled the room.

I'd already tallied the laconite in here, but now I tapped at a piece with the chisel experimentally. A hairline crack, almost invisible, spidered out from the center of the stone. Breath catching, chest thudding, I drew the tools away. The odd little rap every now and then should be enough to degrade it sufficiently—but not enough for the damage to be obvious.

I was more concerned by the Cage's other task: sniffing out information they could use to "influence" Rexim's decisions in the Chamber.

Quickly I checked in all the places *I* might have hidden something secret in this room: beneath the mattress, inside the books, the top of the wardrobe, the bottoms of pockets.

There was paper on Vercha's writing desk, a pot of ink that looked fresh from today. As I searched, I came upon a small wax-sealed envelope, shoved all the way to the rear of a drawer. It was as yet unaddressed, and when I held it to a lamp, I saw faint, close-packed writing inside. But intrigued as I was, I could do nothing with it. The wax seal would break, and she'd know someone had snooped.

Frustrated, I tidied, leaving everything pristine. But when I walked past the fireplace, something else caught my eye. Crouching, I prodded at the cinders with the poker. There was paper here, too, blackened scraps among the ashes. One brownish corner seemed to have escaped the blaze; three spiky words in black ink: . . . *our future depends . . .*

Vercha had been burning letters.

I stood and returned the poker to its stand, remembering when Vercha had dropped a letter at the posting house in Port Rhorstin. How odd it now seemed that she hadn't left it in the culverhouse to be flown to the mainland by one of our crows.

My mind whirred as I moved to Catua's room. It could all be nothing, I supposed. Maybe Vercha just didn't like storing letters. But it struck me as strange that she would go to the trouble.

The urge to pry further was smoldering in me, but there was little I could do, with the letters sealed or burned. Besides, I couldn't linger. I might be missed soon.

Pushing the discovery aside for now, I stepped into the bedroom of the youngest Shearwater.

It was all reds and golds and looked far more lived-in. There were books on nearly every surface, some lying open, others in teetering piles. A blouse hung haphazardly on the back of a chair. Something told me I didn't need to worry so much about putting things back exactly where I found them.

Working quickly, I moved from armoire to dresser, from washstand to writing desk, and finally to her end table. She had far less laconite than Vercha did, less than her father and her eldest brother. What was here was dusty, as though little used, and as those lacework cracks spread outward, my heart didn't pound quite as forcefully as before.

I'd found no evidence, however, to pass on to the Cage. No love letters, no diary mentioning Rhianne . . . Disappointment plucked at me, mixed with cold guilt.

I was about to leave to search the brothers' rooms when my fingers dislodged something in an end table drawer. I crouched, feeling around a bit more, and realized with a jolt what I'd discovered:

A hidden compartment.

I eased it open and reached inside, drawing out a thin stack of paper. It was a slim volume—a pamphlet, really—bound together with fraying string. I flipped it and read the title stamped on it:

THE BREOVAN CHARTER OF ORHA RIGHTS

I dropped the pamphlet as though I'd been burned and stared down at it, pulse hammering. Then, fingers trembling, I picked it up and flicked through it, wanting to see if it really was what it said it was.

And sure enough, it was a charter. A manifesto. Printed in stark black ink, its pages well thumbed.

I didn't know a whole lot about our neighboring kingdom—our Instructors had covered only its infighting, its wars—but I knew materials like these were forbidden in Nenamor. They were seen as proof of the bearer's allegiance to—or at least agreement with—the Cage. Mere possession of them warranted arrest.

I couldn't stay here. I needed to move. But now something else was rooting me to the spot: There were pencil underlinings on a few of the pages, annotations in the margins of the text. I tried to make myself slide the pamphlet back into the compartment and shut it up tight, but with a painful swallow, queasy with nerves, I realized I couldn't.

This was evidence.

These annotations had to be Catua's. How would this look to the rest of the Hundred: Shearwater's own daughter in possession of such a text? Here was a secret the Cage could leverage, one that would damage the Brigant's reputation irrevocably, not to mention result in his daughter's arrest. And a secret, unlike Catua's trysts with Rhianne, that I could back up with something other than my word.

But as I slipped the pamphlet into my pocket, the queasiness morphed into full-blown sickness. That guilt was back, now ten times worse. I'd never had an unkind word from Catua. Was I really going to let the Cage use her for extortion?

I couldn't decide now. Time was ticking on: The clock on the mantel read close to eleven. I stole from the room and made straight for Emment's. A new sense of urgency—and my wheeling thoughts—made me rush, my steps thudding loudly on the stone, but I knew these floors would still be deserted, all the guests and servants below.

The door to Emment's suite was standing open, but it was dim inside and no sounds came from within. I pushed it wider and scanned his first room: empty. Crossing the patterned rug to his bedroom, I saw embers glowing like foxes' eyes in his grate. A lamp was burning, turned down low. The valets must have missed it earlier.

As I stepped into the bedroom, I stopped abruptly.

The doors of his wardrobes were all flung open. His dresser, with its dozens of gilt-handled drawers, looked as though it had been thoroughly ransacked. In the wavering glow from the lamp, something sparkled in the darkness within; moving closer, I realized it was laconite. A few pieces, items I recognized from before, were piled haphazardly over each other. And a brooch on top . . .

I crouched, picked it up.

The laconite hummed, but with a very slight stutter. Peering at the stone, turning it over, I saw a barely there network of cracks deep within. I'd have missed it if I wasn't studying it intently, if I hadn't just caused the same damage in the sisters' rooms. But there was no mistaking it.

The brooch had been tampered with already.

A scrape behind me made me drop the brooch and turn. I just glimpsed a figure rearing above me, a pale object raised high in their arms, before I ducked and lurched sideways with a rustle of skirts.

The object—a vase—smashed down just inches from me. I threw up an elbow to protect my face as slivers of porcelain exploded on the floorboards.

As I skittered backward, belly-up, crablike, it took me a second to take in my attacker. Slim figured. Rich tawny skin. Tight black curls and flashing dark eyes. A handsome face I'd only ever seen smiling. Now it was pulled into a wide-eyed grimace.

"Oh dear," came that silk-smooth voice. "I was very much hoping I wouldn't have to dispatch anyone. And I rather liked you." He tipped his head.

It was Avrix Cormorant, in his fine dance clothes, bearing down on me with a jagged shard of vase.

I rolled, scrambled to regain my footing, but my dress was ridiculous: a plumped-up parachute. Then he was upon me, fabric tearing, and I kicked out viciously, eliciting a grunt.

Staggering up, half falling against the writing desk, I fumbled a hand over its surface in the shadows. Quills, papers, and then—a letter opener. I brandished it like a blade, faced him as he straightened.

There it was: that slow, cocky smile. "I'm sorry," he said. "I can't let you leave." This time, as he came for me, he was focused. Intent.

"Wait!" I cried, stabbing out with the letter opener. It looked paltry, absurd, compared to his wicked shard. "Was that you—the laconite? Did you damage it on purpose?"

His eyes narrowed, but he didn't break his stride.

"I . . ." It was a risk, but I had no other choice. "I came here to do the exact same thing."

I dropped the letter opener—his glinting gaze followed it—and dug in my bodice for the hammer and chisel.

"Here," I said, breathless, holding them out with shaking hands.

When he saw the tools, he went suddenly still. His eyes crawled up to mine, a strange spark within them. After a long, drawn-out moment, he padded to the dresser and placed the porcelain shard on top.

"You wish the Shearwaters harm," he said softly. "Or at least their heir. Why, may I ask?"

"Why do you?" I returned, eyeing the laconite. Right now I could think of only one reason. But it was mad. It couldn't be . . . there was no way . . .

Creases appeared at the corners of his eyes, and his lips twitched slightly. "You're working for the Cage."

I blinked at him. "And you are, too. You're a . . . a cuckoo."

He broke into a smile. That spark was back—almost a delight, flashing across his features. "Of course," he said. "Why else would I have these?" He fished in his pockets and drew out a set of tools similar to mine. *Cage tools,* Kielty had called them, hadn't he? The nabyrium glittered in the light from the lamp.

I gazed at them, and then at him, in bare shock. "You?" I whispered, unable to process it. I couldn't slot them together in my mind: my image of Avrix, the debonair noble, and the shadowy group I'd found myself aiding.

"Your disbelief is pleasing," he said lightly, cheeks twitching. "Means I've not let the mask slip just yet."

"Is your sister . . . ?" I thought of the imperious Morgen, her piercing looks, her condescension.

"Gods, no," Avrix replied, turning away. He cupped his jaw, ran his thumb over the stubble. "As children we were both little radicals. Went to stay with relatives as young'uns and came back spouting things that shocked our parents." He smiled fondly, staring at the floor. "I kept perusing the periodicals they sent us, seeking out like minds, harboring that . . . anger, and eventually got to know a cuckoo in Pontarth. Offered to do what I could, when I could.

"But Morgen . . . no. She 'grew out of all that,' as she was fond of telling me as often as she could." He threw me a glance. "Still, I decided to stay put. I can do more for our cause—albeit less frequently—from the inside. Pass on information, mainly."

His words unearthed what had been nagging at me. "Why would they send another?" My chest had constricted. Kielty hadn't said anything about this. Did the Cage not trust me to help them alone?

"Gosh," he said, "this was all very last minute. When Vercha wrote to invite us to the island, I just had time to dash off a crow to my contact, knowing I'd be spending a good stretch of time in the inner domain of our illustrious next Regent . . ." His countenance twisted, but only for a second. "My contact's response arrived just as we were leaving—a set of instructions that, I imagine, match yours."

The news must not have reached Kielty when I met him, though I still couldn't help feeling a little uneasy. Clearly this Leadership Kielty had mentioned didn't quite have full faith in my abilities. But then, why would they? I was still an unknown. And as for the cause Avrix had spoken of . . . did I really consider myself a convert?

"I thought it was you who suggested this visit," I said, remembering Vercha's "news."

"Vercha said that, did she?" Avrix chuckled. "Probably a ruse to make Rexim more amenable. No. My being here was opportunity only."

As I surveyed him, I began to see the benefits to the situation—glossing over the almost-getting-killed part, of course.

"Then we can work together," I ventured, stepping forward. I'd been growing increasingly anxious about my tasks, about how I was going to get through all the laconite, not to mention dig up more dirt on the family.

"I knew I liked you," Avrix said, tucking his tools back into his doublet. My body warmed at the Cormorant's approval; just like at the sailing race, something in me wanted to impress him.

Noises came from below. Running footsteps. A shout.

My stomach clenched. Just drunk ballgoers? Or had someone noticed we were missing, got suspicious?

"Come on," he said. "Help me put this room back together."

He closed the wardrobe doors and tidied Emment's desk while I arranged the laconite in the many-drawered dresser. As I did so, I came across some false laconite, stored at the back, a few pieces thick with dust.

Kielty hadn't seemed interested in it. But it still needled me. What if it meant something? What if it had something to do with my other task—to dig up any skeletons the family were hiding?

Impulsively, I drew out a small goldwork pin. The blood-red stone set into it was silent, and I pocketed it, shoving it down alongside Zennia's brooch.

Avrix and I glanced at the shattered vase at the same time.

"You felt that quake earlier?" he said, brow lifting.

"Explains the mess easily enough," I said, comprehending, and we shared a brief, triumphant look.

"It's Corith, isn't it?" he said, searching my face. "It's good to have you onside in this ongoing fight."

"You too." I felt a brief flare of comradeship. After nearly a month of cold glances and closed faces, I was glad to finally have something close to an ally.

Another shout from downstairs. We were spurred into motion. Stealing out of Emment's chambers, we headed back down the spiral staircase, to the ball.

25

Something was wrong.

I became aware of it as Avrix and I dashed down the tower steps. Though the spiral staircase was still deserted, I detected a growing tumult below—there were raised voices, rushed footsteps, the barking of orders in a voice very like Rexim's. Surely that couldn't all be for us?

We emerged into an empty corridor and crept toward the imperial staircase. On the landing, the noise intensified. Crowds were gathered in the entrance hall. A drunk guest lurched past and peered out a narrow window.

Avrix slipped by and, a second later, was gone, lost among the revellers. I was left to pick my way down the staircase, trying to blend in, wondering what was going on.

Guests were darting this way and that. Some were clustered in tight, anxious circles, their eyes on the windows, which showed only pitch darkness. I could still hear the drumming of rain on the glass and, under it, the ever-present purring of laconite.

I was halfway down the stairs when the siblings strode into view. Vercha's eyes swept the chamber—I couldn't escape that sharp gaze—and spotting me, she stalked over, handsome features set hard.

"Where have you been?" she hissed, grabbing my elbow.

"Er—" My excuses floated right out of my head. I was still dumbstruck by Avrix's revelation.

"Never mind," she said, tugging me down the stairs with her. Her face was oddly pale. "Come quickly. They need you."

The next figure I was faced with was Llir. Remembering our dance, what I'd admitted to myself after, I flushed, but he only looked as strained as Vercha. Someone had pulled the keep's doors wide, and people milled there like agitated insects.

Behind Emment and Catua, Rexim's burly frame appeared.

"Here she is, Father."

Spots of red colored his cheeks. "Floodmouth." His venomous tone made me falter. "Get down to the east cove and corral the others. *Now.*"

I had no idea what *others* he was talking about, but I willed my legs to move toward the doors. There, the rage of the storm was palpable. A few guests had braved it and stood huddled under parasols, their hems soaked through, their eyes fixed east. Most collected in front of the doorway, and as I elbowed through them I glanced back, glimpsing the siblings. Vercha was gripping Catua's arm. Emment spoke rapidly to a pair of nobles. Llir locked eyes with me, watching me go.

Then I was through, thrown into the furor.

I called to the rain, but my nerves were taut as bowstrings. It half listened, sparing me the worst of the downpour, but by the time I was midway across the outer ward, my dress—my stupid, hells-damned dress—was drenched and heavy, weighing me down.

Thunder cracked directly overhead. I ducked, then stumbled toward the cove path. All around me, the rain sheeted down, the bay invisible, cloaked in black. Slipping and sliding, I made my way east. With the castle lit up like a Feast Day tree, there was just enough glow to see the rough track ahead.

Under the storm, I heard a low, muted roar. It brought to mind the terrifying swells of peak archwater, but I knew that was still a week away. And anyway, this noise . . . it seemed continuous, an insistent droning at the edge of my hearing.

Our tower reared out of the darkness ahead like the neck of some colossal sea beast. I passed it, blinking rain from my eyes, edging forward carefully, conscious of the clifftops close by.

A few moments later, I walked smack into a body.

"Oof. Who's that? Hey, Osprey, we've got another one!"

Voices. Squelching footsteps. Somewhere, a woman moaning.

"How long?" someone said.

"Two minutes. Maybe less."

I turned in a circle, peering through the deluge. Dark, blurry figures moved around me on the slope, muted flashes of color—Orha's vibrant livery.

Then a hand grabbed me. "Hey." Amber eyes. Light brown skin. Curly black hair plastered down over drawn brows. "You're a Floodmouth too?"

"The Shearwaters'," I said, teeth chattering.

"Finally," the young man bit out. "Where were you? We'd have got down here much quicker if you'd been here to guide us. Come on." He urged me onward. "There's not much time."

"Until what?" I demanded, trying to shake off his grip. His livery was the deep orange of House Osprey.

He spun me around, made me face the unseen ocean. "Wait for it," he said, breathless and grim.

I squinted eastward. All was black, thickly cloaked.

"I don't under—"

A stark white flash. Lightning. It streaked down, revealing roiling clouds above.

The place it struck should have been covered by water. I didn't know what time it was, but even at lowest tide, the sea never drew out much beyond the island. I should have seen waves. Fountains of spray. Instead, the lightning illuminated bare mud. A great, horrifying expanse of seabed.

And beyond it, lit up for only a second, a low black wall, stretching out along the horizon.

"What—?" I managed. The roar was growing louder.

"Tidal wave," Osprey's Floodmouth said quietly. "That quake earlier . . . you can't have missed it?"

My core felt cold. My ears filled with buzzing.

"No, but it was nothing. It felt too small . . ."

He looked at me askance. "Yes, if the island had been the center. That's what people assumed at first. But it wasn't. It must have been way out, off the coast." He stared out gravely. "Big one, I reckon."

My hair was sopping, but I hardly noticed. Now I began to realize why we'd been sent out here.

I sensed him looking at me, waiting for my reply. Waiting for the guidance I knew they were expecting, deferring to my authority as Rexim's Floodmouth. But I wasn't a leader; I'd never felt like one. And certainly not facing something like this.

"Right," Osprey's Floodmouth called when I said nothing, "spread out along the cliff's edge. Any laconite on you—ditch it now."

He had a commanding air despite his youth, an easy confidence that made my cheeks flush with shame. I maneuvered forward, again cursing my dress. Every movement was far harder than it needed to be.

"They sent us here to die," a woman was moaning. Fear needled my skin at her words.

"Shut up, will you?" came someone's fraught snap. The rushing out in the bay grew louder. The darkness was total—somehow worse than seeing the wave.

"Will it come up this high?" I said to no one in particular.

"Oh, yes," said another woman beside me. "I'm House Avocet. We know our waves. It won't reach the castle—that would have to be a *monster*—but it seems your Brigant wants to save his storehouses."

I turned, peered back at the shrouded island. The castle flared, a beacon of gold light, faintly illuminating clusters of buildings below. Down here were the fish cellar, the icehouse . . . and the Orha's tower.

Beyond, squatting at low levels around the island, were the boathouses. Those vessels would be expensive to replace. We'd been ordered out here to try to lessen the damage.

But at what cost to us? a voice in my head said.

I thought of the stories Zennia had told me. The Sparkmouths who had choked in her mother's glass furnaces. Her own disappearance amid raging waves.

Was that—here, now—to be my fate, too?

I whirled as a second lightning strike seared down. In its brilliance, I glimpsed that terrible rising wall of water, blacker than the night, bearing down on the cove. My legs went weak. I stumbled backward. Osprey's Floodmouth shouted something, and along the line, others called out, too.

My mind flashed back to Rexim's test. The one I'd survived only by giving up. Those waves had been nothing, just ripples, compared to this one. They'd listened, barely, but only when I thought I'd die . . .

Pathetic. Hot shame bled into my cheeks. I thrust a hand into the pocket where I'd stashed Zennia's brooch. I hadn't been able to wear it openly lest someone, a Shearwater or a servant, recognize it, but I'd wanted it close. A reminder of her. I squeezed it now but still felt horribly alone.

Fleetingly I flicked my eyes closed, hoping the brooch might temper my horror, but my mind's eye was crimson, a raging inferno, not even anything ball shaped to squeeze down. I gulped in air. "Stand down!" I urged the water, my voice cracking, knowing at any second it would reach us, overcome us. "Stand down now—spare this place!"

But then the deeper darkness ahead of me . . . *moved.* Came charging toward me. I staggered backward.

Along the line, the others were retreating, some looking just as panicked as I felt, others more determined, still yelling entreaties. My feet tangled in my dress as I stumbled, and then a great black swell broke over the clifftop.

It hurtled forward, a violent stampede, appearing almost to barrel toward *me* especially. I recalled forgetting to thank the tide. How, in the last few days, I'd been so caught up in everything going on that I'd neglected my usual morning practice.

Rhama's words came to me: *"It takes time, and respect."*

The water reared, towering above us, but for a slowed-down second or two, it seemed to . . . hesitate. The Floodmouths' raw shouts echoed around me. Then, despite their efforts—

The wave hit.

It was like running headfirst into cold glass. I was tossed, upended, like a child's rag doll, my skirts torn and billowing, the momentum shoving me backward.

In an instant, I was under. Salt filled my mouth. I was blinded, enveloped in a rough, icy darkness. Lungs burning, I sensed I was being swept away. In a moment, I'd be cast off the cliff edge to perish. Frantically, I raked out my hands, felt hard earth, a thicket of daggerlike thorns—the gorse.

Another surge broke over me, threatening to finish the job. But it was weaker. Shallower. I clung to the gorse.

The water began to dissipate.

Lying bruised and battered on the sodden soil, I coughed, tasting bitter bile on my tongue. From somewhere a scream sounded. A few hoarse shouts.

Sucking in a breath, I crouched on shaking legs. All was dark, and though the pelting rain had lessened, there was no part of me now that wasn't drenched and chilled to ice.

I'd been tossed some distance but couldn't tell how far. As I clambered to standing, I put out a hand and yelped as a long, wicked gorse thorn stabbed me. I stumbled in the opposite direction, and the ground grew stony under my feet. Then, without warning, it abruptly fell away. I teetered, terrified. This must be a cliff edge. Below, water still pounded savagely on rock.

I turned and pushed my way numbly through the gorse, trying not to think about how close I'd come to pitching down there.

Squelches in the mud. A hand on my shoulder.

"Who's that?" It was Osprey's Floodmouth, voice raw from exhaustion, from all the shouting. "Are you all right? Close call with that cliff. But I think we only lost one." He trudged away, livery dripping. "Come on, they'll want us back up at the castle."

Lost one. Someone *had* died out here.

I followed him, hearing others traipsing ahead of us.

But when we reached the site of the Orha's old tower, we all stopped short. I swiped rain from my eyes.

Before the great wave, it had loomed, four floors high. Now it was a ruin, the upper stories gutted. My room and Mawre's were gone, nothing left but jagged remnants of walls. The front entrance gaped, Tigo's windows had shattered, and around us, among the flattened, mulchy gorse, lay fallen stones and detritus from our chambers.

I stared up at where my room had once been. My only clothes, my livery. The pouch of regals Emment had paid me. Zennia's belongings; the letter she'd left. All now scattered and swept away.

Suddenly panicked, I put a hand to my bodice, digging for my tools—and the Breovan Charter. They'd been there, safely stowed when I'd returned to the ball. But now they were gone, shaken loose by the torrent.

I felt around for Zennia's brooch and was relieved to feel it at the bottom of my pocket, rattling against the false-laconite pin I'd swiped from Emment's room.

But without the other items, I was useless to the Cage. No way to continue damaging the laconite, and no hard proof of Catua's secret.

The voice of Osprey's Floodmouth floated out of the darkness: "Must have been ancient to have collapsed like that."

"It was," I said, surprised at how hoarse I sounded.

"Come on," he replied. "I'll report it up at the castle."

They'd all been safe up there, of course—the Brigants and Brigantesses, the lesser nobles, the other Orha.

By the time we reached the castle, bedraggled and exhausted, the storm had passed over, moving west toward the mainland, but distant lightning still flashed in the sky, and the rain had kept up a persistent drizzle.

Most of the guests had spilled out into the inner ward. With no Floodmouths left to protect them, they'd huddled under parasols or the hoods of their cloaks. There were figures up on the battlements holding lamps, and I wondered bitterly if they'd enjoyed a good show.

A murmur ran through the crowds as we appeared. One Orha fewer than we'd been when we'd gone down there.

As the young man who'd taken charge on the clifftop strode forward, he was met by Damona Osprey and a man I guessed was her son: white blond, his outfit sumptuous. House Osprey were known for ostentation. The family's other Orha, in their flame-orange livery, clustered and fussed around them like oxpeckers. Rexim appeared, inserting himself among them, and as Osprey's Floodmouth reported what had happened, the Shearwater patriarch's gaze cut to me.

"Corith! Thank the gods you're all right."

Vercha had spotted me. She was trailed by Llir, pale face shadowed, along with Tigo, Rhianne, and Mawre.

"Moons, you look terrible," she said, peering closer. "What's that on your—" She gasped. "Oh, Corith, you're *bleeding.*"

With vague surprise, I looked down at myself. There were cuts on my clavicle, a slash on my arm. The gorse thorns . . . they'd been knife-like, but I'd hardly noticed the pain.

As Vercha fretted, seeming now more worried about my dress than my injuries, my gaze slid to the nobles behind her.

I'd nearly died. One of the other Floodmouths *had.* I scanned the ballgoers, trying to spot anyone looking grieved, wondering which House the fallen Orha had belonged to, but everyone I could see was wide-eyed and gossiping. Knocking back the dregs of their pale-green punch.

I opened my mouth to say something like "I'm fine," but nothing came out. Instead I swayed. My limbs burned from the climb up the hill, my dress was waterlogged, weighing me down, and my throat was raw from swallowing seawater.

"Corith—" Vercha started, but a bulky figure blocked her.

"Floodmouth," came Rexim's deep, grating voice, pitched so only the family could hear. He leaned in close, cheeks flushed with anger; and was there a shade of humiliation there, too? "Miss Haney has been lauding your efforts. Though you seemed like nothing special to me, I've been happy, thus far, to trust her judgment. Now I see I was foolish to do so."

His eyes darted to the nobles around us, his tone sharpening even further. "While you were off idling gods know where, the other

Houses' Floodmouths were reporting for duty. One had to step up and lead in your absence."

I took a step back, chest constricting uncomfortably.

"Thanks in part to this sorry excuse for a Floodmouth," he hissed, glancing at Tigo, Rhianne, and Mawre, "your home—a temple *centuries* old—is now little more than a pile of rubble. You'll all have to move into the castle proper. Tell Miss Haney to open up East Tower.

"And as for you . . ." He loomed over me, making me shrink. "With the vote weeks away, I can't be seen to be running anything less than a fully competent household. I'll be writing to Arbenhaw first thing tomorrow to let them know to expect you back. You can spend tonight in East Tower, too, but don't bother making yourself at home there."

Face pinched as though I were a clump of mud on his boot sole, he stalked off, his fur-lined cloak swishing.

Vercha hurried after her father, calling to him to wait. I couldn't bring myself to meet the others' gazes. All I wanted was to curl into a ball.

Llir seemed to rouse himself. "Tigo," he said, voice pitched low, "take some other Mudmouths and inspect the Orha's tower. What's left of it, anyway. Make it as safe as you can. We don't want it collapsing on any gawkers tonight." He looked me over briskly. "Mawre—towels and dry clothes for Corith. And Rhianne—hot brandy. Bring them to Miss Haney's office."

Jerking into motion, they went their separate ways.

I glanced at Llir, caught off guard. It was the first time I'd heard my name on his lips.

"Come on," he said, "you need to sit down." He tipped his chin toward the housekeeper's office. But when I tried to walk, my legs went weak, failing to carry the weight of my dress. After a moment's hesitation, he moved in next to me, sliding a velvety arm beneath my shoulders. I shuffled along, pressed in next to him, acutely—almost painfully—aware of his warm frame.

It was a relief to be out of the drizzle, away from the curious stares of the guests. As I limped into the office, I glimpsed myself in a mirror: dress so wet it was black instead of purple, stained with blood, its lace sleeves shredded. Strands of dark-copper hair over my face. Eyes shadowed with fatigue and smudged powder.

I sank gratefully onto a bench near the hearth—the couch looked more inviting, but I didn't want to stain it. A small fire snapped and crackled in the grate.

Llir leaned tiredly against the wall across from me. As he pushed a hand through his rain-dark hair, I noticed his doublet and hose were soaked, too, his dancing shoes ruined. Had he been one of those watchers on the battlements?

"I couldn't do it," I croaked out, exhausted. "Some of the others, they—they held it back a bit, but—" I faltered, staring down at my chapped hands.

He let out a breath through his nose, resigned. "I don't really know what they expected you all to do out there."

"Why send us, then?" I said, an edge to my voice. I couldn't help but look up at him accusingly.

He frowned. "It was Osprey's idea," he said, tone clipped. "They're very powerful. Lots of influence. The Brigantess said Father should take advantage of it, all these Floodmouths here in one place. Try to ensure nothing important got destroyed."

With a splinter of guilt, I thought of the tower.

"Avocet and Turnstone agreed with them," he added.

"But your father has more influence than any of them, surely? He's about to win the Chamber Seat, after all."

Llir's eyes darted away. "Father . . . chose to assent, too." In the distance, a growl of thunder sounded. "I suppose he wants to keep the

big players onside."

They were all as bad as each other, I thought viciously. Worse when they were together—when they wanted to impress.

I swallowed, remembering Rexim's declaration. It was over, I realized with a creeping sickness: my task for the Cage, any hope of my reward . . . I'd lost my tools anyway. It was all on Avrix now. I'd be sent back to Arbenhaw to await a new placement and never find out what the Cage knew about Zennia.

"They'll send me down to drain the marshes," I said flatly. "Or to sail in some navy somewhere." I met his eye. "I hope your next stint without a Floodmouth is shorter, and less of a burden than it clearly was after Zennia."

Llir stared at me. "A night's sleep can change minds," he said. "Including, with any luck, my father's."

It took a moment for his words to register. "Why do you care if I stay or go? I'm Vercha's little pet, not yours. That's Tigo." My face was warm—a mixture of shame and defiance.

In the firelit gloom, I saw his brows pinch in anger. "Pet?" he repeated, quiet and hoarse. "You have no—" He paused. "Tigo's been like a *father* to me—"

But before either of us could say anything else, the door banged open and people bustled in.

Rhianne's crimson head appeared first, bent over a cup of something steaming. Mawre followed, holding crisp, clean clothes. And barging in past them, navy dress rustling, came Catua, her blond hair hanging in damp ringlets.

"Are you all right?" the youngest Shearwater said. "Llir and I saw the wave from the battlements. We were trying to spot you, see if you made it out okay, but it was too dark. And then all those *vultures* came up . . . Are you still bleeding? Here, look, I have towels."

The blood had slowed, nearly stopped by now, but I let her crouch down and inspect my cuts. Llir was watching me. I avoided his eyes. I'd perhaps been too hasty with my accusing looks, my sparring . . . But that didn't change the fact that others had been up there, delighted by the spectacle, salivating at our peril.

Something fierce had begun to smolder in me. It had sparked—the first licks of it—back in the cove, seeing just how little value Rexim placed on my life. Then, bit by bit, it had been stoked into a fire. All the disparaging words about Zennia: *Inept. Foolhardy. Specimen. Dud.* The way we were expected to stand around like accessories, beholden to traditions born from loathing. Brigant Crake's violent ambitions for us on the borders. And now, this casual, callous disregard.

I'd excelled at Arbenhaw in hopes of an easy placement—but with Houses like Osprey and Shrike wielding influence, nothing would ever be easy for Orha.

I looked blankly at Catua as she dabbed at my skin. *She says big change has to happen slowly.* But I'd been feet away from being cast off that cliff. If nothing changed now, I'd end up like the Floodmouth who *had* been swept away. And so would countless other Orha.

Zennia must have had this fire in her, too. Hers had first kindled before she came to Arbenhaw, and by the time she'd witnessed those fights in Port Rhorstin, it must have grown into a blazing pyre. Hot enough to burn away any fear of the Hundred.

"Corith?" Rhianne's face swam into view. "Drink this. I've added ginger."

I cupped my hands around the mug. I didn't have the energy to think more about this now.

"Come on, let's give the girl some privacy," said Mawre, placing the pile of dry clothes by my side. "They're Rhianne's, so they'll be a bit short for you."

"Only my things survived," the Sparkmouth said sorrowfully.

"Thank you," I managed, my face flushing again. Though I knew the old tower's destruction hadn't solely been my fault, it was hard not to let Rexim's harsh words eat at me.

A thought struck me then. "Port Rhorstin," I said. "The wave . . ."

"They have Floodmouths," said Mawre, "employed by the harbor-master. But the island will have taken the wind out of the wave's sails. I think only our southern boathouse got flooded. You bore the brunt of it."

One of us had paid the ultimate price.

As they filed out, Catua murmured darkly to Rhianne.

Llir pushed off the wall and headed to the door, then paused for a second, catching my gaze. Eventually, eyes flicking down over my ruined dress, he said simply, a little stiffly, "I'm sorry."

I wondered if he was thinking of his father's punishment. Of the fact that this might be the last time we spoke. I half regretted my harsh words of earlier; I supposed I should bid him a final farewell. But when I parted my lips, the words got stuck in my throat.

Instead, I glanced away, fingering the pile of dry clothes, and when I looked back, he had slipped out the door.

I was woken the next morning by a loud, insistent knocking. When I cracked an eye open, I couldn't work out where I was. Then, recognizing my new room in East Tower—pokey, with a whining draft and a drip from the ceiling—the events of the past twelve hours crashed in on me.

Dark thoughts swirled, threatening to pull me under. Last night, as I'd wound my way up here, I'd known I would need to send word to Kielty, admit I was being banished from the island. But now, jolted roughly from a dead sleep, I wondered sickly if I'd missed my chance. Was this my escort fetching me already? A new Egard and Belamy to deliver me back to Arbenhaw?

There were no drapes over the arrow slits here, and a cold, bright light speared through them onto the stone. I groaned and turned over on the uncomfortable cot bed. My limbs were lead weights after the fury of the tidal wave.

Whoever was out there hammering on the door clearly realized no one was going to answer, for they opened it, stepped through, and snapped it neatly shut behind them.

It was Vercha, bundled from neck to toe in a thick riding mantle with white sable trimmings.

"Still abed?" she said, gazing around my sad little chamber.

As I snapped to attention, my blanket fell off me and I realized just how cold it was. The soupy humidity leading up to the storm had sloughed away, leaving a thin, bitter chill.

"No matter," she went on, stepping toward me. "Corith, listen. I've been talking to Father. He agrees that he spoke a little too hastily last night in informing you that your service would end. I've persuaded him to allow you *one week*—no more—to prove yourself an indispensable member of our staff. You'll have to— Oh, Corith!"

She'd come across my still-sodden dress, which I'd left exactly where I'd stepped out of it: a dark-purple puddle, skirts torn, turning musty.

I jumped off the bed. "I'm so sorry," I said. "Let me—"

She waved me back. "Never mind, never mind. Maybe Debry can work some magic on it." She picked it up delicately, laid it over a wooden bench.

Turning, she swept a stern gaze over me. "You're able to crack on with your chores, I take it? I'm aware you were battered around a bit yesterday, but we have work to do if we're going to convince Father . . ."

I thought of Rexim's fond looks at his daughter, how ready he always seemed to agree to her plans. I'd long suspected she was his favorite, and I saw now how much sway she had.

"Of course," I said. My heart was drumming. *One week.* "But, Miss, I must thank you—"

"Please," she interrupted, her smile tight-lipped. "You may thank me by proving I wasn't foolish to argue for you."

I met her stare with a frosty understanding.

Vercha had invested time and money into me, paying for my dress, for the new clothes I'd bought. She'd preened me, paraded me, been seen to favor me. Now she was saving face. Smoothing things over. She didn't want her judgment to appear to have been poor.

I dropped my gaze and set about tugging on some work clothes. Rhianne's breeches were tight and frayed at the hems. "I'll report to Miss Haney straightaway," I said breathlessly.

As I crossed the room, came within touching distance of her, Vercha's arm snapped out and grabbed my elbow.

"Corith," she said quietly, a small smile on her face. "You won't disappoint me. Will you?" Her eyes bore into mine. This close, I saw the elegant sweep of her cheekbones, the sharp cut of her jaw, so like her younger brother's.

My relief at my weeklong reprieve sputtered out, replaced by a cold apprehension. Her fingers were like pincers where they gripped my arm.

"I won't, Miss," I forced out, avoiding that piercing gaze.

She released me, unmoving, and watched me walk to the doorway.

I remembered the fragments of charred paper in her grate. That was one secret I'd decided to let lie. The alternative—crossing Vercha—sent a prickle of fear through me.

I opened the door, my blouse sweaty with nerves, and slipped out, grateful to vanish from her sight.

One week.

Through a window, I glimpsed the glistening mudflats, peppered with gulls delighting in fresh pickings. I thought of the rebels, somewhere out there on the mainland, plotting and preparing for their foray at pallwater. The sixteenth of Undalh was far too late now. In one week, I might be gone from here, unable to pass on the information—the secrets—the Cage would need to "persuade" Rexim Shearwater.

Which meant Kielty's group would have to come early. I had to send him a summons. Today.

I also had to get Avrix alone somehow. Tell him what had happened, and find out how long he'd be here. With my tools gone, no doubt swept off into the bay, he was now my only means of fully succeeding, of finding out what had happened to Zennia.

Shivering, I remembered the eager-eyed guests at the ball. The stark realization I'd come to after the wave.

I'd demanded that Kielty protect me as a source, ensure the family didn't know I'd spied, but now the thought of remaining here—*if* Vercha managed to convince Rexim to keep me—brought an acrid bitterness to the back of my throat.

The alternatives, though—leaving with the Cage, or running, only to be suspected of it anyway—felt weighty, and more than a little frightening.

When Kielty's group *did* arrive, I knew I'd have to make a choice. Decide what I wanted my future to be. But I couldn't bring myself to dwell on that just yet.

In the meantime, I was about to set a fire beneath them.

I'd counted on the Waking Tide rousing me the next morning, but up in my drafty room in East Tower, its roar was muted, just a distant rushing. Instead, as I remembered Catua once lamenting, it was the birds that shocked me awake close to dawn, wheedling as they rode the sea breeze past my window.

The day before, I'd snuck up to the culverhouse and, with shaking hands, scratched out a message:

> K,
>
> THE BIRD IN OUR BOOTH GROWS WRATHFUL. I MAY BE GONE IN A SEVENDAY—YOU MUST VISIT SOONER, AT ARCHWATER.
>
> BLUEBIRD

It was far from perfect, but it would have to do. I couldn't risk explaining any more on paper, and I was even too nervous to sign off as "C," deciding to reference my mask instead.

Restless and tense, I dressed in the dry chill, pulling Rhianne's too-short cloak around my shoulders. The cuts from the gorse had scabbed over but still ached. As I stole out of the keep into a pinkish pre-sunrise, I guessed I had a quarter of an hour before I was missed. I'd have to make sure I woke earlier tomorrow. But I was determined, at least, to make headway this morning. To face archwater again—and this time exert my will. I'd need every scrap of practice I could get to see me through whatever awaited me next. And besides, the routine felt calming amid this turmoil.

I jogged down the path from the castle to the cove, my heart skittering anxiously at the sound of the sea. I forced my feet to carry me to the cliff's edge, the same place Rexim had stood when he'd tested me, and stared down at the water churning in the cove, at the fountains of surf as the waves slammed on stone. Gone were the sedate, suggestible currents of pallwater. Peak archwater was six days away, and its fury was already palpable.

I picked my way gingerly down a steep scramble and crouched on an outcropping misted by spray. In a lonely hour lying awake last night, I'd raked over all the times—all the ways—I'd faltered.

"The ocean is a . . . different beast."

I'd blown into Bower Island with the wind, commanded the tide, and expected it to listen. I was a stranger, and a fool, and it had treated me thus.

Then, when it *had* listened, I'd forgotten to thank it. I'd been so encased in my inner world, so embroiled in my own emotions, I hadn't shown it the respect that Rhama had pressed home.

And now, rightfully, it was angry.

I had to get a grip. I had to rectify this. I shifted forward, dangled my feet in the foam. Stared out at the white swells, the whirlpools and eddies. I emptied my mind of apprehension, then turned my focus outward, to the sea.

"I'm sorry," I said, really and truly meaning it. No commands this time, just conversation. I tried to open myself up, to just *listen*. The tide had moods, too, and I needed to learn them.

It came, then, like the flicker of a sputtering candle. A sliver of an emotion that I knew wasn't mine.

The receding tide was weary but ebullient, gathering strength for its next assault on the bay. I caught wariness, too. A distant suspicion. Resentment that I might get in its way.

I sat with it for a long time—probably too long. I knew Miss Haney would be wondering where I was. But soon I sensed the tide's wariness ease. And then I opened my mouth and spoke: "Show me your power—send up a fountain."

A flash of outrage. Then . . . simmering curiosity. I kept my mind open, stayed tranquil, unmoving.

Then, at last, the next wave rose high, spiralling upward. Droplets refracted the sunrise like jewels. I *felt* the sea's pride, a warm flare in my chest, and though I tried to suppress it, I felt pride of my own, too—a gleam of relief, like a torch in the darkness.

The tide shrank back, growing distant again.

A sudden skitter behind me made me start. Loose gravel tumbled down into the spray. I hopped into a crouch, craned my neck to peer upward. Against the flushed sky, I thought I glimpsed something black. A ripple of fabric, like a cloak's hem disappearing. But the next second there was nothing. I blinked salt from my eyes.

A bird, I expected. A crow, or a shearwater. The black-capped birds liked to follow the tides eastward.

After making sure to thank the water, I clambered to my feet, still bruised from two nights ago, and began the slow, careful climb to the clifftop.

There, cresting the ridge, I saw no one, bird or human—only the craggy hump of the old tower's ruins.

* * *

I practiced before dawn the next morning, and the next. And during daylight hours, I threw myself into my duties.

At first I'd wondered if it was worth the effort. But I quickly realized I had no choice. If the Cage didn't come early, if my note went astray, I had to do whatever I could to impress Rexim, for I'd need to be here when they *did* arrive, at pallwater, the date Kielty had originally planned. How would it look to Rexim if I just gave up?

So I plowed through my chores in double time, ferrying water to the horses and bringing ale from the brewhouse, sprinkling the flowers and vines in the orangery. I made sure to cross paths with Miss Haney at all hours, even calling at her office to ask for more work, knowing she would be reporting back to Rexim.

The Brigant himself didn't approach me again, but whenever I happened to come across him—outside the stables as he handed over his mount, in the high-ceilinged hallways as I scrubbed down the floors—he stared down his aquiline nose at me, and I straightened my shoulders, quickened my steps, and scoured a little harder, avoiding his eyes.

Amid all this, of course, were my social duties, for the Cormorants were still installed in South Tower. It was difficult, among the hubbub and rigors of my work, to find any opportunity to speak to Avrix. But speak to him I must, for he had the only tools. Moreover, if my note *had* wound its way to Kielty, the Cage would be coming in just three days, while the Cormorants were still here—something Avrix didn't know yet . . .

With a pressing sense of dread, an uncomfortable queasiness, I'd been moving around the castle with a note in my pocket:

MIDNIGHT. THE RUINED TOWER. WE MUST SPEAK.

The only chance I had to get anywhere near Avrix was at the Shearwaters' and the Cormorants' first rehearsal for their play.

They'd finally settled on one: *Cithre's Folly.* Tragic, salacious, controversial, it told the story of the eponymous Cithre, a Brigantess, and her affair with her Orha servant—the latter character, of course, being the villain.

Morgen, directing a wink at us Orha, insisted the work was based on a true story. Emment was diverted, Vercha amused, and Llir—as always—hard to read. Catua, I noticed, had gone slightly pink, and Rhianne had crouched to inspect the fire.

I lingered on the periphery with a pitcher of water as the group cavorted with swords they'd taken from the armory and down from the walls of the entrance hall. Emment was playing the villainous Orha, and he stalked the floodboards, flourishing a dusty cloak with a gold fringe. The eldest Shearwater seemed to relish the role, taking on the persona with bright-eyed fervor—almost a wild, feverish devotion.

As I watched him darkly, a fleeting image came to my mind: Emment dragging Zennia; him spitting with rage, embarrassed by her outburst after the fight. Had he hurt her before they got into the boat? Shoved her—dead or injured—into the waves later? Or had it happened on the crossing, out on the water? Perhaps she'd tried to fight back, to escape . . .

Maybe Kielty had followed them to the docks. Maybe he or one of his group had taken a boat out behind them, watching. Keeping tabs on the Shearwater heir, knowing the mission they'd been tasked with by Leadership . . .

I blinked, snapping back to the room. Avrix was passing, twirling a blade.

"Refreshment from the kitchens," I said, stepping forward. "I heard your sister say rehearsing was thirsty work, so I thought . . ." I held out the pitcher of water.

He paused with the twitch of a dark brow, then sheathed the sword in one swift movement. "This one's a keeper," he announced to the room, making the skin on my neck grow warm.

As I handed over the pitcher and goblets, I slipped my folded note into his palm. He hesitated, but only for a split second, before striding over to Morgen, dipping a hand into his pocket. After that, I didn't see what he did with the note.

I could only hope he'd meet me at midnight.

The Shearwaters and the Cormorants stayed up late that night.

I fretted that they would carry on rehearsing, keep drinking and dancing, until dawn lit the sky, and Avrix wouldn't be able to steal away at all. But in the end, as I hovered near the steps to East Tower, I heard them cross the entrance hall a little after one o'clock, Morgen's rich laughter echoing under the high ceiling.

I slipped into the shadows and out a back entrance. The air outside was salty and smoky—Tigo and Rhianne had been burning branches up on the gorse slopes that evening.

Low tide was less than an hour away. The bay was cloaked in inky navy, but I could hear the rushing of the retreating ocean. I jogged down the path in near-total darkness—my feet knew its rises and hollows by now—and soon picked out the deep black of the eerie tower ruins, blotting out the stars.

It wasn't long before footsteps scraped on the path. Avrix's slim figure materialized from the darkness, garbed in a night-robe over a silk shirt and hose. I tried to calm my juddering heart and shoved my hands deep into the pockets of my breeches.

"You came."

He smiled, his eyes betraying a hard glint. Of what—impatience, interest?—I couldn't tell. "But of course. We have a job to do together, do we not? And time is moving on. You were right to summon me."

I stepped a little closer. "Yes, that's what I needed to talk to you about. I've had to ask the Ca–"—my eyes flitted around us, the darkness disconcerting—"the *people* we discussed to come earlier. In three days, actually."

He merely squinted, contemplating me in silence. "Oh?" he said eventually, lightly. "And why might that be?"

"Brigant Shearwater wasn't pleased the night of the ball. Because of . . . well, because of this." I gestured to the crumbling tower, or what was left of it. "He wanted to get rid of me, but Vercha spoke to him. I have one week to impress him, but he could change his mind at any time."

"Yes," Avrix said, raising a thick eyebrow. "Vercha said there'd been some trouble. I was sorry to hear it. But why should that matter?" He gazed at me as though trying to decide something. "Forgive me for saying it, but should you be . . . dismissed, *I* shall still be here to complete the assigned task."

I frowned. "You're leaving, too, aren't you, in a few days? Our . . . friends were originally going to come at next pallwater. They told me I need to time the damage just right, and I'll need to be here to pass on my information. The secrets. Besides, there'd be no one left to warn them if anything changes, if Rexim leaves . . ."

He was nodding shallowly, brow furrowed in concentration. "As I said, my own contact and I were rather rushed. I'm sure you were given more instruction than I was."

Up at the castle, lamps were burning in West Tower, but aside from that, the fortress was shrouded. As I looked back at Avrix, my cheeks grew hot. "There's something else I need to tell you. My tools . . . they got washed away when I . . ."

He gave me a pained look. "I'm sorry they sent you down there. Lucky I'm here, eh?" The grimace became a grin. "The family's bedchambers will have to wait until daytime, but the armory and the statues . . . I was going to go there now."

"I can be your lookout," I said, mirroring his smile.

Pulse speeding now, I followed him up the path. Working as a pair, we might actually crack this. In three days, if Kielty had got my note, I'd finally get the answers I craved about Zennia. Rexim Shearwater would get what was coming to him. And Morgen and the siblings . . . they'd be caught up in the fray.

The thought of it should have buoyed me onward. Despite the setbacks, all was getting back on track.

So why did unease still prickle at me like an itch?

28

Somehow, between my meeting with Avrix and the first sallow slivers of dawn the next morning, I managed to snatch a few hours of restless sleep. Eventually I mustered just enough energy to climb from my bed and tug on some clothes.

I'd heard nothing from Kielty in response to my note, and my unease was snowballing as each hour passed. What if someone at the Veil recognized the crow and sent the note back to Miss Haney, or even Rexim? By now I'd worried at my lower lip so much that the skin was cracked and tasted of iron.

Intending to head to the cove again to practice, I rubbed my tired eyes and glanced out the window. It looked down over the deserted outer ward, which was picked out in grays, the stones swathed in shadow. Satisfied that there was no one about, I made to turn, when my eye caught movement.

A figure. Striding out across the sparse grass below.

I stepped to the window, squinting down through the glass. It was Llir again, clad in a night-robe and mantle. Just like the last time I'd seen him this early, he crossed to the same round, ivy-covered tower, pulled a key from his pocket, and slipped through the door.

Seconds ticked by, and I saw no more of him. That burning curiosity sparked in my core.

Miss Haney kept copies of every key in the castle. I'd seen them hanging just inside her office door. My pulse picked up, my blood thrumming with opportunity.

No, my mind commanded. *Absolutely not.*

But the thought was there now, insistent, like an insect. A fly careering around in my skull.

You could be silent, a persuasive part of me murmured. *In and out quickly. He'd never know you were there.*

I dithered. It was risky; he'd already caught me once. But I told myself I had to know what Llir was doing. I had the false laconite I'd stolen from Emment's room, but I still didn't know if that was proof of anything. The Charter was gone. I had nothing else. I'd told Avrix about Rexim's accounts, and we'd both tried to get into the study to obtain proof, but the Brigant kept the room locked tight at night.

What if this was something the Cage could use? Or even something that could threaten their plans? I'd be doing my duty. Kielty would *want* me to check.

Squashing my misgivings, I stole from my room.

Miss Haney's office was locked at this hour, but she—more fool her—had trusted me with a key. All that time spent buttering her up was paying off in more ways than one. The copies hung from hooks on the wall, helpfully labelled, and I found the one I needed quickly.

Locking up the office, I crept to the ward. A blustery breeze tossed my sleep-rumpled hair, and I tugged the hood of my cloak up over it.

The air was bitter, a prelude to winter, and Rhianne's patched breeches with holes in the pockets, her thin cloak, which dangled around my mid-calves, did little to keep it from chilling my skin.

I stared at the tower, at the slits in its stone, and thought of the nightclothes Llir had been wearing. Was he meeting someone? My neck grew hot. I remembered Morgen Cormorant's flirting, the murmurs the two had exchanged at the ball. It hadn't looked very significant at the time, but what if I stumbled on something I shouldn't?

I sensed the heat in my neck creep downward—and another curl of that strange and shocking envy.

With fingers that trembled not just from the cold, I slid in the key and turned it slowly, wincing as the inevitable *clunk* rang out. I paused, listening to the huff of my breath. Silence. I eased the door open carefully. Stepping through, I was faced with a spiralling staircase, an arrow slit facing out to the bay. I stilled again, listening, but heard only the wind, which whined ghoulishly up in the eaves of the tower. Trying to keep my footsteps light, I padded upward, hugging the wall.

The tower was high, and before long I was panting. Despite the chill, strands of hair stuck to my neck. There were round chambers visible through open doorways—for archers, I guessed, to aim down at the causeway—but dust lay thick on their bare wooden floorboards.

At the top, I was faced with another heavy door, cracked open, revealing a strip of slate sky. The roof. I heard the thin whine of the wind. And below it, just audible—

A murmur.

A voice.

I knew I should turn around and leave, but my smoldering need to know all the secrets on this island spurred me to take the last step up to the gap.

The door was set into a small, low turret. The roof of the tower, all stark stone and battlements, stretched away to my right, curving out of sight. Tugging my hood further over my head and sidling through the doorway, my whole body tensed, I peeked around the wall—and saw Llir, facing away from me. I could hear him speaking, and my gaze flashed around the roof, but there was no one there.

He was talking to himself.

Puzzled, breath hitching, I tried to catch what he was saying but couldn't make the words out over the droning of the wind.

The wind.

With a sick shock, the truth crashed over me—*Llir was a Gustmouth*—and I stood frozen, dumbfounded.

The air was swirling messily around him. A chaotic vortex. He muttered to it again.

Heart kicking wildly, I turned to leave. I was still clutching the heavy tower key in my fingers and, without thinking, I dropped it into my pocket, intending to vanish the way I'd come.

Thunk.

The noise was gunshot clear.

I looked down. The key was lying at my feet. I thrust my hand into the pocket—*it had no bottom.* These breeches were Rhianne's, and the stitching had come loose.

A scrape behind me. A grunt of surprise. I lurched for the door, but a strong gust slammed it closed. Falling against it, I wrestled with the latch, but a second later, I felt Llir's hands on me.

"Show yourself!"

He dragged me backward, his arm snaking up to try to hook around my throat.

I stumbled and fell, pulling his arms down with me, and we rolled, limbs knocking, my cloak tangling in his legs.

Before I really knew what I'd done, I thrust out my elbow, snapped it up into his jaw. He jerked back, grunting, and I staggered to my feet.

Breathless, we faced each other, Llir in a crouch. At some point in the scuffle, my hood had come down, and I saw fierce recognition flare in his eyes.

"Of course it's you," he said, the corner of his mouth quirking, sneerlike. His gaze was knife sharp, his hair tumbled by the wind. "Tigo said he'd come across you lurking. You were in *my* room, too, weren't you? A week ago. What is it this time—come to scrub bird droppings off the battlements?"

I scowled back. Excuses whirled through my head—the ones I'd prepared in case I was caught in the castle—but none of them were going to fly up here.

Instead I stepped back, my shoulders sagging. "I . . . followed you," I said eventually. "I saw you from my window. Wanted to know what you were doing."

He stared at me, taken aback by my bluntness. But I couldn't summon even the flimsiest lie. "Zennia—your old Floodmouth. She left a sort of diary. Said she'd spotted lights up here, and I . . . I guess I just got curious."

At last he rose, flicking his tongue over his lips. "I suppose we should have just told you from the start. The others know: Tigo, Mawre, Rhianne. But"—his eyes darted intensely—"we didn't know if we could trust you. Father . . . doesn't like people knowing."

Of course he wouldn't. Goose bumps rose on my arms, and not because of the chill in the air.

This was it: the secret I needed. The secret the Cage could use against Rexim.

"It was obvious, then?" he added, massaging his jaw. He winced. "That hurt quite a lot, you know."

"Sorry," I said, flushing. I'd elbowed a *Shearwater*. "I mean, it was obvious something was going on. The furtive looks. The way you all cut off speaking. You haven't exactly come across as . . . normal."

Cogs now clicked into gear in my mind. "*That's* why Tigo tails you so closely. So anyone near you who's wearing laconite thinks it's *him* setting it off. We're your cover."

"Congratulations," he said brittlely, "on your powers of deduction."

"But if I noticed," I said, "surely others would, too?"

He turned slightly, glancing out at the sunrise. Dragged a hand through his wind-tossed hair. "Not necessarily. Not the Hundred, at least. It's tradition for us to have Orha with us. We don't really bother when we're not in company, but now, with the Cormorants, and back at the ball . . ." His eyes ran over me. "Well, you've seen the charades we have to keep up."

I studied him sidelong in the sun's pink glow. I was seeing him anew. It all slotted into place.

I thought of Rexim's luncheon. The ball guests. Morgen. If even one member of the Hundred found out, it would spread through the Houses like ink in water.

And as for marriage within the nobility, even a mere liaison with one of them . . . As much as I'd found myself envying Morgen, their murmured remarks, their comfortable banter, it was clear now: Llir could never allow himself to be alone with her. Or anyone else draped in laconite.

"No one can know," I said slowly, quietly, "because it's . . ."

Shameful.

The unvoiced word hung between us.

He looked awkward; angry. I thought he'd tell me to leave. But a few seconds later, he rubbed at his eyes. They were shadowed; I remembered the siblings' late night.

When he finally spoke, it was with that same meditative quality that had crept over him when he'd watched Emment sleep.

"Father pretends it doesn't exist. Always has. Won't countenance any mention of it, let alone use of it." He frowned, adding, with forced dismissiveness, "Not that I need to anyway. When I was young, I was scared of it. After that, I hated it." Something black entered his eyes, which were fixed on the dawn sky. "Now . . . I don't know. I got curious, I suppose." His eyes flicked to me, almost resentful, as though that curiosity was somehow my fault.

"Your father would lose everything if people knew he'd kept this secret."

Llir had no idea, I thought uncomfortably. No clue what this revelation meant, how I could use it . . .

He winced at my matter-of-factness. "Only one of us," he said eventually, "out of all the Hundred, is openly Orha. Iovawn Crake."

The towering Mudmouth flashed into my mind.

"But he's a soldier," Llir went on. "A warmonger. He uses his . . . talent . . . to subdue their enemies. His father was open about it. Brazen. Took hold of it before it could be used against him."

"And that won't work for you," I said. Prejudice, I knew, was rarely consistent.

He gave a hollow laugh. "Do I look like I enjoy violence?"

My cheeks warmed a little. I looked away, at the sunrise.

"No," he continued. "The Crakes, they're like that. But Father styles himself as above that kind of thing. We weren't always. Grandmother Velda was a skirmisher. But Father thinks time is moving on, that the Houses are growing tired of the constant fighting."

"Are they?"

He was silent a moment. "It was close at first. But then Father pulled ahead in the vote. He's still a traditionalist, and the Houses like that, but he prefers to settle squabbles in the Chamber. In the courts."

His mention of the vote brought the Cage to my mind, and my own secret—the reckoning that could be two days away. As much as

Llir insisted Rexim didn't default to violence, I was pretty certain the Brigant would make an exception for me if he discovered my part in what was coming.

I hugged myself under my cloak and thought of the laconite Avrix was working on. At once, another cog moved into place in my mind.

The false laconite. It was all there for Llir.

"We don't really bother when we're not in company . . ."

Of *course* the family would want fake laconite. Just as Llir had to ensure Orha were near him whenever he was in the presence of anyone wearing laconite, so, too, as a noble, would he have to wear it himself. And what could be more annoying than that? Even my stints with the pendant on my journey here had irritated me, set my nerves on edge. I couldn't imagine a lifetime of it. And his family . . . they clearly found it bothersome, too. With false versions, they could keep up appearances, adhere to all the latest fashions, while not having to endure that constant buzzing.

And, I realized with a burst of adrenaline, *I had some,* sequestered away in my room. The pin I'd taken from Emment's bedchamber on the night of the ball, when I'd run into Avrix. It was proof. Hard evidence that Llir was Orha. I had what I needed for the Cage.

I'd succeeded.

My gaze must have drifted, as Llir gave me an odd look.

"I . . . I have to go," I said. "I have to get on with my chores."

He stepped toward me. "I don't suppose I need to tell you not to speak of this to anyone."

His proximity reminded me of our dance at the ball. Seeing the way the sun's rays lit his cheekbones, my insides knotted and my tongue went dry. I managed to shake my head. "No, of course not. I won't."

He seemed about to say something else, but then he clearly thought better of it, for he frowned faintly and shifted away.

I took the opportunity to turn and leave, snatching up the key as I hurried past it. But I was halfway down the spiral stairs when quick footsteps sounded on the stone behind me, a voice at my back, slightly breathless.

"Corith."

My stomach did something strange, as if I were about to plunge from a great height—or was already falling. Llir hovered in the shadows above me, one velvet-clad arm braced against the curving wall.

"Yes?"

His jaw worked as though he was arguing with himself. Finally he forced out: "How do you do it? Control your emotions? Enough to make it work—properly."

I stared at him, wide-eyed. "What? Why?"

I couldn't quite tell if I was imagining it, but the faintest hint of rose seemed to enter his pale cheeks.

"Does it matter why? I just want to know."

I frowned. "Haven't you asked the others?"

"I did," he said reluctantly. His face was guarded. "But Tigo and Mawre, they seem to be naturals. And Rhianne—she told me what they taught her, at that . . . school, but it's never really worked for me. What did they teach *you*?"

My gaze skittered. "They tell us lots of things. But, well, for me, nothing's ever worked quite as well as a trick a . . . a friend once taught me."

He watched me from the shadows, silent a moment. Then he said, "I saw you. Down at the cove. Practicing."

It took me a second to process what he meant. That flutter of black; a cloak's hem disappearing. "You saw me," I said, frown deepening. "You followed me?"

"Looks like we have that in common." He raised an eyebrow.

As my face warmed, he sighed and scrunched at his hair. "I won't say anything, if that's what you're worried about. My silence for yours."

After a pause, I nodded.

"So, will you share that trick with me? Here, tomorrow. Same place, same time."

My heart thudded dully in my chest. Two days until the date I'd told Kielty to come. Two days until the Shearwaters' lives could be upended. The nauseous dread that had been clawing at my insides returned. I found I couldn't look Llir in the eye.

"All right. Tomorrow." Everything had to appear normal.

"I'll leave the door unlocked," he said.

We stood there. Something in the air felt charged.

"Goodbye, then," Llir said, oddly formal. I nodded; I didn't trust my voice not to waver.

I turned, practically running down the steps, not waiting to see if he was coming down after me.

I woke the next morning under a shroud of foreboding.

I'd still not heard even a whisper from Kielty. I had no idea if my note had found him, if he and his group would be coming tomorrow. Maybe he'd thought it safer not to reply. Or perhaps, I brooded as I pulled on some breeches, the day itself would come and go and Rexim would decide he was better off without me.

I'd risen early again, planning to go down to the cove, then remembered with a lurch that I'd agreed to meet Llir.

My chest felt heavy as I tugged on Rhianne's clothes. I never normally paid much attention to my appearance, but now I found myself in front of my cracked mirror, peering blearily at my bird's-nest hair. I dragged a brush through it, braided it, fiddled with it. I half wished I had Vercha's powders from the ball. Then I frowned, flicked my gaze down to the washstand, knowing that how I looked hardly mattered. Tomorrow, if the Cage had heeded my message, they'd descend on the island. And what then, for me?

By now, after what I'd witnessed of the Hundred, I felt queasy at the prospect of continuing to serve them. Perhaps Kielty's people could smuggle me out. I could bargain Llir's secret for a placement elsewhere, far enough away to be anonymous, to be out of Rexim's reach . . . Surely, with all their contacts, including at Arbenhaw, the Cage could wrangle something like that.

But if it turned out Rexim couldn't be persuaded? What would the Cage do to the Shearwaters then?

I shivered. I had to admit to myself that the prospect of Catua or Llir coming to harm, or Rhianne or Mawre or even Tigo, unsettled me. My loyalties felt muddied, my allegiances blurred.

Fighting to wrestle down my unease, I straightened my bodice and hurried from my room. The outer ward was cast in shadow, and the solid, leaden clouds above the battlements threatened rain. The door to Llir's ivy-clad tower was ajar, and when I pushed it open, I found him within, a few steps up the spiralling staircase, leaning his back and shoulders against the wall.

I noticed he'd made something of an effort, too. No sleep-ruffled hair, no velvety night-robe. He was dressed for the day in a black doublet and hose, brownish-gold locks swept back off his forehead.

I knew the normal thing to say would be "Good morning," but I'd never seemed able to make small talk that wasn't stilted. Greetings that tripped off the tongue for others always sounded somehow disingenuous from me. I'd long learned to default to silence instead.

He surveyed me for a moment in the dimness of the stairwell. After our run-in the day before, something new seemed to have settled between us. A private knowledge—an understanding—and it made my skin fizzle with a strange, awkward intimacy.

Eventually he came down the steps toward me. "I'll lock us in," he said, "so we're not disturbed." As he leaned past me, turned the key in the lock, the shadows gathered beneath his cheekbones. He turned and started back up the stairs.

As I followed, I found myself pondering just why he wanted—or even needed—to know this trick. Since I'd been stationed on the island, he hadn't seemed to have much trouble controlling his emotions. I was thinking of Emment, of the contrast between the brothers: the elder's chaotic whims; the younger's inscrutability. But how much of that had been the secret Llir was keeping?

I knew all too well that appearances could be deceiving. People had always claimed *I* was calm. At Arbenhaw the Instructors had praised my impassivity. Only Zennia had known the turmoil that bubbled beneath the mask.

A thin drizzle was falling as we emerged onto the roof. Llir walked to the center of the round stone space and turned to face me, his gaze assessing.

Lowering myself to the floor, I neatly crossed my legs. "It's easier to sit at first," I said. "It grounds you."

He copied me, folding his long legs together.

I eyed him, trying to mask my discomfort. I felt supremely unsuited to this situation. I'd never, in all my eighteen years, *taught* anybody anything before.

"What are you feeling?" I asked. "Right now?"

He looked at me with a shade of suspicion. "Uncertainty, I suppose," he said after a moment. I could almost sense the conflict within him: the curiosity he'd mentioned; the years of resentment butting against it.

"All right. Take that uncertainty," I said. "Now, close your eyes."

He closed them with a slight frown.

"Try to picture the uncertainty in your mind's eye. As though it were in front of you. What does it look like?"

With his eyes firmly closed, I was at leisure to study him. I took in his lithe frame, his rain-flecked features, the crease between his brows, his damp, now-curling hair. I usually avoided looking too long at other people; it almost felt forbidden to be staring this way. I watched his Adam's apple bob upward as he swallowed, saw his tongue flick over his narrow lips before he spoke.

"It looks like . . . wings," he said in a low voice. "Like hundreds and hundreds of fluttering wings."

I blinked, surprised, pulled out of my reverie. "Wings," I repeated, falling silent for a moment. It felt like knowledge I, of all people, shouldn't have of him. "All right. Can—can you try to force them together? Into a group? Maybe a ball?"

His brows quirked together. "Yes, I suppose so."

"Keep forcing them. As though you're stuffing a load of birds into a—a sack."

I felt foolish, but the ghost of a smile touched his face.

"Imagine clipping their wings. Or—or baking them into a pie, I don't know."

To my sudden, soaring delight, a single peal of laughter escaped him, echoing off the stone into the damp, chill air.

"Okay," he said, eyes still closed. "Fine. I'm doing it."

"Keep going," I said, "until the wings aren't flapping anymore, or until they're all gone, wherever you've put them. When I do this, I picture a . . . a scarlet ball. Like lightning, or a fire. I squeeze it down to a pinprick."

My neck was growing warmer as I spoke. Aside from Zennia, I'd never shared this with anyone.

Llir's eyes snapped open. He held my stare.

"How do you feel now?" I asked with trepidation.

His shoulders had lowered; his frown had smoothed out. "Not . . . uncertain anymore," he said, watching me.

"Then try it now," I pressed him. "Speak."

His chest rose and fell shallowly with his breaths. His eyes found the battlements, the clouds stretching out beyond.

"Circle us," he murmured. It took only a few seconds. The air stirred, and a breeze wafted against my face.

"And you," I said to the strengthening drizzle, which had turned our hair curly and soaked into our cloaks.

As we sat there cross-legged, facing each other, the breeze picked up, swirling in a vortex around us. Flecks of dirt were whipped up with it, a few feathers left by perching gulls. The rain reluctantly trailed after the wind, encircling us in a haze of fine droplets. It spun faster, catching the edges of my clothes.

And then it came. The first genuine smile he'd given me. It was slow, spreading like dawn light over his features. It took me a second—I felt pinned, off-balance—but I flashed one back at him, my insides swooping.

But hot on its heels, that dread crept back in, the recollection of everything already set in motion. My anxiety flared like a white-hot flame.

Llir looked as though he was struggling, too. His smile had faded, and an odd look crossed his face. The wind died, sputtering out like a rushlight, and the rain once again encroached onto our heads. I blinked water from my eyes and dropped my gaze. "Sorry," I mumbled, feeling my hair stick to my neck.

He shook his head, rolled his shoulders stiffly. "I need to focus more," he said. "I lost it."

"Positive emotions can spook it, too."

He caught my eye. That strange look flashed again.

A moment later, he climbed to his feet. "Let's go. We're getting soaked up here."

I hurried after him to the shelter of the doorway, where he held the door open for me to go first.

"Thank you for this," he said as I passed him, and I paused, my elbow brushing his doublet.

"It's nothing," I said, glancing up at him. "Like I said, just a little trick."

He was watching me, studying me, face etched with a small frown. Then he blinked and stepped back, and I slipped through the door, grateful to descend into the dimness.

30

The following afternoon found me in the corridor with the statues. I was strung out like wire, my whole body aching. My lack of sleep was catching up with me.

I'd managed to train in the cove in the morning—an hour in the predawn shadows and stillness—but it wasn't enough; the archwater waves were growing fiercer. Over the past week, I thought I felt a tenuous connection, a disgruntled acceptance of my grovelling apologies, but it was frail. The tide was still capricious.

The previous day, I'd been Avrix's lookout again.

Much of his time was taken up rehearsing, or lounging in the snug or parlor with the Shearwaters, but yesterday he feigned a headache and left—"A glass too many last night, I fear." I lingered, jittery, within earshot of the others as Emment and Vercha argued about a scene. In the end, none of them set foot near West Tower, and Avrix reappeared later, face unreadable.

Now, as I manually washed down the floors, I stepped close to the statues, to their laconite eyes. The faint ringing I'd by now grown accustomed to seemed quieter, intermittent, almost forlorn. Would the other Orha servants, or Llir, notice? I had to hope they'd learned to tune the noise out by now.

And then there was the treacherous sliver of me that hoped that someone *would* notice. That this reckoning would never come.

When I peered closely at the eyes, I could see Avrix's damage: hairline cracks, barely visible in the stone, spiralling out like spiderwebs. I thought of the armory, the bedchambers, even the gatehouse . . . all that laconite rendered weak, near useless.

Soon the only working laconite on the island would be the smallest beads, which were difficult to crack. In anticipation of the Cage's arrival—the turmoil that would hit the island in a day—Avrix and I had pilfered some each: two bags of gems from the backs of dusty drawers, which I fervently hoped wouldn't be missed before tomorrow.

"Corith!"

I jumped, dropping my washcloth. Vercha was striding determinedly toward me, and I clasped my trembling fingers behind my back.

"There you are." She was bright-eyed, turned out perfectly in black sable. "The Cormorants' Gustmouth has wrenched his ankle. He was out with the twins shooting birds this morning. Quite lame, poor thing. But it means we need you."

I opened my mouth, but she pressed on, gaze glinting.

"We're putting on *Cithre's Folly* tonight—you know, our little theatrical? But their Gustmouth can't walk, and he had a small part . . . I said you'd be more than happy to stand in for him."

She smiled at me delightedly, as if she'd done me a great service. My stomach dropped, and my face must have shown it, for she patted me reassuringly on the arm. "Don't worry, it's not a speaking part. They're tableaux scenes, just poses in the background. But the banqueting scene . . . it just won't *work* without you."

Her eyes were beseeching. I had no choice. Nothing could seem suspicious until the Cage came tomorrow. And if they didn't, if they stuck to their original date, I had to endeavor to remain on the island . . . Rexim would decide on my future tomorrow, and an angry Vercha would surely sway his mind. I swallowed and nodded, forcing a fake smile.

"Wonderful. Meet us in the ballroom at eight."

Eight o'clock rolled around far too quickly. The chimes were like a funeral knell as I dragged myself across the castle to the ballroom.

"Ah," came Morgen's voice as I entered. "There's our spy."

I stared at her in horror.

She laughed lightly. "Your role, in our banqueting scene. The informant who tells the heir his cousins are plotting to have him killed." Her dark eyes glittered with amusement in the lamplight. "She looks like she's being sent to her execution, Vercha. Should we spare her the ordeal?"

I sucked in a long breath.

Vercha pursed her lips, came striding toward me. "Come now, Corith. You're doing us a great favor. Here. Put this on. And here's your mask." She handed me a neatly folded white bundle.

Two sets of wooden screens had been erected. One was tall and elaborately painted—a scene of hanging gardens, distant towers, curling vines. The second set hid what I guessed was "backstage." There were leather cases spilling over with costumes, a rail of cloaks, a nest of thin swords. As Ferda loped past with an armful of more weapons—props, I supposed, for some battle scene—Vercha propelled me to a full-length mirror. There stood Llir in a mask and black shirt.

"Move," Vercha trilled. "Corith needs to get changed."

He caught my eye briefly, and my stomach gave a tug. "She's taking this very seriously," he said in an undertone, and his sister swiped his arm with a fan as he strode off.

I dressed quickly. My costume was a long white gown, like something an ancient acolyte might have worn. My mask, too, was plain white, expressionless. As I fixed it to my eyes, surveyed myself in the mirror, it brought to my mind the jester at the Veil.

I shivered. I was glad of this false face tonight. I worried my treachery was painted across my features.

Before long, Catua made an appearance, trailed by the families' remaining Orha and, at last, an already tipsy Emment. The heir seemed jovial enough this evening, but ever since our encounter after the ball, his jaunty veneer had begun to slip. Something within him seemed to have altered. I thought I could see doubts—a new, wretched darkness—and I couldn't interpret his fixed, hollow stares as anything other than guilt about Zennia.

I'd found myself weighing up whether, when the Cage came, I could use the opportunity for a reckoning with him.

Rhianne and Mawre were tasked with special effects, helped by Orran, the incapacitated Gustmouth, who perched on a bench beneath an open window and coaxed in breezes for the scenes on ships' prows. Rhianne had started a fire in the hearth. "Atmospheric lighting," she murmured as she passed me.

A few other servants had minor parts, and they primped and paced, repeating their brief lines. Soon the ragtag audience arrived. The Brigant himself, closely trailed by his wolfhounds, settled in a gilt chair in front of the stage, pipe in one hand, wine in the other. A cluster of footmen perched behind him, and I even saw a gaggle of guards from the gatehouse along the back wall, bantering with each other.

"Ahem," came a voice. A costumed Avrix Cormorant, his matchlock pistol strapped to his belt. Emment played a series of trills on the spinet.

"Cithre's Folly," Avrix intoned deeply. "A theatrical. Performed by Houses Shearwater and Cormorant. Long may they be allies." He gave a sweeping bow, and on his way up, he cut a swift glance in my direction.

Rexim looked amused.

And thus it began.

Morgen was the eponymous Cithre, the Brigantess embroiled in an affair with her Orha. Emment played his nefarious role with great zeal, despite the effects of a few goblets of wine. I watched as lines tripped off his tongue with no prompting, his gestures expansive—he wore the character like a cloak.

Avrix was the tragic hero, the spurned husband, but there were subplots galore involving the others. Llir played the heir, Catua and Vercha his cousins. The girls took on their murderous personas with gusto, kitted out in helmets and swords. And scattered throughout the melodramatics were tableaux: still life scenes laid out behind the actors.

About halfway through, I was tuning out. The names were all blurring—Eulix, Aumar—and my thoughts were bent toward what tomorrow would bring. I was only jerked from my ruminations by Vercha hissing my name from the stage.

"Sorry," I whispered, adjusting my mask. I hurried into the tableau. Rhianne brought up the light.

The scene was a sumptuous feast, an imaginary banquet. I was to walk across it and bend to whisper in the heir's ear in front of Vercha and Catua: the traitors, the betrayers. Vercha held up an invisible platter, while Catua mimed taking a great gulp of wine.

It hit me suddenly: The heir was Llir. Cheeks burning—but hidden by my mask, with any luck—I approached him, bent toward him, held a palm to my lips. We all froze in place, holding the tableau, as Avrix and Emment strode into the foreground.

"Faithful steward! Mine eyes see true now." Avrix twirled one of the swords, advancing. "Hold! Thou shalt get thy requital."

Llir had stilled with his face tilted toward me.

His mask was silver, the eyes edged in black, the nose slightly pointed: an owl's snub beak. I could see every strand of golden-brown hair, slicked back for the role but curled around his ears. I stared at the stubble dusting his jaw, the pale skin peering from beneath his high collar.

Though he didn't move a muscle, his eyes slid to mine. He could probably feel my warm breath on his ear. I held it in, gnawing my lip reflexively, and his gaze flickered downward to my mouth. He blinked.

"Woe! Oh, torment!"

Emment had "stabbed" Avrix, who lay groaning and twitching on the ground. Rexim chuckled. Morgen hovered on the sidelines.

The scene broke up. The tableau was over.

The four of us at the banquet jumped into motion, and as I moved away, my leg brushed Llir's knee. I stole off the stage with my heart banging wildly, the skin on my thigh tingling, my damp gown clinging to me.

As the final act of the play unfolded, I donned a cloak and hid backstage. Morgen had taken the floor for the finale; her rich voice rang out like an orator's under the rafters.

My thoughts were whirling. What was *happening* to me?

I didn't seem able to be anywhere near Llir Shearwater without a zinging in my skin, a stutter in my pulse, a burning need for him to look at me, to notice me.

It had worsened since I'd discovered he was Orha. He was *like me*. I wanted to speak to him again. To know about his childhood, his relationship with Rexim. I wanted to know his fears, his desires . . .

His desires.

At that thought, and with trembling fingers, I decanted a measure of wine into a tumbler. It was impossible. Foolish. Llir was Hundred. I was Orha.

And the possibility remained—stark and bone cold—that tomorrow, absolutely none of this would matter.

After the play came the dancing and cavorting.

The stage and screens were cleared away, but we stayed in our costumes, masks still in place. Rhianne shrank the fire down low and lit the torches. The servants brought in platters of food.

By the time Catua began to play at the spinet, a pleasant tingling sensation simmered in my stomach and I was already starting to forget about the Cage.

Although the rational part of me knew I should try to get some rest before the approaching storm, the foolish, reckless part—normally suppressed—was winning, and I poured myself a drop more wine. I liked the way it was blunting my edges, making me fonder of everything and everyone.

The notes of the spinet were spiralling, melding, and soon a wine-fuelled galliard began. Images lurched out at me: Morgen and Emment twirling; Llir, mask glinting, goblet in hand, dancing with Vercha, lips stretched in a smile.

"Top up?" came a voice. I looked up to see Avrix. His gold mask sparkled as he filled my glass, and behind it, his eyes were flashing knowingly. But before I could sip from it, Vercha was before me, pulling me from my chair, saying something that didn't register. I was tugged into the dance, my white skirts swishing, the music sounding exquisite to my ear.

As we stepped and spun, circled and clapped, I couldn't help turning my gaze to Llir. It was hard to tell through the silvery mask, but I thought I caught him watching me, too. A strange anticipation fizzled in me, as if something was on the cusp of happening between us.

Morgen took Catua's place at the spinet, the pretty trills of country jigs giving way to a slower, more sedate pavane. We stepped near and around and away from each other like courting birds putting on a display.

Outside the windows the sky was ebony. Time had seemed to flash by in an instant. Distantly I heard the clock chime two—Rexim was gone, as were most of the servants. I looked around for the other Orha, but only a few of House Cormorant's were left, lurking in shadow, silently watching. Avrix and Catua were playing a duet, Morgen and the other Shearwaters still dancing.

My legs were burning, the bones of my feet aching, and I was tired—so tired—after my snatched hours of sleep. I would fall down in a slumber where I stood if I stayed here, if I didn't head up and get some rest soon. Reluctantly I slipped out of the ballroom, a small smile touching my lips as I went. The notes of the songs ran in loops through my head, my mind pleasantly buzzy, all thoughts of the Cage banished.

As I climbed the spiral steps, I was so preoccupied that I barely registered the padding of footsteps behind me. It wasn't until a hand caught my arm, spun me gently around, that I realized Llir had followed me.

"Corith," he repeated. He'd been calling my name.

His mask flashed silver in the glow from the lamps: an owl swooping up at me out of the darkness.

I stumbled on the lip of the stair, put my hands out to steady myself. He caught me by the upper arms, gripping them lightly.

"Whoa," he said. "Steady." He was two steps below me. As I found my balance, he stepped up, our eyes level.

I smiled. "Following me again," I accused him.

He cocked a thin eyebrow. "How much wine did you have?"

"Just the right amount," I said contentedly, smiling wider.

Beneath his mask, his mouth quirked into a smirk. His eyes were intense, the color of a storm. "I came to ask you something," he murmured, voice deep.

I leaned in. "Is it something secret? Is that why we're whispering?" A new, thrilling boldness had infused me.

He looked surprised for a second; then his gaze grew darker. Our masked faces were inches apart.

"Very secret," he said, in little more than a thrum.

My eyes flicked downward. His did the same. There was a hot curl of something like fire in my abdomen.

I knew I should take a step back up the stair. That tipping toward him was a terrible idea. But his fingers were on my waist, each one a brand, and they were pressing me incrementally, inexorably nearer.

"Corith," Llir huffed out. His breath was warm spice, his tone halfway between want and warning. Our lips brushed together; our masks bumped gently. It was almost a trial, to see if we wanted more.

And it wasn't enough. He deepened the kiss, something almost fierce in the movement.

Then—a peal of laughter from below.

We both started and glanced down the stairs. But the sound had come from the ballroom—Vercha's high cackle.

I shook my head, a strange buzzing in my ears. What in hells was I doing? This was dangerous.

"I was going to ask if you'll meet me again." His gaze locked onto mine once more. Where his hand still gripped me, my skin felt scorched. "Tomorrow morning. To practice that trick."

I swallowed, feeling suddenly uneasy.

Tomorrow.

My thoughts jumped jerkily to the Cage.

As I stared at him, the lamplight limning his hair, a dark and dreadful longing came over me—a longing to spill everything out to him, right here and now. To tug out this wicked fishhook of a secret and bleed the truth, no matter the damage.

I wanted to warn him. To tell him to run. Or perhaps running was what *I* ought to do. My part in all this was finished, wasn't it? Avrix and I had prepared the way for the Cage . . . Did I really have to linger for what came next?

He watched me, eyes narrowing in confusion. "If you'd rather not . . ." His tone was guarded.

I opened my mouth to say, "Of course I'll come," for I knew I couldn't give in to that longing, nor could I run, abandoning my only chance of ever finding out what had happened to Zennia. But my throat was dry; the words stuck fast.

"All right," Llir said quietly. "Good night, then." He turned.

"Wait," I bit out, moving after him. I could save this.

But Llir, now three steps down, had frozen. An arrow slit there looked down over the bay, and slowly he walked over to it, staring.

"What is it?" I said dully. It looked pitch-black out there to me. My thoughts were fuzzy, my lips buzzing after that kiss.

He wrenched off his mask, let it drop to the floor, gripped the stone with white fingers as he gazed through the opening.

"What is that?" he muttered, more to himself than to me, but I dutifully joined him, peering out, too.

From our lofty viewpoint, looking southwest, we could see the island, deep black on navy, sweeping down to the edge of the mudflats.
The moons were out, nearly converging, casting a weak, silver glow on the bay, but the pinewood and the beach were wreathed in white mist. It was low tide—it must have been later than I thought—and the flats were vast and yawning and empty.

But there, halfway along the causeway—

Muted yellow lights approaching the island. Eight or maybe ten in total, spaced out in a long, snaking line, like fireflies.

"Torches," Llir breathed.

My thoughts felt sluggish. "Why . . . why in intervals like that?"

"Look," he said, shifting, giving me more room. "You see the darker areas, black clusters around them? Men. Groups of them. One torch at the head of each."

Like a procession.

Or a fighting force.

My insides flopped. My pulse picked up.

No. They were a whole night early. I'd said a sevenday—not to come till full archwater. My panic was mixed with irrational anger. Though I knew, in truth, it would make little difference in the end.

"Ten torches," he whispered. "And the way they're spaced out . . ." I watched as his lips moved silently. "Eighty, maybe a hundred men."

A hundred men.

My lips clammed up. Llir stared at me for a few long seconds, then wheeled, almost pitching forward. He took the steps downward two at a time.

His frantic shouts, when they finally came, echoed sharply under the high ceiling.

"Father . . . *Father!*"

It made no sense. It made no sense at all.

I stood, paralyzed with shock, in the stairwell. A hundred men. Far more than I'd expected. That was an infantry company, a small army . . . I'd thought the Cage would just send Orha. I moved to the window as though in a trance and stared, disbelieving, down at the causeway. Why had they come that way? Out in the open?

They had to have tracked across the flats at first, to avoid a march right through Port Rhorstin. But I'd envisioned the Cage keeping more of a low profile, sneaking in from the unguarded east. Even at archwater, when the tide was well out, boats could be floated on the slow-moving rivers. It was daring, and they'd have to be quick about it, but with a couple of Floodmouths, it could be done. There were safe areas on the sands they'd know about if they'd done their research.

Shouts from below. The scudding of feet. I jerked into motion.

Avrix. I had to find him.

I hurried back to the imperial staircase, down the wide steps and into the dark entrance hall. There, as I was crossing the flagstones, a figure barrelled out of the shadows and shrieked, "Oh!"

I threw out my hands, staggered backward, but it was only Debry, her brown curls askew.

"Who's that?" She sounded panicked, and I realized I was still wearing my eerie white mask.

"It's me," I said, tugging it off and dropping it.

"Corith. Have you seen Tigo?" She was wide-eyed, breathless. "Master Llir sent me to fetch him. Oh, Moons—do you know?"

She meant the intruders. "I know," I said quickly. "Why do you need Tigo?"

"For his *speaking*, of course." She wrung her hands, terrified. "Will you help me? Will you stay with me?"

I hesitated. I had to find Avrix. But I also knew that I couldn't seem suspicious. I nodded tersely. If we did find the Cormorant, I'd just have to think of some excuse to get rid of Debry.

"Let's try the servants' parlor," I said, crossing the hall.

Debry trailed after me, breathing rapidly. "What's happening? Who is it? When will they get here?"

I didn't reply, though I thought on her last question. The Cage had been more than halfway down the causeway. That meant they'd be here in an hour, maybe less.

Enough time for the Shearwaters to mount a defense—but we had less than half their men. And even if the family sent Tigo out . . . I was certain the Cage would have more Mudmouths than we did.

We.

My treacherous mind snagged on the word. Why was I counting myself among the Shearwaters?

I tried to push away thoughts of the coming clash. With a hundred men, this wasn't "a little chat" with Rexim . . . and it didn't appear to be extortion either. I couldn't bring myself to think about what it meant. About the Shearwaters—Llir—finding out what I'd done . . .

As we jogged toward the servants' parlor, we passed Miss Haney's office door. To my surprise, it was open, light spilling from inside.

"Miss Haney?" called Debry, making for the door.

I followed. The housekeeper didn't usually stay up, even if the family were having a late night.

An odd noise reached my ears: something muffled, unnerving.

"Debry . . ."

But the maid had walked right in. As I stepped around her, she let out a gasp.

The room was lit with smoldering torches, but the grate was cold, the desk clear of papers. A little way inside, I saw four figures. Three on the ground. One sitting in a chair.

Miss Haney, Tigo, and Mawre were kneeling. They were gagged, their wrists and ankles bound. Tigo had a nasty burn on one cheek, his hand ax lying a few feet away. He and Mawre were wearing laconite pendants. As I took them in, their eyes widened; they struggled.

The figure in the chair stood up as I entered. Tall, paper pale, hard-set features, white-blond hair in thick, tight braids. It was the Cormorants' Sparkmouth, Nemaine.

"Good. It's you," she said, her ice-blue eyes taking me in.

My stomach twanged with a horrible confusion, before Debry whimpered and wheeled around. "Wait," I hissed at her, seeing what Nemaine was holding. But the maid seemed determined to disregard me tonight.

As Debry fled the room, Nemaine sighed and pushed past me, raising the light crossbow she held in her arms.

"What are—"

Snap.

My words cut off at the shot.

I cried out, staggering through the doorway into the hall. Debry lay sprawled out on her stomach, a bolt in her back, long and knifelike and terrible.

I sagged. "What did you do?" I bleated thinly. It took everything I had not to sink to the ground.

"Be grateful," the Sparkmouth said. "Clean and quick. I could have burned her, I suppose, but that would have been rather noisy."

She gestured with the crossbow, shepherding me back inside.

"I don't—I don't understand," I stammered. I backed into the room, where the captives looked horrified. "What are you doing?"

She quirked a pale brow. "What do you think?" she answered calmly. "Lord Cormorant told me all about you. We work together; we share the same . . . sentiments. I take it you know our *mutual friends* are arriving. I am helping to prepare the way. To remove . . . obstacles."

"Debry wasn't an obstacle," I said, my body shaking.

A sick, guilty relief washed over me at the realization Nemaine wasn't going to kill me, too. But something about all this didn't sit right. I couldn't think through it—I was unbalanced, my mind sluggish.

Nemaine smiled slowly at me, cocking her head. "Of course she was. She would have alerted the castle. It's best those still abed remain . . . unaware."

Mawre, I saw, understood already.

Our mutual friends.

She stared at me, wide-eyed.

Tigo caught up, and then Miss Haney. I could see the confusion, then the hatred, in their gazes.

"Where's Rhianne?" I forced out, looking away.

"Their Sparkmouth? I don't know," Nemaine said, irritated. "Why don't you make yourself useful and look for her? I tried, but this lot take too much minding." She kicked at Mawre, who glared in response. "Find her. Subdue her. Bring her in here. We need to move stealthily, in this calm before the tempest."

I stayed where I was; my feet felt stuck to the floor.

"Come, now," she said, flashing white teeth at me. "We are allies, though we didn't know it before. We must be quick. Our friends will be here in less than an hour."

I backed away, stumbling over a downed coatrack.

Not long ago, I'd thought I might feel triumphant when the time came. When Rexim, Vercha, and Emment realized there'd been a cuckoo in their nest this whole time. But the rest of them . . . there, everything was gray.

I stared at the captives. At least here they were out the way. Safe—for now—from the Cage's unexpected army.

But in return, their gazes were as sharp as Tigo's hand ax, flashing with that new and awful understanding.

I couldn't stand those stares any longer. I turned and fled.

Pressing the back of my hand to my mouth, I skirted Debry's body and ran full tilt for the stairs.

First order of business: I needed defenses.

The weapons in the entrance hall had been cleaned out, all the sabers and rapiers commandeered for *Cithre's Folly*. There was the armory, of course, but that was back past Debry . . . past Nemaine . . .

Instead, I lurched up the steps to my room, where I levered up a loose floorboard under my bed and brought out two items I'd sequestered there.

The first was the pouch of laconite beads I'd liberated from the backs of the Shearwaters' drawers, for defense against Orha when the day arrived. The pouch buzzed faintly as I pocketed it, its promised protection reassuring me slightly.

My fingers trembled as I drew out the second item: a knife from the kitchens, stubby but sharp. I'd placed it there a few days ago after watching yet another of the siblings' rehearsals, seeing Emment stride back and forth across the stage, playing the villain so convincingly. The ominous feeling that had curled deep within me had become something dark and resentful and wicked. I'd gone to the kitchens to get this knife, hoping that just a few days later, I'd find out—whether from the Cage or from Emment himself—what part he'd really played in my friend's disappearance.

I'd hidden it here with a vague, wild intention to use it for something that scared me: revenge.

Pulling it out now, it looked inadequate, pathetic. Not just for threatening Emment but for defending myself.

I gripped it tight anyway. It was better than nothing. But the feel of the handle against my skin made me pause. So far this night had been a dream, then a nightmare—the dancing, that kiss, then the horror of Debry's death. Now the cold metal on my skin brought it home. It was real. It was happening. And I didn't know if I'd make it out.

Briefly I crouched and let out a sob. Let the panic and misery overwhelm me, just for a second. Then I swallowed, swapped my gown for some breeches, and, with shaking hands, tucked the knife into my belt.

Second order of business:

I had to go and meet the Cage.

I slipped out a side door, avoiding the inner ward. It was a cold, crisp night, the air rich with pine. The twin moons were half veiled by cloud, and the island was bathed in eerie silver. For a moment, glancing out at the bay, I stood puzzled—the clouds were hanging so low. Then I realized it was sea fog, growing denser by the minute.

I hurried west to the causeway, taking a circuitous route, for the guards were probably swarming around the gatehouse. Fingers of mist clawed at me as I ran. I could just see the windows of the ballroom burning gold.

At last, a furnace of adrenaline in my chest, I crept under the low-hanging boughs of the pinewood and picked my way forward through the mist-wreathed trees.

In front of me, the vista unfurled like a blanket: the black, empty bay, the rivers choked by fog. Through the thinner haze that clung to the island, I saw the causeway arcing out like a blade.

And on it, the Cage. Their marching forces. Closer, maybe half an hour off.

Except, I saw now . . . something looked wrong.

Muted moonslight glinted off steel plate, off swords, halberds, helmets, cuirasses. A pair of figures was riding up front: one squat, the other one towering, wide shouldered. Behind them, banners I hadn't spotted before. They fluttered silver gray, dun green, and black, and on them . . . I could only just make it out. A small, plump bird: black feathered, crimson eyed.

My legs were shaking. I sank to the damp ground, grasping at the trunk of the nearest tree.

The army on the causeway wasn't the Cage. It was a House. And there was only one House it could be.

With a monumental effort, I pulled myself up, turned tail, and sprinted back to the castle.

This time I didn't bother to avoid the gatehouse. The guards there couldn't know I'd been spying for the Cage, and in any case, my caution was eclipsed now by shock.

Crake.

I lurched up the path as guards ran back and forth. One, a rat-faced man I recognized—one of the three who'd carted me to the cove all those weeks ago—stalled and sneered, hefting a longbow and quiver. "You," he shouted, "get that Mudmouth! Where is he? He needs to throw up some earth defenses!"

I didn't, couldn't, force out a reply. I darted past him, ignoring his yells. My chest was thumping; every breath burned my lungs.

My mind flashed back to Rexim's luncheon: our unexpected visitors, the knowing glint in Crake's eyes. Had their intrusion been a ploy to scope out the island? And his request that Rexim stand down as a candidate . . . maybe that had been a last chance.

And these were the consequences of refusing.

Behind me guards barked orders, hauled weapons. They were organizing themselves as best they could around the gatehouse, lining the ramparts, readying behind the arrow slits, but the forty or so of them wouldn't hold off Crake's men. Even with the drawbridge, the moat, the barbican . . . with Tigo out of action and the laconite useless, Iovawn Crake would crush them all.

The inner ward was surprisingly empty, only the odd soldier streaking through the fog. As I loped toward a servants' entrance, trying to ignore the roaring in my head, I heard shouts from inside. The *crack* of a pistol. My stomach pitched, and my thoughts flashed to the siblings.

I changed direction, digging out my knife.

As I slipped into the keep, Nemaine's words drifted back to me: *"I take it you know our* mutual friends *are arriving . . ."* I remembered her captives' grim understanding. They must all assume I was allied with House Crake. Nemaine had never mentioned the rebels. The thought of it made nausea rise in me.

Then—shouting. It was coming from the ballroom. I stopped short, my stomach roiling with dread.

Part of me wanted to flee, find somewhere to hide. The ruins of the old tower might suffice. Rhianne's dark cellar, with its nooks, its hidey-holes . . . Crake surely wouldn't venture down there.

But another part of me—a part that frightened me—was urging me to the ballroom. To do what I could. For now, in this moment, things were starting to become clearer. I cared about Rhianne, Mawre, even Tigo. The siblings . . . my thoughts there were blurry, jumbled. But Rhianne loved Catua, and Catua had always been kind to me. And the prospect of Llir getting hurt made me feel ill.

As though propelled by some unseen force, I jogged to the ballroom, where the great doors stood open.

I glanced inside, and for a few dizzying seconds, I thought the Shearwaters and the Cormorants were acting again. Playing out another scene, spouting lines at each other. But then I saw the grimace on

Emment's wine-stained lips. Catua's pale, almost colorless complexion. The haze of pistol smoke wafting over their heads.

The tableau was laid out like a painting before me: Avrix, gun in hand, aiming it at Rexim. Swords, the same ones used for the play, and crossbows in the hands of the Cormorants' Orha. Morgen, flanking her brother with a blade. Vercha and Llir in the wings, wan faced.

I'd expected to see someone bleeding on the floor, but Avrix's shot, it seemed, had been a warning.

I staggered, trying to take in what I was seeing. My feet scuffed the floorboards as I caught myself on the doorframe.

Avrix's head whipped around. "Ah, there you are." His dark eyes glittered, as genial as ever. "I'm glad you popped up. Means we get the chance to thank you."

Beside him, his sister was smiling at me, something almost predatory in her gaze. "Indeed," she added. "Our efficient little helper. You've made our job, and House Crake's, much easier." She frowned slightly. "I'm sorry, I don't think I ever caught your name?"

I stared at them as the others turned their gazes on me. I must have looked like a fish caught on a line: eyes bugging, mouth opening and closing mutely.

Morgen laughed. "Never mind. Now, where were we?"

"What do you mean, *Corith* has made your job easier?" It was Catua, her white face now blooming scarlet. "Your job of coming here under the pretense of a visit, scrutinizing our defenses and doing *gods* know what else, sending word back to Crake, plying us with drink, making sure all our weapons were here, where you could take them? Your job of *betraying* us? What's *Corith* got to do with that?"

I was frozen, a statue. I couldn't look at Llir. I didn't want to hear what the twins would say next, but I was pinned to the doorway by the Shearwaters' stares.

"Believe me," said Avrix with a strangely sad smile, "I know how much of a shock this must be."

"Especially for you, Vercha," his sister continued. "So much time, so much *effort*, put into your little protégée here. I remember your telling me what an asset she'd been."

I chanced a glance at Vercha, who was standing stock-still. She was looking at Morgen, face bleached, brows pinched.

"Speak plainly," Rexim barked at the twins. His hair was sleep tousled, but he looked sharp, alert. He'd pulled on a laconite-studded doublet, one I recognized; one Avrix had surely tampered with. Though he had no weapon, his hand hovered at scabbard height. "What does the Floodmouth have to do with this?"

"Why, she's a little baby cuckoo, of course," said Morgen. "Bedded down right here in your nest. An informant for the Cage. And, lately, a saboteur."

Avrix. He'd told his sister everything.

"The Cage," repeated Rexim, shaking his head. "It's Crake who's coming down that causeway. So I say again: *Speak plainly*."

"As you wish," said Avrix irritably. His aim hadn't faltered; his finger stroked the trigger. "Your little cuckoo here has been spying for the Cage, preparing the way for a visit they've been planning. Don't know all the details, but I know she's been digging . . . ferreting out all your dirty little secrets, probably so her conspirators could use them against you."

Heads whipped around. Sharp gazes fell on me. Had Catua noticed her Charter was missing? Was Llir thinking of when he and Tigo had caught me?

"As for what they were going to do—likely something drawn out and painful. Something to do with your winning the vote, which won't be happening now, of course." He cocked his head. "You know, we've actually *saved* you all . . ."

"No."

I'd spoken—it shocked me as much as them.

"No, you don't understand," I forced out. "They weren't going to be violent. At least, not unless they really had to." It was Crake who'd brought the army, not the Cage. I so wanted to believe the words I was uttering. "They were going to try to persuade—to bargain—"

"You," Rexim spat. His voice was poison. He raised a finger, pointed it at my face. "Be silent. You don't get to speak."

In my peripheral vision, I saw Llir staring, but I still couldn't bring myself to meet his eyes.

"You say you saved us?" Emment said to Avrix. His skin was grayish, his eyes unnaturally wide. "You'll have to explain that one to me. *Friend.*"

"From the shame of being yet another Cage casualty." Avrix was smiling, gaze still locked on Rexim. "Far more noble to go down to House Crake."

"But why?" Catua hissed. "You still haven't told us why."

The smile on Avrix's face turned pained. "Little Cattie. We don't relish having to do this, you know. Our families have been allies—friends—for decades. But that friendship has rarely borne fruit for us. All those years, and what have we Cormorants received? What gifts? What patronage? What buoying up, even, in the wake of the growing power, the growing popularity, the growing *success* of the mighty Shearwaters?" He shook his head sadly. "I tell you: nothing."

"That's a lie—" Rexim tried to cut in, but Avrix spoke louder, intoning over him.

"*Nothing.* And so when Uirbrig Crake, boor though he is"—Avrix winced slightly—"made us a very generous offer, it was hard to refuse. And I'm sorry for that."

"Like hells you are," Emment growled in response. He looked unsteady, reckless in his tipsiness.

"Father's going to win the Seat." Catua's voice was a blade's edge. "Then you'll get the *rewards* you seek."

Morgen laughed, high and clear. "Oh, no, I don't think so, my dear. Your little cuckoo has seen your accounts. Daddy's extra income will pay off his debts, save him from the shame of having to sell off your heirlooms, but there'll hardly be any left over for *friends*."

The family turned their eyes on me again. Rexim's lips were twisted at the corners, bitter and knowing. My face burned crimson.

I'd not slept for nearly a full day and night, and with all the wine that had flowed after the play, my mind was sluggish, like the streams out on the flats. But my shock was subsiding, leaving shivers in its wake. I thought back to Avrix's story, the night of the ball. All lies, of course. My skin prickled shamefully as I wracked my memory. Had *I* mentioned the Cage first or had he? I'd just assumed . . .

And before that, when we'd met in the culverhouse. He hadn't been sending a message to the Cage. He'd been contacting Crake.

I'd been so stupid.

Distant shouts. I turned, glanced behind me. By the sound of it, the Crakes were at the gatehouse already.

A scuffle in the room made me whirl back around. Emment had lunged for Avrix's pistol, taking advantage of his momentary distraction. The Cormorant swung his arm; there was an almighty *bang*. Emment and Avrix yelled out together.

Rexim threw an arm up to shield his face. There was shouting now, a shriek from Vercha. My eyes raked their forms, expecting to see blood, but the gun had backfired in an explosion of powder. Avrix dropped the pistol, his hand a black ruin. Burns marred one of Emment's cheeks.

"Out!" roared Rexim, and he gestured to his children. As one, the Shearwaters sprinted for the door.

For me.

“Tsk,” Morgen snapped out behind them. “Should’ve kept Nemaine here. Daiman! Orran!” The Cormorants’ Orha began to advance.

I pressed myself against the doorframe as Rexim hurtled toward the exit. He looked like he wanted nothing more than to eviscerate me, but since he had no blade, he could only glare cold murder.

He swept by me, followed swiftly by the siblings, and at last I sought Llir’s gaze as he passed me. He was pale as frost, his cheeks hard planes. In his eyes, disbelief warred with hot anger.

“Useless,” I heard Morgen mutter. Their Mudmouth was speaking, and I could feel the ground rumbling, but it was too late. Dust spiralled in the Shearwaters’ wake.

“Come on,” barked Avrix. I tried to back away.

Though I’d inadvertently aided them—I felt sick at the thought—we certainly weren’t allies, and I didn’t think they’d show me mercy. I brandished my stubby knife, but Avrix barrelled straight into me, unperturbed. I fell and rolled, my shoulder jarring painfully. When I clambered to my feet, they were past me, pursuing the Shearwaters.

Not knowing where else to go, what to *do*, I trailed after the Cormorants, fingering my knife.

“This way,” Catua shouted in the distance. “Get to the laconite—and then the armory.”

My stomach dropped. Avrix hadn’t told them what we’d done . . .

The Cormorants skidded into the main corridor, lined with the statues I’d spent so long polishing. At the far end was the door that led to the armory, but as I staggered in behind them, peered into the gloom, I saw Emment and Llir trying in vain to open it.

“My apologies,” called Avrix between harsh breaths, “but of course, we couldn’t leave that room unbarred.”

Catua said something low and urgent to her father, and Rexim glanced down at his laconite doublet.

With mounting horror, I watched the Orha move forward. Daiman, the Mudmouth. Orran, the Gustmouth. Orran was limping; I recalled he'd sprained his ankle. Their Floodmouth, Ebba, must be somewhere with Nemaine, no doubt to provide a counter to Rhianne . . .

As though my thoughts had acted as a summons, a hand touched my back. I jumped, whipped around.

"You're here!" came a voice. "I thought their Sparkmouth had got you." I found myself staring into Rhianne's freckled face. "I've been lying low, trying to get to Tigo and Mawre . . ."

"I—" My tongue was dry; the words wouldn't come.

But Rhianne was no longer paying attention to me. She was staring, white-faced, into the shuddering hallway. For the Mudmouth was muttering again, under his breath, splinters erupting from the dark, polished floor. Slivers of plaster, wickedly sharp, speared down from the ceiling, making the Shearwaters cower.

"I don't understand," Rhianne whispered. "The statues . . ."

"They've all been tampered with." My tone was flat. I turned to her. "Rhianne. I have something to tell you—"

But she ignored me, striding forward, speaking under her breath. I watched as the torches on the walls all flared.

"What now?" Avrix snarled, still cradling his hand.

Morgen turned, smiling brittlely at Rhianne. "Well, now," she said, "aren't you a clever little squirrel? It seems some harsh words with Nemaine are in order. She was supposed to corral you all."

"I'm afraid she failed in that," bit out Rhianne. "And I'm afraid I'm about to incapacitate your Mudmouth."

As she took a step forward, my heart swelled with hope. I retreated, knowing my hidden laconite might hinder her.

She spoke a few words, and a flame shot downward from one of the torch brackets, making straight for Daiman.

"We leave," shouted Morgen, turning toward us. To Avrix, she hissed, "Let Crake handle the Shearwaters."

They ran for the door, brandishing blades. Something whizzed past us: a crossbow bolt.

Behind them, a shriek: Daiman's cloak was on fire. In an instant, he was down on the floor, tearing it off, but Rhianne was still speaking. More sparks descended.

We dodged the Cormorants and their limping Gustmouth. Before long Daiman came streaking after them.

"Come on," Rhianne said, her eyes flickering between Catua and me. "It might take a while, but I can get into the armory . . ."

I stared at her, my former flare of hope dying.

"Corith." She was holding her hand out. Beckoning.

My eyes found the Shearwaters, still shouldering the door. Rhianne didn't know yet. I couldn't tell her.

"I'm sorry," I whispered. And I turned and dashed away.

There was nothing left for me here, or anywhere. All I could think to do now was run.

Crake had upended the Cage's plans. The rebels surely wouldn't be coming here now, and I'd never find out what had happened to Zennia. My only hope of *that* lay with Emment, but he was gone, holed up somewhere, soon to be facing down Crake.

I thought again of the tower ruins, Rhianne's little basement. If I hid out there until the Waking Tide retreated, ran ahead of the Morning Tide, all the way to the mainland . . . The prospect both tempted and depressed me in equal measure. Miserably I pictured handing myself over to Arbenhaw, and the placement that no doubt awaited me after: something brutal, backbreaking . . . short-lived.

But I realized grimly, as I stumbled from the hall, that my treacherous feet were heading that way: taking me out past Miss Haney's office to the rear servants' exit, which led to the cove path . . .

Smack.

I'd been so caught up in my brooding, I'd walked straight into a tall, solid figure. With twin grunts, we staggered back. I looked up. And froze.

"You." Nemaine's voice was tinged with disappointment. "Are you still here? Please tell me you subdued that Sparkmouth."

I didn't reply, merely backed away slowly.

She surveyed me critically, then cocked a pale eyebrow. "Ah. So you've figured it all out at last?"

No sign of her crossbow. Maybe she'd left it with whoever was now guarding Tigo and the others. But as she came toward me, matching my pace, a fierce-looking flame floated behind her down the hall.

"That Lord Cormorant lied?" I said, my face heating. "That he's nothing to do with the Cage at all? Yes, he made that quite clear just now."

I noticed her flame fading, flickering weakly. My pouch of laconite: It was doing its job.

Nemaine's face twisted into a crooked smirk. "The Cage. You and your little cuckoo friends. You think you'll make any real difference in this Queendom?" She shook her head. "You and I, working for the Hundred—we have it *good.* The best job an Orha can ask for. Or at least you did, until you fell in with those murderers. You should have been grateful for where you were. Proud. Not scheming against the people who see and appreciate your power."

"You think they appreciate us?" I said, thinking of Rexim. Of Vercha and Emment. All those Floodmouths up on the cliffs. Of what Zennia had seen before she'd come to Arbenhaw. Of the fights at the Veil. Of Uirbrig Crake. "The Hundred don't appreciate us. We're objects to them."

I was breathing heavily, my hands curled into fists. "You know what they think? That if we got even a *sniff* of power, we'd murder them all and seek to rule the world. Like they claim we tried to do before the Great Revolt."

Out of Nemaine's eyeline, her flame was guttering. "I don't know why I'm wasting my time arguing with you. Now. Are you going to stay here and cause trouble, or run away and hide like a good little mouse?"

Mouse.

My cheeks flared. It was what my classmates had called me.

I recalled the way my feet had been heading, the plan to flee that had wormed its way into my mind. I swallowed, my limbs as tense as spinet wire. I couldn't—wouldn't—run from this now.

When I didn't respond, Nemaine stepped toward me, lips parting. She would try to get rid of me. Burn me alive. But her flame had winked out; nothing happened when she called to it.

"Not as stupid as I took you for," she murmured, eyes raking over me. She knew I had laconite on me somewhere.

I backed away steadily, remembering my hidden knife. In the absence of her power, she advanced on me bodily. She was a full head taller than me, far broader at the shoulder. And the way she moved . . . she'd had training, I could tell.

I darted backward, moving my hand toward my knife, but as well as being strong, she was frighteningly fast. She launched herself forward, grabbing me by the shoulder. Grunting, I tried to twist from her grip, but her arm, leather clad and solid as steel, slipped around my neck and held me fast.

She had no weapon—she'd been relying on that flame—but I didn't think she'd have a problem removing me if she chose to. Our standoff had pushed us toward Miss Haney's office, and my stomach flopped as I glimpsed the dark hump of Debry's body on the floor. I could see no sign of Tigo and Mawre. Had Nemaine disposed of them, just as she was about to dispose of me? The thought made my pulse sound louder in my ears, made my palms go clammy. *My fault. My fault.*

I felt Nemaine's hand dig around in my cloak. The knife wasn't there—that was in an inner pocket—but the laconite was, and she tossed it away.

Then, in the near distance: ragged shouts, hoarse cheers. The gatehouse guards fending off Crake's attack? Or, more likely, Crake's forces celebrating breaking through.

The Sparkmouth paused, though she didn't break her hold.

"They're here," she said, her voice low. Fervent. And she began to drag me to the nearest window.

35

Nemaine pulled me to a tall, unglazed opening that looked out into the shadowy inner ward. The chill air was like a slap to my cheeks, smelling of brine and acrid smoke. The mist had thickened, drifting wraithlike through the cloisters, and I stopped struggling, peering out fearfully. Clangs and shouts rang out from the darkness. Somewhere a man shrieked, over and over.

It wouldn't be long now.

As Nemaine looked on eagerly, I pictured Crake sweeping in. Cutting down the Shearwaters; Catua and Llir. Uirbrig Crake sitting in the Chamber, any chance of rights crushed beneath his armored boots. He and Shrike would fill the Court with their cronies, with those who shared their penchant for violence. And then . . . Breova. We'd soon be at war.

What future for me, others like me, in that world? For Rhianne and Mawre and Tigo? For Llir?

Scant guards streaked from the curling mists, staggering into the ward, seeking shelter. A few of them made it to the keep's main door and disappeared through it, barring it behind them. But Crake's forces were roiling up behind the rest, a tide of bristling blades and axes. One by one, those left were cut down, skewered at swordpoint or battered around the head.

A cheer went up as two men rode through the barbican. Dark dread bubbled over in my stomach. The one in front was squatter, uglier: Uirbrig Crake, showing teeth as he smiled. Behind him came the man I feared much more, at least here, on this isolated island. Six and a half feet, hair black as charcoal, he sported a silver breastplate and a cloak. His gaze swept over the ward, the walls. I tried to shrink away, but Nemaine held me tight.

Crake's soldiers soon filled the yard, holding torches. The fog was thin, hanging motionless, ghostlike. They brought in the battering ram I'd known was coming and carried it, chanting, to the keep's main door.

Iovawn Crake murmured to his father, and the older man laughed: a croaking guffaw. Then the Mudmouth spoke again, his eyes on the ground, and a shiver ran through the stones beneath my feet.

Boom.

The ram began its work, each deafening thud making my teeth knock together. And in between them, a growing judder. Cracks appeared in the walls around the door.

"Shearwater!" Uirbrig's voice rang out over the ruckus. "Show yourself! I hadn't pegged you for a coward."

The ram pounded a few more times. Then, on the third floor, near to West Tower, a window opened and Rexim leaned out.

Uirbrig gave a wave of his hand. The battering ram stilled, and the ground stopped shuddering. For a moment, there was only mist and muffled silence.

"Coward?" Rexim called. My stomach flipped over. Was Llir there, standing just behind him? Emment, Vercha, Catua? Rhianne? I felt a sudden longing to see them, to be with them, a burning want like a torch in my chest.

"I, the coward?" Rexim continued. "When you are the one too afraid to wait for the vote?"

Uirbrig chuckled as though he'd expected the reply. "You know me, Rexim. I'm a man of action." His watery eyes narrowed, his smile turning pinched. "I'm what this nation really needs."

"And when they find out what you've done? You think they will vote for you?"

"Come, friend. We both know many of them would. The Hundred, much as you try to deny it, are still a bloodthirsty rabble at heart." Uirbrig shifted heavily in his saddle. "But in any case, they won't find out. As far as they'll know, House Shearwater's unfortunate destruction will have come at the hands of that scourge, the Cage."

The bottom fell out of my stomach at his words. Rexim, stunned to silence, simply stared. Nemaine must have sensed me stiffen, as she chuckled. With disgust, I felt her breath tickle my ear.

"Oh, yes," Uirbrig continued, looking gleeful. "Sending the Cormorants turned out to be fruitful indeed. Your old allies would have the run of the island for an extended time, where my son and I couldn't. Access to all your weapons, your laconite.

"And then, just a week ago, I received a crow . . ." He smiled, showing his teeth, slowly shaking his head. "You should keep a closer eye on your own servants, Rexim. I'm told there was a cuckoo under your beak all this time. Shameful. And now, for all the Hundred will know, your downfall has been yet another violent victory for those"—he spat on the stone—*"traitors."*

His eyes, and Iovawn's, roved the high windows, perhaps wondering if I—the cuckoo, the traitor—cowered somewhere behind the thick walls. I tried to rear back but was blocked by Nemaine.

"Don't worry, little mouse," she said. "You'll meet them soon."

Her solid body pressed into me, trapping me, but with a start, I felt something sharp prick my hip. *My knife.* In my panic, I'd forgotten all about it. I went still, not wanting to alert her, and began, with agonizing slowness, to move my hand to where I'd stashed it.

Rexim had vanished from the window now. Uirbrig gave a disappointed shake of his head and lifted his fingers. The onslaught resumed.

Iovawn Crake was muttering again, his eyes fixed ahead of him, his lips barely moving.

Ordinarily the laconite over the doorways in the ward, inlaid into the moat, reinforcing the archways, would have dulled and deadened any Mudmouth's assault. But as it was . . . there was a rumble, a low growl, that reminded me, bloodcurdlingly, of the quake before the tidal wave. The ground in front of him seemed to *ripple* . . .

With a series of reports like pistol shots, the stone around the keep's entrance split open and crumbled. The ram then made short work of the door, which splintered and fell inward, smashed to tinder.

I could only watch as House Crake's forces marched through the inner ward and into the keep.

"Time to get acquainted with our real masters," said Nemaine, drawing back from me, shifting her grip.

The split second of freedom gave me time to whirl around and grab my knife, now inches from my fingers. I stabbed out at her, my hand twisting awkwardly, but the blade connected and sank into her side.

She gave a cry and clutched the knife's handle. The wound didn't look life-threatening, but it was enough distraction to allow me to run. I pitched away from her, almost tumbling, then bound down the hallway, my strides uneven.

I heard her spitting curses behind me, then the sounds of her fumbling with something—a tinderbox. I had to get away before she struck up a flame. But there, ahead of me: my pouch of laconite. I snatched it up and held it close as I streaked down the corridor.

I now knew these halls nearly as well as I'd known Arbenhaw's, and I darted from corridor to storeroom to stairway, taking the maids' passages, the footmen's hidden doors. Soon the Sparkmouth's heavy steps and snarls of rage faded. Perhaps her wound had slowed her down. Or perhaps Nemaine had other matters to pursue—and didn't think this "mouse" presented enough of a threat. All the same, I was sure Crake would post guards in the keep. Safer, for now, to be outside its walls.

I slipped out a side door, steadying myself against the stone. My legs dragged, my exhaustion overwhelming, but though my body was tired, my senses were buzzing.

The thought came to me: *I have to* do *something.*

There had to be some way I could help House Shearwater. Do something to prove to myself—and them, maybe—that I wasn't who they thought I was: a traitor and a coward.

I took in the vista that opened ahead of me: a wide view east, looking down on the cove. The mist had thinned over the hillocks on the island, the fog moving westward, farther into the bay. And within it . . . lights at the far end of the island.

I squinted, wondering who would be down there. Crake must have sent men to cut off our retreat. Not that there was any escape at high tide, but when Crake arrived, the tide was lower. Uirbrig clearly wasn't taking any chances. I was glad now that I hadn't fled for the tower's ruins.

And then I saw the boats.

There were three, pulled up high above the cove. I could just see dark figures moving stealthily around them.

Why would Crake have brought boats with them? They'd marched down the causeway. They couldn't need vessels.

I recalled my confusion when I'd thought Crake's army was the Cage. The Cage wouldn't use the causeway; they'd come over the flats. Follow the high tide back out to the island, use the rivers, maybe, to get across the bay—undetected until the very last moment.

My pulse pattered rapidly as I peered through the gloom, watching as the tiny figures unloaded items.

Understanding came like a plunge into icy water.

A second later, I ran for the cove path.

I had to take the long route around, and I didn't want to risk a torch. My feet didn't know all its dips and rises, as they did with the shorter, well-trodden tracks, and with the mist still wadded in the hollows like gauze, I had to pick my way carefully, eyes on the ground.

As I approached the cove, I edged forward, concealing myself behind tall gorse and rocky outcrops. I caught whispered voices, the light steps of feet, strained words being exchanged as the figures milled ahead.

From what I could see through the haze and the dimness, the boat people were armed with bows and arrows, rusted short swords, battered-looking crossbows. They were dressed drably, wrapped in dark hooded cloaks, not a Crake banner or a piece of armor in sight.

I swallowed thickly, steeled myself to step forward, but before I could, an arm snapped around my throat.

"Got one!" hissed a voice by my ear.

The speaker was female. She sounded young. My mind seemed to seize. That voice . . . it was familiar.

We were quickly surrounded. Torches were held high. A man

stepped in front of me and tugged down his hood—bright gold hair roughly caught in a low bun, days-old stubble, a face startlingly handsome. The last time I'd seen those cornflower-blue eyes, they'd been glinting at me from behind a lion mask.

"Kielty," I said. It came out as a rushed breath.

He moved toward me, clapped a hand onto my shoulder. "It's you. Good. I got your note." He cocked an eyebrow. "You gave us the shock of our lives, you know. Well. Now I have one for you."

His gaze moved deliberately to the girl restraining me.

She let me go, took a few steps backward. As I turned, she slowly lowered her hood.

Round, tan cheeks picked out by torchlight. Dark eyes I'd looked into so many times. Even in the dimness, I knew that face. I knew that hair, pulled up into bunches. I knew that figure, compact and springy.

"Corith," came that voice again.

And all at once, everything crashed down on me.

I **staggered** forward, nearly slipping in my haste.

I couldn't speak. Couldn't even say her name. My chest was bursting; my breath snared in my throat. As Zennia fell toward me and we clutched each other's shoulders, she gazed into my face, eyes roving my features.

"You—you're—" The words wouldn't come to me.

"I'm sorry," she was saying fiercely. "Corith, I'm *sorry*."

I gripped my friend hard. I could hardly believe that she was here, that I was touching her. Then the scene seemed to come into focus around me: Zennia. Alive. With members of the *Cage*.

I studied her. Her face was leaner, the skin on her lips chapped. I saw now that her eyes were pricked with tears.

"Beautiful reunion," said Kielty behind us. "But I'd rather like to ask you—what in *hells* is going on out here?"

I turned reluctantly, still grasping Zennia. "You—you let me believe she was dead," I said. "You said you had nothing to do with her disappearance—"

For the first time, his cheery demeanor faltered. "I'm sorry about that," he said, frowning. "I truly am. Leadership's orders—we didn't know you. This one"—he jerked his chin toward Zennia—"tried to persuade us to tell you everything, but we couldn't risk it. We had to . . . test you. And besides," he added, eyes twinkling now, "I believe I said, 'We played no part in the death of your friend.' Technically true." He lifted a shoulder.

"Test me?" I whispered. "Bribe me, you mean? Dangle the truth about her like a carrot on a stick?" I turned back to Zennia, wide-eyed, disbelieving.

"I'm so, so sorry," she said, face crumpling. "I tried. But they said you might report us."

Us.

I felt like a puppet again. Like my legs might give out at any moment.

"You're with the Cage," I said dully. "You . . . joined them. How?"

She nodded. "It was all Instructor Rhama. He's a cuckoo, like Kielty, but I didn't know he was with them, not till the night before my exam . . . And Corith, I'm so sorry, I had no chance to talk to you. Rhama said not to—"

Kielty moved toward us. By now the rest of the group were clustering around us with hard, narrow gazes. "Explanations later. I'm going to have to insist. Before whatever's happening up there comes down here." He lifted an eyebrow at the distant castle, where fires flared and faint yells sounded.

"It's House Crake," I told him, scrubbing dampness from my cheeks. I hadn't even noticed my eyes were leaking. "Arrived in the night. A hundred men. I thought they were *you* . . ." I gave a hollow laugh.

Zennia slid in next to me, arm tight around my shoulders. She was staring at my face as though trying to read there everything that had happened in the last few weeks.

An angry murmur fizzled through the group. Kielty shook his head. "We'll have to abandon ship. Send a crow back to Pen Aryn, say we were beaten to the punch." He stared fixedly at the castle. "We'll lie low here for now. See how this pans out. We don't really have much choice."

The waves were pounding on the rocks below us. The Waking Tide, cutting off any retreat.

"Hells," he continued, "I could *skewer* Crake for this. If we had more people . . ."

"How many are you?"

"Less than twenty," said Zennia. "And not all Orha. Some Floodmouths, a couple of Mudmouths, one Gustmouth. And Kielty, of course." She flashed him a grin.

Still not enough to challenge Crake, not to mention the Cormorants and their Orha, too.

"They're wearing their own laconite," I said, grim faced. "Except their Orha, and the son . . . Iovawn."

Kielty's face darkened. "He's with them, is he? Fabulous."

I thought of Llir, somewhere in the keep. Barricaded in with his family, maybe. Had Crake got to them by now?

Something in me had stoked into a blaze. As much as I wanted to stay stuck to Zennia, I'd made a promise to myself up there, hadn't I? I'd vowed I would do what I could to help the family.

And I realized now, with a shudder of shame, how wrong I'd been about Emment Shearwater . . . His hesitation, his hollow stares and dark moods. That hadn't been guilt; it had been uncertainty. *I'd* planted the creeping suspicion in his head that he might have done something horrible to Zennia. He'd played a convincing villain in their play, but that was all it had been: an act.

"I need to go back up there," I said. "See what's going on."

Kielty eyed me. "You'd be much safer down here with us. There's nothing we can do. Crake'll sweep through them in minutes. Trust me, he won't leave anyone alive. Well, maybe the Orha, but he'll find a use for you."

"I have to," I said. "I can't just—" My limbs were trembling.

Kielty's gaze now seemed almost knowing, and I wondered if he'd guessed what was drawing me back. Either way, he said nothing.

"I'm coming with you," Zennia said.

I shook my head, turning toward her. "No. I already thought you were dead once. I don't want to be the cause of it actually *happening* this time."

"Too bad," she said with an infuriating smile. "Because I'm not letting you out of my sight again."

My shoulders slumped. I couldn't exactly stop her.

"What do you have in the way of a weapon?" Kielty was examining my crumpled garments.

I reached for my knife before remembering what I'd done with it: stabbed Nemaine in order to escape. My blank face must have given me away, because he shook his head and handed me his own rapier: a little rusty but still pin sharp.

"I don't know how to use one of these."

"It's better than nothing," Zennia said, at the same time as Kielty quipped, "Point and stab."

The three of us laughed, all a little nervously.

After that the rebels turned back to their boats, from which they were unloading more weapons, leather armor. A few scouts fanned out, seeking hidden places to safely wait out the assault raging above.

Zennia and I began the hike up to the castle, keeping to the mist-wreathed, rarely used paths. Kielty's rapier felt odd at my side, an unfamiliar, unbalancing weight. For her part, Zennia had a crossbow in a holster. It looked strange to my eyes after a decade of desks and black uniforms at Arbenhaw.

"You sure you don't want to just leave them all to it?" she murmured, gazing warily up at the castle. More shouts drifted down toward us, the crash of something splintering inside.

I followed her gaze. I couldn't find the words. I hardly understood how I was feeling myself, let alone felt able to explain it to another. The silence was heavy, and after a moment, I looked back at my friend, taking her in. "They all said you'd drowned." My voice came out hoarse. "Rexim, Tigo . . . Emment said he *saw* it."

Zennia stiffened but didn't break her stride. "Emment," she repeated, scowling slightly. "Yes, he did. He saw me drown." She met my stare. "Because that's what I wanted him to see."

I opened my lips to say, "I don't understand," but she must have seen my bafflement.

"I decided to do it before we got into the boat. Before we headed back to the island." She paused. "How much do you know already?"

"I know about the fights," I said, hugging myself. "I saw one of them, too. I know you spoke up." A hot flare of pride, of admiration. She'd done what felt right, despite the danger.

"Okay. I need to go further back." She chewed her lip. "Remember when I said it was all Instructor Rhama? Well, it was him who got me this job. The spying, the sabotage . . . that was meant to be me. He told me about it the night before my exam; said he was putting his life on the line, but that something told him I'd be interested . . ."

That memory again: the lecture hall. *"Is it true we used to call ourselves Tidespeakers, sir?"*

I wondered now if that had been when it started. When he'd started watching her, hearing her quiet scoffs. He must have pinpointed her as an asset: the best of us, a talent too strong to waste.

After Owyn, I made Zennia promise never to run. Never to take her chances with the gallows. I supposed she hadn't really broken that promise. She hadn't had to; Rhama had made sure of that.

"The letter hidden in your room," I whispered. The one I found soon after arriving, only for it to get swept away by the wave. "You said you couldn't talk about everything you wanted to . . . and the dates on the back. They were meetings with Kielty, weren't they?"

"Yes," she said brittlely. "I'd just got started. But after . . . what I did at the Veil, Emment said that was the end of my placement. That he'd tell his father and I'd be sent back to Arbenhaw. He said they'd put me in the cellars overnight, then bundle me straight into a coach the next morning.

"That's when I knew I *had* to do something. Kielty wouldn't be able to save me, and there was no guarantee I'd escape on the journey." She looked at me, brown eyes glinting in the gloom. "I decided to fake it. Fake that I'd drowned."

"Why didn't you just run from Emment?" I asked. "He was drunk, wasn't he? You could have slipped through his grip."

"No," she said, thick black brows drawing downward. Her eyes were on the path, picking out where to place her feet. "My likeness would've been everywhere. Etched in the papers, on posters in the streets . . . '*Missing Orha.*' Remember Owyn? This way no one would go looking for me. Safer for me; safer for the Cage."

My thoughts were jumping, making new connections. Everything now seemed clear as glass. "*You* called up the waves in the bay. But how? Emment would've heard you, wouldn't he?"

Her lips twisted. "I made sure I had my back to him. Pretended I was whispering to the water to propel us, when really, I was riling it up, agitating it. Soon it was choppy enough to toss us."

"And then you could get far enough away from him to—"

"Make it seem like I was in real trouble."

Rhianne's words echoed in my mind. *"He was shaking harder than I've ever seen anyone . . . Got us all up, made us go out there looking . . ."*

A mixture of guilt and pity sloshed in me. Emment *had* seen what he thought he'd seen.

"Then what?" I said, imagining that night: the darkness, the chill, the rippling waters.

"Swam back to the harbor, then sprinted for the Veil. Kielty was just closing up. I was lucky. Another few minutes and he'd have vanished—I had no idea where he slept at night.

"After that we sent word to Rhama. And Leadership." She shivered, shoulders lifting. "They weren't too happy. Sent me down south to help raid laconite shipments, but Kielty persuaded them to let me back. For this."

And that, I guessed, was where *I'd* come in.

"It was Rhama," I said, thinking back to my exam, the memory making my cheeks warm with shame. "My final exam. It was all going wrong. But he couldn't allow that—he needed me, didn't he?"

Zennia paused on the path, reaching out. "I told them it had to be you," she said. "I knew it would mean I had a chance of seeing you, a chance to stop you being sent somewhere else. But this job—" She came closer, gripped my arm hard. "Corith, it suited you *perfectly*. You know what I'm like: My face says everything. That's probably why Rhama knew he was safe to approach me. And it was hard—*so* hard—to be around the Shearwaters. But you . . . *you*, Corith. You're what this job needed. I knew you'd be better at keeping your cool."

I tried to picture Zennia sucking up to Vercha and found myself smiling. My friend's lips twitched, too.

"I told them I knew you better than anyone. They agreed to have Rhama send you to the island, but they outright refused to tell you about the mission. In case you went straight to Instructor Caerig, I suppose."

I thought of Rhama's assessing looks that day. I knew I was far more of a closed book than Zennia. He must have been wondering if they'd made the right choice.

"Corith," she said, "I put you in danger—"

"It's all right," I said, taking her wrist and squeezing it.

The sight of her jerkin's buttons glinting suddenly brought something else to my mind. I dug in my pocket and brought it out: the brooch I'd given her for her eighteenth birthday, the one Kielty had used to entice me, to prove he knew more about Zennia.

She took it and turned it over in her fingers. "I'm sorry," she said again, her voice breaking slightly, and I tugged her to me and hugged her close. We stood there a moment, enveloped against the chill, then reluctantly drew back and set off up the path.

"So you went to join the rebels. What's it like, living rough?" Sidelong, I noted her new, wiry leanness. Her thin, frayed garments. Her hard-set face.

"Not easy," she said a moment later. "But it feels right. What we do feels right."

I fell silent. I thought of the headlines in the pamphlets. Bombings. Poisonings. I didn't know what to believe.

Murderers. Traitors.

I hadn't thought I was like them. I'd helped them only for information about my friend. But now? I'd seen the Hundred's actions firsthand. Was I still only aiding the Cage for Zennia?

My thoughts were in a jumble. Pushing them away, I focused on placing my feet among the hollows.

We were near the castle now, near enough to see Crake's soldiers; there were two pairs of them patrolling the curtain wall.

“Come on,” I said. “We have to get inside.”

We waited for a brief gap in the patrols and sneaked forward. The castle passageways were burned into my brain, and I intended to lead Zennia past the rarely used storerooms. But as we skirted around the barbican, I saw the inner ward lit up with torches. A bonfire crackled. Men shouted within. We couldn’t cross the archway without being seen.

“Look,” Zennia hissed, nudging my elbow. “Listen.”

Soldiers were marching from the keep into the ward. I heard boots hitting stone, a harsh laugh I recognized. Uirbrig Crake. He was back outside.

Zennia gripped my arm. Two figures were approaching: guards emerging from the shadows under the gate. We flattened ourselves against the barbican wall, where the thin mist laced the towers like cobwebs. If we ran, they'd surely spot us.

"Up there," I whispered, sliding along the wall, jerking my chin toward an upper window. The barbican's towers were squat and thick walled, but the stone was rough with jutting reinforcements, arrow slits where we could place our feet.

Zennia boosted me, clasped hands under my heel, and I hauled myself up, remembering the cove. If I could climb out of *there*, I could scale this wall. The thought lent a warm, fierce strength to my limbs.

"Hurry," Zennia murmured from below. I knew she wouldn't have spoken unless it was urgent. I squeezed through the narrow window, its sides scraping me, and a moment later, Zennia tumbled in behind me. We kneeled on the floorboards, breaths coming harshly.

A mutter; another man's short, grating laugh. They hadn't seen us. They were moving away.

Heart thudding, I unbuckled the rapier from my belt and moved to the opposite side of the tower. Peering through an arrow slit into the ward, I hissed through my teeth. "What is that down there?" But there was no real need to whisper up here—the space below us was teeming with activity.

Zennia came up behind me, grim faced. "It almost looks like . . ." She cut off, squinting downward.

A platform had been hastily erected in the inner ward: a wooden deck held up with piled timber. Placed upon it, right in the center, was a block of stone.

Just then, a small party emerged from the keep. I angled myself so I could see them more clearly. Iovawn Crake, following his father, and behind him, surrounded by soldiers—the Shearwaters.

My hands gripped the ledge, and my chest constricted. Rexim, out front, was grave faced, stoic, no longer in his useless laconite doublet but in shirtsleeves only, his collar flecked with blood. Behind him came Emment, nervous and jittery, with a cut lip and a rapidly forming black eye.

The sisters came next, Catua's cheeks wet, Vercha's face bleached of all color. Vercha's eyes were on Iovawn's back, and she was holding herself stiffly, her gaze remote.

Last came Llir, limping slightly. His face was wan, his green eyes darting. When his gaze fell on the platform, with its ominous stone block, his Adam's apple bobbed a few times, slowly.

My own throat and tongue had turned horribly dry.

"Looks like they're going to finish them off," Zennia whispered.

All I could do was shake my head. This couldn't be happening. Not now. Not yet.

Below, Uirbrig Crake stalked toward Rexim. "Wonderful of you to join us at last," he said. "You realized, eventually, it would be folly to resist. Good man. Although it seems your sons did not."

Emment, with his battered face and bruised eye, leaned forward and spat as far as he could. A burly woman next to him, decked out in steel plate, reached for her weapon, but Crake stilled her with a gesture.

Crake's eyes narrowed as they roved over Emment, taking him in critically. He shook his head.

"Get the Brigant up there," he snapped at last, and Rexim was hauled toward the platform.

"I do apologize," Uirbrig continued, his voice rising over the siblings' protests. "This is all going to be rather uncivilized. But as I said to your father, I *am* a man of action. Of the here and now. This is, regrettably, necessary."

Emment was trying to shake off his captors. Llir's mouth opened; Vercha went even paler. *"Scum,"* Catua bit out savagely, her voice shaking, but Uirbrig ignored her, turning to watch Rexim's progress.

Iovawn Crake was lurking nearby, shrug shouldered like a vulture, overseeing the proceedings. At his father's order, at the words that followed, I thought I saw surprise flicker faintly on his face . . . but a second later, all trace of it was gone.

"Take me instead," Emment choked, stepping forward. The woman in plate yanked him back with a grunt. "Take me, and let my father live. Hells know I deserve it." His voice cracked miserably. "More than any of the rest of them."

My fingers pressed the ledge until they hurt. My chest burned horribly. He thought he was a killer.

"If you spare him, and the others"—Emment glanced at his siblings—"my father will agree to step aside as a candidate. No one has to know about any of this." He looked to his father, face drawn in desperation, but Rexim, implacable, merely shook his head narrowly. Emment seemed to crumple, swaying where he stood.

Uirbrig chuckled. "Noble sentiments. I'm impressed. But you see, your father's a sensible man. This is simply the way it has to be."

I sensed Zennia shift beside me as Rexim was forced to kneel before the block. "Corith," she murmured, a barely there warning. "Don't look." But I couldn't drag my eyes from the ward.

"Stop!" came a high, brittle voice. It was Vercha. She was stiff-backed, staring at Iovawn Crake.

He met her gaze. Something passed between them. The others didn't see it; they were distracted, devastated.

Iovawn said something inaudible to his father, but Uirbrig ignored him, a smile on his face. Uirbrig raised a hand, gestured to his soldiers, and one of them hefted a greatsword above his head.

As the siblings' cries pierced the air below me, I felt a hot, sick lurch and turned away, squeezing my eyes shut. But I'd forgotten to stop up my ears with my fingers, so that when the noises came—a horrible slicing, a meaty thud mingled with Vercha's raw screams—they cut right through me, making me dizzy.

I knew I would never forget those sounds.

Then I felt Zennia's warm hands on me, heard her voice in my ear: "We have to go. Now."

I shrugged her away. Uirbrig was speaking again, his throaty voice raised over the siblings' sobs.

I dragged myself up just enough to see them but angled my face to block out the platform. Black spots swam in my vision like flies.

"Now," said Crake, pacing into my eyeline, "here's what's going to happen next. I need to get off this godsforsaken island, share the unfortunate news of your father's run-in with the Cage. I'm told your Morning Tide—is that what you call it?—will be heading for the mainland before too long. I want us to be just ahead of it. We'll turn south, move over Cormorant land."

I couldn't see the fog-cloaked bay from here but knew the Waking Tide would be receding by now.

"But before that, you, my noble friend"—Crake was pointing a finger at Emment—"are going to tell me, right now, where your family keeps your hoard. I know it's hidden somewhere on this island, and I know your father hasn't sold it off. You know as well as I do that's a last resort. The greatest of shames among the Hundred." He grinned, showing small yellow teeth. "It's not in your cellars—your coffers are too bare. Many families stash it away somewhere secret. I'm on a deadline here, so I'm going to need your help."

I looked at Emment, who was hollow eyed, haunted. His expression flickered with uncertainty for a moment, then his shoulders stiffened, his features closed tight.

"If you're so foolish as to decide not to cooperate, I'm afraid we shall have to take measures to persuade you. And your dear siblings, if required."

A weighty silence. Uirbrig sighed. He crooked a finger, and Emment was dragged forward. The Shearwater heir offered little resistance.

I barely caught Uirbrig's next signal: a twitch of his chin, directed at his soldiers. As one of them hauled Emment's tall frame straight, another delivered a roundhouse crack to his jaw.

Catua cried out. Llir's eyes closed briefly.

Emment grunted, spat on the ground, but this time it was blood that stained the cobblestones.

"Feeling any more amenable?" Uirbrig's tone was feather-light.

"Rot in hells," came Emment's drawl, his words slurring, his body listing.

All Crake did this time was glance at his soldiers. Another plated fist smashed into Emment's face. I sagged again and turned, staring at the opposite wall.

"Corith." Zennia's voice was distant, buzzy. "Surely you don't want to stay to see this? We have to get back. In case they decide to search the towers."

A roaring sound was filling my head, Uirbrig's words bubbling up beneath it: *"I need to get off this gods-forsaken island . . . Your Morning Tide . . . I want to be just ahead of it."*

I looked dully at Zennia. She was crouching over me, her cloaked form just visible in the chamber's thick shadows.

Something—an idea—was burgeoning in my mind.

I didn't want to grasp it too forcefully, surprise it, for fear it would slip from my thoughts like water. My eyes roved the tower as I prodded at it, nurtured it, encouraged it to firm up and grow more substantial . . .

Zennia watched me, silent, understanding. We'd known each other for a decade now—she was used to my taking more time to process things. To germinate, and only later vocalize, a thought.

Below us, Emment's beating had stopped. There was some sort of commotion. More people arriving. I folded my idea away gently, carefully, turned and peered back down into the ward.

"Crake!"

It was Avrix and Morgen Cormorant, flanked by their Orha and a few bored-looking soldiers. I spotted Nemaine, blood staining her jerkin.

"How long is this going to take?" barked Avrix. Seeing him, hatred and shame speared through me. "You said you'd get the hoard. I need to have this seen to." He was cradling his hand, the flesh burned black, lines of pain etched into his forehead.

Uirbrig surveyed Emment, who'd collapsed on the ground. "I don't have time for this idiocy," he grated. "Take him up there. Start on the other boy next."

Bustling activity. More cries from Catua. As a soldier grabbed Llir, my core turned to ice.

Emment was hauled up onto the platform—I glimpsed a red stain, a dark, slumped body—but before he could be made to kneel, like his father, Vercha stepped forward, face white as bone.

"It was buried beneath the old tower," she said, her voice clear. "Deep below the cellar. But the tower collapsed. You'll need a Mudmouth"—her eyes flicked to Iovawn—"but you'll still reach it, if you don't destroy it first."

Emment's shoulders slumped. Catua shook her head, despondent.

"Sensible girl," Uirbrig said, smiling. And he walked to his son, who was standing just below us.

"Take some men and get the hoard." His voice was low, but the words drifted upward. "I don't care how long it takes. Then, when you have it, you can get rid of the whelps. But we need to make sure she was telling the truth, first."

"And if she wasn't?" Iovawn's voice was deep, unsettling.

"Then start on them again. One by one. They'll crack. Like I said, take as long as you need. Meet me on the mainland when it's done. Do it properly."

A shout from a guard broke through, drawing their attention.

"Sire. Sire! This one's Orha!"

Uirbrig frowned. "What is it now?"

"This one's Orha, sire. The second son."

They were shoving Llir forward, his long legs buckling under him. One of his guards had a laconite cuff, which must have given the secret away. It was ringing faintly in the silence of the yard.

"Move away," said Crake to his son, who obeyed.

Once it was just Uirbrig, the guard, and Llir, the Brigant stared down at the cuff in amazement. "Well, well, well," he murmured, smirking. "Shearwater had a dirty little secret all along. All this time. We were more alike than I knew."

"My father was nothing like you," said Llir, his tone arctic.

In response, Uirbrig brought his meaty arm upward, smacking Llir's chin. I heard his teeth knock in his head.

"We take the Orha with us," Crake called. "Including this one."

Llir raised his head, flexed his jaw with a wince. He flitted a dark, uneasy glance at the Brigant.

Behind him, the Cormorants were staring in shock. Morgen turned, murmured something to her brother, and Avrix, eyes fixed on Llir, shook his head.

"We've wasted too long here," said Uirbrig to his son. "Go. Find this ruined tower. I'll have men guard the rest of the whelps till you return."

Iovawn gave an almost imperceptible nod and strode away, his long cloak fluttering.

The inner ward became a hive of activity as the majority of the troops prepared to depart. Soldiers darted back and forth, beginning to load wagons, to pack equipment onto mounts. Llir was led away, kept separate from his siblings, and for a second his gaze seemed to dart around the walls, the windows, as though searching for something—or someone. I drew back, fearful that his guards would notice, and leaned against the stone, meeting Zennia's dark eyes.

I took a breath, trying to center myself.

"Listen," I said tentatively. "I think I have a plan."

It was far too risky to leave the barbican by the door, so Zennia lowered me, with surprising, wiry strength, from the lowest window at the rear of our tower. I fell half the distance, jarring my ankles, pressing myself against the stone once I was down. Zennia passed Kielty's rapier to me, then hung expertly from the ledge and dropped lightly to the ground.

She looked at me. "Are you absolutely sure about this?" Her eyes were wide, reflecting the pink sunrise.

I nodded. I wasn't sure I trusted myself to speak.

She still looked unhappy, but she'd agreed we had no choice. None save hiding and waiting this out. Leaving the siblings to the same fate as their father. Leaving House Crake to sweep up the spoils and escape unharmed—with the Cage taking the fall.

"Kielty will agree," I said, "when he hears Crake's plan. If he doesn't . . ."

I didn't want to think about that.

"Okay," Zennia muttered, more to herself than to me. "Let's do this." She took a deep breath.

“Remember,” I said, “watch for their retreat. And tell the Mudmouths—”

“I remember,” she cut in, smiling. She pulled me into a fierce hug. “Be careful. Okay?”

“And you,” I said, my voice little above a whisper. I tried to commit the warm feel of her to memory.

A noise off in the yard made us jump, pull apart. And with that, I watched as my friend—my sister—turned and disappeared into the haze like a shadow.

For a moment, as I stood there, frozen, I recalled the sick, fleshy slicing of the greatsword. The thud on the platform. Vercha's high-pitched shrieks. I went dizzy, swayed, pressed a hand into the stone. Then I blinked and sucked in a breath of cold air.

Pull it together. You have work to do.

I sidled along the barbican wall, keeping to the shadows, tugging up my cloak's hood. In the distance I saw dim figures in the mist, the to-ing and fro-ing of soldiers, of horses. As I watched the activity, I bit my lip until it was bloody, steeling myself, feeling my heart thump painfully. I knew what it was I needed to do. Knew what it would mean, and what would happen after . . . Doing it, however, was another matter entirely.

Finally I straightened, pulled my hood down lower, and strode brazenly away from the wall, circling the barbican. Making for the inner ward.

Voices echoed off the lofty stone, beneath them the ever-present rushing of the ocean. The cloying dampness in the air clung to my clothes.

“Hoi! You there!”

I'd known this would happen, but that didn't stop the unpleasant knotting of my insides.

"Yes?" I snapped, forcing my eyes to narrow. I drew myself up, ran my eyes over my accoster.

He was young—*good*—and fair haired, his armor gleaming.

He looked taken aback by my cold reception but planted himself in front of me anyway. "Speak your name. Your business." He touched his blade.

"I'm not one of the Shearwaters, if that's what you're insinuating. You think I'd be walking around out here if I was?" I tried my hardest to channel Vercha. And Nemaine. "As for my business—isn't it obvious? I'm preparing to leave this hells-cursed island, just as your dear leader has ordered." I inclined my chin toward the inner ward behind him. "I'm Ebba, the Cormorants' Floodmouth. Let me pass."

A handful of soldiers strode past us, leading horses. A few hauled the battering ram that had splintered the door. Their eyes passed over us, fleetingly curious. If enough of them saw him let me go, maybe they wouldn't bother questioning me again.

He fingered the rough laconite hanging around his neck. It was ringing faintly, backing up my story. He took in my cloak, the set of my mouth, then waved me on. "All right. Hurry, then."

I fought to keep the relief off my face. Instead, I said brusquely, "Crake's Orha—where are they? I've been told to liaise on positions for the march back."

He was already stepping away, distracted, and glanced back at me with an impatient frown. "The inner ward. West side, I think." And then he was off, jogging to catch up with the other soldiers.

Legs shaking, I strode in the direction he'd indicated, avoiding anyone else's eyes. But no one was paying attention to me now. There was something to be said for holding yourself confidently.

I was grateful for my hood as I entered the inner ward, slipping in just as a gaggle of soldiers marched past. The space was thronged with people and mounts, with piles of weapons and banners in Crake colors. Nearby, a horse munched meditatively in a nosebag while a burly woman inspected its hooves.

I walked past a wagon being loaded with valuables and recognized an ornate clock from the keep; the Shearwaters' silverware; an engraved fencing sword. As well as seeking the family's hoard, they were clearly looting everything they could from the castle.

Though the sight made my throat burn with indignation, I forced myself to look away. Time was short—I could be stopped again at any moment.

Carefully avoiding the east side of the ward, where the Cormorants were busy preparing their mounts and the Shearwaters were huddling, closely guarded, I moved through the hubbub to the western end, where I quickly identified House Crake's Orha.

They were the ones with little, if any, armor. Though Iovawn Crake was his father's general, and Mudmouths and Sparkmouths could be useful on the front lines, most of the time, Orha were kept to the rear. We needed quiet, concentration; to be away from the harrowing anxiety of battle. Otherwise any speaking we attempted wouldn't work. That was why they made good use of us in the navies—Floodmouths and Gustmouths sinking ships from afar. But a battle-hardened Mudmouth, impervious to stress, was a real asset if an army could get one. Which was perhaps the only reason Uirbrig Crake valued his son.

The Crake Orha were garbed in dull greens and browns, some standing around talking, others loading up supplies. I spotted their packs on the ground against the walls, and I sidled among them with an outward confidence I didn't feel.

A stone here, a stone there . . . I ducked and rummaged among the belongings. With all the soldiers moving around us, no one was paying me any real mind, but I tried to look as though I was searching for something.

The laconite beads Avrix and I had stolen vibrated in my fingers as I slipped them into the packs, sliding them secretly into loose hems and stitching, pushing them deep down below bedrolls and clothes. I didn't know which packs belonged to the Floodmouths, but it didn't really matter. I had plenty to go around.

I even managed to drop some into pockets, deep into the heavy folds of their cloaks. At Arbenhaw, the rare times we'd been allowed into town, Zennia and I had practiced slipping hands into pockets. It was easy, among the throng, to go unnoticed. To stumble against someone and mutter, "Sorry," under my breath.

But a moment later, before my pouch was empty, a viselike grip enfolded my upper arm.

"You."

A chill prickled down my neck. Turning, I found myself looking upward. At Nemaine.

"What are you doing, skulking in the shadows?" She was limping, a dark stain near her hip where I'd stabbed her, but her face betrayed no sign of the pain.

Raising her voice, she hauled me roughly along with her. "Who let this traitor wander freely out here?"

By now the fair-haired soldier I'd duped was back in the inner ward, loading valuables onto wagons. He and a few others glanced over. His face dropped.

"She—she told me she was Cormorant," he stammered.

Nemaine glanced back at me, her blue eyes flashing. Was it all bitter anger, or was there surprise there, too? Almost as though my daring had impressed her. "Perhaps not a mouse after all but a weasel," she murmured, tugging me to the east side of the ward.

I struggled for effect. Though I'd predicted this would happen, it didn't stop my heart hammering dully against my ribs. What if Uirbrig changed his mind? Decided, in the end, to lop off everyone's heads?

"Another prisoner," Nemaine intoned as we reached the east wall. "Managed to give us the slip until now."

In front of me, Tigo, Mawre, and Rhianne were trussed up and gagged, sitting sullenly on the ground.

At the sight of them, warm relief flared in me, but that quickly dissipated as I took in their expressions. They were glaring, murderous, their eyes like blades. Above her gag, Rhianne's nose wrinkled in a scowl—the siblings must have told her, or she'd figured it all out.

Once I'd been relieved of Kielty's rapier, I was thrown down beside them, gagged and shackled. Guards loitering nearby watched over us.

I looked at Rhianne. Surely she should understand? The girl she loved had rebel sympathies. She herself had said she understood their cause, even if she didn't approve of their methods. In my gaze, I tried to say, wordlessly, *I'm sorry*. But Rhianne only shook her head. I knew what she was thinking.

It wasn't so much that I was working for the rebels. It was the fact that I'd tried to sabotage the Shearwaters. To prize out their secrets and use them against the family. And who knew what Kielty's group would've done if it hadn't worked?

In any case, I thought, it was too late now. Rexim was dead, and the siblings were about to be . . . unless my reckless plan somehow worked.

Hollow-eyed, I avoided Rhianne's accusing gaze—

Only to find myself staring into the face of Llir Shearwater.

Now that he'd been identified as Orha, he'd been separated from his bloody and beaten brother and from his sisters, who huddled pale faced across the ward, to await Iovawn Crake's eventual return. Llir now sat with his chained-up ankles in front of him, his back against the wall, his wrists tightly bound.

I winced to see his gag drawn tight under his cheekbones. Somewhere along the way, he'd lost his doublet, and he sat now in grimy, baggy shirtsleeves, his collar hanging open, his head tipped back.

We held each other's gaze for one long moment, my stomach jumping queasily as I remembered last night. The tableau we'd held, the stir of his breath, how close I'd been to that curve of pale neck that now stood out sharply against the castle's dull stone.

And after, in the stairwell, before everything had gone awry: the glint of his eyes through the holes of his mask, those stretched-out seconds when his lips had met mine, the feel and taste of him, warm and wine tinged and too brief.

But the memory was already blurring in my mind. Had that really only been a few hours ago? Had it even happened at all?

Now, rather than those smiles on the tower roof or his surprised, slightly teasing look after the play, his expression was closed, his stare a stony challenge. He looked deliberately away, flicked his eyes around the battlements; closed them, after a while, resting back against the stone.

I, in turn, hunched down on the cobbles, burying my head in the gap between my knees. I didn't want to meet any more ice-cold stares, see the judgment in the faces of those I'd deceived.

I told myself I shouldn't care what the Shearwaters or their Orha thought of me. I wouldn't be seeing them again after this. Even if all of us made it out of here alive.

Alive.

That was what I needed to focus on.

I stared hard at the ground and waited for Crake to give the order.

39

Not long after, preparations were complete.

Mounts had been readied. Stolen goods had been packed. Crake's soldiers moved into formation, ready to march home ahead of the Morning Tide.

I strained my ears as I was hauled to my feet, trying to hear the sea's distant buffeting, but the shouts all around me, the clinking of armor, drowned it out. I was jostled into place with the others.

A satisfied-looking Uirbrig Crake rode past, heading to the front of the line. Rhianne, just ten feet or so ahead of me, looked as if she wanted nothing more than to spit at his feet, her gag the only thing stopping her. Beside her, Mawre looked on stonily. Tigo was some way ahead of us, tightly bound, specially guarded by three hulking soldiers. Llir was behind. I couldn't quite spot him—only the flash of a white shirt, a bent head, tousled hair.

My own guard, a man, stood close beside me. Stringy hair in a ponytail; grinning yellowed teeth. As I shivered, the chill seeping into my garments, he hung a laconite pendant around my neck. "Don't want any of you Orha filth trying anything funny on the march."

I gave him a flat stare. My gag rendered me useless anyway, and besides, although he couldn't know it, there were still a few laconite beads in my pockets.

Morgen Cormorant trotted past us, head held high, followed closely by her brother. Avrix's hand had been bandaged, and he held it close to his chest as he rode. His gaze caught mine, and his lips twitched slightly, his uninjured hand rising in a small mock salute.

Before I could scowl, a call came: "Move off!"

My stomach flipped. Were Kielty and the others ready? Had Zennia even gotten to them to relay the plan?

We trudged off, the soldiers laughing and bantering, the horses snorting, the wagons creaking. Soon the bay opened out ahead of us, fog cloaked and eerie, a ghostly white mire. Around and in front, the mudflats glittered, and behind us came a low, murmuring roar.

Thud, thud. Leather soles hit the causeway. Greaves reverberated. Blades clanked against armor.

If this didn't work, what awaited us on the mainland? A brutal placement in the Quagland marshes? A short-lived stint in Crake's or Shrike's armies? For some, no doubt, a quick execution. Those who refused to work. To comply.

I suspected Llir Shearwater would be among that number. Though I didn't look around, I could almost sense his gaze. Could he see me ahead of him, my shoulders hunched? *Traitor. Cuckoo.*

He didn't know what was coming.

I flicked my gaze north, then south, to the sides of us. There, close by on the mudflats, I saw them: Dark humps of sand. Jagged furrows in the dimness. Someone—or more than one person—had been there. People who could bend the ground to their will.

My pulse picked up, sweat prickling between my shoulders.

Step one. They'd done it. Kielty had come through.

I flashed a quick look over my shoulder, hoping the Cage were even now back east. They hadn't had much time, but if they'd split their resources . . .

"Eyes forward."

A sharp smack connected with my cheek. My head whipped around as my guard shoved me ahead of him.

I staggered, raised my bound wrists to my face.

Step two. This part required something from me.

The guard's blow had been fortuitous. I slowed, then stopped short and swayed where I stood.

"Hoi," came the gruff voice again. A calloused hand gripped me. "No loiterin'. Get on with you, Orha vermin."

I bent, put my hands on my knees, sank downward. I mumbled something, but my gag turned it to nonsense. The guard reached down, ripped the gag from my mouth. "I can't go on," I moaned. "I'm going to be sick."

A frustrated sigh. He hauled me upward, but I loosened my muscles like a rag doll, slumped lower.

"What's the bloody holdup?" came a woman's hoarse voice. Behind us, because of the narrowness of the causeway, a bottleneck was forming. Faces peered over shoulders. I lay on the slick stone, my clothes soaking up seawater, and curled inward as my guard shoved me roughly with a boot.

"Got a sick one!" he called to the soldiers ahead of us. A few had stalled, staring back through the thin mist. "Shall I just get rid of 'er?" he added. My insides lurched.

As long as they didn't slit my throat, I hardly cared how they decided to deal with me—throw me on the sands to be taken by the tide, load me on horseback, chuck me in a wagon. All I needed, right now, was a delay.

And with the group stretched out in such a long line, with the horses at the front and the wagons at the rear, I was getting my wish. Shouted orders were passed back to us.

"Nah, Crake says he wants to keep the Orha. Pass her back. Get her on one of the wagons."

My guard wasted no time in hauling me up and hoisting me over his shoulder like a sack. "Get on, then," he barked, heading back the way we'd come as the rest of the line filtered past him, finally moving.

From up here, I had a better view behind us, but the sea fog mostly hid the island from sight. I could hear the tide, though, roaring ever nearer, chomping at the bit to sweep out into the bay.

I was jittery, feverish, as the guard bore me onward, and I suddenly glimpsed Llir's face as we passed him. His green eyes sought mine, brow furrowed in confusion. I knew I didn't look sick. I held his gaze.

Then he was gone, and there was only dull armor, the rhythmic marching of boot soles on stone.

I looked out—and felt my heart leap when I saw it. The tide. Swirling in, racing level with our group.

My delay. It had worked, bestowed just enough time. And Crake didn't realize, because of what the Cage were doing . . .

I could see it now, the way the water was warping, thundering ahead to the left and right of us, but lagging behind us in a great, strange U shape. Like a tumbling avalanche, it roared up the channels, filling the ditches carved out by the Cage.

And the waves held back by the Floodmouths behind us, back at the island, were racing to catch up . . .

For that was what Zennia had relayed to the Cage, the hasty plan we'd hatched in the tower. I'd remembered Rhianne's words when we'd talked on the clifftop: *"Sometimes the sands, they can change their shape, and that makes the water swirl in differently . . ."*

The Floodmouths—more experienced with the ocean than I was—had leashed the tide where it flowed around the island, while at the same time, the Mudmouths had caused a series of small quakes, shallow tremors in the sands that would push the waves higher. The tidal wave at the ball had impressed itself on my mind.

And then . . .

Release.

The Floodmouths had stood down, leaving the tide to barrel in at our rear with pure fury.

I thought I could see it: that first foam-tipped wave, eager to catch up with its fellows either side of it. It was high—head-high—soaring dark out of the sea fog, and now I heard the shouts of panic down the line.

I struggled, causing my guard to lose his footing. As he staggered, I managed to leap down from his arms, but a second later, he was no longer looking at me. His eyes, like everyone else's, were fixed behind us, on the towering wave that was now almost here . . .

The roaring was louder, almost deafening, and the bay on either side of us was a tumult of water. My heart hammered as though it would burst from my chest. I was lightheaded. What in hells had I done?

I'd been thinking only of destroying House Crake. My own survival, and that of Llir and the others, had been a niggle I'd squashed, something to deal with later.

Now I saw I'd underestimated the ferocity, the violence, with which the tide was advancing. The Cage must only have held it back for a few minutes, but that was enough. It was spitting with rage.

It was done now. Things were too far gone. I'd have to see this through—however it ended.

The line of soldiers, of Orha, was fragmenting. Awkwardly, for my wrists were bound in front of me, I shrugged off my pendant and kicked it away, then dug in my pockets and got rid of the remaining laconite.

A figure appeared next to me. Llir, face white. He'd managed to tug his gag down around his neck.

"What is this?" He was staring out at the tide.

"Take that off," I said, nudging his pendant, and he looked at me, wild-eyed, as he pulled it over his head.

"Was this you?" His voice was cracking with fear. But suspicion, too—a simmering resentment. My betrayal hung between us, unspoken.

"Kind of," I muttered. "Come on. Get these off." They'd freed our ankles, but our wrists were still lashed, and I scrabbled at his bindings. "Gods. We need a knife."

A distant shout came then, echoed down the line: "All Floodmouths! To the rear! Stop this nonsense!"

I suspected it had originated with Uirbrig Crake.

But it was hopeless, trying to organize this rabble. Panic had gripped his forces like a fever. His soldiers were trying to remove their armor, but time had run out, the wave was here. The Orha, the Floodmouths, were already shouting, but their words went unheeded by the oncoming tide. An Orha fled past me, spitting commands, and I remembered pushing laconite deep down into her cloak. Another still had his pack on his shoulders, a pack I'd laced with the beads in the ward.

"We need to get away from them," I said to Llir. "They have laconite."

He looked at me, uncomprehending. I pulled him with me. "All the Crake Orha. I put laconite on them. They won't find it. It's too small. Too well hidden."

"It's too late," Llir said. He was staring above my shoulders. And when I half turned, flinching, I saw he was right.

Boom.

The first wave smashed into the wagons, splintering wood, sending sacks into the air. There were yells down the causeway, horses whinnying. There was no sign of Rhianne, of Tigo or Mawre. The next wave reared, dark and ominous, and though it wasn't as tall as the tidal wave, it still sent a zigzag of ice through my insides.

Llir was backing away, looking horrified. "What did you do?" he said. "How did you do this?"

I looked around wildly. We needed a blade. And there on the causeway, cast off by its owner, I saw one: a short sword, its edges glinting. But as soon as I spotted it, the next wave reached us, towering over us, about to crash down.

I threw myself forward, reached out my bound wrists, just grasped the hilt as the gray wall descended.

Smack.

I flashed back to my test in the cove. To the towering wave on the night of the ball. That same stinging shock, that same bone-deep chill, slamming the breath from my lungs in an instant. Salt filled my nose, my mouth, my eyes. I was tossed, tumbled, knees over shoulders, but somehow my fingers still gripped the sword.

My side knocked into something, the causeway maybe, and jarred my elbow so hard I cried out. But my voice was lost, brine pouring through my lips. I could only struggle to keep upright in the water.

Around me, other bodies were tossed by the tide. Weighed down by their armor, they sank like stones, hands scrabbling desperately, eyes stretched wide in fear.

The next wave swelled, carrying me upward. I could sense the tide's ferocity, its singular focus, its fervor to make up the distance it had lost. I kicked my legs, trying to stay above water, but it was nearly impossible with my wrists still tied.

"Llir!" My voice splintered. "Llir, where are you?"

I knew I couldn't use the short sword alone. But it was more than that. I needed him; I needed Llir to be all right.

My head whipped around. I could see no sign of him. But off to the north, I saw men . . . stuck in mud.

The sucking sands. The ones that had caught Emment.

The soldiers had fled, left the solidity of the causeway, and headed toward the mainland, trying to outrun the tide. But it was foolish—the sea was around and ahead of us, curling inward and trapping us like hares. Tidal bores boiled up the Cage's channels, flooding the mudflats, drowning those who'd got stuck.

My eyes raked their forms—I was terrified I'd see Llir—when one burly figure among them caught my eye:

Uirbrig Crake.

He was still in his heavy armor. As I watched, he roared like a bear, spitting foam, yelling hoarsely to his soldiers, "To me! To me!" His legs were stuck fast, sinking rapidly—and then the next wave plowed into him, unforgiving.

The water level was rising fast. Suddenly, as the next wave lifted and dragged me, I realized I could no longer touch the causeway with my toes. A moment passed, but Crake didn't reappear. And soon, bodies began to float past me, face down.

"Llir!"

My voice was hoarse, torn ragged. It took all my strength to hold on to the blade. My legs were on fire, my muscles rebelling, but I pumped my elbows to stay afloat. I dipped down briefly, felt my head go under, then reared up, forcing my body to obey.

And then: a hand, two hands, on my shoulder.

I turned. Llir was behind me, bone pale.

Relief flooded through me. "I have a blade," I gasped. "Quick. I can't hold it up for very long."

We rose with the bulge of another huge wave. We were like dolls, utterly at the sea's mercy. Llir sawed his bindings against the sharp edge until, after what felt like an age, they frayed apart. Then, wrists free, he grabbed onto the sword, and I cut my own ropes. He let the blade sink, panting.

"I have to get back," he gulped, turning in the water. "Emment . . ." He took up an exhausted-looking front crawl.

It was all I could do not to sink down like the sword. "Wait," I croaked, "we shouldn't use all our energy. *Llir.* We need a float—" But he couldn't hear me through the tide's roaring.

I struggled after him, searing pain in my limbs. Pieces of leather floated past me, shards of wood.

In sheer desperation, I spoke to the water, pleading with it in a whisper as I swam. But I knew it was hopeless. I was too overwrought. And the tide wasn't listening; it was bent on its assault. I needed to stay put, save some of my energy. Find something to hang on to, some timber, a raft . . .

Ahead, Llir began to dip lower in the water, his legs now sinking, his strokes more frantic. His head went right under, then emerged, sea slick. I heard him coughing. I fought to keep up.

Just as I came within arm's length of him, he gulped some water and went down, choking. I dived, grabbed him and yanked him upward, adrenaline granting me one final burst of strength.

He came up gasping, shaking water from his eyes. His hair was dark, plastered to his head, and his shirt was billowing around us, cloudlike. I didn't let go, afraid he would go under again, and we floated, gripping each other's arms tightly, legs kicking beneath us. He looked wild, half crazed.

"Speak to it!" he yelled. "Speak to it now! Tame it!" His gaze flashed in the direction of the island, of his siblings.

Had Iovawn Crake excavated the ruins by now? Was he back at the castle? I pictured that stone block.

A wave broke near us, showering us in surf, and a jagged wooden board tumbled past, barely missing us.

"Do it!" he shouted, face inches from mine, as we soared together on the next great swell.

"I can't," I yelled over the crashing of the water, the rumble of the wave as it carried us with it. "I can't—can't concentrate in this—"

"You have to!" His grip on my arms was like iron. "Do you understand? I *have* to get to them!"

I could see it in his face: that same look from the inner ward, from the causeway after. *Cuckoo. Betrayer.* I closed my eyes, tried to summon my red ball, but his anger, his anguish, was leaching into me.

"I don't think I can," I choked out. "I'm sorry. I'm *sorry*."

"Then what in hells use are you?" he cried, his voice cracking open, his face soaked by spray.

Something in me broke in two.

I knew it was the desperate outburst of a boy whose family might be dying—or already dead. But that didn't stop the bitter indignation, and then the black hopelessness, rolling over me.

He was right. What use *was* I if I couldn't even do the one thing I'd been born to do?

My arms were lead weights; my legs kicked feebly. Only Llir, now, was stopping me sinking, and I wanted to tell him to just let me go.

Seeing me crumple, feeling me sag, he tugged me upward, his sharp features tensing. "Corith," he grated, dipping his head. "Listen to me. I know you can do this."

But his words were muted and my vision was blurred. I closed my eyes again . . .

And was back in the cove. Rexim's pinched smile. Vercha's delight. The writhing water. The oncoming tumult. I remembered that unnatural *ceasing* I'd felt . . . but I knew that this time, giving up would mean death.

"Hey," I heard Llir shout, "stay with me."

But now I flashed back to the tidal wave. That terrible roaring. The dark wall of water. I'd failed then and knew I would fail now, too. Archwater was far too feral to be tamed, at least by me. We would both drown here.

I felt Llir shift. We were closer now. The cold seemed to have reached the core of my being.

Another memory came to me, this one much calmer. One I'd thought back to a few times before: Zennia's profile, her hand rising into the air. Rhama staring at us, blank faced, across the lecture hall.

"Tidespeakers," I mumbled, the word lost in the sea's rushing.

As though through thick glass, I heard Llir answer, "What?"

"Tidespeakers," I said again, opening my eyes. They stung, and I dragged my wrist across them. "We used to be called Tidespeakers. Before the Revolt."

He gazed at me. Water dripped from his sodden hair. "Yes," he said. "I know. I've read the histories. See? You were *made* to do this. I *know* you can."

His words swam together in my mind. *Made to. You can.*

"Remember what you taught me?" he called over the tumult.

I did remember teaching him my trick up on the tower. And I recalled, now, the progress I'd made in the cove. When I squeezed my eyes shut, Zennia's face swam in the darkness.

"You, Corith. You're what this job needed."

I had to do something. And not just for her but for him now, too. For Llir. For his family.

A new image burst into my mind's eye: my red ball. I'd never seen the lightning so bright, so swollen. All my panic, all my despair, streaking out like flames: a great pyre of emotion.

I cracked my eyes open, gripped by renewed fear. "It's too much," I spluttered. "I can't shrink it. Not this time."

"You can." Llir pressed his forehead against mine. Another wave lifted us, bearing us skyward, but his green gaze was steady, an anchor in the maelstrom.

I closed my eyes again, saw that red blaze burning.

And slowly, methodically, I began to squeeze it down.

All my shame, all my anger at House Crake. All my regret at deceiving the siblings. My disgust at the Cormorants. My fear for my life. My frustration at my weakness, and my heart-swelling hope . . . It was all there, and I let myself *bathe* in it briefly before squashing it, shrinking it, forcing it inward.

Slowly a preternatural serenity came over me. The ball got smaller, the lightning less frantic. It was an egg now, smoother. Then a nut. Then a pea. And finally, with one last monumental effort, I pinched it into a pinprick: a star in the night sky.

"Stop, now," I said to the water tiredly. I took a deep breath, lips stinging with salt. "You'll let us pass. You'll give us safe passage. You'll carry us east."

I opened my eyes.

My senses zinged with a new awareness of the tide, a *mutual* awareness. It was finally listening. All that work I'd put in down by the cove . . . the ocean remembered me, had deigned to pay attention.

We were dipping, the wave beneath us diminishing. Llir drew away, staring around us in surprise.

In a perfect circle, ten feet in diameter, a stillness had descended, like the eye of a storm. The waves lapped peacefully, the violent currents gone. As we floated, the sea gently buffeted us eastward.

"Come on!" Llir had struck away from me already. I could see from the fevered glint in his eyes that all his thoughts were bent toward his siblings. He took up his loping front crawl again, and I followed, trying to block out the pain, the fatigue.

The island loomed larger but was still frighteningly far off. Outside our bubble, the waves reared, crashing down angrily. I didn't know how long they would give us.

A shape in the distance caught my attention: two humped figures on a . . . boat? No, a raft. One was waving both arms in the air, but I couldn't make them out through the spray and thin fog.

Despite the tide's nudging, I was tiring, faltering. My muscles were corded, seizing with cold. I tried to call out, to warn Llir I was lagging, but my voice wasn't working. Sea slopped past my lips.

At that moment, I felt a grip on my ankle, heard a croak from behind me: "Floodmouth. Thank the gods."

I wheeled. A figure was tugging me backward, deep-brown eyes unnaturally wide, ebony hair waterlogged and stringy.

Avrix.

He looked half drowned already. Sucked in cheeks, wrinkled skin, like a corpse that had floated up from the seabed. He was low in the water, legs down below him, injured hand floundering as the other clung onto my foot.

"Morgen's gone," he gasped, kicking wildly. "And Ebba. But you're a good girl. You'll save us both, won't you? I won't let go." His grip was strong as a hawk's talons.

Revulsion rose in my gullet like bile. *No,* I tried to say. *Let go. You'll drown me.* But nothing came out; the words wouldn't form.

I went under.

Freezing salt filled my mouth. I managed to surface, just glimpsed Llir's head turning, but then I was down again, deeper this time.

I kicked out, tried to shake Avrix off me, but he clung on desperately, sinking along with me.

My lungs were burning, screaming for air, and I remembered the last time I'd felt this: my exam.

I'd almost failed then. Now I was going to.

My arms moved weakly. My legs were like lead. At least, I thought, I'd gotten rid of Crake. And it was oddly peaceful down here . . . strangely pleasant. I could almost ignore the crushing weight on my chest.

But at last I couldn't fight the urge any longer.

I opened my mouth, tried to suck in a breath, and choked, instead, on icy water.

The next thing I was aware of was a scratching beneath my cheek.

A cough spasmed out of me, followed by a dribble of seawater. My head was pounding, my limbs like loose rope. A brisk breeze was blowing, and I could hear gulls shrieking—I wasn't under that grave-cold water anymore.

I shifted and realized it was gravel against my face, scraping my skin, bruising me through my clothes. I blinked salt from my eyes, my vision slowly clearing, and saw a figure lying stretched out next to me.

Llir.

He was on his back, his chest rising and falling as he panted, but his eyes were squeezed shut, his face drawn with exhaustion.

"Here," I heard a familiar voice say, and another figure—suntanned skin slick with sea spray—bent down between us and offered a metal flask. Tigo. "It survived the swim. Who'd have thought it?"

I heaved myself upright as Llir grasped the flask. He took a swig and coughed out a painful-sounding guffaw. "It's tea," he croaked. "I was hoping for brandy."

"Tea is the elixir of life," Tigo admonished, looking mightily relieved that Llir was speaking.

"You want some, too?" came another voice, flinty. I looked around and saw Rhianne nearby, her red hair darkened to burgundy by seawater. We were on the island's shingle beach, and she was dragging a makeshift raft up the slope—the jagged base of a wagon, it looked like.

A hand appeared in front of me, holding out the flask, and I took a quick swig, my eyes finding Tigo's. Though the burn on his cheek still looked nasty and must have stung horribly in the salty water, his gaze was impassive, and he quickly glanced away. With a sick sort of feeling, I remembered how we'd left things.

"What happened?" I said, the words coming out wheezy. "Avrix . . ." I recalled his iron-strong grip.

Rhianne trudged over, brushing grime from her palms. "He went down—Morgen, too, earlier—but Llir managed to get to you. Lucky we snagged that driftwood."

I looked quickly at Llir, but he avoided my eyes. He stood stiffly, bent over, spat on the shingle.

"Where's Mawre?" I asked, feeling a clawing foreboding. I wasn't used to seeing the others without her.

No one said anything for a few long, drawn-out seconds. Then Rhianne shook her head, her face bleached ivory. "We don't know," she said. "We looked, but we couldn't find her."

My vision swam. I curled forward, hands on the pebbles.

"Come on," I heard Llir say. He was upright, moving. "Emment. My sisters . . . We have to get up there."

"Wait," said Rhianne, looking hard at me, stepping nearer. "First she tells us what the *hells* that was." She pointed to the bay, where the tide was still raging. "That wasn't a normal Morning Tide. It never *lags* like that . . . never floods that quickly. And the height of those waves . . ." She squinted, frowning.

Tigo said frankly, "You can't have done that alone."

My limbs trembled weakly as I hauled myself up. I had no energy to keep the truth in me, to come up with some alternative story. "It was the Cage," I said quietly, waving a hand to the east. "They're here. Arrived just after Crake did. And Zennia is with them—she was always one of them."

The others, Llir included, stared at me in shock.

"Our old Floodmouth." Rhianne had gone even paler. "She's alive?"

Tigo and Llir exchanged a glance.

"Yes." I looked at Llir, a weight on my chest. "I thought your brother might have done something to her, but I was wrong. He *did* see her go down. She faked it."

Llir said nothing, unbalanced by the news, seeming to see me anew—yet again.

"Zennia was working for the Cage all along, like you," said Tigo, folding his arms. His voice was hard as the stones beneath our feet, but as he looked at me, the corner of his mouth quirked strangely. "I knew there was something you were hiding, but I never thought . . ."

I dropped my gaze.

"Hells know what your Cage would have done to us," he continued. "What they still might do. Tell me why we shouldn't have just left you in the water."

"Tigo," Rhianne said. "Corith did save us from Crake." She peered at me, jutting her chin toward the ocean. "I'm guessing it was you who came up with that plan. You're the only one of them who knows our tides that well . . . who could have predicted just how it might work."

After a pause, I nodded. Tigo's lips pressed together.

"Enough," snapped Llir, his patience clearly spent. "We can do this later. Right now I'm going up there."

Without waiting to see if any of us would follow, he turned and jogged for the path up to the castle. His face was screwed up with pain, with weariness.

Tigo set off immediately behind him, while Rhianne dithered a few seconds before joining them.

I stared after them, my heart beating a fast, hollow rhythm. Time seemed to slow. The moment felt heavy.

I could skirt around the island, go east, meet the Cage. They were probably still returning from the bay, recovering. Some Floodmouths would have had to guide the Mudmouths out on boats, while others would have been speaking to the tide, urging it onward. We could all wait this out . . . let the siblings face Iovawn Crake . . .

I almost laughed as that thought crossed my mind. I felt wild, cut loose. I knew my decision.

With a loping, limping, painful gait, I forced my legs to run upward, after Llir.

I tried not to think about when I'd last slept, tried to ignore the fiery burning in my body. My clothes were sodden, and they weighed me down, making me shiver in the cold, crisp air.

It was as we approached the Crake-manned gatehouse that I suddenly realized we had no weapons. Llir and the others were forging ahead, and there was no time to cry out before the soldiers spotted us.

But then I stumbled; stopped and stared. Tigo was speaking, saying something to the earth, and it rippled, great cracks shooting up toward the walls.

There were three guards, more of a lookout than a defense. Two on the ground and one up on the ramparts. As I watched, one of the gatehouse towers shivered, at the same time as a hillock of earth burst from the ground. The guard on the tower lost his footing, fell out of sight, and the ones on the ground toppled over like wooden pins.

Rhianne had pulled out her pocket tinderbox, but she was scowling: Seawater was pouring out of it. There was little *I* could do to help Tigo either, but I followed at a short distance, wishing I still had Kielty's rapier.

Llir sprang forward, kicking a downed guard's sword away, then darted after it before the man could get up.

Tigo was speaking to the earth again, carving a crevasse under the second man. A grave. The man shrieked as soil poured in over him. I swallowed. Tigo was burying him alive.

Llir was on his knees, crawling forward for the sword, but its owner had now grabbed tight onto his ankle. The soldier's other hand snaked down, pulled out a dagger, and I lurched toward them, yelling out, "Llir—behind you!"

Tigo had seen, too. Earth erupted in the man's face. He staggered upright, but now Llir had reached the fallen weapon, and before I could really register what had happened, Llir had spun, thrust out the sword like in his fencing lessons.

The man choked, the blade buried deep in his stomach, and Llir stepped back, abruptly paling.

As the soldier went down again, gasping and twitching, Tigo went to Llir and gripped his upper arm. "You had to do it," the Mudmouth said to him quietly. "He would have killed you."

Llir was nodding, his lips pressed tight.

A shout came then, from the direction of the castle. A woman. Catua?

"Come on," urged Rhianne.

Llir gripped the sword, and I picked up the dagger. We hurried up the path, dodging great clods of earth, and slowed, now cautious, as we entered the outer ward. But the stretch of hard-packed dirt was empty, the only sounds coming from beyond the barbican: the inner ward.

"If we go up that tower," I whispered, "we can see what's happening." I pointed to the one that was wreathed in red ivy.

Llir looked swiftly at me. His tower.

Our tower.

The door stood open, splintered in places. Crake's forces must have searched the interior. We took the steps quickly and silently, and crept slowly onto the rooftop in case more guards were up there. But with only the Shearwater siblings left, it seemed Crake the Younger had been left with few troops, as there was no one on the battlements—and less than a dozen guards below.

"Look," said Rhianne, pointing to the east. The ruined tower was all but gone, its stones piled nearby, its foundations exposed. Trenches had been furrowed in the dark, springy loam, great mounds of earth deposited near the clifftops.

Voices from below drew my attention, and along with the others, I sidled to the ramparts.

Iovawn Crake was directly below us. He was pacing, looking vaguely troubled. Near him, ten feet away, was Vercha, her wrists still bound but her ankles unshackled.

As I watched, Vercha hissed something at Iovawn. Pleading? But she didn't look desperate . . . just angry. There was a bloodstain on her gown, and her dark hair hung loose. Purple shadows ringed her eyes as she watched him, trembling.

Iovawn spoke, but again, we couldn't hear him.

"Can we get any closer?" whispered Rhianne. "A lower window?"

Llir shushed her. His eyes were on his older brother, who, I now saw, was kneeling on the platform. Rexim's corpse had been removed, though the dark stain remained. I swallowed as I spotted it.

"He's going to get rid of them," Llir muttered, face strained. He dragged a hand through his wet hair. "One by one."

Rhianne said, "Shouldn't we just—"

"Llir's right," I interrupted. "I was here before, when I made the plan with Zennia, and I heard Uirbrig Crake tell his son to 'kill the whelps.'"

They all looked at me, surprised. Fear flashed in Llir's gaze. "Then we have to do something," he said, jerking upright.

"Wait," said Tigo, pulling him down. "There's nearly a dozen of them down there. Look. They have crossbows, swords. And Iovawn . . . he's a Mudmouth. We can't just go barging in there without a plan. Besides, if they spot us up here, we're trapped. Like rats in a barrel. They'll pick us off one by one."

Llir's face was haggard. Below us, Vercha was murmuring. She'd stepped closer to Iovawn, their expressions intense. But now Iovawn was striding away from her, cloak billowing. He said something to the men guarding Emment on the platform, and shortly after, the Shearwater was shoved off it.

"Where are they taking him?" Rhianne asked, puzzled. "Maybe he's decided not to do it in front of your sisters."

"Seems unlikely, for a Crake," murmured Tigo.

I blocked out their voices. I was thinking. Assessing.

In the middle of the ward was a burning brazier, left over from the assault. The guards were loitering, looking bored, unalert. With their prisoners cooperative, there was little for them to do.

Catua was huddled, hollow eyed, against one wall, near a line of barrels that I knew contained water. Only two days past, I'd been filling one of those . . . at this moment, my chores seemed a lifetime ago.

Tigo's words turned over in my mind: *"Like rats in a barrel . . ."*

"Are you thinking what I'm thinking?"

I turned my head to see Tigo looking at me. The reticence, the anger, in his eyes were still there, but there was grit, too, now. Determination.

"Maybe," I said.

And we began to hatch a plan.

It was bold. Messy. Obvious, really. But it was all we had. And we'd had to think fast.

We hastened down the steps and out of the tower. As we skirted the curtain wall, approaching the barbican, Llir twirled his sword, adjusting his grip. I had the dagger secured in my belt, and as we crept forward, peering cautiously into the ward, I took a deep breath, flicked my eyes closed briefly.

I'd been keeping my ball of emotions crushed tight, and I checked it now, bringing to mind the crimson pinprick. It had grown a little, streaks of light lurching out of it, but I batted them, squeezed them, until my skull pounded painfully.

"Ready?" Rhianne was glancing between us.

In the ward, guards manhandled Emment and Catua.

"Ready," Llir said grimly, lifting his blade, and a second later . . .

All four of us spoke together.

Crack!

My barrels were the first to go.

Crack! Crack! One after the other.

They exploded in fountains of timber and water, bursting on the cobbles, sending splinters soaring high.

Distraction complete, the brazier flared next, a shower of embers streaking upward and outward. Rhianne remained under the barbican, where she could coax them where she wanted them: right toward the guards.

Tigo thundered forward, the earth already shuddering. Iovawn Crake, who'd been striding away from us, now spun just as cobbles cracked beneath his feet.

And Llir had called up a sharp, cold wind, which streaked in past us and made Vercha totter. Arms raised to protect her face, she cowered against the wall, out of harm's way—for now.

I followed Tigo and Llir into the ward, gripping my dagger, remembering my part in this.

There was no more water—no more words I could speak—but we needed to take down the Crake guards. And quickly.

One man was already aflame, his doublet charring as he threw himself to the ground. Another, a woman, was screaming shrilly, her skin black where her eye had once been.

Terrifyingly, Iovawn Crake was still standing. He'd kept his footing despite Tigo's efforts. He skirted the jagged rent that had opened in the ground and began to mutter darkly. The earth gave a rumble.

Rhianne had moved into the ward now. Her lips moved unceasingly, and the fire obeyed. A spark hit a guard who was aiming a crossbow, and his shot went wide as he batted at his clothes.

Nearby Llir was tackling a group of three guards, speaking to the wind as he stabbed and thrusted. The gale he'd whipped up was messy, imprecise, but it did a fair job of distracting them, wrong-footing them.

"Over here! Corith!" A voice was calling me. I'd somehow ended up near Emment and Catua. The guards who were clutching them were looking around wildly. Wondering if perhaps they should be fighting instead.

I took advantage of their hesitation and launched my dagger at the nearest one's head. The throw was poor, but it made him flinch, allowing Emment to snap his wrists up and smash the man's nose.

At the same time, Catua whirled, throwing her head back, catching her guard a glancing blow to the chin. Emment, who had pilfered his captor's short sword, stabbed out with it as best he could with bound hands.

I retrieved my dagger and darted over to them. "Here," I said breathlessly, cutting their bonds. "Listen. Zennia's alive. She's here, with the Cage." I gazed hard at Emment as his ropes fell away. He had two black eyes, grazes on his cheekbones, bruises covering his jaw and neck. "And I'm sorry," I huffed out, "for—well, for some of it." I thought of the bets, the money he'd stolen. Just because, in the end, he hadn't harmed my friend, it didn't mean Emment Shearwater was a saint. But I couldn't let him think he'd killed a person.

Before, with Rexim and Crake in the ward, Emment had looked for all the world like a broken man. But now, as my words registered in him, something new and resolute glittered in his eyes.

"Fortuitous timing, little cuckoo," he said, and brandished the short sword, bearing down on the two guards.

"Do you know how to use one of these?" Catua asked me. She was wrestling with a light crossbow her guard had dropped.

"No idea," I said breathlessly.

Boom.

Another great rent in the cobbles. Another jagged tear, more dark earth exposed.

Tigo and Iovawn circled each other, each trying to topple the other, to trap him. But the ground couldn't seem to decide who to listen to. It shivered, grumbled, opened up then closed over.

My chest jolted as new flames streaked from the brazier—three, no four, heading straight for the Crake heir.

Rhianne had realized what I'd realized, too. That the longer Iovawn was standing, the more danger we were in.

Tigo had seen the flames, was momentarily distracted, and that was enough for Iovawn to try something new.

Our Mudmouth had wandered too close to Llir's tower. Now the structure gave a sudden, violent shudder, cracks streaking up it, the ancient mortar crumbling. All I could do was freeze and stare as great blocks of stone tumbled—right onto Tigo. Dust whipped up. His figure disappeared. Dimly I registered a scream from Rhianne.

Free from his main challenger—at least for the time being—Iovawn Crake hefted the broadsword at his side. Glancing around, looking more irritated than anything, he stalked toward Llir, who'd finished off a third guard.

I watched, helpless, as Iovawn muttered under his breath. The ground under Llir disintegrated to powder, and his legs sank into it. He yelled in frustration.

By now Rhianne's flames had reached their target and whipped around Iovawn, teasing and caressing him. One caught his cloak, setting it rapidly aflame, but the hulking warrior merely shed it like a snakeskin. Another worried at his face, burning his ear, and he batted at it angrily, snapping to his remaining guards, "Shut that hells-damned Sparkmouth up!"

Like a hungry bear, he barrelled toward Llir, sweeping his sword fluidly, raising it head-high.

"No!" I cried out, and just at that moment, the brazier *whooshed*, went up like a firework. Huge streaks of flame shot out, soaring skyward, crackling with heat and belching out smoke. Rhianne. I caught sight of her: pallid, furious. Everyone ducked—even Iovawn flinched—and I watched as flames burst through the keep's windows. Others chased the remaining guards, sending them shrieking from the ward or rolling on the ground.

The heat was intense, and I coughed on the smoke. The side of my face stung where a flame had shot past me. But Iovawn Crake had collected himself already, and now, teeth gritted, raised his broadsword once more.

Llir still had his own sword, stolen at the gatehouse, but it looked like a needle compared to Crake's blade. Iovawn swung down; Llir tried to block, but the force of the impact sent his weapon spinning.

"Corith! By your feet!" It was Catua's hoarse voice. She was aiming the crossbow she'd acquired at Iovawn. I glanced down, saw another one lying near me, and snatched it up, my heart thumping wildly.

As I fumbled with it, trying to make sense of the mechanism, I saw a tall figure running straight toward Iovawn.

Emment.

Face black and blue, shirt streaked with blood, he was limping slightly but hurtling in fast. Llir shouted something—trying to warn his brother off, maybe—but Emment ignored him, his face twisted with hate.

Iovawn flashed his sword around lazily, blocked Emment's first strike, then swept a slashing arc. Despite his injuries, Emment kept his footing, dancing out of reach of the blade.

He went in again, and I felt a dark foreboding. Catua loosed a bolt, but the shot went wide.

Iovawn thrusted, then heaved his blade upward, and the edge caught Emment, slashing open his cheek.

Llir bellowed at his brother. His sisters were screaming. I raised the crossbow, looked at the levers.

With a small smirk, Iovawn turned back to Llir, brought his sword up, then down in a powerful strike. Somehow it hit the earth, sending gravel flying, but already Iovawn was preparing another blow.

Shouldering the crossbow, I pulled one lever. Nothing happened. I pushed another and heard a strange click. Then I saw something that looked like a trigger, and I squeezed it, aiming for Iovawn's bulk.

Miraculously the crossbow fired its heavy bolt, bucking in my arms. Iovawn let out a grunt. The bolt had buried itself shallowly in his side, and he staggered, glancing across at me curiously.

Llir pulled his feet from the broken earth, gave a howl—a war yell—and brought down his blade. Once, twice, on the Crake heir's sword arm. Chopping deep through muscle and tendon, the wrist almost severed right through. Blood gushed; the broadsword clanged to the ground. Iovawn looked surprised, then dropped to his knees.

"He can still kill us all," Catua was shouting, but by now Emment had approached from behind. His chin, his neck, his shoulder—all were scarlet. But he didn't seem to care, lips stretched: half grin and half grimace.

Before the giant could speak again, could bury us, Emment stuffed his bloodied linen shirt into Crake's mouth. The man didn't resist. He looked around dully. It was clear he was outnumbered.

And then we heard voices.

Figures emerged from the fading mist.

They were dressed in dark colors; most seemed to be sodden. Kielty was at their head, Zennia jogging by his side. The rest of the Cage trooped wearily under the barbican, and behind them, keeping a wide, wary distance from the rebels, came Ferda, Miss Haney, and a handful of other servants.

"Where's Tigo?" came a voice. A tall figure strode toward us. Hot relief bloomed in my chest to see Mawre, a crack in her spectacles, her black hair still dripping.

Tigo.

Llir was already running, almost pitching over in his haste.

The Cage's Mudmouths were tired, and cautious, but willing to help rescue one of their own. Leaving a few Orha to guard Iovawn Crake, Kielty came with us, joining in our digging, and eventually we uncovered a prone figure choked with dust.

My mouth tasted of bile and my innards were sick with nerves, but it seemed Tigo was alive—just. His legs were trapped, broken by fallen blocks, but his upper body had been spared, ending up in a dark cavity. Bruising now joined the burn on his cheek. He spoke only once, to ask after Llir, who climbed down next to him as the blocks were removed.

Only now did I notice the smoke trailing upward, hear the ominous, far-off crackling in the keep. Somewhere nearby, a window shattered, and I glimpsed licks of red flame inside.

"That was me," a voice said—a trembling Rhianne. She stepped tentatively toward the castle, then flinched as something crashed down inside.

"Come on," said Catua, ashen faced but calm, putting an arm around the Sparkmouth and leading her away.

I made to follow them, my hand tight around Zennia's, when Emment's tall frame stepped in front of us, blocking our way.

Face and neck still painted with blood, he pressed his fingers to the slash on his cheek. "You," he said, eyes roving Zennia. "You let me believe you'd died out there. And you"—he turned to me, lip curling—"*you* convinced me I'd murdered her."

My shoulders slumped. I was too tired for this. "I was wrong," I replied. "I said I was sorry."

He was quiet a moment, studying us. Then, to my surprise, he shook his head wearily. "You know, as unhappy as I am about—all this"—he waved a hand at the huddle of cloaked rebels—"I think what you said was . . . good for me, in a way." He'd sagged a little, too, gaze growing distant. "It forced me to confront the consequences of my actions. Made me realize I'd been failing my family, over and over. Failing myself."

Catua suddenly appeared behind him. "You need that cheek stitched," she said to him gently. Catching Zennia's eye, she smiled. "I'm glad you're okay."

Zennia nodded gratefully.

We all regrouped just beyond the outer ward, a safe distance away from the fire and smoke. A tourniquet was tied above Iovawn's sliced arm, and Kielty, face hard as he surveyed the Mudmouth, cauterized it, provoking a bitten-off cry. Vercha, her shadowed eyes flickering between them, paced at a distance, looking jittery.

Emment and Catua soon struck up a debate about whether to keep Iovawn Crake alive.

"We can put him under the gatehouse for now," suggested Llir, who looked more exhausted than I'd ever seen anyone. "There are two cells under it."

"I don't like that," said Emment darkly. "If he gets the gag off somehow . . ."

The arguments resumed.

"What's this?" Zennia remarked. There were chests piled on the ground, gold coins spilling out, the head of a jewelled scepter. She nudged a velvet bag that was hanging from a chest, and a laconite cuff tumbled out onto the scrubby grass.

"That belongs to us," snapped Vercha, stepping in front of her. "The Shearwater hoard. Get your filthy traitor hands off it."

I felt a flash of anger. "They're not here for your treasure."

Vercha turned on me. "Then what, may I ask, are they still doing here? And, for that matter, why are *you* still here? You need to get off this island. You and all your *murderer* friends."

I glanced at the siblings. Llir and Emment looked on stonily, but Catua stomped over. "Verch, they saved us. Corith and her friends stopped Crake. She saved Llir"—she glanced at me fiercely—"and risked her *life* to come back for us."

Vercha looked poisonous. "Have you forgotten why they came here? Their original plan—before Crake killed Father *for* them?"

"We were never going to kill Rexim Shearwater. We needed him." Zennia's jaw thrust forward belligerently.

Kielty was watching with folded arms, a small smirk. "We'll leave you in peace," he said, "just as soon as we're ready. In the meantime, why don't you use that laconite there to solve your little, ah . . . problem?"

He indicated Iovawn, and Vercha flushed pink. Catua shook her head and began to unload laconite—a jewelled chain, a studded coronet.

As Iovawn Crake was taken down under the gatehouse, laden with enough of the stone for a king, Kielty told his people to make ready to leave.

"You're coming, right?" Zennia said to me suddenly. Vercha was hissing angrily at Catua, Llir trying to persuade Emment to have his cheek stitched. "Corith." She looked hard at me. "You *are* coming with us?"

I rubbed a grimy hand across my face, closed my eyes.

The last few weeks flashed through my mind in an instant. I thought of Rexim, of the nobles at the ball. Of the anger that had unfurled in me after the great wave. I remembered all the times I'd pushed away thoughts of the Cage, too uneasy, too afraid, to face things head-on. All the times I'd thought a comfortable bed or a nice, hot breakfast trumped roughing it in the woods . . . That, I knew now, had been only my fear talking.

I'd seen with my own eyes what the Hundred really thought of us. I couldn't, with any conscience, step back into that world now.

My eyes fluttered open. Llir was staring at me.

I turned to Zennia and said, "I go where you go."

"As do I," came a brisk voice. Catua. She was pale, grim faced, but looked brutally determined. She stepped up to Kielty, held one hand out to him. "Catua Shearwater. I'd like to come with you."

I'd never thought I'd see Kielty caught off guard. But now he did a double take, blinking rapidly. "I'm . . . sorry?" He shook her hand automatically.

"I've read the Breovan Charter. Many times. I want to help you." Behind her Rhianne was hovering. She looked unhappy but not surprised. "Truthfully I don't like some of your . . . methods, but I do know that the people you target have done wrong. And I think you might need someone who really *knows* the Hundred. Who can help you with the politics. That's—if you'll have me."

Kielty looked as though Feast Day had come early. But the siblings reacted with a violence of emotion.

"Cat," barked Emment, "you *cannot* be serious."

Llir's shoulders had stiffened. He'd frozen in place. Vercha stared at Catua as though she'd grown an extra head.

"I won't apologize for it," Catua said defensively. "Of course I don't want to leave you all, but you saw what Crake did. How he rounded up the Orha. Llir—gods know what he was going to do with you. The families like that . . . they need to be stopped."

"Cattie," said Vercha dangerously, "this is insane. You're not going anywhere with these barbarians."

Catua sniffed. "I am, Verch. My mind's made up. If you don't report me—which I really hope you won't—we'll see each other soon, I promise. On the mainland."

Emment looked shattered. He glanced at their burning home. "Cat, all we have left is each other." He paused, his silver eyes flicking to mine. "I know I've not been . . . the heir I should have been. But I promise—I *promise* you—I'm going to do better. Listen. We'll go to Breawr, tell everyone about Crake. The vote . . . We can help someone like Father win—"

But Catua shook her head, tears pricking her eyes. "That's not enough," she said. "Not for me, not anymore." She pulled him into a fierce hug. Beside them Llir stood, stunned.

Vercha, I noticed, had walked away stiffly, but no one was paying her any attention.

"I'm going, too," said Rhianne, stepping forward, and when Catua finally pulled away from her brother, she grasped the Sparkmouth's hand tightly in hers.

"And you?" Kielty said to Llir.

My stomach clenched uncomfortably. I willed Llir to look at me. My eyes skipped over his ash-stained skin, the rips in his shirt, his blood-splattered blade. But Llir's gaze only slid slowly to Kielty.

"You'll leave this island before the next high tide." His voice was lower than I'd ever heard it before. "And you're lucky we're not sending alerts ahead of you, telling the authorities to intercept you on the mainland."

"Really?" Kielty said. His blue eyes flashed a challenge. "You're one of us, friend. Aren't you proud of what you are? Don't you want to shed that shame you've clearly been living with?"

Llir moved toward him, his gaze unwavering. "I'm not your *friend*. And you know *nothing* about me." His eyes were pure ice; his shoulders trembled. "If Crake hadn't murdered my father today, I have no doubt at all that you and your people would have."

"I'm sorry you believe that," Kielty replied peaceably. In contrast to Llir, his posture was calm, open. He seemed to realize that here was a lost cause and moved off to oversee the preparations for leaving.

Gradually most people filtered away, the Cage to retrieve their boats and supplies, Rhianne and Mawre to help tend to Tigo, Emment to continue pestering Catua. I was left alone—or so I thought—to stare, hollowed out, at the burning castle. But when I turned, I saw that I wasn't alone. Llir was behind me, his eyes on his ruined home.

Despite the spots of dried blood on his jaw, his hair salt tousled and wild over his forehead, he still somehow managed to look regal. Even beautiful. Finally his green eyes sank to meet mine.

I swallowed, remembering the dance. The tableau. The feel of his fingers gripping my waist. A lifetime ago—or at least it felt like it. All that was gone up in smoke, like the keep.

"I'm sorry," I offered. It was all I could think of to say.

He stared at me. Emotions warred in his expression, but the only one I could reliably pick out was anger. When he eventually spoke, his voice was hoarse with fatigue.

"Sorry for what? For betraying my family, sabotaging our defenses, or sorry that someone else got in first?"

I felt my face flatten. "Only the first one. And sorry in the sense that I wish I hadn't *had* to do it."

He studied me. "You didn't follow me that morning because you were curious. You followed me because you needed dirt on my family. And you got it, didn't you? *My* secret was the one. The one thing my father would do anything to keep hidden."

"I didn't want to use it," I said. It was true. "I didn't really want to use anything I found out."

His top lip curled; he looked away from me briefly.

"I was going to tell you, before you threw in your lot with *them*"—he inclined his chin to where the Cage were packing up—"that I'm sure I can persuade Emment and Vercha to keep you on." His eyes sought his brother, who was having his wound cleaned. "Like Emment said, there's still the vote. We can back the most progressive candidate. Rebuild. Move to my father's house in Breawr in the meantime."

He finally looked at me, saw me shaking my head. His next words were said all in a rush, gaze intense. "We could use your talents. And you'll have everything you want."

Anger spread crimson wings in my chest, but beneath it was a horrible, hot bubble of shame . . . shame that a sliver of me *wanted* to accept him. To go back to my cushy, familiar placement, to be adjacent to that luxury I'd half grown accustomed to . . .

"Still so wedded to Hundred tradition. Still speaking of us as though we're pieces of furniture." I shook my head narrowly, felt my breath coming faster. "You still can't imagine any other kind of life, can you, than the wool-wrapped one you've been living out here?"

His expression closed up, a shutter coming down, but before he could reply, a cry rang out.

It was Zennia, sprinting toward us from the gatehouse.

"He's gone. Iovawn Crake. He's *gone*."

A ripple of shock went through those of us who heard her. Emment and Catua ran over from nearby.

"What do you mean, *gone*?" Emment grated. "The laconite—"

"Discarded. He's spoken to the earth, burrowed a tunnel. I'm sure if we search, we'll find the exit, but there's no sign of him anywhere. He's just disappeared."

"Impossible," Llir breathed. "He was chained, he had laconite . . ."

"He was gagged, too," said Catua, "and the cell was locked tight."

I spun in a circle, a dark weight settling on me. "Where's Vercha?" I asked, my voice breaking slightly.

I was remembering a writing desk stuffed full of paper. An unopened letter. Charred flecks in a grate.

"She stormed off," said Catua, frowning. "Why? I haven't seen her since . . ." She trailed off, staring at my face.

"What are you implying?" Emment snapped, turning in a circle. "*Verch!* I'll find her. She'll be here. She will."

He jogged off, calling his sister's name, but Catua gripped my arm with cold fingers. "You know something," she said, gazing hard into my face.

"I think—" I said slowly, "I think they were writing to each other."

The tide was nearly out by the time Emment called off the search.

Vercha was gone. And Iovawn Crake with her.

We'd found the exit to the tunnel he'd bored—it would have spilled them out beyond the pinewood, near the causeway. There we saw the remnants of a raised mud track, which could have been used to cross the last of the Morning Tide.

"If she got him out, why didn't they just attack us?" Catua was sitting with her chin in her hands.

"Probably knew how outnumbered they were," put in Kielty, who'd returned with the rest of the Cage.

"I don't understand," Catua replied. "Vercha wanted us dead? Her own sister, her own brothers? The father she loved?"

"No," I said, crouching down next to her. As much as I disliked Vercha, I didn't believe that. "I think maybe she . . . aligned with Uirbrig Crake more than with your father. But I think, perhaps, what Uirbrig did . . . the—the execution. That surprised her and Iovawn both."

Emment and Llir were standing over us, arms folded, disbelief etched onto their faces.

"Maybe Iovawn thought the plan was imprisonment," I said. "Maybe that's what he told Vercha when he wrote. That they'd say you'd all been kidnapped by the Cage but ultimately keep you alive—keep you safe—until Crake's and Shrike's plans were already in motion. But then, when Uirbrig killed your father and told his son to kill the rest of you, too . . . maybe Vercha tried to persuade Iovawn to lock you up. And pretend to Uirbrig that he'd actually done the deed."

"He took me off the block," murmured Emment, "in the end."

The sight of the mudflats glittering in front of us was a stark reminder that it was time to leave.

The boats were loaded, ready to be wheeled down the causeway, where, near the mainland, we'd hike north over the flats. According to

Kielty, we'd be meeting a special contact somewhere in the wilderness near the estuary of the River Tiva.

Of course, Emment and Llir didn't come to see us off. They held a private goodbye with Catua, and when she jogged down to join the rest of us waiting on the shingle, I saw the Shearwater brothers on a rise near the castle, staring down at us all from on high.

I climbed stiffly and wearily into a boat, one of three on wheels being pulled by a gray horse. Ferda, who'd been among those the Cage had safely shepherded, had lent us the mount—with Emment's reluctant permission.

As I sat there, our makeshift caravan trundling off, the weight of the last few hours descended on me.

I leaned sideways, resting my head on Zennia's shoulder, and at the touch of her hand, her firm arm around my shoulders, a wonderful, searing relief suffused me.

"Everything's going to change now," came Kielty's voice. He was opposite me, looking down the boat at Catua. "With her on our side." His eyes held a strange glint.

I didn't want to think about the future just yet. I couldn't wrap my mind around this bright, bitter freedom.

Instead, I looked back at the dark hump of Bower Island, at the crumbling castle guttering smoke, at the spray as the tide chased our heels to the mainland.

And saw a watching figure still outlined against the sky.

Acknowledgments

The idea for *Tidespeaker* was born not long after my first daughter was, on endless pram walks trying to get her to sleep. It was written over the course of her second year of life—in naptimes, after bedtimes, during grandparent visits and snatched hours on weekends—and edited during her third. Thank you, R, for sharing me with this book, for inspiring me to follow my dreams, and for making the last four years the best of my life.

A thousand thank-yous to my agent, Marina. I still remember the giddy thrill of seeing that first email from you. Since then, you've been the most passionate champion, stellar editor, and patient guide any debut author could ask for. Thanks, too, to Benedict at the Soho Agency; to Peter, Stuti, and Danielle at Park, Fine & Brower Literary Management; and to Clementine and Elizabeth at ILA.

To Lydia at Delacorte Press, my editor and fellow Austenite: Thank you for seeing something special in this story and knowing how to make it a hundred times better. You helped me hone *Tidespeaker* into a far better reflection of my original daydreams on those long pram walks. I really appreciate your talent, kindness, and unwavering positivity. Thanks also to the wider team at Delacorte: Wendy Loggia,

Mallory Loehr, Judith Haut, Gillian Levinson, Trisha Previte, Megan Shortt, Tamar Schwartz, Liz Sutton, Colleen Fellingham, Candice Gianetti, John Adamo, Dominique Cimina, and Joe English.

Katie and the team at Rock the Boat: As you know, I've long admired Oneworld, and to be published by you is a dream come true. Thank you, Katie, for your eagle eye and your belief in this story, and to the wider team for all your work.

Thanks to Alexxander Dovelin for the absolutely stunning cover illustration, to Virginia Allyn for the beautiful map (another dream come true!), and to Judit for her incredible, squeal-inducing character art.

Thank you, Jamie, for beta reading an early version of *Tidespeaker*—your comments helped give me the confidence to query this book—and DV for the much-needed critique of my first chapter. Darlene: I'm so lucky to have got to know you. Bori: Thank you for your wisdom and wit. Anna, Caitlin, and the rest of the 2026 Debuts Discord/WhatsApp: Thanks for your support—you've been an absolute lifeline. And to Rachel Griffin and Leanne Schwartz: I'm so grateful for your wonderful and generous jacket blurbs.

Tom: You mean more to me than I can ever express. Thank you for believing in me and supporting me unreservedly. Mum: Thank you for introducing me to Narnia and *The Hobbit* as a child, and a million more thank-yous for your help with R and H—this book wouldn't exist without the time you gifted me. Dad: Thank you for never doubting I could do whatever I put my mind to. And to Mike: I actually finally did it! Lastly, thanks also to Steve, Jo, and Rachel for all the good times, and for your help with the kids.

About the Author

Sadie Turner grew up in the Welsh Borders and now lives in Hampshire, England, not far from the former home of one of her biggest inspirations: Jane Austen. She is a copywriter, mother of two, and author of gloomy, romantic, neurodiverse YA Fantasy. When she can find the time, she loves reading, cooking, and classic CRPGs, and she is rarely seen without a cup of tea close at hand. She is the author of the Tidespeaker duology.

sadieturner.co.uk